Lie Lay Lain

Bryn Greenwood

Lie Lay Lain

ISBN 978-0-9888777-6-4

This book is a work of fiction. Names, characters, places and incidents are the products of the author's fevered imagination or are used fictitiously. Any resemblance to actual, real life events, locales or persons (living or dead) is entirely coincidental.

STAIRWAY PRESS

A Curva Peligrosa Book
STAIRWAY PRESS—SEATTLE

www.stairwaypress.com
1500A East College Way #554
Mount Vernon, WA 98273

Cover Design by Guy Corp www.grafixCORP.com

In memory of Rilya Wilson

CHAPTER ONE

Jennifer

JENNIFER WOULD HAVE walked more quickly if she hadn't been wearing new shoes, but she couldn't stop glancing down to admire the way the slender black t-strap bisected her foot. They were easily the most elegant shoes she had ever owned.

Then again, if it had happened on the first day she wore her new Louboutins, maybe she would have been walking even more slowly. Maybe it would have happened to her.

As it was, Wednesday was the second day she wore the glistening black pumps. She was thinking about payday and buying a new purse. A Coach. Or a Prada. Intent on debating the merits of the two handbags, she didn't notice the Lincoln Navigator roaring around the corner of Platt and Franklin. Jennifer reached the sidewalk, just as the SUV hit. Not her, but the woman walking behind her. The woman's solid weight struck Jennifer's back with the violence of a football tackle.

Jennifer staggered, as the sidewalk came up at her. At the last second, some instinct for survival kicked in and her hands pushed out to stop the fall. The concrete tore at her palms and chewed her knees, but the pain lasted for only a moment, before it was wiped away by the sight of a limp body in a blue shirt tumbling over her. The body landed a few feet in front of Jennifer.

Silence welled up like a bubble, encased everything, and then through it burst chaos. People screamed, car brakes squealed, and glass broke. Someone shouted, "God, call for an ambulance. Call 9-1-1!"

"Get his tag number!" a woman screamed.

Shoes shuffled all around Jennifer, and a man stepped on her hand, gawking at the woman in the blue shirt. Jennifer jerked her hand out from under a Bruno Magli wingtip, and crawled forward uncertainly. When she had been thinking of her own shoes, she had imagined people behind her catching a glimpse of the shiny red soles. Everyone could see them now.

Jennifer's mind refused to send its usual signals, to prompt her to get up or cry out. She stayed on her hands and knees, staring at the woman.

Then the woman opened her eyes, and her mouth gaped, full of blood. One hand scrabbled at the sidewalk, and the people who had gathered around her stepped back uneasily. "My baby," she moaned. "I want my baby."

"It's okay, Jennifer. I called for an ambulance. There's an ambulance coming," someone said. Jennifer looked up and recognized one of the tech support guys from work. She thought his name was Mike.

No one dared to touch the woman. The lower half of her body was skewed at a sickening angle to her torso, and blood oozed out onto the sidewalk. Only her face moved, and the hand that didn't seem to be getting the right signals from her brain.

"My baby, my baby, my baby," she said, and then, "baby, baby, baby." Her voice took on a frightening pitch—reaching for high notes—and she reduced her plea to a single syllable: "Bay, bay, bay, bay, bay."

It was a ghastly metronome of dying, and its rhythm broke through Jennifer's trance. As though someone flicked a switch that she'd never known existed inside her, she rose on her knees and scanned the sidewalk.

She snapped her fingers, pointed, and said, "Her purse."

Mike from tech support scrambled for it and thrust it at Jennifer. It was a cheap bag, floral fabric with vinyl trim. Jennifer fought the worn out zipper open and spilled the contents of the bag onto the sidewalk. The wallet came easily to hand, as tattered as the purse. Inside were plastic pages of snapshots.

"Is the ambulance coming? When's it going to get here?" Jennifer pawed at the slippery plastic covering the pictures.

"I don't know," Mike said.

"My baby, oh, please," the dying woman said. "I want to see my Shanti."

Stalling, Jennifer flipped to the driver's license: Gayle Prichard.

"It's okay, Gayle. The ambulance is coming," Jennifer said. She wanted to reassure the woman, but fear made her voice raw.

Gayle's right hand stopped scratching at the concrete, but her left leg started to twitch, an involuntary movement. Wishing she didn't have to, Jennifer knelt outside the growing pool of blood. She looked at the people gathered around and saw curiosity and horror, but no one who wanted to help.

"Which one is Shanti? Gayle, which picture is Shanti?" Jennifer asked.

"You know Shanti. Why you got to act that way, Renee? I never meant to hurt you," Gayle said, her eyes rolling. Her hair was bleached blond with gray-brown roots two inches deep. Her driver's license said she was 32, three years older than Jennifer, but she looked forty, with deep lines in her sallow face.

Of course, it would be the first photo. A little girl, pale brown, with her curly hair up in pigtails. She stood on a playground, her hands on her hips. Jennifer pulled the photo out of the plastic and crawled closer, her gorge rising at the smell of blood. Resting her elbows on the sidewalk, feeling blood soak through her blouse, she held the picture steady for Gayle to see.

"Oh, my baby girl. Sweet, sweet girl," Gayle said.

"Is that Shanti? She's so pretty."

"Oh, God, oh, please. Renee, Renee. Renee, you got to promise me. You got to promise," Gayle said. She must have thought Jennifer was Renee.

"It's okay."

"You got to promise you'll look out for my baby. Promise you'll take care of Shanti."

"It's okay, Gayle. Shanti is fine. She's fine. She's safe at school right now, I bet," Jennifer extemporized. Desperate for someone to guide her, Jennifer looked at Mike, who knelt nearby. He stared at her, his lower lip clamped between his teeth.

"No!" Gayle cried. It was a sound of anguish that made Jennifer's jaw clench. "You got to promise."

"Say it," Mike said.

Jennifer had wanted him to share the burden, but now things were unraveling. If she did this thing, she was not sure she would be fully herself after it. Some part of her might become this Renee. She glared at Mike until he looked away.

"I promise," Jennifer said.

"Promise me, Renee. Promise you'll take care of Shanti. You're all she's got left. Say it. Promise."

"I promise I'll take care of Shanti."

"Oh, Renee. I love you. I always loved you. You were my best friend." Gayle's eyes stopped rolling wildly. They settled on the picture Jennifer held. Her tongue crept out to her lips, wiping at the blood there.

"Tell her," Mike whispered.

Jennifer choked down the knot in her throat and said, "I love you, too, Gayle. Best friends."

"Oh God, it's here. Thank God. Here!" Mike stood up and waved his arms.

The paramedics broke through the crowd, and one of them lifted Jennifer out of the way, setting her aside on the curb. A second ambulance came, the police arrived and cleared the crowds, all while Jennifer sat looking at a small patch of pitted asphalt. Two bits of plastic from a car's headlight lay in her field of view, and a few inches away, a discarded wad of gum.

Too late, Jennifer thought of praying, but dismissed it. Either God knew what was happening and would help, or he didn't know, or he wouldn't help. Pastor Lou said it wasn't that God didn't want to help. He said, "I believe that tragedies break God's heart, too." Maybe God wanted to help but wasn't able. Thinking of that confused Jennifer, but it was easier to think about God than to sit empty-headed, listening to the woman choke on her own blood.

Jennifer didn't resist when a paramedic took her by the arm and walked her toward an ambulance. Several times, the paramedic spoke to her, once saying, "Lay down. Lay back." Only when he put his blue-gloved hands on her shoulders and pushed did she obey. Then he flashed a light in her eyes.

He wiped away enough of the blood to see that most of it wasn't Jennifer's, and doused her knees and hands with disinfectant. Distantly, it burned, making her numb hands tingle. The pain was a relief, distracting her from everything else.

At the hospital, a vague figure in purple repeated the ritual. The light in the eyes, the swabbing, the bandaging. Jennifer lay motionless in a nimbus of light and noise, until the person in purple led her to the waiting room, where she sat unseeing, unhearing. The only thing she was aware of was her heartbeat. She counted it, sometimes reaching as high as 300 before she lost her place and started over.

Some time later, a hand squeezed her arm, and someone said, "Ma'am? Ma'am?" Jennifer blinked at the wall of purple in front of her. A large woman in scrubs, a nurse. When their eyes met, the nurse smiled. "Can you talk to me now, ma'am?"

Jennifer nodded.

"What's your friend's name?"

"Is she okay? Is she—?" Jennifer saw it in the nurse's eyes. Gayle Prichard was dead.

"Honey, it was quick. She didn't suffer long."

"You don't know how long it took the ambulance to get there," Jennifer croaked, and she heard in her own voice that she had been crying. She looked down at the wallet in her lap. The paramedic had returned it to her, probably thinking it was hers.

"Honey, can you tell me your friend's name?" the nurse said.

"She's not my friend." A cold flash ran through Jennifer's

brain. The switch that had been shifted on returned to its original position. "I don't know her. I was just there when it happened. Her name's Gayle, but I don't know her."

The nurse lifted the bloody wallet and opened it to the ID.

"You don't know her?"

"I never saw her before today. I was just there. She hit me. I was right in front of her. What do I do now?"

"You don't need to do anything, hon. We'll take care of it. Are you still feeling okay? Any pain? Any stiffness in your neck or back?"

"I'm fine. I'm okay."

"Do you have someone you can call to come pick you up?"

"Sure. I'll call my fiancé."

"Okay, hon," the nurse said.

Jennifer still held the picture she had removed from Gayle's wallet. It was smeared with bloody fingerprints—Jennifer's. She reached for her cell phone, first with one hand and then the other, searching around her mid-section for her purse. It was gone. Her purse. Her Louis Vuitton. Was it lying on the sidewalk in front of the Bank of America building? Of course not; that was stupid. Someone had picked it up and made off with it. Her credit cards and license and cell phone.

Getting to her feet, she almost staggered, surprised to find she was barely strong enough to walk to the nurse's counter. Another nurse said, "Are you okay?"

"I need to use a phone."

The woman pointed to three cubicles at the far end of the waiting room.

"You can use one of the yellow phones over there."

It took Jennifer half a dozen tries to remember Kevin's number and, when he answered, he was drunk and indignant.

"We've been here since 5:30. Where are you?" he roared. In the background she heard music blaring, people talking and playing pool, and Carrie's braying laughter. "You're the one who always wants to go to The Rack anyway, so here we are eating sushi. Where are you?"

"The hospital," she murmured, hating to speak too loudly in the waiting room.

"Where?" he shouted.

"Tampa General. I'm not hurt," she said, answering a question he hadn't asked. "But my car's downtown and I don't have my keys. I don't have my purse."

"You what with your car? Get a cab and come down here if you don't have your car."

"I can't. I don't have my purse."

In the background, Kevin's best friend Nathan said, "Get down here, you little bitch. We ordered all your favorite fucking bait and you're not even here. I'm not eating any fucking raw fish."

"That's all you won't eat," Kevin said loudly, and there was more laughter. Someone belched, and then Kevin said, "Are you coming or what?"

"I'm going home." She couldn't bring herself to explain it all. "I'm not dressed to come out."

"How can you not be dressed to go out?"

It was pointless to be angry with him, and it exhausted her. She heard Nathan shout, "She's not coming? Bullshit. Where is she? I'm going to go get her. That's bullshit."

Nathan came on the line and said, "I'm coming to get you. Where the fuck are you?"

"Tampa General. The emergency room."

Nathan repeated it and then someone muffled the phone. After a few moments, Kevin came back on the line and said, "You're at the hospital? What happened, Jenn? We're gonna come get you. Hang on."

"Will you please come by yourself, Kev? Please?"

"Jenn, baby, I can't drive. We'll be there in twenty minutes, okay?"

"Please, not everybody," she tried again, but he'd hung up. With careful steps, she walked back to one of the preformed plastic chairs. It wasn't the one she'd started with. That one had been taken by someone with more serious problems. Jennifer wanted to cry, to give up and lie down like the woman next to her, who slumped across three seats, sobbing into her hands. They would all come. Nathan and his foul mouth. Kevin, too drunk to drive. Carrie's braying laughter. Tracey's jiggling cleavage and cigarette smoke.

Unsteady on her feet, Jennifer shuffled to the automatic doors, which slid open obediently. Silly how she'd been waiting, like she was locked in, when it was that simple to get free. Outside, a labyrinth of chain link fencing encircled the hospital. The sun had already sunk below a mound of dirt, and on the other side hulked the construction of a parking garage.

Jennifer made it across the bridge to Davis Islands, like a shambling homeless person. When she reached the building manager's door, she knocked and heard the sound of a television. He opened the door, a bottle of beer in one hand, and stared at her.

"I'm Jennifer Palhete. In apartment 317. I lost my keys."

"Do you need to go to the hospital?" the manager said.

Jennifer flapped her gauze-wrapped hands. "I've already been. I just need into my apartment. I know there's a lock-out fee, but I lost my purse. If I could pay you later…."

"Don't worry about it."

It wasn't until she was alone in the bathroom, undressing, that she understood the manager's deferential tone. She looked like a zombie: hollow-eyed and dressed in clothes fresh from the grave. Her pantyhose were nearly severed at the knees, one giant run held together at the waist. Her shoes, her beautiful red-soled shoes, looked as though they had been run over. The toes were scuffed down to the grain of the leather. The soles were unscathed.

The rest of her clothes were similarly destroyed. Her skirt had a quarter-sized clot of blood imbedded in its sea green suede cloth, just at crotch level. In back, the stitching on one side of the zipper was ripped out, and a black slash of filth crossed the hip. Dried blood stiffened the sleeves of her blouse and a shoulder seam hung open. On the back, below the right shoulder blade, Jennifer imagined she would find the imprint of Gayle's body, but there was nothing there. In fact, it was the only part of the blouse that was still clean.

She forgot about her bandaged hands, found herself in the shower, trying to wash her hair with dripping mummy paws.

She forgot about Kevin, until she heard him shouting, "Jennifer!"

"Maybe we should call the fucking cops," Nathan said.

"I'm here," she called out feebly, pulling on a t-shirt over wet skin. She twisted off the bandages, dropped them in the sink, and smeared blood on her pajama bottoms as she pulled them on.

"Jenn, what's the matter?" That was Carrie, tapping at the bathroom door.

When Jennifer stepped out, Carrie gasped and reached for Jennifer's arm, like she was touching a ghost.

"Oh, chickie, what happened to you?" Tracey said. She was like a doll with hands molded for specific accessories; she looked odd without a cigarette or martini glass.

"I got...." It was too hard to explain. "I didn't get run over, but this woman got run over and she ran into me."

"Jesus," Kevin whispered. He folded her into a drunken embrace and kissed her forehead and her bloody hands, saying, "Oh, Jenn, baby. You're all banged up."

Tracey offered a bottle of pills and Jennifer swallowed one, not knowing what it was. After that, she floated in a haze, numb. It was not the numbness of childhood illness, where familiar hands take on the task you cannot do. It was like the well-meaning but alien care people offer an injured or abandoned baby animal. How you scoop and coddle a tiny rabbit, cupped in your hands.

The rabbit is not comforted—you're a giant monster booming, "Aw, look at his little earsies," with none of the familiar shapes and smells of its mother. Even so, the baby rabbit is relieved to be dry, to be fed, to be unharmed.

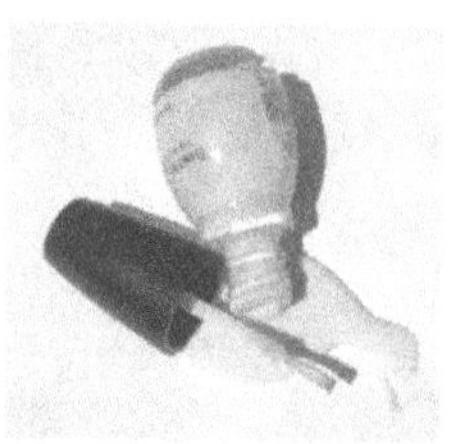

CHAPTER TWO

Olivia

OLIVIA HOLLEY WAS born with a third thumb, which was removed before she entered kindergarten. The sickle-shaped scar remained, a ghost tucked into the webbing between the forefinger and thumb on her left hand. When she drew her thumb alongside her fingers, the scar disappeared into a fold of skin. For most of her childhood, she believed the extra thumb was a sign from God that something was wrong with her. If you asked her about it now, she would laugh and say, "It's just an oddity. Like people who have extra canine teeth."

If you asked, that's what she would say, but after a few hours, her mind would travel back to a time when her brain was a five-year-old turtle in a not fully hardened shell. She would remember not that she had once *believed* something was wrong with her, but that something *was* wrong with her.

Her mother occasionally forgot and called her Mitten, her baby nickname. Standing at the kitchen sink, hurrying through the dishes to get to church on time, Mrs. Holley sometimes said, "Mitten, did you get your dad's coffee cup?"

When it happened, Olivia grabbed the mug off the table and set it on the kitchen counter, instead of slamming it down. In that instant of restraint, Mrs. Holley often realized what she had done, and instead of letting it go, which was what Olivia wished for, her mother apologized. In the course of the apology, she invariably used the nickname again.

The name itself didn't bother Olivia, but the lie surrounding it did. When you have a baby with an extra thumb, it's easy to cover up. You slip a mitten on the offending hand, and when people ask, you say, "She's a thumb-sucker. The doctor recommended the mitten." Olivia's mother told the lie often enough that she seemed to have convinced herself. The first time she slipped and used the nickname in front of one of Olivia's high school classmates, Mrs. Holley told the lie without a moment's hesitation: "When she was a baby, she used to suck her thumb, so we made her wear a mitten over it."

Over them! Olivia wanted to shout. Instead she said nothing, but she worried that her mother was going to hell. Not in a hurtling ball of fire, like a murderer or a rapist, but in a slow, steady slide, like other liars. Olivia knew it should not be a big deal—everyone lied—but her mother lied all the time, and never about anything important.

That was why what happened with the paramedic was so painful.

Olivia was the kind of girl who never managed to break the ice, even at parties where she knew everyone. The paramedic, on the other hand, leaned out the ambulance window every day for weeks and said, "Morning." Or sometimes, "Hey there."

Startled out of her pre-dawn reverie each time, Olivia nodded, half-smiled, and kept walking. She walked every morning for an hour, looping around the river park trail before the sun made it up over the tree line. The ambulance parked at the edge of the river, its driver leaning back in the seat, arm propped on the window. He had been parking there as long as Olivia had been trying to lose weight. For all she knew, before that. She supposed he was on his break.

She accepted the exchange of greetings as an unavoidable annoyance. Then one morning, as she stepped off the curb to start her walk, he got out of the ambulance cab and walked toward her. Standing in the middle of the sidewalk, he seemed to be waiting for her to cross the street and reach him. Or perhaps he hadn't noticed he was standing directly in her path. Except that he was looking at her.

"Hey there," he said.

Olivia dropped her gaze, giving her half-smile and trying to step to the side, between the trash can and him. He side-stepped to match her and then there was no place to go. She flushed. She hated games like that. Resigned, she muttered, "Morning."

"Nice and hot, huh?" he said.

"Global warming. That's what they say." She hesitated, her foot seeking the curb, trying to gauge if there was enough room to squeeze past without touching him.

"Yeah, you right."

He had the hint of an accent, something exotic to Tampa. When he said *hot* it sounded like *hawt*. *There* was *dere*. New Jersey?

Belatedly she felt nervous. There it was, practically dark, and she was alone.

"You new to Tampa? Dis neighborhood?" he asked. He rocked back on his heels like he was enjoying himself. Daring a quick glance at him, she guessed at a nice tan. Or swarthy—Italian? Hard to tell in the pre-dawn. His hair was close-cropped, military style, dark blond or brown. Embroidered on the right side of his uniform shirt was his name: James.

"Excuse me, James, I need to go for my walk." That at least startled him. He looked down at his chest and laughed. She stepped up on the sidewalk and, bracing herself for it, pushed past him, her shoulder brushing against his.

Behind her, he said, "James is my last name. I'm a paramedic, not a Quick Lube guy."

The next morning, she walked a different route, annoyed at being displaced from her own neighborhood. There was too much traffic on the other side of Hillsborough Avenue, and the change in routine threw off her timing. She prided herself on being punctual, because so many people took advantage of the pastor's leniency. Nancy, who was in charge of the computer network, usually came in an hour late and often left early.

Olivia kicked her hair-drying efforts into a higher gear and rushed into her clothes. She forgot her deodorant and had to backtrack, working the deodorant stick up under her shirt, past her bra to her armpits.

By the time she got into the car, she was sweating again. Tampa in July.

Despite all her hurrying, she missed the window of opportunity. She left four minutes late, and in traffic the gap opened wider and wider. Leaving on time meant arriving at church at 8:25. Leaving four minutes later meant arriving at 8:41. Pastor Lou was already in his office when she got there.

"Good morning, Olivia," he called. "How are you?"

"I'm great. How are you this morning?" She forced the cheer into her voice and got back Lou's usual joyful answer.

"I'm blessed."

She stepped into his office, her blouse stuck to her back, and the day started. After her meeting with the pastor came a steady drone of computer work: weekly newsletter, donation entry, membership files, typing requests.

In the afternoon, Beryl Magnuson-Croft came in with the twins. Olivia, after four years on the job, was still considered the "new Beryl," because Beryl had the job before her. Everyone made a big fuss over the boys, who were almost a year old. Beryl usually waved and said hello on her way to Pastor Lou's office, but that afternoon she squeezed the stroller into Olivia's cubicle and sat down. One of the boys was asleep, drooling down his jumper front. The other grunted and frowned, cranky from the heat.

There was no reason for Olivia to feel flattered by the visit, but for a moment she did. Olivia's older sister, Cynthia, and Beryl had graduated from Plant High School the same year. Like Cynthia, Beryl had been popular, athletic, pretty, and smart. Olivia considered herself only marginally one of those things. The feeling of flattery, of being sought out, dissipated as soon as Beryl said, "I need to schedule the boys' baptism. Time to get these little heathens sprinkled."

Olivia laughed dutifully, the way she did at Pastor Lou's jokes, without bothering to evaluate whether they were funny. Then she opened her baptism calendar and inserted a fresh page. She jotted down Beryl and her husband's names, then the boys' names and their birth date.

"What date were you thinking of?" she said. She scheduled baptisms and weddings all the time, but it left her feeling outside the flow of life, which was silly. At 27, she still had plenty of time. All the same, she felt uninvolved. She had no stories of her own to offer nervous brides or proud parents. A scribe, that's what she was, someone who wrote down names and dates.

"October 12," Beryl said, whisking out a bottle and popping it into the one boy's mouth. He looked surprised, but didn't follow through with his opening threat to cry.

"But that's Youth Sunday."

"Oh, I know." As always, Beryl looked supremely confident, one leg crossed over the other. Below the cuffs of her capris, her ankles were evenly tanned, her toenails done professionally.

"It's just that we don't schedule baptisms on major Sundays," Olivia said. "It's too crazy, with the youth doing the services and the two choirs...."

"It's been done before." Beryl would know.

"I'm sorry. Pastor Lou asked me not to schedule any baptisms on major Sundays." Olivia hated having to fall back on Pastor Lou's authority, but no one accepted what she said, unless she cited him as the source. "Is there another Sunday?"

"No, there isn't another Sunday. Look, is he here? I'll talk to him."

"He should be back at four o'clock. He's on hospital visitation."

Beryl grasped the stroller handles, jerked it back sharply, making the twins' heads lurch, and drove it out of the office. She returned twinless at four o'clock and, without stopping to speak to Olivia, went into Pastor Lou's office. Fifteen minutes later he walked her out to the lobby, saying, "As always, it's lovely to see you, Beryl. So sorry I missed the boys."

After Beryl was gone, he paused outside Olivia's cubicle, but didn't meet her eyes. "Go ahead and schedule the Croft baptism for October 12."

"Which service?" she said.

"I didn't think to ask. Call Beryl and find out."

After four years, Olivia found the little daily betrayals wore her out the most.

CHAPTER THREE

Jennifer

KEVIN, IMPERVIOUS TO hangover, called Jennifer in sick. Before he left, he leaned over her in bed and kissed her forehead. He looked sleek, successful, like a magazine ad. His suit was subdued, and capable of hiding the little paunch he was getting at 34.

On his way out of the bedroom, he shot his cuffs, checked his tie and hair in the mirror, and said, "Now, promise me you'll be okay while I'm at work."

"I promise."

By one o'clock, she had done four things: gotten up to pee, drunk a glass of water, and answered two telemarketing calls from mortgage companies.

She turned on the TV and found that all the afternoon talk shows shared an algorithm of human stupidity and misery. Too tired to move, she watched a string of revelations about infidelities and bastardy. She wondered if the guests on the shows were paid actors or if they actually suffered from the humiliating subtitled personal problems ("Wife is pregnant by father-in-law") and a complete lack of shame. This woman was in love with her sister's new husband, and pregnant by the sister's ex-husband. That one was going to marry a soon-to-be transsexual. This man was going to reveal his $400,000 in gambling debts to his fiancée. The next woman had just learned of her husband's obsession with midget pornography. Or was that rude? Little people erotica, then.

When the phone rang again, Jennifer prepared herself for another mortgage sales pitch, but the caller ID said HillCo Holding, the old name for the real estate division of TampaFuture, Inc. She answered, expecting her boss, Lucas.

"Um, Jennifer?" said the voice on the other end of the phone. "This is Mike Renner, Tech Support at TFI, you know?"

"Yeah."

"I left you a message last night, but I figured you might not be up to calling me back. I didn't want you to worry, because I picked up your purse from the sidewalk."

Shock and relief crashed down on Jennifer. She had forgotten about her purse, her cell phone, her credit cards, her house keys.

"I could bring it to you after work," Mike said.

"Yes, thank you. That would be great."

Jennifer fell back on the sofa and slept until the doorbell woke her. It seemed to take forever to gather her body and drag it to the apartment door. Mike stood on the other side, squinting at the peephole, clutching her purse in both hands. At the moment she opened the door, she recognized him, not as a witness to Gayle Prichard's death, but as the person who had installed her new laptop docking station a few months before.

"Oh, hey," he said. He smiled, or tried to, and gulped air. Jennifer imagined that she saw tiny reflections of herself in his eyes: hair tangled, face creased from sleep, handprint of blood smeared on her pajamas.

"Thanks so much." She took the purse from his hands, wondering if she needed to invite him in. That would be the polite thing to do.

"You know, she worked for TFI," Mike said. "The woman, Gayle Prichard. She was a custodian for TFI. She was leaving work, going to the bus stop. They sent an email about it."

Looking at his sad eyes, Jennifer decided she'd rather invite Gayle Prichard's corpse in. It would have been the same thing.

"Thanks again," she said. Before he could answer, she closed the door.

When Kevin came home, he sat on the sofa beside her, frowning.

"Jenn, baby. Is this what you've been doing all day? Have you even combed your hair or showered?"

He meant well. She couldn't keep sitting around like that. After a shower, she slathered ointment on her hands and knees, and let Kevin take her to dinner. She ordered soup and spring rolls, wanting something insubstantial. Something that could be forgotten as soon as she swallowed it.

Later, when Kevin got into bed, she pressed against him, caressing him with her bandaged hands.

"Are you sure you feel okay?" he said.

"I feel fine." She didn't, but she wanted something to blot out her thoughts, and sex always did that. Even when he rolled on top of her and made every aching muscle and joint in her body twinge, it was better than lying awake thinking. The sex worked, leaving her comforted and sleepy, but the feeling didn't last. She slept in small slivers of calm, interrupted by sudden dark images and long periods of wakefulness.

In the morning, her purse lay on the kitchen counter. As recklessly as she had dumped Gayle's purse, she emptied her own. To one side she gathered her cell phone, keys, and the cards from her wallet. When she had salvaged the important things, she swept the rest of it into the trash on top of her clothes from the day before. After a moment's hesitation, she dropped the purse and wallet in. The purse had a minor scuff on one side, and the wallet was pristine, but they were both irremediably tainted.

She felt like a stranger handling her own things, in part because of the gloves she wore. They were plain white cotton, intended to be worn at night with lotion, but she used them to hold her bandages in place.

Leaving the house with the salvageable contents of her purse in a plastic bag, Jennifer took a taxi to the mall. At the Prada counter, she chose without a thought for practicality, but with an eye to luxury: gold buckles and rivets on buttery cream leather. For a wallet she chose brittle red alligator with a series of whispering zippers and clasps. She declined a shopping bag, asking instead for a pair of scissors to remove the tags. Indifferent to the sales clerk's curious gaze, Jennifer transferred the contents of her plastic bag to the new purse with her alien gloved hands.

From there she traveled back in purse-time, first to the make-up counter, before moving on to a hair accessories store for a new brush, and then to a pharmacy for eye drops and all the other things that made up her "necessaries." Newness was the trick to wiping away the events of yesterday. By the time she reached work, she was a new woman.

The effect was brief.

Before, she had always enjoyed the ascent from the lobby to the TampaFuture, Inc. offices. The glass front of the elevator worked as an observation deck and a display case. She liked to stand with one hand elegantly draped on the brass railing, watching the atrium fall away below her.

That morning, she cowered at the back of the elevator, shivering uncontrollably, having just walked past the spot where Gayle Prichard died.

In Jennifer's office, a gorgeous floral arrangement attested to the institutional concern for her well-being. Ensconced in his executive suite, the big boss, Mr. Kraus had declared that she should have flowers for what she'd been through. In her inbox there was an email from her immediate supervisor, Lucas, saying she should take it easy if she didn't feel well. He had cc'd Mr. Kraus.

Taking advantage of their concern, she left work early to meet Carrie for drinks. Reversing her course down the corridor to the elevators, Jennifer felt the cumulative gaze of her coworkers. The executives in their sleek Danish offices with views of the bay, and the peons in their windowless cubicles on the other side, lifted their heads, then dropped them quickly, so that when Jennifer turned her head to either side, she met no one's gaze.

She felt like her feet were made of glass. The slightest misstep would break her. Obviously, the solution was new shoes.

At the International Mall, she and Tracey and Carrie killed three hours and more than a thousand dollars on four pairs of shoes. While Carrie fussed over Jennifer's hands and knees, Tracey made every pair of shoes Jennifer tried on feel fabulous.

"Oh, those make your legs look so long," Tracey cooed, with an iced latte accessory fitted into her martini hand. "I'd kill for ankles like yours. You look so delicate in those shoes."

The same with the boots in glossy black leather, crisscrossed with laces and buckles, nearly knee-high.

"Those would look so amazing a swishy skirt. And you always look so elegant in skirts. The contrast will be fabulous."

Except for the casual sandals, they were all technically out of Jennifer's budget. She'd intended to replace the destroyed Louboutins, but with Tracey encouraging her, the shoes gleamed with the promise of oblivion.

Kevin winced when he saw the receipt, but said, "If it makes you feel better, and as long it's not going to be a regular thing."

"It does and it won't," Jennifer said. To clinch his acceptance, she modeled the shoes for him. The two pairs of pumps and the sandals with her work clothes. The boots with nothing at all. He stopped frowning after that.

Beyond the immediate benefit of spending hours with Carrie mothering her and Tracey complimenting her, the shoes worked. The sleek t-strap pumps with Cuban heels made everything feel new and elegant. On the way into the building the next morning, Jennifer didn't have to make a conscious effort to avoid the square of pavement where the woman had died.

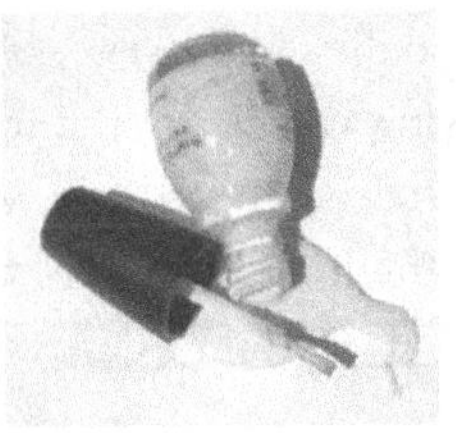

CHAPTER FOUR

Olivia

ON WEDNESDAY NIGHT, before her Bible study class, Olivia ran into Carrie Lewis and Jennifer Palhete in the lobby of the Education Building.

"Olivia, we miss you at the Singles Group. Are you going to come back?" Carrie said.

"Oh, probably not," Olivia said.

Carrie gave Jennifer a sly smile. "First Jenn and then Mandy, and now you, too, Olivia? If you stop coming, I'll be the only one out of the original group left. Are you ditching us? Are you dating someone?"

Olivia wished she could fall into a sinkhole. In the three months since she'd stopped attending the Christian Singles group, she had been on as many dates as she went on in the last year she belonged to the group: zero.

Jennifer looked tired. She smiled wanly and said, "Who is it? Anyone we know?" Jennifer was a real Florida girl: thin, blond, and tan. It was ridiculous that she'd ever belonged to the Christian Singles group. Olivia made a valiant effort not to enjoy seeing her looking haggard. *Poor Jennifer*, she made herself say in her head.

Later, she wondered if the urge to lie was coded in her DNA, deceit inherited from her mother, because instead of telling the truth, Olivia said, "I doubt if you know him. He's a paramedic."

"Is it serious? How long have you been seeing him?" There was a hint of surprise or disbelief in Carrie's voice that rendered Hell entirely unnecessary. Lying was its own punishment.

Before Olivia was forced to answer, a handful of parishioners stopped on the way into the building. One woman said, "Jennifer, are you okay?" Jennifer nodded, trying to deflect it, but the other women began to fuss over her.

"You poor thing," someone else said. "I heard about what happened."

Olivia slipped away, kicking herself mentally, but grateful to escape without building on her lie. What was there to be ashamed of? So what if she hadn't been on a date? Who was she trying to impress? Jennifer? Carrie? Beryl Magnuson-Croft *in absentia*?

It only got worse when Olivia's mother came out of choir practice and said, "Livvie, what's this I hear about you dating an ambulance driver? How come we haven't met him yet?"

"Oh, Mom, just one date. We met for dinner. No big deal." She'd forgotten that Carrie was in the choir, and the lie opened like a gaping maw.

"Well, we want to meet him. Invite him to dinner."

"Sure, okay, if we go out again. I don't know if we will." Olivia was nauseated by the time she went into the fellowship hall for supper. Sitting down to a plate of salad and dry barbeque chicken, she longed for the lie to disappear.

Her brother Rich sat down with a plate full of potato salad, cole slaw, and chicken dripping with sweet sauce. Around a mouthful of food, he said, "Who's this ambulance driver? There's that guy who takes his break down by the river. Is that him?"

Luckily, no one ever listened to Rich, so she managed to ignore the question.

For the first time since her diet resolution, Olivia skipped her walk the next morning. When she went down to breakfast, Mrs. Holley said, "Do you feel okay, honey? You didn't go on your walk."

"The barbeque chicken didn't agree with me," Olivia said. That made five lies she had told in the service of one stupid, prideful mistake.

And the lie wouldn't go away. The problem was not that other people kept bringing it up; her father hadn't even mentioned it. Olivia couldn't let it go. She couldn't forgive herself for telling such a ridiculous lie.

The next morning, she left for her walk with a mission. She couldn't untell the lie, but she could make it true.

The window on the ambulance was down and the paramedic had the seat leaned back as he listened to the radio.

"Hi. I'm Olivia," she said. He sat up, blinking, like he'd been asleep.

"Hey there, Olivia. I'm Randall." He put his hand through the window and she thrust hers up at him. Their palms glanced together, but before he could get a grip on her sweaty fingers, she pulled them back.

"Oh, I thought your name was—oh, that's right—you're not a Quick Lube guy. James is your last name."

"Yeah, you got it. I'm glad you decided I'm not too scary to talk to."

Olivia blushed. "I wasn't scared. I just...."

"You what?"

"I'm not very good at meeting people."

"Seem to me you doing okay, Olivia. I enjoyed meeting you."

"Would you like to go out sometime? To dinner?" she said.

Ever so slowly, the paramedic brought his arm to rest on the window ledge. His shirt sleeve rode up, revealing the edge of a tattoo on his left biceps.

"Did you just ask me out on a date?" he said.

"I—yes." She had just asked a stranger with a tattoo out on a date.

She forced her gaze away from his arm and up to his face. He smiled. His teeth were even and white. In the dimness before sunrise, it was almost all she could see of his facial features. For a moment, Olivia panicked. What if he said no?

"Sure," he said. "I'd go to dinner with you. When?"

"I don't know." She was so stupid she had not planned ahead.

"How about Saturday?"

"Yes, okay. No, wait, I can't on Saturday."

"You tell me," he said and, miraculously, he was still smiling.

"Um, Friday?"

"Okay. What time?"

It was a complete disaster. She hadn't been on a date in so long that she didn't even remember how to arrange one. When he asked for her address, she nearly flailed in embarrassment. The thought of her parents quizzing him was unbearable.

"Maybe we could meet somewhere," she suggested.

"Where?"

She picked a restaurant at random and regretted it as soon as he agreed. Everyone she knew ate there. It was a catastrophe, and by the time it was settled, she was so exhausted she finished her walk at a trudge.

CHAPTER FIVE

Jennifer

WHEN SHE EARNED her new office, Jennifer had viewed the floor to ceiling window that looked out on the main lobby as an inconvenience, but one she welcomed. The knowledge that she was on display to anyone walking by schooled her to wear her public face all the time. No nose-picking or pantyhose-crotch-tugging, two bad habits she didn't need anyway. Nobody ever died from having their pantyhose creep up. Better to learn to suffer with a smile on her face, because that was all she could do when she was front and center at an event.

She missed her old windowless office as she hunkered down at her desk to call the Department of Children and Families. She lost her nerve twice and hung up, but the third time she said, "I'm trying to find out what happened to a little girl after her mother died."

"And?" said the woman on the other end.

"And I thought she might have ended up in state care?"

"You should check with the girl's family."

"I don't actually know the family. I knew the woman who died, and that she was a single mother. I wanted to find out about her daughter."

"You need to check with the deceased's family. Sorry."

The woman didn't sound sorry, and she hung up without waiting to hear what Jennifer would say.

Embarrassed, Jennifer tried next with Human Resources. Linda was a little Buddha, all belly and jolly smile, sitting at a desk awash with candy dishes and figurines, offerings at the shrine of Equal Opportunity. Jennifer barely knew Linda, but she pretended she had dropped by the office to chat. After five minutes of small talk, she said, "So what happened with Gayle Prichard?"

"Who?" Linda said.

"Gayle Prichard, the custodial worker who was killed."

"Oh, her. Hit and run, I guess. I don't think they've caught the guy yet."

"Oh," Jennifer said, her hands going damp. For a moment she stared at them, raw but healing. "I meant, what happened with her little girl. I wondered who ended up with custody of her daughter?"

"I guess I didn't realize she had a daughter. Did you know her well?"

"A little," Jennifer lied, and abruptly cut to the chase. "Look, could you get her family's contact info for me? Whoever her emergency contact was?"

Linda sat up straighter, pulled her jacket together over her belly. "That's confidential. It's against policy to give out personnel info."

"Couldn't you give me a name and phone number? Just whoever she had listed in case of emergency?"

"I don't think so," Linda said. Her hands automatically straightened papers on her desk, obscuring them.

"Please, Linda. I'd just like to make sure her little girl is okay. Please. Please?" The desperation broke through, surprising both of them.

Linda kept her eyes down. "No, I couldn't. I'm sorry."

Close to tears, Jennifer hurried away and locked herself in the handicapped restroom at the end of the hall. She stayed there until she acknowledged it was ludicrous. Fifteen minutes, then twenty, then thirty. The sort of bathroom stay that could only be justified by food poisoning or a total emotional breakdown. She needed to go back to her office and finalize arrangements for the Strategic Planning Conference.

When Kevin called to ask if she wanted to go to lunch, she was relieved. He was only doing it to check up on her, to make sure she was getting through the day, but it offered a reprieve. After she ate lunch, she would come back to the office and it would all be new. A fresh start.

After they ate, while they waited for the waitress to bring back Kevin's card, he checked messages on his Blackberry. Jennifer would have done the same, but now she dreaded going back to work. The fresh start of the afternoon looked threatening. As she stared at the thin spot on top of Kevin's head, she dared to mention her failed conversation with Linda. She made it sound as casual as she could, but when Kevin frowned, she knew she'd failed.

He said, "Well, you should hire a detective."

"Do you think so?"

"No, Jennifer. I think you should forget about it. It's not your problem."

If it wasn't Jennifer's problem, she didn't know whose it was. After Kevin dropped her at the office, she read through the dozen emails Lucas had sent her during lunch. An hour later, she had done nothing else.

Someone knocked uncertainly at the door frame. A pale hand with knobby knuckles.

"Yes?" Jennifer said.

"Oh, hey." Mike from IT. He bobbed his head through the doorway, but kept his body outside. "I was just—I wanted to see how you were. Can I do anything for you?"

Jennifer knew she should say, "Oh, thanks for checking. That's so sweet, but I'm fine." She'd had enough practice lately saying it. Except Mike had seen what happened. Mike was as responsible as she was.

"Come in," Jennifer said.

He entered with one long step and several little shuffles. Then he stood at the corner of her desk, like a kid called up to the front of the classroom.

"You know, if there's anything I can do to help," he said.

"Maybe you could close the door."

With a herkity step backward he pushed the door closed, before returning to the desk. His head turned, as he surveyed the wall of glass.

"I need some information," Jennifer said.

"Oh, um, oh. Like what?"

"I need to find out where Gayle lived. I need to talk to her family. Find out what happened to her daughter."

"I could do some looking online. You know, Spokeo, that kind of thing."

"What I need is her emergency contact info. I asked Linda in HR about it, but she said she couldn't give that out."

"Oh." Mike swayed on his feet, clearly searching for something to do with his hands. They didn't want to stay down by his sides, but he didn't seem to want them drifting up to his face. It must have been habit. He didn't have any pimples, but Jennifer could see he'd been through acne hell and come out the other side permanently marked. He jammed both hands into the pockets of his baggy chinos. His gaze went back to the window, and she recognized on his face the hypervigilance she'd worked through in the first week in her office.

"It's all on the computers now, right? All the personnel files?" Jennifer said.

"Yeah, the new HR software does it all."

"Don't you have access to that?"

"Oh. Hey, I don't know if that's a good idea. I mean, if Linda says she can't give that stuff out," Mike mumbled. His eyes darted around the room before going back to the window.

"Look, it's not like I'm asking you to do something *wrong*. I need to find out about Gayle's daughter. Okay? You know what happened. You know."

Jennifer stood up and her legs felt shaky the way they did after she worked out too hard. She stared at Mike, to force him to look at her. For a few seconds, their eyes locked, before Mike looked away. He coughed, or cleared his throat. A low rumbling sound that could just as easily have been the precursor to tears. He stared at his feet, alternately shaking his head and nodding.

"I know," he whispered.

"That's all I need. If you can get it for me, it's not like anyone would know. Nobody would know it was you."

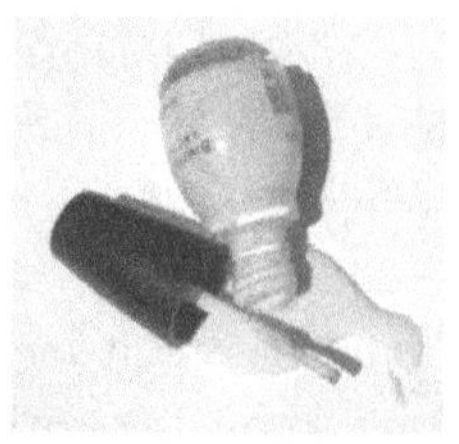

CHAPTER SIX

Olivia

WHEN OLIVIA LOOKED in the mirror she saw a bulldog. Snub nose, jowls, frowning mouth. No matter how hard she tried to smile or lift her chin, the bulldog always returned. In an act of desperation before her date, she went out and bought a fashion magazine to help with her hair and make-up. She ended up with one intended for black women, because it was the only magazine in the whole rack that featured models approaching Olivia's size.

To her amazement, the cover photo solved half her problems. As promised, on page 47, the magazine gave her instructions on how to pull her hair up and back with a zigzagged part, just like the model on the cover. It took her almost half an hour to make her hair look the same, but when she was finished, she was startled by how good it looked. Flattering, even if it didn't solve the bulldog problem.

On page 129, there was a graphic about clothing accessories the magazine referred to as "Waist Defining." Like the hairdo, it had seemed unlikely to work, but a lunchtime trip to Saks in the WestShore Mall proved otherwise. A "slimming" garment and a four-inch wide black patent leather belt, combined with a V-necked blouse and a narrow skirt, produced an hourglass figure Olivia had never known she had. The fact that this also didn't address the bulldog situation confirmed her suspicions that there was nothing to be done about it. If some girls were blessed with feline grace, hers was all canine.

Ironically, her hands were her best feature. They were plump, soft, smooth and white, marred only by the thin scar where her third thumb had been. As a consequence of her very nice hands, her fingernails were her main vanity. She had an elaborate manicure station, and each week she painted her fingernails fresh. As she typed at work, preparing the transcript of the previous Sunday's sermon, she typed 35 words per minute. Never faster, although she could go faster. Every two minutes, she stopped and checked her nails for chips.

On Friday night, they looked perfect. Borrowing another tip from her fashion magazine, Olivia glued a starburst of tiny rhinestones on each thumbnail, just like the model on page 71. When her nails were dry and the rhinestones set, she realized they were too flashy for a casual dinner date, but there was no time to undo it.

Constitutionally incapable of doing anything else, she arrived early at the restaurant. Once there she began to think of all the things that could go wrong. In fact, she couldn't imagine how things could go right. She had never gone on a date with a stranger. A friend from church. A friend of a friend. Never a stranger.

As much as she wanted to chicken out, she didn't have a choice. Either she went into the restaurant or she was a liar who stood people up. She got out of the car and walked across the parking lot with her stomach flopping violently. As her hand fell on the restaurant door, a more horrible prospect occurred to her. If he was early, he would know she had come early. Worse, if he was late, or didn't come at all, she'd be sitting at a table waiting, making excuses to the waitress. Pathetic. Exposed.

She wanted to wait in the car, but that put her a moment away from escape, so she settled for the weathered bench next to the restaurant's front door. The skirt had been a good decision. When she sat down, it covered her knees, dimples and fat included, but it revealed how pale her legs were, how solid her ankles. Just as her hand was on the second button of her blouse—fastened it was too prim, unfastened it revealed cleavage—someone came up the sidewalk, backlit by the setting sun. It was him. Olive tried to do half a dozen different things as he approached: stand, smooth her skirt, straighten her blouse, check her nails, look at her watch. He was six minutes late.

With her hand extended, she squinted into the sunset, trying to make out his facial expression. He clasped her hand and leaned forward to kiss her cheek. Surprised, she took a step back out of reflex.

"Hey, Olivia," he said, and the quiet of his voice embarrassed her as much as the kiss. It was too intimate, and to counteract it she spoke loudly.

"Hi! How are you?" To her relief, he opened the door and she hurried ahead into the air conditioning.

Behind her at the hostess stand, he murmured, "You nervous?"

"Oh, no," she said, not daring to turn around. A ridiculous lie. Was that six? No, there were all the lies she'd told to get out of the house.

"You look real good, baby."

The soft compliment and the endearment caught her off-guard. She looked down at herself to see what he saw. By chance, her final decision had been the second button undone. She spent the first five minutes at their table wishing there were an unobtrusive way to button it, but he was too attentive. Leaning forward on one elbow, he looked at her, while she stared down at a menu she'd long since memorized.

He was too suave. He ordered for her. "The lady is gonna take the crab enchiladas suizas," he said, having asked her the moment before the waiter came. That was a lie, too. She'd said it to sound more interesting, knowing she was a coward who would fall back on the familiar chicken enchiladas.

He ordered a beer, which startled her. Olivia didn't know anyone who drank beer. In college, her older sister Cynthia had a dating rule about that. If the guy ordered alcohol, it was the last date.

"You know what I do, but you didn't tell me what you do with yourself all day," he said.

"Oh. I'm a secretary at Church of the Palms."

The bottom of his beer bottle clunked on the table. He laughed. "Oh, man, nobody gonna believe I went out with a church secretary."

"Oh, well," she said. "What about you, Randall? Now, you're a—"

"Rindell," he corrected, the stress on the second syllable. "I'm a paramedic."

Olivia looked at him, really looked at him, and hoped her sudden realization wasn't plastered all over her face. He was black. Well, obviously, he was not literally *black*, but he was not Caucasian. What she'd assumed was a tan was his natural color. His hair was that indeterminate blonde-brown because. He. Was. Black.

African-American, she corrected, feeling stupid and bigoted.

Standing next to the ambulance in the near dark before sunrise, squinting into the sunset as he came toward the restaurant, she hadn't looked at him closely. He was an obstacle to get past. His name should have been the hint, if she'd been listening carefully. She had assumed—what? That he was white, by dint of the fact that she was white and she had asked him out? That he was white, because it suited her purposes that he should be? Would she have asked him out if she'd realized he wasn't? There were, she knew, white women who preferred black men. Did he think that about her—that she had asked him out because he was black? Oh God, and then the fashion magazine, the hairdo, the rhinestone manicure. A deeper flush crept up over her bare neck toward her face.

He was smiling, showing his dimples, waiting for her to speak.

"You gone a million miles away, didn't you, O-livia?"

She made a squeaking, embarrassed apology, and dropped her voice, at long last wanting some intimacy. "I was wondering where you're from. Your accent. Are you from New York?"

"New York? I get that sometimes. Brooklyn, people say, or New Jersey. I don't know why. I was born and bred in New

Orleans." He said it with four syllables but no *r*.

Olivia followed the obvious conversational track: "So, you came here after Katrina?"

"Yeah. I was an EMT in New Orleans, in Chalmette. The Red Cross helped me finish the paramedic training and get my Florida certification. Did that up in Gainesville and then I got this here job about six months ago."

Olivia clasped her hands together on the table, but Rindell reached over and untangled them. She managed to extract the left one, but he held the right in both of his, looking at it closely.

"Those some fancy nails. That don't get chipped doing typing and stuff?" he said. His hand was so warm, but she shivered as he ran his thumb along the tops of her knuckles.

"Oh, sure, some, but it's just my vanity, keeping them painted."

"You got soft little hands."

"Well, you know, being a secretary. It's all indoor work."

"I bet you got teeny tiny feet, too, don't you?"

"I don't know. I guess. I wear a size five, but I don't think that's all that small." Olivia had no idea what she was saying. She was only talking until she could figure out how to get her hand back out of his. "So did your whole family relocate to Tampa?"

As soon as she said it, she realized the mistake. If he had wanted to volunteer the information, he would have. His gaze went inward and he lost the friendly look on his face. When she tugged on her hand, he let it go.

"I'm so sorry," she whispered.

"Let's don't talk about that tonight," he said in a low voice, and took a drink of beer.

Eager to move away from that subject, Olivia pitched herself into safe conversation: Tampa traffic, Tampa weather, Cuban food, movies, Hemingway cats. Dating was hard work, chatting and smiling, looking for clues about what to say. It was what she always did to make things go smoothly. It required so much effort that by the time the check came she barely had the strength to fight about who would pay. She won by saying, "I did ask you out."

"Awright," he said. "But I'm paying next time."

Next time. Olivia hadn't thought that far ahead. Focused on expiating the lie, she hadn't considered the consequences of the truth. When her cell phone rang, she was grateful.

"Where are you?" her mother said.

"I told you I was going out to dinner."

"Oh, I didn't know when you were coming home. Daddy and Rich went to a softball game, so I'm here all alone." There was a plaintive element to the statement that irritated Olivia.

"I'll be home in a bit, okay?"

"I don't want to ruin your evening."

"You're not." To Rindell she said, "I suppose I need to get home. That was my mother."

"You live with your mama?" he said with a dry smile.

In the parking lot, Olivia breathed deeply, seeing how close she was to escape. Her car was twenty feet away and she counted them down in her mind as Rindell walked her toward it.

Standing at the driver's side, she was nearly home free until he leaned toward her and she pulled back. He glanced away, resting his elbow on the roof of her car. "Why'd you ask me out, Olivia? I get this feeling you don't want to be here with me, and that ain't a feeling I like. Why you here?"

The prospect of another lie sprawled before her. Not just another lie, but an avalanche of lies. She would not tell another. Not one more. Two fat beads of sweat rolled out from the bottom of her cleavage and soaked into her blouse.

"I'm nervous." She exhaled in relief. That was true.

"You don't need to be," he said.

Olivia laughed, feeling slightly hysterical, and fished in her purse for her car keys. "I need to get home. My mother…."

He laughed, too. Not in an unkind way, but distinctly at her. Either her nervousness, or because of how threadbare her escape plan was.

Wallet, lip gloss, nail polish, cell phone, dental floss, sunglasses case, compact, change purse, hair brush. Her fingers tripped over all of them, scrounged at the bottom, collecting purse lint under her perfect nails.

Watching her fishing expedition, Rindell said, "I get you don't like to meet strangers, but I don't get why you'd go and have dinner with one."

"I think I've lost my keys." That at least forced the conversation away from the question. She plowed through her purse again, and Rindell peered into the car.

"They're in the ignition," he said, a smirk hiding in the corner of his mouth.

"I'll call my mom and have her bring me the spare keys. You don't need to wait. I don't want to keep you."

"Why don't I take you by home? That way you don't have to bother your mama."

"Oh, no. I don't want to take you out of your way."

Rindell leveled his hand between them, like punctuation, or a traffic sign. Stop. "I came out to see you. Nothing is outta my way if you're with me, right?"

When she persisted, the hand came up again. He said, "You starting to piss me off, O-livia. I understand, I really do. You don't know me. Fine. But I don't like how there got to be this ongoing suspicion."

"No, it's nothing like that. I just...."

His wallet was out by then, and he began to hand her its contents piece by piece. His driver's license. His hospital ID card. "See? I got a library card, which I know don't guarantee I ain't a psycho, but you asked me out. So maybe you could give me the benefit of the doubt."

"It's not that," she whispered. "I didn't want to inconvenience you."

"And I said it's not. So what's the problem?"

"At Disney World, on the Space Mountain ride, there's a sign to show how tall you have to be. You must be this tall to go on this ride. When I was a kid, I was too short. That's how I feel. About being here. About dating. I don't think I'm tall enough for this ride."

Olivia was prepared to be laughed at again. She was not prepared for the slow, easy smile that spread across Rindell's face and lit up his eyes. He raised his arm and held it straight out, so that his palm barely brushed over Olivia's piled-up hair.

"No, no. You definitely tall enough for this ride," he said.

As his hand slipped down to her shoulder, he closed the gap between them, until Olivia had to tilt her head back to look up at him. She was so astounded by the development that she didn't remember to close her eyes until his mouth touched hers. His lips were soft, but at the corners of his mouth he had fine beard stubble. Where it grazed her skin, it set off shocks that burst all through her body, potent and sly, sneaking past her practicality. He followed up the main kiss with a smaller one on the end of her nose.

She clutched his ID cards in her sweaty hands. Looking down at his driver's license, she frowned.

"You live really close to me," she said.

"Then that's foolish for me not to take you by home."

"Okay."

Of all the things she feared about Rindell driving her home, the one that had not occurred to her was that he drove a motorcycle. There had been one opportunity to say no and she had failed.

She buckled on the helmet he offered her, then hiked her skirt a little. When she lifted her leg to straddle the bike, she discovered the skirt was too tight. She hiked it higher, then higher, aware that he was watching the steady migration of fabric up her thighs. So much for hiding her chubby knees.

Balanced behind him she felt ridiculous, a feeling that didn't abate as he pulled out on Florida Avenue. She held onto him more tightly than she wanted, and at the stoplight at Hillsborough, he patted her hand reassuringly where she clutched his shirt over his abdomen.

"I ain't gonna lose you." He laughed, his teeth sparkling in the sodium lights. His helmet strap hung loose, useless in a wreck.

She shouted directions to him as they went, and too quickly he pulled into her driveway. The cycle's headlight played across the front room windows, but to her relief, he silenced the engine and turned off the light.

"Go on get your keys," he said.

Running up the front stairs, she pulled the helmet off and left it on the steps. Although she slipped in as quietly as she could, and unhooked the extra car keys from the rack in the kitchen, she didn't get away clean. As she reached the front door, her mother came out of the Florida room and said, "Mitten, what are you doing?"

"I locked my keys in the car. I came to get the spare."

Mrs. Holley rubbed at her eyes; she'd been sleeping in front of the TV. "Well, who brought you home? Why didn't you call me?"

"What's that noise? Is that the phone?" Olivia said, like a rabbit trying to draw a predator away from its nest.

"Oh, it's just the TV. Who brought you home? You didn't walk, did you?"

"No. It's no big deal. I'll be back in a minute." Olivia tried to slip out the front door, but Mrs. Holley came after her doggedly, shuffling onto the porch in her slippers. Her head jerked up when she saw Rindell in the driveway.

"You came on a motorcycle? You know that's not safe."

"I wore a helmet," Olivia mumbled, and snatched it up from the front steps.

Her mother kept coming. Olivia walked backwards toward the bike, trying to block Barb's view.

"Have we met?" Mrs. Holley called to Rindell. He was smiling as he removed his helmet. In the steamy twilight, she squinted, offering her hand, and he took it. "I'm Barb Holley, Olivia's mother."

"Rindell James. Pleasure to meet you, ma'am."

"Motorcycles are so dangerous. After what happened to Rich, I don't like you being on one, Livvie."

"I know, Mom. He's going to take me back to get the car. Before it's too dark. I'm sure it's much more dangerous to be on a bike after dark."

Olivia would have done anything to bring the encounter with her mother to an end, but Mrs. Holley put a smile back on her face and said, "We'd love to have you for dinner on Sunday. I know my husband wants to meet you."

Olivia cringed and Rindell must have seen it, because he hesitated.

"Thank you. I appreciate the invitation," he said. He did not say that he would come.

"Well, we better go," Olivia tried again.

She struggled with the helmet strap until Rindell reached out to help her, his fingers warm under her chin. Then, with her mother to witness it all, he kick-started the bike in one elegant movement, and Olivia hiked her skirt in a series of inelegant movements. As they pulled away, Mrs. Holley waved.

Olivia slumped against Rindell's back. There, where he couldn't see her, his anonymous warmth was comforting. Waiting for a green light, he rested his hand on her bare knee. She shivered when he slid his hand down her calf to her ankle and back up.

Back at the restaurant, she unlocked her car with resignation, dreading her mother's inevitable inquisition. There might be tears over the motorcycle and certainly there would be awkward questions. Thinking of it, Olivia hardly noticed Rindell leaning against the car until he touched her shoulder.

"Thank you," she said. "For taking me to get the keys."

"Thanks for supper."

"You're welcome. This is one of my favorite restaurants."

"Look, we don't gotta play games. I seen the look on your face when your mama invited me for dinner."

"They're very old-fashioned. I don't expect you to…."

"You don't need an excuse," he said. "You don't wanna go out again, say so."

"No. I didn't say that."

A tight knot of heat formed under Olivia's sternum, and honesty—the real variety, not the kind she'd forced on herself as restitution for a lie—nearly percolated to the surface. She wanted to tell it all, even the self-deceptions that lay between the exact truths.

Before she could confess, Rindell leaned in and kissed her. The urge for honesty dissipated, leaving behind a vague warmth. It was that easy. Her lie was expiated. They could start over.

"I don't have to go home right away," she said.

"You don't, Cinderella?"

"We could go somewhere. For coffee. Or a drink."

Olivia glanced past him, at his motorcycle, and thought of the heat from his back soaking through her blouse.

"Didn't I say you was tall enough for this ride?" he said.

CHAPTER SEVEN

Jennifer

JENNIFER NEARLY CRIED when Kevin told her he'd invited her parents over for Sunday. He meant well. Maybe he thought her parents could comfort her. Her father, yes, but her mother, unlikely.

Jennifer had always been proud of her father, a high school history teacher. He had never done anything out of the ordinary, but he was always respectable. At school he wore plain grey suits and inoffensive blue ties. In the summers, it was khakis with creases, subdued plaid button-downs, brown loafers and a matching belt. He got his hair trimmed every week and shaved every day. Just like Kevin.

Her mother, however, was an embarrassment.

Jennifer was still trying to live down a childhood full of jeers and questions like, "Is your mom that crazy lady who drives the bus?"

Yes, that was her mother. Moira, the school bus driver with the obnoxious hair, who wore wild mismatched clothes and belted out embarrassing old songs.

Jennifer knew it was useless to ask her father to control Moira's wardrobe. In thirty-five years of marriage he had never said anything but, "You look nice, Moira." He was a gentleman, or blissfully oblivious to his wife's fashion crimes.

Even as they hugged at the front door on Sunday morning,

Jennifer couldn't stop the flood of embarrassment.

Moira was sixty, but she dressed like a retiree with an advancing case of dementia. Other women her age tried to cover the gray in their hair. She experimented with ways of accentuating hers. No trips to a salon to touch up her roots for Moira; she preferred to buy Silver Fox temporary dyes at the Dollar Store. Her most recent experiment had produced a violent pink tinge, spotty in the places where her previous home coloring job had not washed out.

She wore gold sandals, like an aging Hollywood starlet, and sparkling blue polish on her toenails. On the bottom half she wore maroon stretch-velvet track pants, and on top a leopard print velour top with sequins around the neckline. On her arm she carried the five-hundred dollar calfskin Coach handbag Jennifer had given her for Christmas.

Like a diamond on a dog turd, Jennifer thought, hating herself for it. She covered her mouth and hurried to the bedroom.

Doubling her usual preparation time, she wasted twenty minutes changing her mind about what to wear. When she was ready, there was just enough time to drive to church and hurry into the back of the sanctuary, as the first hymn began. She kept her eyes front and center, to avoid the gaze of anyone who tried to acknowledge her. By the second hymn, Moira was rustling in her purse for candies, which she offered in a stage-whisper to the people all around her.

Jennifer scooted closer to Kevin, opening the distance between her and her mother.

After the service, Jennifer herded her parents toward the parking lot, dodging conversations that required introductions.

Olivia Holley prevented them from making a clean getaway. As the Palhetes went down the ramp toward the parking lot, they met the Holleys coming from the education building.

"Hi," Olivia said.

"Hi," Jennifer said, relieved. Olivia wasn't the sort of person who forced you to stand talking for ten minutes after services.

As they passed, however, Olivia paused and turned back.

"Jennifer, I was going to call you Monday, but you'd probably like to know now. The DeLeon wedding is cancelled."

"Oh, that's too bad," Jennifer answered on autopilot. She had no idea who the DeLeons were.

"I'm sorry. I thought the DeLeons were the ones who ended up with the date you wanted for your wedding. I guess I have you confused with someone else." Olivia frowned, clearly puzzled.

"What?" Jennifer felt a flutter of excitement. "Were they on June 13th?"

"That's right. Is that you?"

The flutter of excitement turned into a rush of joy. In the six months since Jennifer and Kevin had gotten engaged, they hadn't picked a compromise date. The next June 13th was the ideal date, and now it was available. The world had been wobbling on its axis, but it began to even out.

"That's great!" Kevin said. He slipped his arm around Jennifer's waist and kissed her on the cheek.

Olivia smiled, enjoying the moment of being the bearer of good news. "I went ahead and penciled you in, but we have to have the first deposit to be able to hold the date."

"She'll bring it to you on Monday," Kevin said.

"That'll be perfect. Have a good day."

"Thanks!" Jennifer said. She and Olivia moved apart, but it was too late.

As Jennifer turned to give her parents the good news, Mrs. Holley said, "We heard what happened to your poor Jennifer. So horrible. So so horrible seeing something like that."

In an instant, Gayle Prichard's bloody face entered Jennifer's mind. Her mouth opening, saying, *My baby. My baby.* Jennifer shuddered.

Kevin interrupted with the news about the wedding date.

The two mothers went from concerned murmuring to gushing over the impending marriage. Before they could be extricated, they were hugging like they were at a Wimauma church supper. Which was probably what Moira thought.

"We're just going to lunch," Mr. Palhete said.

"At The Colonnade," Kevin said.

"Oh, yes, it's a landmark," said Mrs. Holley.

"Why don't y'all come?" That fast, Moira had arrived at the *y'all come* moment.

"Nonsense," said Olivia's father. "We're having fresh corn and homemade crab cakes for Sunday dinner. We'd love to have you."

"Oh, we wouldn't want to impose," Mr. Palhete said.

As always, her father was the blessed voice of reason, Jennifer thought. She glanced at Kevin for back-up, but he was smiling. Only Olivia looked as uneasy as Jennifer felt.

"No imposition," Mr. Holley boomed. "My brother is always over-generous with the crab, so we have enough to feed an army. I vouch that it will be at least as good as The Colonnade, and although I may be biased, I wager it'll be better."

Olivia brought one perfectly manicured hand up to cover her mouth, but met Jennifer's gaze and pulled it away. She plastered on a smile and said, "I thought you'd be happy about the date. It's too bad for the DeLeons, but it's nice for you."

"Nice for me," Jennifer said stupidly, but her words were lost in the growing volume of conversation between the Holley and Palhete parents. The address was given, directions repeated. In the car, driving toward the Holley house, Jennifer saw the meal with the Holleys for what it was: a way to limit the number of people exposed to Moira.

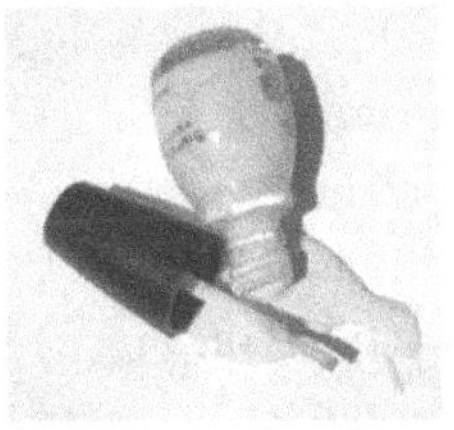

CHAPTER EIGHT

Olivia

FOR RICH THERE was no embarrassment in living with his parents. Since the wreck, he couldn't live on his own. Olivia's excuse for living at home had evolved over the years. During college, her parents assumed she would live at home until she married, like her sister Cynthia had. As that prospect dimmed, Olivia decided to save money to put down on a house of her own. Then after Rich's accident, her parents hinted that she should stay to help with him.

Six years of working full time and her father's refusal to take rent had paid off her car and put eighty thousand dollars in her bank account. Now, with Rich settled into his life, Olivia didn't know what she was waiting for. The prospect of never moving out frightened her, but so did the prospect of moving out alone. The impending arrival of witnesses to her living situation heightened that sense of panic.

She brazened through first few minutes with the Palhetes by going into mindless hostess mode. "Make yourselves at home. Can I get you something to drink? We'll be ready to eat in about half an hour."

Mrs. Palhete and Mrs. Holley talked like old friends. The camaraderie between Mr. Holley and Mr. Palhete was equally enthusiastic, if not equally distributed between the two men. In ten minutes, Mr. Holley had the other man out in the back yard, discussing citrus trees.

Overhearing her mother say, "Oh, did you see the Veatch baby getting baptized? Such a sweet little black baby. They're so cute," Olivia blanched. The Veatches were one of three black families at the church, but why did her mother have to put it that way?

"So, Kevin, you're still working at Grange Toyota?" Olivia pitched her voice loud enough to drown out her mother.

"I'm actually at the Lexus showroom down on Dale Mabry now, and I owe it all to the church," Kevin said. Jennifer elbowed him, but he ignored it. "When I came here, people told me the best place to network in Tampa was Church of the Palms."

"Well, I'm sure it's been good for more than networking," Jennifer said.

Kevin winked. "Olivia knows what I mean. Besides, I didn't just meet David Grange at church. I met Jenn there, too."

"Oh, well, congratulations. I'm so happy you'll get the day you wanted for your wedding," Olivia said.

"We're putting you on the guest list," Kevin said.

"We're about ready to eat," Mrs. Holley called from the kitchen.

"The crab is very good this year." Olivia wanted to offer a condolence prize for their suffering. "Come eat, Rich. Turn off the TV and come into the dining room."

At that moment, the doorbell rang.

Rindell.

Olivia's guts went nearly liquid with fear, and she was grateful for Jennifer and Kevin's presence. She tried to steady herself on the walk to the front door, but in that instant the house went from warm and familiar to cramped and hostile. *White.* The house practically screamed, "White people live here!" Of course, all the family photos were of white people, but the frumpy furniture, the floral air freshener, her mother's ridiculous pitcher collection, all seemed so hopelessly, categorically Caucasian. It could only have been worse if it had been December and her mother had been playing *White Christmas*.

Before she could speak to Rindell, her father waddled into the foyer, winded from the effort. Olivia swallowed hard and said, "Daddy, this is Rindell James."

Her father clasped Rindell's hand, saying, "Jim Holley. Welcome to our little corner of Tampa."

"Thank you. Real good to meet you, sir."

Seeing her father's raised eyebrow, Olivia realized that while Mrs. Holley was happy to trumpet the race of the Veatch baby to anyone who would listen, she hadn't told her husband that Olivia's "suitor" was black. Olivia checked the handshake, to see if her father was giving Rindell "the grip." Could black people be white-knuckled? She wished she could thump herself for being so stupid. It wasn't as though Rindell was literally black, and it was clear that Mr. Holley was giving him a crushing handshake. And it was Olivia's fault. She should have warned Rindell. She should have warned her father.

The other introductions were easy. Jennifer and Kevin were perfectly friendly, Rich indifferent, and the two mothers shook Rindell's hand while wearing over-eager smiles. From there, Olivia herded everyone into the dining room, eager to get food into peoples' mouths.

"So, Rindell," said Mr. Holley, as Olivia knew he would. He had done it to all of her sister's boyfriends. "Tell us about yourself."

Rindell laughed. "What did you have in mind, sir?"

"Now, a father needs to know certain things about his daughter's young men. You're employed as…."

"I'm a paramedic." Rindell took it well, but he spared a glance out of the corner of his eye, to check on the whispering between the two mothers.

"Well, it sounds like I picked the right day to have a heart attack, with a paramedic at lunch."

"Jim," said Mrs. Holley.

Jennifer jumped in with: "I always thought being a paramedic would be such a stressful job. I mean, having people's lives in your hands."

"There's that movie, that Nicholas Cage movie, where he's a

paramedic," Kevin said. "I mean, it's not like that, I guess?"

"It's kinda stressful sometimes, but not too bad. You got to balance things, accept that you can't control everything. People do die, no matter how hard you try sometimes."

"Well put," said Mr. Palhete. "We simply have to put some things in God's hands."

They turned as a body to look at him in surprise. The sentiment seemed at odds with his quiet professorial demeanor.

"Do you see a lot of people die?" Jennifer said, but it was no longer friendly conversation. The look she gave Rindell was intense. "There was a woman who was run over across from the Bank of America parking garage downtown."

"Jennifer," Kevin said.

Olivia heard the warning in his voice, but couldn't think of how to change the subject. Jennifer looked pale and she clutched her fork with a bite of crab cake skewered on it, forgotten.

"What?" Jennifer said. "I wanted to ask if he—"

"I don't think we need to talk about it at lunch. I'm sure he doesn't want to talk about it."

"It's awright," Rindell said. "I heard about that. Sounded pretty bad. I wasn't there, though. I usually work the third shift. I just got off duty a couple hours ago."

"Is it hard to forget about it, when you come home from work?" Jennifer said.

"It's not too bad. I seen a lot worse things when I was in Iraq."

"You served in the Army, then?" said Mr. Holley.

"Marine Corps."

Although Olivia tried to will him not to, he lifted the sleeve of his polo shirt to reveal a complicated blue and red tattoo with the letters USMC below it.

"Oh, my father was in the Marines," Mrs. Holley piped in. A lie. Her father was in whatever service branch she wanted him to be in, depending on the conversation. Olivia doubted he'd been in the military at all.

"So you went to Iraq," Mr. Holley said, frowning about the

tattoo, although it was already hidden again.

"Two tours, fifteen months each," Rindell said.

"Were you a paramedic in the Marines?" Kevin said.

"No, the Marines don't got medical personnel. That's the Navy. I was a fifty cal gunner."

"Decided not to reenlist, eh?" The insinuation in her father's voice irritated Olivia. As though three years weren't enough?

"I'd seen all I wanted to see." Rindell took a bite of his lunch. "The crab cakes are real good, Mrs. Holley."

"Oh, thank you. It's an old family recipe." A lie. The recipe came out of *Southern Living*.

"Toyotas, right? That's what you work with?" Rich said to Kevin. He'd caught up on the earlier conversation, or he'd only now thought of what he wanted to add.

"That's right. Lexus is a Toyota brand," Kevin said.

"It's a mistake."

Everyone laughed, including Kevin, who said, "I don't know. I think I'm doing okay."

"No, no. Toyota's mistake. A mistake to get sidetracked with hybrids."

"I'll just have to take your word on that, buddy." Kevin looked around at the Holleys for guidance.

Olivia laughed with relief and patted Rich's shoulder. He shrugged it away and leaned closer to Kevin. His left hand, the one he never seemed completely in control of, swooped up and picked at his eyebrow.

"The future is hydrogen—hydrogen—hydrogen fuel cells. It's the low volumetric energy density—that's the trick," Rich said.

"Is that so? That's interesting."

The laughter started with Kevin and spread to everyone else.

"Kevin's in sales. He doesn't make the cars, Rich. He sells them," Olivia said. She felt badly for Rich, who frowned in confusion, but it lightened the mood.

After lunch, as they cleared the table, Olivia whispered to Rindell, "I'm so sorry. I didn't mean for you to have to meet so many people. It was just chance that the Palhetes came to lunch."

"It's awright." He leaned in to take a pile of plates from her and stole a kiss, his lips warm and secretive below her left ear.

"Oh, don't let her foist those dishes off on you." Mrs. Holley maneuvered in between them.

"Sorry," Olivia mouthed as she took the plates into the kitchen.

After the Palhetes left, Rindell seemed eager to escape.

"Let's go set out on the stoop," he said. "Or we could walk over by my house, get some fresh air."

"We're going for a walk if anyone wants to come," Olivia called into the living room. He closed his eyes in dismay, but she knew it was safe. No one would join them for a walk on a humid July afternoon.

"Did that go okay?" he asked as they walked.

"I'm sorry. Like I said, my parents are old-fashioned." She couldn't bring herself to tell him the exact truth. Instead, she tried to explain her family and apologize for them. Her father's pomposity, her mother's lies, Rich's oddness. "Rich had a bad motorcycle accident. It caused permanent brain damage. That's why my mom was weird about your motorcycle."

"Yeah, I get you," Rindell said.

Olivia refused to confess the main source of her parents' weird behavior at lunch: Rindell was only the second boy she'd ever brought home. Dan was the first and, although he'd fit in well with her family, he had disappeared out of her life without saying good-bye. Not that she blamed him.

When Rindell turned the corner, leading them toward the river, she had a sinking feeling. Their destination lay ahead. He lived at the Eyesore.

Like most of the houses in the neighborhood, it was a frame bungalow with a broad front porch. Where most of the bungalows near the river had been maintained or rehabilitated to their original charm, the Eyesore stood alone in its unrepentant ugliness. Two of the brick porch pillars had heaved outward, skewing the porch supports, while a live oak sapling had grown to a tree near the front steps. The growing tree had buckled the porch floor, and ruptured the front edge of the roof. Every time it rained, the two shattered halves of rain gutter emptied a torrent of water on the front steps.

The ugliness of the house could have been easily remedied—the tree cut, the broken porch repaired, the battered lap siding painted fresh. The house, however, was not the only problem. What Mr. Holley complained about, and what had earned the house its nickname, was an assemblage of fifty years of junk: rusted cars, abandoned appliances, rolls of orange safety fencing, and beyond that, a hail-dimpled Airstream trailer sitting on moldering tires, with a lean-to shed affixed to its side with tin sheeting, tar paper, and caulk.

Rindell called it home.

"It's temporary," he said, reading the dismay she couldn't conceal. "When I got here I needed to find a place quick and he needed a tenant. I love living down here and no way I can afford a house in this neighborhood. And it's cheap, so I figure if I can stick it out for a while, I can save up enough money for a down payment on a house."

"That's why I live at home, so I guess that makes us equal," Olivia said.

"Yeah, only I didn't have that look on my face when I found out you live with your mama."

She laughed and covered her face, but he put his arm around her and gave her a squeeze.

"You know, my dad has been at war with Mr. Batson about this trailer ever since I was a kid."

"Welcome to the demilitarized zone then," Rindell said.

The lean-to housed the kitchen, its rough plank floor giving onto the trailer, where a living room and bedroom were cobbled together. It was dilapidated, but neat. An open cupboard held some folded clothes and his uniforms on hangers. She took one of the two chairs and regretted it as the cane bottom sagged under her. The air inside was stagnant, but cleared quickly when he turned on the window air conditioner. Rindell sat on the bed across from Olivia and smiled.

"Why you look so worried? I don't scare that easy," he said.

"My family is not always on their best behavior. Or their best behavior is questionable."

"It's all good. Why don't you come over here?"

After all, she had come back to his house with him. What had she expected? What was he expecting? She sat on the edge of the bed next to him, close enough that his arm fit around her. The kiss came as a relief, effortless, but she nearly came undone when he slipped his hand up under her blouse to caress the naked roll of fat above the waist of her skirt.

"Whoa," he said, when she jumped back from him. "We can slow this down."

"You—it tickles." Taking the amusement in his eyes as a challenge, she kissed him. She liked it, more than she remembered liking any other kiss, but she had no clue what to do next.

Rindell did. Until the moment Olivia stopped worrying and began to enjoy it, she was shocked by how comfortable Rindell was. He didn't fumble at her clothes, the way Dan had. Rindell took her blouse and her bra off as easily as she could have, before he went to work on her skirt zipper. With daylight streaming through the curved window above the bed, Olivia was almost afraid to open her eyes, to witness the steady removal of her clothes.

What she didn't want, though, was a repeat of the embarrassing and embarrassed coupling in the dark of Dan's bedroom. She made herself look at Rindell as he kissed her breasts and stroked her thighs on the route to removing her panties. Rindell wasn't even embarrassed to have her watch him put on a condom. He grinned at her as he rolled it on. Then his smooth back was under her hands, his breath warm on her neck, saying, "Oh, sweet Olivia." Not painful at all and, after the initial shock of him pushing into her, very nice. No, nice was too simple a thing. It was sweaty and wonderful, but anxiety-producing, especially when he stopped.

She was content to lie back and let him do whatever had to be done; that was how it happened with Dan. Except Rindell stopped and said, "What do you need, baby?"

"I—it's fine," she said, no longer brave enough to look at him. From his breath she knew he wasn't more than two inches from her face.

"Fine? What's that mean?"

"I meant what you're doing is fine."

He laughed and she opened her eyes a slit to find him smiling down at her.

"It's supposed to be better than fine. Just give me hint: slower, harder, faster, more to left, what?"

"I don't know."

That made him laugh more. He thrust in and out of her, slower and harder than he had before. He was right. It was better than fine. Sex with Dan had been about the level of disappointment Olivia expected from life. Sex with Rindell was more like the magazines made it seem, right down to the almost impossible-to-grasp and then suddenly everywhere orgasm.

For a few minutes afterward, she floated on a cloud of pleasant amazement until she realized she was lying naked next to a veritable stranger, exposed.

While he disposed of the condom, she sat up and hunted for her clothes.

"Where you going?" he said, as she put on her blouse.

"Um." She had planned to make as graceful an exit as she could, but he put his arms around her and pulled her back into bed.

"So, how long did you say you'd been in Tampa?" she said.

"You don't got to make conversation, Olivia. You don't. Your mama teach you that? To keep filling up the quiet so nobody feels uncomfortable? Nod okay. Don't say anything. You try it for five minutes."

She nodded, already desperate to break the silence. They lay face to face and, because he looked into her eyes, she looked back. His eyes were light brown with flecks of green. She opened her mouth, intending to tell him that he had nice eyes, but he put his finger on her lips. He watched her squirm, his mouth twitching in a smile. The silence was agony to Olivia. Not speaking was like being asked not to breathe. In the grips of it, she clutched him violently, grinding her face in to his shoulder. It was torturous, but her shyness passed off and left her unafraid to manhandle him. She wrestled against him, as though he were physically preventing her from speaking. He was lean, but strong, and he burned stripes around her wrists with his bare hands, pinning her under him. Then for a few minutes he kissed her, relieving her of the urge to talk.

He released her and wiggled his fingers into her sides, until she screamed with laughter and said, "Stop! Stop! Before I pee my pants."

He collapsed on her laughing. "That's about the first real thing you've said to me all day."

"I don't mean to. I—I'm not very good at dating."

"You doing fine." He undid the first button on her blouse. "You need to get naked more often. That's the real Olivia under those church secretary clothes."

The real Olivia. The remark stayed with her long after Rindell walked her home in the dark and left her on the porch with a kiss. Her parents had gone to bed, but Rich was watching TV. He turned off the set and blinked half a dozen times. For a moment she worried about what he saw: her rumpled hair and clothes.

"Dad doesn't like him."

"Big deal," Olivia said, but it was pure bravado.

"Dad'll make you break up with him."

"Is that why Tanya broke up with you? Because her dad didn't like you?" Olivia regretted it as soon as it was out of her mouth.

"Fuck you," Rich said dismally. Tanya had broken up with him because after his accident, he wasn't the guy she loved.

"I'm sorry. Do you remember when we built the fort under the dining room table when we had chicken pox?"

"Yeah," he said, his frown already fading.

"You tickled me so hard—"

"You wet your pants!" He guffawed, pleased at the memory and at remembering it. It pleased her, too, and she leaned over to kiss his forehead.

"I love you, big brother."

"Yeah?"

"You know I do. Come on, let's go up to bed. Work in the morning."

"Yup." He puffed his cheeks out and exhaled loudly. "Gotta build some bookcases." It almost brought her to tears. A degree in mechanical engineering and that was all he was capable of now.

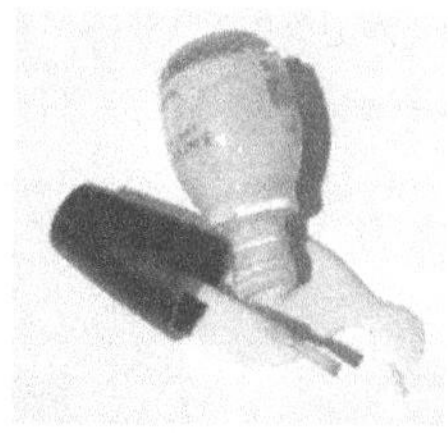

CHAPTER NINE

Olivia

OLIVIA WOKE UP drenched in sweat from an anxiety dream. Having sex with Dan had been a stupid mistake, but one she made with forethought. Too much forethought, not enough knowledge, it turned out. She'd planned on that one sexual act making their relationship more serious. Instead, it sped up the rate at which the relationship turned lukewarm. Dan stopped calling her and he stopped coming to church, too. That was the sum total of the break-up. She foisted her virginity off on him and he stopped showing up.

With Rindell, she had made a stupid mistake without any planning. It was official: she was the sort of girl who had sex on the second date, if she stretched the definition of "date" to include a Sunday dinner with her family.

On Tuesday morning, at the weekly staff meeting at church, they prayed for refugees in Darfur, Bernadette's elderly mother, and the Children's Ministry Director's marriage. Olivia enjoyed the staff meetings, which were an hour of quiet in the dim, multi-colored light of the small chapel. She didn't have to pay strict attention, as long as she murmured along with the prayers. That day, she felt twangy with nerves. Clasping her fingers together over and over, Olivia longed to ask for prayers, but worried over how to phrase the request. *I had sex with a guy I barely know, and now I'm worried he won't call me* would cause more problems than it solved.

Belatedly, Olivia thought to pray for forgiveness for the actual sin of fornication. It was a half-hearted prayer, buried under a wave of anxiety. She almost wished someone would ask her what was wrong, but as long as she did her work, no one noticed her. If the newsletter and the Sunday bulletin were right, and the membership and attendance numbers were properly reported, she could have been a robot.

She indulged in feeling Alone and Miserable for a few minutes, but she had work to do. Starting up the computer, she opened the manila folder full of attendance cards. Right on top: Beryl Magnuson-Croft and her husband. Ugh.

Olivia was twenty or so records into the file, when someone knocked at her cubicle. She looked up and found Jennifer in the doorway, looking pale.

"I thought I'd see you yesterday," Olivia said. She didn't want to be unpleasant, but it was the sort of lapse that created problems for her. People forgot to pay the deposit and lost their reservations. Then they blamed Olivia.

"I'm sorry. I just got so busy." Jennifer lowered herself carefully into the guest chair and reached into her purse for a checkbook. For several moments, she fumbled with it, flipping to a fresh check, uncapping her pen.

"You can write it to COTP, so you don't have to write it all out. It's six hundred even."

Jennifer scrawled the check in sloppy penmanship, which surprised Olivia, who thought of Jennifer as stylish in every way. Only as she took the deposit check did Olivia notice her scabbed and red palms.

"Your poor hands," she said. "How are you?"

"I'm okay." Jennifer didn't seem okay, and she stayed seated even after Olivia gave her the receipt for the deposit.

"Would you like some hand lotion?"

She offered the bottle and Jennifer took a squirt of it. With a confused look she pulled off her engagement ring off and laid it on the corner of the desk.

"Are you sure you're okay?"

Olivia expected a nod, but Jennifer said, "Did you ever make a promise and then not keep it?"

"I'm sure I have." At that moment Olivia was particularly willing to commiserate on sins and failures. She was a fornicating liar.

"I'm worried I'm going to forget. It would be so easy to forget. That woman who got run over." Jennifer circled her hands around each other long after the lotion had been smoothed on.

"That was so sad. I'm sure that was horrible for you."

"Not as horrible as it was for her." Jennifer looked like she might laugh, but then she clapped a hand over her mouth and began to cry. "Oh God. I just—when she was dying, she thought I was someone else. Her sister. And she asked me to promise to take care of her daughter. She was dying. What was I going to do? She was dying. I promised. Now I can't find out where her daughter is."

Instinctively, Olivia glanced up, but Pastor Lou's office was dark, as she knew it would be. He was at a conference in Lakeland. Watching Jennifer smear her make-up with tears, Olivia grabbed a box of tissues from the bookshelf and pushed them toward her.

"It's okay, Jennifer," she said. "You did a good thing. What if she'd died with no one there? You helped her."

"That's what Pastor Lou says, but I'm not doing what I promised. I need to keep my promise and I don't know what to do. I made the promise and now I can't make it come true."

"Can I help?" Olivia said.

Jennifer's head came up slowly and the look on her face was clear to Olivia: no one else had asked yet. It made Olivia's heart go soft. She felt willing to do anything, to be the person who helped Jennifer keep her promise. To make a lie true.

"I have the address where she used to live. I got it from a guy at work—he kind of broke the rules to get it—but I haven't worked up my nerve to go."

"I'll go with you," Olivia said.

"Don't offer until you hear where it is."

The address, on a street called Avon, meant nothing to Olivia, until she pulled up a map online. It lay west of Central, south of Martin Luther King, dead center of the public housing projects.

"I'd ask Kevin, but he says I have to stop obsessing, but you see, don't you? You see how important it is." Jennifer's voice dropped to a quiet plea.

"I do see," Olivia said. If making a lie true mattered, keeping a promise to a dead woman was far more important. "I have a friend who might go. The guy you met at lunch." That quickly she volunteered Rindell, when she wasn't even sure if he would call her. That was how much she wanted to help.

"You wouldn't mind asking him?"

"Not at all."

Olivia never saw the ambulance on Mondays or Tuesdays. His days off, she guessed. On Wednesday, though, she would ask him. Regardless of what had happened between them, she would ask him to help Jennifer.

Olivia plodded through the rest of the morning's work and then got lunch from the staff refrigerator. She was opening her salad container when she heard Bernadette say for the fifth or sixth time that day: "The assistance program only takes applications on Wednesdays and Thursdays. You'll have to come back then."

Olivia was glad it wasn't her job to turn away homeless people all the time. Bernadette seemed to like it.

"Pardon me, ma'am," came the answer. "I'm looking for Olivia Holley."

Relief washed over Olivia with such force that she felt shaky and wet between the legs. She turned away from her computer, expecting to see Rindell come around the corner, but her phone rang first.

She answered with a sharp, "Yes?"

"Olivia?" It was Bernadette calling from ten feet down the hall to say, "There's a man here to see you. What was your name?" A pause. "Randall to see you. Are you available?"

"I'll be there in a minute." Olivia used the minute to check her teeth, her breath, her nails.

When she saw Rindell in front of the reception desk, the depth of the insult sank in. He looked professional, wearing a polo shirt and khakis. He was clean-shaven and neat, but Bernadette's chilly behavior was a simple matter of categories: he was black, therefore Bernadette assumed he was there for the assistance program. That Was Why Black People Came To Church Of The Palms.

"Come down to my office," Olivia planned to say, but before she could, Rindell crossed the lobby and kissed her on the cheek. Wanting to erase Bernadette's insult, Olivia turned her head and kissed him on the mouth. He tasted like cinnamon.

"Hey. I wanna take you to lunch. I'm not too late, am I?"

"Let me get my purse." Grabbing the purse and her keys, she stuffed her salad into a drawer and hurried back to the lobby.

"I'm going to lunch," she said to Bernadette and breezed out the front door with Rindell. She had never "gone to lunch." It felt thrilling and evocative. Going to lunch with a man. A lunch date. Even the sight of his motorcycle couldn't trip her up. Taking his arm, she said, "Let's go in my car. I have air conditioning."

"Now, see, that's what I'm talking about," he said in the car. "You actually seem glad to see me today."

"I am." Too eager, she thought, as she leaned across the console and kissed him. Did that make her seem desperate?

As though he knew all her secret desires, he took her to Mema's, the temple of forbidden indulgence. Alaskan Fried Tacos were not part of her diet. She stood before the shabby menu board tacked to the tiny shack, scanning hopelessly for something similar to the salad she'd abandoned.

"You been here? I recommend the shrimp tacos, or you don't like shrimp, the grouper tacos are real good." The grouper tacos were her favorite. Rindell had already ordered and was waiting to the side of the window, his wallet in hand.

"Um, okay," she said. "Two grouper tacos and an iced tea. Unsweet."

"Two won't get you through the afternoon. Give her three and let's have some of the black bean dip, too."

The day was miserably hot, but in the shade of a live oak, Olivia felt shivery with happiness. When he brought their food to the picnic table, she took a long drink of iced tea and made a sound of pleasure.

While waiting, she had thought of the perfect opening question, and she released it as soon as he sat down: "So, what's Mr. Batson like? We were so scared of him as kids, but I don't know anything about him."

"He a crazy old bastard. You was right to be scared," Rindell said. As she'd hoped, he launched into a story about his landlord.

While he talked, Olivia paced herself over the tacos, so as not to inhale all the succulent greasiness and crunchy shell doused with sour cream that she had been denying herself. As she licked her fingers, she found him watching her with a smile.

"Now I been doing all the talking and you haven't hardly said nothing to me."

"I thought I was supposed to be quiet."

He laughed, shook his head. "You so contrary. You look happy, though."

"I am. Thanks for lunch." She fished an ice cube from her cup to wash her hands.

"You welcome." It surprised her how his accent, his grammar, which had seemed so glaringly alien at first, felt familiar now. Like she was privy to an inside joke, included in a club.

When he came around the table and sat next to her, she wiped her hands on a napkin and prepared to ask for a favor.

CHAPTER TEN

Jennifer

"YOU LOST YOUR ring?" Kevin said in a restrained shout. He replayed the voicemail for Jennifer, angrily stabbing at the phone's buttons until the message repeated.

"Hi. It's Olivia at Church of the Palms. For Jennifer. I hope you're feeling better. You accidentally left your ring here. I had Luanne lock it up in the safe. Let me know when you can come get it."

"I didn't lose it," Jennifer said. "I took it off to put on some hand lotion and I forgot to put it back on."

"You got lucky the secretary found it first."

"It wasn't lost. It was on her desk. Who else would have found it?"

"And what were you doing at the church today? Were you lying when you said you took the deposit on Monday? Did you lie to me?" The shout was no longer restrained, but it reached Jennifer through a haze. She put her head down, turned away.

"No, I...." She shrugged. "I forgot. It's no big deal. I went today and wrote the check and it's all reserved now. Okay?"

"No, it's not okay. How am I supposed to feel about the fact that you forgot to reserve the church for our wedding? That you left your ring on the secretary's desk? Did you call Asturiano about the reception? Miss Special Event Planner?"

"Why can't you do anything? I'm supposed to believe you're

so busy all day that you don't have five minutes to call Asturiano?" Jennifer tried to respond with heat, but her anger was cool.

"You said you'd take care of it."

"No, I didn't. You *told* me to take care of it. Well, guess what? I don't take orders from you. So, you know what? I made the deposit. You can call Asturiano tomorrow."

"Nice," Kevin muttered.

Finally Jennifer felt the anger she'd been feigning, a hot vein of disgust that throbbed in her throat, wordless and futile. She turned away from Kevin and walked into the bedroom.

"What is going on with you?" he yelled after her. He couldn't be bothered to follow her and have a conversation.

"Nothing."

"Nothing? Don't play dumb with me, Jennifer. I get that the woman's death upset you. I get that, but you have got to stop being so morbid."

"What am I doing that's morbid?"

"Oh, let's see. How about asking the paramedic about that woman while the poor guy was trying to eat lunch?"

Jennifer peeled out of her work clothes, but instead of hanging them up, she left them on the floor where they fell. Rummaging through the other clothes on the floor, she found her pajamas and put them on. The whole apartment looked like a disaster, because if she didn't do it, it didn't get done.

"You're putting on your pajamas? At six o'clock? What about dinner?" Kevin stood in the doorway, watching her.

"I'm not hungry."

"Jenn, you need to eat something."

"I'm fine." She flopped down on the bed, but he didn't go. He stood there, hovering, worrying.

"Where's all the stuff for the invitations?" he said.

"It's in the file cabinet. I'll call tomorrow, okay?"

"I can do it. I'm not trying to dump everything on you."

"I'll do it." That was what he wanted. For her to do her job.

"I want to make sure Asturiano still has the date open. That has to be settled, so we can order the invitations."

"I know," Jennifer said.

"Okay. I just think we need to get moving. Now that we have the date, we need to light a fire."

That was one of Kevin's phrases: *light a fire*. He was always going to light a fire under someone. Now it was her.

"Something, something, something," he said. "Okay?"

"Okay." She didn't know what he'd said, but it was easier to agree.

"I'm going to get something to eat. Do you want anything?"

"No, I'm fine."

After he was gone, Jennifer dragged herself out of bed and went into the living room, where she turned on her laptop. First things first: update the wedding to-do list. No, first things first: send a message to Wendi, her best friend. They were roommates all through college, and at Wendi's wedding two years before, Jennifer had been her maid of honor. Wendi had promised to do the same when Jennifer got married. Then she moved to Vermont with her husband, got pregnant, and went silent. Jennifer understood—having a baby took a lot of time—but she'd counted on her wedding being a perfect chance for them to catch up. She typed a quick message about finalizing the date and fired it off with the subject line "Time to find a babysitter! I'm getting hitched!"

Half an hour later the response came, stingingly short: "That's great, Jenn! Sorry but it isn't going to work out for me to come then."

Just like that, Carrie Lewis was promoted to maid of honor. So much for best friends.

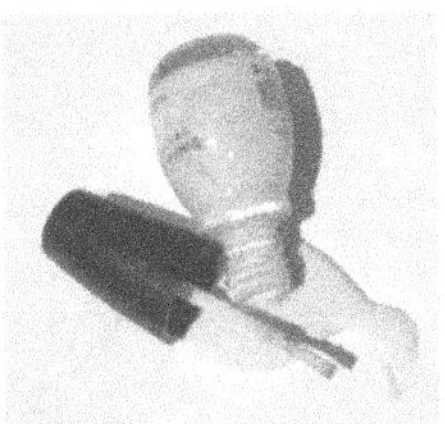

CHAPTER ELEVEN

Olivia

PUBLIC HOUSING WAS not as frightening as Olivia had imagined, but it was more depressing. Outside a battered store that had "MEAT MARKET" painted on its stucco wall, three young black men hung around, drinking out of paper sacks. The streets were original red brick and beautifully shaded by live oaks, but the apartment buildings were grotesque: white concrete block with turquoise trim and a smattering of graffiti. Grass refused to grow in the front yards, where people in lawn chairs watched the car go by.

If any of it unnerved Rindell, he didn't show it. After she parked, he hopped out of the car and started down the sidewalk. She hurried after him, as he walked along, reading apartment numbers, dodging a pile-up of plastic kiddie cars and bikes. When he ducked into a dark stairwell to the second floor, Olivia followed closely, panting from the heat.

By the time she caught up to him, he had already knocked on an apartment door, which swung open. Faced with a frowning, dark man in boxers and an undershirt, Rindell stuck out his hand and said, "Hey, pardner, where y'at? I'm Rindell, dis Olivia."

The man shook hands and mumbled his name warily: "Freddy."

"We looking for somebody knows Gayle Prichard."

The man's eyes tensed up and his lip curled—a prelude to tears that he cut off. "Yeah, I knew her. She's dead. Got killed in a hit and run. Motherfucker drove off and left her there."

"I'm real sorry for dat, cap. We trying to find her sister."

"Renee," Olivia offered.

"You can come on in, if you want."

Inside, the room was dark and humid. Uneasy at invading a grieving man's home, she sat close to Rindell on a cracked leatherette sofa.

"You going to see her sister?" Freddy said as he walked out of the room.

"Yeah, we can find her, we'll go see her. Need to talk to her 'bout Gayle's little girl."

"Sure, social worker picked up Shanti couple days after it happened," Freddy called from wherever he was. "You know, 'cause me and Gayle wasn't married. I don't know if Renee even knows what happened."

Freddy returned with a cardboard box under one arm. He sat down in the recliner opposite them, and placed the box between his feet. His boxer shorts gaped, but he didn't seem to care.

"My friend's worried about her," Olivia said, glancing away. "She wants to talk to Gayle's sister."

"This all the stuff I meant to send with Shanti, but the social worker didn't take it." He dug around in the box and pulled out a few photographs.

"I'm so sorry, but I appreciate any help you can give us."

"I think Renee's address is in here somewhere." Freddy nudged the box toward Olivia and Rindell.

"Thank you," she said.

Freddy ignored her and looked at Rindell, maybe in commiseration. "I tell you, man, that Renee is a crazy white girl. She moves around all these state park campgrounds. Living in a trailer. All year round. Doesn't have a real home. There're some addresses in there. I don't know if they're any good.

"We went to have supper with her, like for Labor Day last year. Went down to that Fort Something. Fort Soto. Down there south of St. Pete. Didn't even eat yet when the two of them started fighting about Shanti's daddy. Right off, then, Renee wanted us to leave. Only time I saw her."

Freddy seemed done, but Olivia waited for Rindell to stand up.

"You'll give Shanti that box for me, huh? I figure she might want the pictures anyway."

"Yeah, you bet, pardner. We'll take care of it for you."

"Thanks, man." Freddy slumped back in the recliner.

"Thanks for your help. I'm so sorry," Olivia said. The sadness hovering around him was so palpable she struggled not to cry.

Rindell tucked the box under his arm and laid a hand on Freddy's shoulder as he passed. "Sorry about what happened. You take care of yourself."

Olivia would have driven away as soon as she could get the car into gear, but Rindell leaned across the console and took her hand off the gear shift.

"Was you scared to come by yourself?" he said, kissing her hand. "Because of going to talk to black folks?"

"No! You know, it's not a very safe neighborhood for a woman alone."

"For a white woman alone...."

"For any woman." She turned on him, hot and angry, but he smiled against her knuckles.

"But you figured you'd be safer with a black man, huh?"

"I didn't even know you were black when I asked you out. I hadn't seen you in daylight," she said.

"Damn. White girl telling me I ain't all that black. You cut me real deep."

"I'm sorry! I didn't mean it that way. I only meant...."

"I'm just teasing you," he said.

"Oh."

He bit her knuckle, then the inside of her wrist, and then the plumpness of her arm, hard enough that she yelped.

"You know, I don't think you daddy thought much of me. He give me *the look*," Rindell said later. They lay on his bed, half undressed, working on the other half.

"What look?"

"The one you get when you go to a white girl's house."

"I don't know." Olivia wasn't willing to commit to a defense of her father. For all she knew he had given Rindell *the look*.

She hesitated, staring down at his brown hands against her white fatness. Memories of her family's off-color jokes tainted her view of the world—sealed off, but present—like some monstrous fetal deformity, floating in the murky fluid of a specimen jar.

"You know how people his age are. My uncle, my stupid uncle used to say, 'You better watch out or that black'll rub off on you.'" She said it with her guts in knots, but Rindell's response was to nod appreciatively.

"Sounds like my maw-maw. Said I wasn't to trust white folks. Told my daddy the same thing, but he never listened. Didn't keep him away from my mama."

Olivia tried to keep her face neutral, but he must have seen something in her eyes.

"That surprise you my mama's white? How'd you think they get black boys my color?"

"I don't know. I didn't think about it."

"I admit, I always had me a thing for white girls, and my maw-maw used to make out how it was that I wanted to be more white. She used to say, 'Dating dose white girls don't gonna make you whiter.' Well, that's nicer than what she said. She said, 'Rubbing up on dose white girls.'"

"Well, you can't get much whiter than me. I'm so pasty and flabby." She hated herself for the total failure of her self-respect. Whatever she thought, there was no need to have said it.

He laughed and, rolling on top of her, said, "I like you all white and pillowy. You're like a marshmallow. Gets me all worked up like I wanna make some s'mores. Be the chocolate in a s'more sandwich."

She let his laughter win, let him sweet talk her with ridiculous marshmallow endearments, but the only pigment change produced by so much rubbing together was that Olivia's face turned bright red. Going home for dinner later, she still felt that blush of pleasure and wondered if her parents noticed it.

CHAPTER TWELVE

Jennifer

IF JENNIFER'S BOSS, Lucas, noticed her distraction, he didn't mention it, but Mr. Kraus, the big boss, must have noticed. At the end of a Bay Day planning session, Mr. Kraus waited until they were alone in the conference room to say, "Do you need to talk about what happened?"

He removed a rectangle of glossy card stock from his inside breast pocket and tapped it on the table in front of her. A brochure for the Employee Assistance Program.

"I want you to call, get some help. Your focus is slipping. There were three typos on the agenda."

Seeing it as no different from any other assignment he gave her, she called and set an appointment.

The counselor, Andrea, was a bony woman with short black hair and wrinkly, earth-tone clothes. Probably, Jennifer guessed, she had once wanted to make a difference, to help people. Instead she ended up in a dimly lit office filled with comfortable chairs, counseling the highly-paid, neurotic employees of a multi-billion dollar real estate development company. Everyone had to pay the bills, and maybe those shabby clothes were more expensive than they looked.

The first half of the session was spent talking generally about how Jennifer felt, but by the end of the hour, Andrea was instructing her on how she ought to feel.

"It's natural that you should feel shocked by this. Death is the most shocking thing we ever face."

"It's not that I'm shocked." Jennifer had been trying to explain that for the last ten minutes. It wasn't shock.

"What do you think you are?"

"I'm not keeping my promise."

"You mean what you said to Gayle?" They called her that, as though they had known her personally.

"Yes. When she was laying there—lying there? Which is it?"

"It doesn't matter," the counselor said, which meant she didn't know, Jennifer guessed. If she knew, she would have said. It mattered.

"When she was dying, I made a promise, and I haven't done anything to keep that promise."

"Now, be fair to yourself. It wasn't exactly your promise, was it? You, Jennifer Palhete, didn't promise to take care of Gayle's daughter."

"But I did," Jennifer whispered, knowing she was about to be subjected to something terrible. "She thought I was someone else, but I made the promise. Her sister doesn't even know I made that promise. I'm the one. I'm responsible."

"You choose to feel responsible, but you're not. You tried to offer help to someone, to offer her comfort, which is a very noble thing to do. That doesn't make you responsible for her sister's actions. You are you. You're not her sister. I want you to try saying it, even if you don't feel it. *I'm not responsible for other people's actions.*"

"I'm not responsible for other people's actions," Jennifer said.

"Good!" Andrea beamed. "Try this: I, Jennifer Palhete, am not responsible for other people's actions."

"I, Jennifer Palhete, am not responsible for other people's actions."

She said it another half dozen times, with Andrea nodding along encouragingly. Saying it, using someone else's words, made Jennifer feel brainwashed. Or hypnotized by all the fluttery linen fabric and bobbly wooden jewelry Andrea wore.

"Just don't make me cluck like a chicken," Jennifer said.

Andrea gave her a blank look. Apparently she'd never been to a Vegas hypnotism show.

"I, Jennifer Palhete, am not responsible for other people's actions."

"Very good. I'm going to print that on a card for you, because I want you to remember it."

Jennifer took the card, which had a fuzzy green forest scene printed on one side above the counselor's name and phone number. The blank side held the "key phrase" she was supposed to remember. *I am not responsible for other people's actions.*

She wanted to believe it. With her boss frowning in one corner of her mind and Kevin scowling in another corner, she needed to believe it. On the drive home, she repeated it to herself out loud. Stopped in traffic, waiting to cross the bridge, she couldn't help it that another phrase kept sneaking in: "Ba-GAWK!"

By the time she got home, the laughing and the crying had both tapered off. She took a few minutes in the car to freshen up her make-up before going upstairs to meet Kevin. While he drove them back over the bridge for Wednesday night church, she made herself repeat the key phrase. Without the chicken cluck to punctuate it, and only inside her head. If she told Kevin about it, he would say that he was glad she had seen a counselor, but he would worry about her needing to see a counselor. That's how he was.

The parking lot was almost full by the time they got to church. As they crunched across the gravel, Kevin reached out and put his arm around her. It startled her, brought her back from the quiet place where she was supposed to have been reciting her key phrase, but had been counting her heartbeat instead.

He kept his arm across her back, all the way into the courtyard between the church offices and the education building. Claustrophobia settled around Jennifer like fog. The church was so beautiful, but today the arched doorways around the courtyard felt like a cloister. Closed. Kevin's arm steadily wilted her blouse against her back, re-igniting the spot where Gayle Prichard's body had made contact.

"Jennifer!" Normally she would have turned automatically at the sound of her name, but tonight she kept walking, afraid of being trapped.

Kevin stopped, though, and turned to see who had called her name. Jennifer smiled and waved vaguely in the right direction. *The beauty queen is not responsible for other people's actions.* Then she kept walking toward the front doors and Kevin followed.

"I'm hungry!" she said. "I had to work through lunch today."

"Aw, are they working you that hard?"

Kevin never looked back. He was that easy to lead. In the fellowship hall, Jennifer steered them through the dinner line, keeping a pleasant but distant smile on her face.

After dinner, Kevin went off to his meeting about renovating the playground at the domestic violence shelter. All Jennifer had to do was get through her Bible study class.

At the education building, she reached the front doors as half a dozen people exited in a flurry of noise and air currents. Chilled air from the inside pushed back against the oppressive heat outside and rippled the posters tacked to the walls. Jennifer entered the foyer and nearly ran into the back of a woman with her hair twisted up into a fancy bun like a seashell.

"Oh, I'm sorry," she said, barely managing to avoid impact.

The woman turned and said, "Oh, Jennifer!"

Olivia. Out of her natural cubicle habitat, Jennifer hadn't recognized her. Too late, Jennifer remembered that she had changed her hair. Not a boxy blob-bob to her shoulders, but a sleek up-do that looked like a good hairstyle for the summer heat.

"Rindell and I went to—"

"I'm sorry, Olivia, but I'm running late. Can we talk later?" Jennifer put on her best smile, careful not to make eye contact. Even though she had to sidestep around Olivia, she kept going. Sell the lie. You're not in a hurry unless you're moving fast.

"Oh, okay. Sure."

Jennifer left her behind, walking as quickly as she could, toward the safety of Bible study. There she could get sympathy, without the price of responsibility.

And how did that work? If she, Jennifer Palhete, wasn't responsible for other people's actions, who was responsible? She'd made it Mike's problem, then she'd made it Olivia's problem.

What was the difference between *not responsible* and *irresponsible*? Was there one?

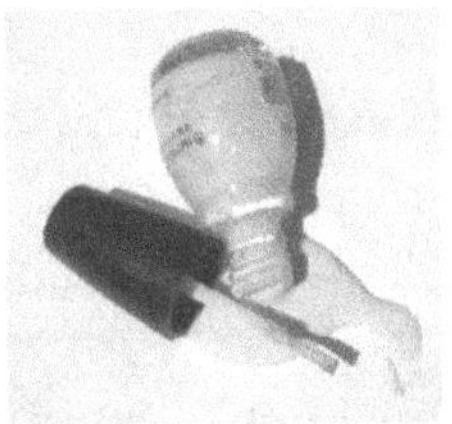

CHAPTER THIRTEEN

Olivia

THE FIRST WEDNESDAY of August started perfectly: clear, not too humid, and not yet hot. Olivia felt ridiculous wearing make-up, a good bra, and a V-neck t-shirt to go for a walk. She was sweatpants and business from the waist down, but from the belly-button up, she was in allurement mode, as far as she could manage it.

When she reached the river park, a total stranger sat in Rindell's ambulance. Olivia pulled up a few feet short and stared indignantly at his slicked back hair and diamond earring.

"You must be Olivia," he said.

"This is my partner, Luis," Rindell said. Coming up behind her, he kissed her neck while she stood squinting at the stranger.

"Oh."

"Come on, I'll walk with you."

He took her hand and led her the way she usually walked, reminding her that he had seen her walking nearly every day for months. At least he was under no delusions about the size of her backside. He'd had a perfect view of it.

"I didn't know you had a partner," she said.

"Yeah. Usually I drop him off by his girlfriend's house. She lives over on Powhatan, east of Nebraska. But they had a big fight, so now I'm stuck with him on break."

As they walked, Rindell steadily worked his arm around her. When his hand crept down past her hip, she caught it nervously and returned it to her waist. He laughed.

"What is this, the military? No PDA?"

"What? It's—it's very public," Olivia said. She didn't have an official policy on public displays of affection. The concept was that alien to her.

"I was gonna say that I got twenty-eight minutes left on my break and we're two blocks from my bed."

Olivia didn't know how to say no. She didn't understand why her default setting was no, so she went with him. To her relief, Rindell was oblivious to her awkwardness. He grinned as he hustled them both out of their clothes, shushing her with his mouth when she tried to talk. Afterward, as he jumped up and stripped off the condom, he laughed maniacally.

"Crap," he said. "Now I know why Luis always look like he gonna panic when I pick him up. Ain't hardly enough time to take care of things."

He hauled his uniform on, and she tried to match his speed, smoothing her hair and getting her exercise pants back on. She was putting on her shoes when he'd finished, although his collar stood up and his ID badge was skewed. He took her face in his hands and kissed her twice with loud smacking noises.

"You made my day, Olivia. Hell, you made my whole week." He was already going, stepping into the lean-to.

She followed him in time to see him jump down from the porch and take off running across the park, legs pumping gracefully. When he reached the ambulance, he turned and waved.

At home, Mr. Holley was in the dining room, the newspaper and a plate of bacon and eggs in front of him. To one side lay a plate with the crusts of cinnamon toast. As Olivia headed to the kitchen, he called out, "Come have breakfast with me."

She hesitated, but the only excuse she could think of was a lie. She wasn't running late. Sex with Rindell had taken less time than her walk usually did. She was fifteen minutes ahead of schedule.

"Sure, Daddy. I'll just get my yogurt."

In the kitchen, she splashed water on her face and checked herself in the mirror over the stove. Perhaps her eyes were more shifty than usual, but the red cheeks and sweaty ringlets of hair around her face were normal for her morning walk.

The moment she sat down, Mr. Holley folded his paper and pushed his plate away.

"Now, Olivia. I want to talk to you about this Rindell character."

"He's not a *character*, Daddy."

"Don't get defensive. I just want to ask you if you're getting serious about him. You should take it slow, be sure you don't rush into anything."

"He's a nice guy and I'm not rushing," she said, dangerously close to a lie. If sleeping with him wasn't rushing, she didn't know what was. To hide her blush, she tore open the yogurt container and gave it a vigorous stirring with her spoon.

"I'm sure he is, but is he the kind of man you're looking for? Would you be comfortable introducing him to the folks at church?"

"Well, sure." She hadn't thought of it at all, and he had already been to Church of the Palms to get her for lunch.

"I'm worried about my little girl," Mr. Holley said. For a moment, Olivia was touched, but he immediately burst that tender bubble. "I want to be sure he's interested in you, for you. There are some black men who are interested in white girls, any white girl."

There it was. Olivia knew what she was: chubby and plain. Naturally, that meant someone like Rindell would only be interested in her for what she was. She didn't waste her breath on indignation. There was no changing her father's mind and Rindell had said something very like it. He had a *thing* for white women, whatever that meant.

"I can take care of myself. And he is a nice guy," she said.

"Okay, but I want you to be careful. He's not like us. He's not the kind of boy you're used to dating. He may expect you to do things...."

"Daddy! Please, can we not talk about that? I'm being careful, okay?" A lie.

She ate the rest of her yogurt in four quick bites and went upstairs, where the scale waited for her. It had to be wrong. She got off and back on twice before she believed what the scale said. Three pounds in a week. Maybe sex was better exercise than walking.

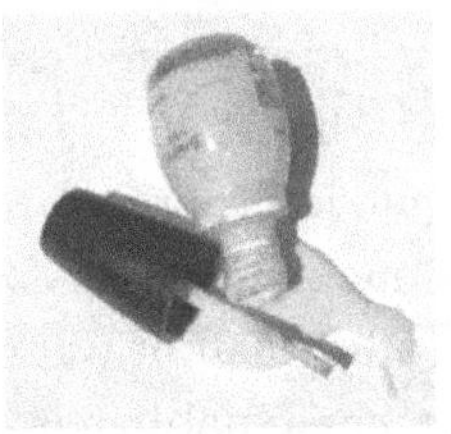

CHAPTER FOURTEEN

Olivia

THE HURRICANE WAS going to miss Tampa. They always missed, but the church sat in a flood zone at the very edge of the bay. Even with a miss, there were dangers: heavy rain, high winds, and storm surge. As the cone of probability progressed up the Gulf that Friday, Olivia went through the usual precautions. She lifted computers and put them on desks, relocated books to higher shelves in the ministry staff offices. By noon she was taping windows alongside the maintenance and housekeeping employees.

After Pastor Lou decided to send people home early, the ministry staff disappeared in an instant, gone home to make preparations of their own, while Olivia pushed the new photocopier up the ramp to the stage in the fellowship hall. Maintenance was too busy boarding up the stained glass windows in the sanctuary.

On top of that, Olivia still needed to prepare for services on Sunday, which might or might not be canceled. Close to three o'clock, Pastor Lou stepped into Olivia's cubicle with the final draft of the Sunday bulletin.

"We'll get you out of here as soon as we can," he said and patted her shoulder.

He meant well, but there was no way she would be going home soon. Fridays always ran long, and preparations for the hurricane had eaten away at the day. In the past, Olivia had enjoyed staying late, being needed. Then she turned over the bulletin to see what changes Pastor Lou had indicated on the back. In his careful penmanship he'd written, "Insert: A big thank you to church staff for their teamwork in hurricane preparations." Olivia gritted her teeth. Everyone talked about teamwork when the ministry staff needed help, but for the office staff, it was every man for himself.

She didn't leave for home until almost eight, and she was the last one out the door except for the second maintenance man, Steve. A year before it would have been a special treat, a moment spent alone with Steve, Olivia's secret crush since he was hired.

"Here's hoping we don't have to come in until Monday," he said as they stood in the cloister, zipping up rain jackets and prepping umbrellas. She was about to step into the rain when Steve said, "Where are you hurrying off to? You got big plans?"

"Date night." Just a few months before, she would have grasped at the opening in desperation.

"Oooh, hot date, huh?"

"Have a good weekend!" Stepping off the curb, umbrella in one hand, shoes in the other, she waded out to her car. The parking lot drained slowly into brick streets that were already filling with rain and storm surge.

Not until she saw the Hillsborough River did she think of Rindell's living situation. The river ran high and fast after the day's rain. As she drove by, she stared out into the dark, trying to make out the line of water moving up the lawns of houses along River Boulevard. The Holley house sat higher on pillars, but the Eyesore lay only twenty feet from the river. The Airstream trailer stood even further down the bank.

When Olivia called, she got Rindell's voicemail.

"I'm home. Give me a call if you want to do something. We could go for coffee or something," she said.

"You're not going back out, are you, Livvie?" her mother called from the Florida room.

"Just for a little while."

"But the weather's so bad."

"You'd better invite your young man to come here. I don't

want you out in this," Mr. Holley said. The voice of authority.

Part of Olivia knew she should obey, because he was her father and she was living under his roof. Another part of her dug in her heels and decided that her father could disapprove as much as he wanted. If Rindell called, she would go out with him.

If he called. It got to be nine o'clock, then ten o'clock, and Olivia sat on the sofa next to her mother with the silent phone on her leg. She resisted offers of popcorn, cookies, hot chocolate, chips and salsa. She sat numbly through her father's relentless channel changing and two sitcom reruns. Then the news ended and Mr. Holley heaved himself up out of his recliner.

"Guess your boy decided he didn't want to get out in the weather," he said.

"I guess not."

"Good night, honey. Don't stay up too late," Mrs. Holley said.

Olivia didn't, because it didn't seem worthwhile. Worse, it seemed pathetic, sitting around waiting for him to call. She trudged up the stairs, brushed her teeth, washed her face, and crawled into bed.

Rainy Saturdays were Olivia's idea of Hell on Earth: trapped in the house with her family all day. Her father prowled around, trying to pick a fight, Rich trudged up and down the stairs, between the kitchen and his video games, while her mother drafted her for a sewing project. Often it was quilts, especially baby quilts for church members or her niece and nephews in Atlanta. By Olivia's estimation, each of her sister's three children had a dozen quilts. After five years, Olivia was still muddling her way through what was known euphemistically as her "wedding quilt." She blamed her slow progress on all the Saturdays she helped her mother cut out and piece baby quilts, but in truth, she had a file box full of half-sewn bits because she had given up on romance and marriage. Mostly.

She hadn't given up enough to leave her cell phone in her bedroom. As she helped lay out and pin squares on the latest quilt, she reached down to touch her phone every few minutes. She wasn't brave enough to take it out of her pocket, because that would invite her mother's curiosity, or her father's disbelief. The instant she took it out, he would be there, blotting out the light in the dining room doorway, asking who she thought was going to call.

The new quilt had a zoo theme. Pastel monkeys and elephants and giraffes made seams with polka dots and fuzzy floral squares. Her mother was making it for "that cute little black baby." It set Olivia's teeth. Couldn't it just be for the Veatch's baby? Olivia had told her mother their name often enough. But no, it was always, "that nice black family." The Sawamiphakdis were always "that nice Asian family," possibly because her mother couldn't pronounce Sawamiphakdi. Or because her mother believed a person couldn't be racist if she were careful to compliment the cuteness of little black babies and to invite nice Asian families to sit in the same pew.

"What about your wedding quilt, Mitten?" The moment always came, but it came early that day. Olivia would have to make some half-hearted attempt to work on the doomed quilt.

Although the rain kept falling, it was like the clouds opened and the sun broke through, because as Mrs. Holley lifted the lid off the box that contained Olivia's disappointment, her phone vibrated in her pocket.

She stood up and clutched at the phone through the leg of her sweatpants. Steeling herself for a call from Pastor Lou, she pulled it out and stared at in disbelief and joy.

"Hi," she managed breathlessly.

"Where y'at, baby," Rindell said.

"I'm at home. Where are you?"

"Damn, what a night. I'm sorry I didn't call you. Things got all kinda crazy."

"Are you okay?"

Across the dining room table, Mrs. Holley frowned. Olivia turned around and headed into the kitchen, but her mother followed.

"Yeah, but I'm flooded out," he said.

"Oh no!"

"Who is it?" Mrs. Holley said. Olivia ignored her.

"Nah, it's okay," Rindell said. "Just a mess, water and mud. Didn't get up in my locker or nothing."

"But the water came up in the trailer?" Olivia tried to backtrack, wanting some privacy, but her mother stood in the doorway, blocking her. It was talk there or go out in the rain.

"Not too bad. But for a while now I gotta sleep in the old man's back room. Til I can get it dry and clean out there."

"I could come help." Olivia plunged, not caring that her mother was pouting now.

"You'd do that?" he said.

"Sure. I could come right now."

"Livvie." Mrs. Holley's hands came to rest on her hips.

"Well, water ain't come down enough yet to do much, but you could come over."

"Who is it?" Mrs. Holley said, loud enough to be heard over the line.

"That your mama?"

"Okay, I'll be down in a bit. Bye," Olivia said to Rindell.

"Where are you going? With the weather like this? I thought you were going to work on your wedding quilt." Mrs. Holley's voice was full of a familiar mixture of indignation and hurt. She'd never used that voice on Olivia's sister, Cynthia, but then Olivia was not Cynthia.

"I'm just going to take a walk."

"With Rindell?"

"Yes." Olivia nearly followed it up with an "If that's okay," but swallowed the three words of surrender. She would not ask permission.

Before her mother could say anything else, Olivia darted up the stairs and put on some better clothes. She went for a pair of lemon yellow capris and a sweater set that had been too tight a few months before. It was still tight, but now the right amount. She tiptoed down the stairs, hoping to avoid her mother, and nearly managed it. Mrs. Holley was in the living room, tattling on Olivia, but when she heard the rustling and stamping of Olivia getting into her old, yellow raincoat and galoshes, she hurried back into the kitchen.

"You're going?"

"Just for a while." Oh, that was a lie. Olivia was going for as long as she could stay away.

She was already on the back steps, about to launch herself into the maelstrom when her mother called, "Don't forget to invite him to church tomorrow."

Olivia darted into the rain, wishing she could outrun that command, but it tagged after her, clinging to the dripping hem of her raincoat, when she sloshed ashore at Mr. Batson's porch. Braving the front steps was like ducking under a miniature Niagara Falls. On the other side, Rindell stood smiling, a beer in his hand.

"Hey, lemon drop," he said.

Glancing down at her all-yellow ensemble, she laughed.

"I'm a human banana."

"Come here, banana pants." Rindell help her off with her raincoat as she stepped out of her galoshes. Against the faded gray floorboards, her feet were bright white with sparkling pink toenails. When Rindell tugged at her hand, she sank down beside him on the battered hulk of a porch settee that was spared all but the mist of the waterfall. The settee groaned at the additional weight, but didn't budge, its springs rusted solid.

"You look like sunshine. I need me some sunshine on a day like this." Rindell put his arm around Olivia and eased her in close until her head was on his shoulder.

"You smell tired," she said.

He laughed until she ducked her face in embarrassment.

"You saying I need a shower?"

He did smell sweaty. The sweat of too much work and worry. The sweat of someone who has had too little sleep, and that in a strange bed.

"No. Not that, just tired."

"Yeah, you right. I am that."

"It was a long night?" she said.

He sighed and was quiet. It was a thoughtful silence that reminded her she didn't have to chatter.

"Long old night, for sure," he said at last. "Hadda go in early 'cause of the weather. Stay late 'cause of the weather. Crazy night. People don't got the sense to get out when the water comes up. Old folks givin' they hearts a workout trying to move stuff up off the floor. You know, that kinda thing."

"Lots of calls?"

"Yeah, even had a call out to by you."

"Bayou?"

"Out to by your church. Water all up over Bayshore. Man, I hate this kinda rain, the way it keeps coming and coming. Streets filling up with water, and the wind blowing, and trees falling over."

"The hurricane's going to miss us. It always does," she said to reassure him. If he had been through Katrina, he would worry about hurricanes.

"Dat's what I hear. Don't make me like it no more, though."

He sighed and kissed her forehead. Sitting up, she shifted on the settee and began to rub his shoulders. When he turned to give her better access, she slipped her hands under his t-shirt. She had often given Mr. Holley shoulder rubs, but for the first time she discovered pleasure in the chore. Rindell's skin was warm and his muscles slowly softened in relief. Once her hands grew tired, she returned to her original spot beside him, with his arm around her and her hand resting on his leg.

For a long while, they watched the rain fall and talked about small things. Once, Mr. Batson came to the front door and looked out at them. He looked exactly as he had when Olivia was a little girl. A wiry, hollow-cheeked black man with a rash of stubble on his cheeks, although his hair was more white than gray now.

"Hey dere, cap," Rindell said.

"Ayuh. You gonna set there all day?"

"Not if it gonna inconvenience you."

Olivia tensed.

"Nope. No skin offa my nose," Mr. Batson said.

"Awright. You need us to move, you let me know."

After the old man was gone, Rindell snorted and shook his head.

"Should I go?" Olivia asked.

"Nah. Stay for a while. Whyn't you come in? Try out my bed."

"I better not."

"Come on. We could give the old man a cheap thrill. This house ain't seen any action in a long ass time."

She giggled, but she didn't dare say yes. Doing that in his trailer, where there was some privacy, that was one thing. The thought of doing it under the same roof as Mr. Batson made her squirm.

Either Rindell was only teasing, or he was that tired, because he didn't push it. They sat on the porch until the afternoon gloom started to turn into darkness and the wind picked up, turning the mist into a cold shower.

Olivia's phone vibrated in her pocket. Rindell laid his hand on her leg, pressing her phone between her thigh and his palm.

"I bet that's your mama, huh?" he said.

"Yeah."

"Goddamn, I guess I better try to sleep before my shift."

"Is it hard, sleeping during the day?"

"Oh, not too much. I don't mind it, except for the rain. I s'pose you gotta get home?"

"Probably she wants to know if I'm coming home for dinner. She wants you to come to church tomorrow." Olivia made it a statement, not a question, so he could ignore it without saying no. He was quiet for a while, the warmth of his hand seeping through the damp cotton to her leg.

"Don't know if I'll be all that awake after another night like last night, but I can do that."

"You don't have to."

"Nah." Rindell sighed, but leaned over and kissed Olivia's cheek. "I wanna keep your mama happy. Lesson number one: don't get crossways of a girl's mama."

"Not her daddy?"

"Oh, girls' daddies. You can't make them happy. You gotta soften up they mamas."

"I'm glad you have a plan," Olivia said as she stood up. "We leave for church at 9:45, assuming the hurricane doesn't hit us."

"I hear they never do."

With her raincoat and galoshes back on, Olivia leaned down to kiss Rindell, raining on him the rivulets of water that had been trapped in the seams of her jacket.

"Good night, banana pants," he said.

CHAPTER FIFTEEN

Jennifer

"WE'LL GO TO the late service tomorrow," Kevin said on Saturday night. That was his answer when Jennifer turned down another drink. The last thing she wanted to do on Sunday morning was stare down a raging hangover while jammed into a pew full of good Christians who hadn't closed down two different bars the night before.

"Oh, come on. You'll have the comfort of knowing I'm there, just as hungover as you are," Carrie said. "If you play your cards right, you'll still be drunk when the first hymn starts up."

"Don't you always wish you were drunk when I start singing?" Kevin's joke struck Jennifer as mildly funny, but Carrie's laughter was so obnoxious that people down the bar turned to look.

Jennifer took the drink, but standing up to go to the bathroom later, she tottered dangerously on the high heels of her magic shoes. They were the shoes that had pulled her out of her funk and made her feel ascendant again.

"Magic shoes, you are going to break my ankle," she told them. She sat back down and started to unbuckle them.

"No, no!" Tracey cried. "Don't let the booze win. You cannot take off those fabulous shoes just because you're afraid."

"I don't have Barbie feet like you, Tracey. I can't walk in these drunk."

"Yes, you can." The way Tracey said it, the words sounded like some ancient Hebrew invocation. Yeshukan. "I'll teach you. Patented Tracey Ohmquist Drunk Slut Walk."

Tracey rose on her Barbie legs and proceeded to mince around the table without wobbling.

"See? Come on. I'll show you."

Clasping Jennifer's wrist in her martini hand, Tracey pulled her to her feet and led her through a strange dance. The precise placement of each foot, the rotation of each hip in conjunction with certain arm gestures. Jennifer felt disembodied, as though she had left her body and been replaced by a runway model. Following Tracey's lead, she sauntered down the hallway toward the restrooms, trailing her fingers along the river rock wall.

"Touch things," Tracey said. "It looks soooo sensual, and it helps keep your balance."

Jennifer couldn't keep from giggling, and Tracey's laughter drifted back to her, inviting. Nothing like Carrie's aggressive braying.

Jennifer got the hang of walking, but she couldn't find the brakes when they reached the door of the ladies room. Trying to slow down with tiny steps, she bumped into Tracey, who bumped into the heavy swing door. They tumbled into the cavernous over-chilled restroom, laughing.

"I love you," Jennifer said. She did, in that moment. Tracey was a creature of infinite mystery, but real kindness. Peace Corps Barbie.

"I love you, too, sweetie." Tracey hugged her, and Jennifer marveled that she was soft and warm instead of hard and plastic.

Jennifer managed to steer herself into one of the stalls, but struggled to unfasten her slacks. They were too tight, because of Kevin's casual sabotage. *Have another drink. Let's have Chinese.* Staying in a size six was an ongoing battle, especially as she had to wage it in secret. Kevin didn't understand that there had been a lot of deprivation involved in maintaining her figure before she moved in with him. He seemed to think she was naturally that size.

She eased herself onto the toilet, gasping as bare skin made contact with the seat, which felt like a block of ice. Tracey and she peed in companionable silence, but Tracey finished first, and in the whooshing moment of the toilet flush, she said, "Didn't she have a little girl or something? Is that what Kevin said?"

"Who?" A chill washed down Jennifer's back, more powerful than the cold blasting out of the air conditioning vent over her head. She had been about to stand and pull up her slacks, but she settled heavily onto the toilet seat. Even sober, the reminder would have unsteadied her.

"He said you were worried about it. That we were supposed to take your mind off it." As sweet as Tracey was, she didn't grasp that she'd done the opposite.

"Did he?" Jennifer managed to stand, but as she was zipping the too tight slacks, the automatic toilet flushed behind her, loud enough to drown out Tracey's answer.

When Jennifer stepped out of the stall, Tracey was checking her make-up in the mirror. She smiled when she saw Jennifer behind her. Hugging her again, she said, "Well, I'm soooo glad you're doing better."

Jennifer felt newly, unpleasantly sober as she walked toward the bathroom door. There she met Carrie coming in.

"Hey, you," Carrie said.

Jennifer stood outside for a few minutes, waiting on the other two women. Pushing the door back open, she was about to call for them, when she heard Carrie saying, "It's because she has *issues* about her mother. That's why she's so worried about this woman's daughter."

"What do you mean? What kind of issues?" Tracey said.

"Her mother basically had nothing to do with raising Jenn. Her father raised her. So I think that's why she's so obsessed about this woman dying. Because of her mother."

The presumption of it rankled Jennifer. Carrie's promotion to best friend status didn't give her the right to play amateur psychologist. Jennifer pushed the door open hard enough to knock it against the wall.

"I do not have *issues* about my mother," she said.

"Yes, you do." Carrie's answer was almost musical. "Do you not remember saying to me, 'I wish I had a real relationship with my mother like you do'?"

"That was in college."

"I'm just saying, I think that's why you're freaking out about this woman dying, because it bothers you that another little girl is going to miss out on a relationship with her mother. Okay?"

"Whatever," Jennifer snapped. While the other women headed toward the dining room, she backtracked to the bathroom. Locked in a toilet stall, she couldn't stop shivering. Not from the air conditioning now, but with remembering how Gayle Prichard had said, "My baby. My baby."

Jennifer's mother had said the same thing, but not to Jennifer. To Jennifer's older sister, Rebecca. Rocking Rebecca on her lap, Moira had kissed her hair and said, "My baby. My baby."

Rebecca had gotten sick not long after Jennifer was born, and Jennifer mainly remembered her sister as a pale, thin girl who couldn't play, and was in and out of the hospital. The one who got all of Moira's attention.

After Rebecca died, Mr. Palhete did everything for Jennifer. Made sure she drank her milk and brushed her teeth. Taught her to ride a bike and bake cookies. When she started kindergarten, her father was the one who braided her hair and made her breakfast and took her to school.

Moira became a ghost. A woman who only came out of her bedroom at night. Then one night when Jennifer was in second grade, she woke to her father pounding on the bathroom door and screaming her mother's name. An ambulance came, its blue and red lights washing through Jennifer's bedroom window. It took Moira away.

The Moira who came home before the start of Jennifer's third grade year was no longer a ghost, but she was no one Jennifer remembered. She wore bright clothes and laughed loudly, but her hands shook all the time. Jennifer readjusted to the new Moira, but they never made up for the lost opportunity of being mother and daughter. Moira had never called Jennifer *my baby*. Moira was Rebecca's mother.

In the morning, while Kevin was in the shower, Jennifer knelt in front of her nightstand, just as she'd knelt in front of the toilet half an hour before. She was somewhere near functional, but no amount of toothpaste or mouthwash could flush out the wooly dead taste on her tongue.

The day after Gayle's death, Jennifer had taken Shanti's picture and tried to throw it away. She'd stood over the bedroom trashcan and tried with all her might, but the picture might as well have been glued to her hand. It wouldn't go into the trash can, but she managed to shove it to the back of her nightstand drawer. Even there, it was magnetized to her. Reaching past lip gloss and Mentholatum, ear plugs, a tangle of jewelry, a new package of hose, and half a dozen other things, Jennifer's hand went readily to the photo.

The bloody fingerprints had partially flaked off, and a new crease marred the photo. Shanti was still giving the camera attitude, her hair in frizzy little poofs, her mouth set in a defiant line. In Jennifer's mind, Shanti was still going home from school to find out her mother was dead. Hearing Kevin turn off the shower, Jennifer pushed the photo back in the drawer and hurried to the closet to find something to wear.

The wind had died down as the hurricane bypassed Tampa, headed for landfall in Alabama, but the streets around the church were full of water. Kevin volunteered to drop Jennifer off at the front and find parking, which she was grateful for, but after fifteen minutes of waiting under the portico she wished she had stayed home. Trying to make nice with people, she had to squeeze her lips together and force a smile on them. She hoped it looked pleasant and not queasy. Like an enormous balloon full of water, her head felt too heavy and floppy to stay up on her neck, and fragile enough to break open with the slightest provocation.

As Kevin slogged up the street with a flimsy foldable umbrella, Olivia and her family came down the walkway, leaving from the early service. Mr. Holley wore a grumpy scowl, but Olivia was smiling as she held her boyfriend's hand. Jennifer wondered if those two things were connected.

Whatever Mr. Holley was upset about, Olivia didn't seem to care. She leaned close and whispered to her boyfriend. He laughed and loosened his tie with his free hand.

"Go get a seat. I'll be in in a second," Jennifer said to Kevin. He nodded as he shook off his umbrella. As much as she wanted to hide in back, she knew he would sit in the front pew where his boss always sat. He never lost a chance to brown-nose.

Jennifer caught up to Olivia as she was about unfurl an umbrella. Her parents and her brother were already heading toward the parking lot, but Olivia turned back when Jennifer called her name.

"Oh, hi." From the stilted way Olivia spoke, Jennifer knew their last awkward encounter hadn't been forgotten.

"I'm sorry about last week," Jennifer said. "Things were chaotic. I appreciate you going to see about that."

"It's okay. I've got a box of stuff in the trunk of my car. Do you want to swap it over to your car?"

Jennifer had the perfect excuse ready.

"Oh shoot, Kevin's got the car keys. Could I come by later and look at it?"

"Sure, okay. Just, um, call me before you come over," Olivia said.

"Oh, great. Thank you. Well, I better go in."

Jennifer felt like she was in high school again, searching for the right thing to say that would make her seem normal. Olivia didn't seem to expect any more than that. She was already turning away. Her boyfriend slid his hand down Olivia's arm to relieve her of the umbrella. He popped it open and put his arm around her, sheltering them both as they stepped into the rain.

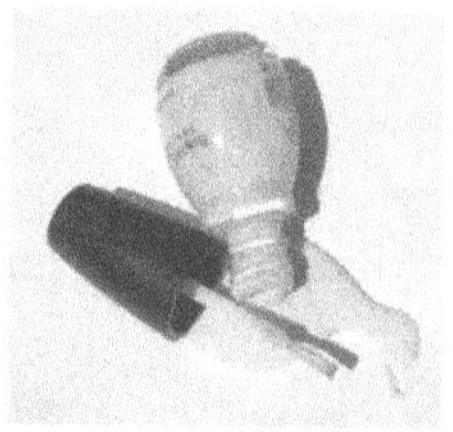

CHAPTER SIXTEEN

Olivia

THEY MADE IT in the back door and through the kitchen without attracting Mr. Batson's attention. Olivia hoped if they were quiet enough, he wouldn't hear them at all, but as soon as the bedroom door was closed, Rindell caught Olivia from behind. His hands went around her waist, squeezing her fat, making her squeal. So much for being quiet.

"Mitten," he said into her ear with his cinnamon breath. He kissed her neck and her pulse jumped. "Why didn't you tell me they call you that?"

She put her hands on his and tried to pry him off, but he wouldn't budge.

"It's just a stupid nickname. Only my mother calls me that." Olivia should have known that her mother would eventually call her that in front of him. Useless to hope he wouldn't notice.

"It's not stupid. It's sexy. Mitten."

She stopped fighting his hands and stood flat-footed, bulldog head down. "Don't make fun of me!"

"Why'd you think that? I wouldn't make fun of you." He loosened his hands on her and turned her to face him.

"Well, there's nothing sexy about being called Mitten."

He came back from the injury, slipping his arms around her, and nuzzled the rainy damp of her neck. Into her ear, he said, "Mitten. Rhymes with kitten. And then all those fingers close together, rubbing against each other. Not sterile like a rubber glove. Now quit your fussing and let's go to bed."

"This is such a nice old quilt, we better pull the sheets down." Resting one knee on the bed, Olivia leaned across, intending to pull the quilt back, but Rindell grabbed her from behind. He pressed his hips against her hard enough that she toppled forward onto her hands and knees. He worked one hand under her shirt to her breasts, while the other hand slid between her legs. It flustered her, and she was already breathing hard from wrestling around with him.

"Get these church clothes off, why don't you?" He unbuttoned her shirt and got it off, unhooked her bra, unzipped her skirt. Undid her altogether. As she wiggled her skirt down to her knees, he pushed her down to all fours again.

On the wobbly, old mattress, she felt unwieldy and uncertain, just as she had started to think she was sure about a few things. He grasped her hips and pulled her back against him.

"Damn," he said. "Goddamn. You could stop a fucking train with this, baby."

The expletives made her ears burn, and then he smacked her. It wasn't a light tap, but a slap, his whole palm striking her buttocks. She gasped and an instant later, he had her panties down and had slapped her naked skin. He did it twice more as she hung her head down, trying to stop the tears that burned in the corners of her eyes.

When he let go of her, she stood up on her knees and started to drag her panties back up.

"Here now, don't be doing that," he said. He opened the nightstand drawer to get out a condom. "Them panties need to come off."

She didn't want him to see her crying, and so when he put his arms around her, she didn't try to push him away or turn around. He went on kissing her neck and squeezing her breasts in his hands. Not as gently as he had been before. More rough, more demanding, but still familiar. Then he pushed her back to all fours. Stroking his hand over her belly, he reached between her legs, and pressed his fingers up into her. It shocked her, because it was easy. She was aroused, ready for him, despite the shock and humiliation. So when he stopped to put the condom on, she waited.

She didn't know what to expect, and exhaled raggedly when he pushed into her.

"Damn," he said again. "You feel so good. You like that okay?"

She nodded, not sure if she did. Wicked, that was how it felt, to be on her hands and knees that way. Dirty. But good. She tried to focus on that, but then he smacked her again. That time, she said, "Ow!"

He laughed.

"Was that too hard? I'm sorry, baby."

He pulled out of her and she almost said, "No, it's okay," but she wasn't sure it was. Before she could decide what to answer, he'd kissed the spot he spanked. Actually kissed her bare behind, like an apology, but one that didn't last long, because then he sank his teeth into her buttock. Hard.

She squeaked in protest and he laughed again. As he eased back into her, he worked one hand between her legs, made her gasp.

"That feel good?" he said. She didn't bother to nod, because he knew it did. The next slap was so hard, it cracked and echoed in the room, but she didn't protest. She was breathless and confused, and the spanking seemed to fit that. It reminded her of being in trouble as a little girl. Doing something forbidden and being punished for it.

Afterward, he was as gentle as he hadn't been during sex. He lay curled against her back, kissing her shoulders and running his hands up and down her.

"You okay? You're awful quiet," he said.

"I'm fine."

He propped himself on his elbow and looked at her.

"Did I do something wrong?"

"No, I didn't—I wasn't sure why you—why did you spank me?"

He flopped back on the bed, laughing. "Spank you? I wasn't—I didn't spank you. Anyways, that wasn't what I meant. You thought I was spanking you?"

"Wasn't that what…" She felt stupid, and he was laughing.

"I just like slapping your ass. You didn't like that? I thought you was kinda into it."

There was no simple answer, and that confounded her. If she said, "I didn't like it," would he think she was a prude? Or would he just be disappointed? If she said she liked it, would he think worse things about her? Did she like it? He was looking at her, waiting for her to answer.

"I don't know," she said. That at least wasn't a lie.

"Okay. Well, you let me know when you decide." He took her chin in his hand and kissed her. A second later his hand was gliding back down her side. He lingered on her buttock and she tensed, half expecting another slap, but he only squeezed it. "See? I can't resist."

Olivia settled her head on his arm and sighed with contentment. He answered her with his own sigh, a little sad.

"I'm glad you're here," he said.

"Me too. I'm sorry you had to go to church."

"Aw, better than me laying here listening to the rain by myself."

"I like the rain. As long as I'm inside and warm," she said. He squeezed her again and then sat up to pull the covers over them. To keep her warm, she guessed.

"I didn't used to hate the rain. I guess I don't hate it now. Just this kinda rain. With the wind, knowing there's a storm on the backside of it."

"Because of Katrina?"

He sighed again, and was silent for several minutes, before he mumbled against her shoulder, "You don't wanna hear about that."

"I'm here. If you wanted to tell me."

"Yeah, you are here."

When he started talking, it came in pieces, as though he had never told the story before.

"Well, my folks lived in the Ninth Ward. Chalmette. That's

where I grew up. You know, after I got outta the Marines, I was back living with them, working as an EMT. My cousin was living with us, too. My mama, she had emphysema. She was on oxygen and couldn't get around too well. We'd kinda, you know, started getting used to knowing she wasn't gonna be with us a whole lot longer. We figured we'd hunker down, wait the storm out, and I could take care of my mama if she had any troubles.

"Except the storm got worse. Like a lot worse, really fast. Water pouring into the house. Ankle deep before we even knew what'd happened. Then the power gone out and my cousin and me—my cousin, DeVaun—we got to talking, like what we should do.

"What we decided was, I was gonna go out with my daddy. He had one of them old jon boats. For fishing. We decided, DeVaun and me, we'd move my mama up on the dining room table. Further away from the water. Then me and my daddy, we'd take the boat to the hospital, see about getting help to evacuate my mama. And I figured, it'd be better for my daddy, too. He was too heavy—big, like your daddy—and his heart wasn't good.

"So my cousin, he stayed there. He trained to be an EMT, too. He stayed with my mama, so he could take care of her til we could get her evacuated."

Rindell was breathing harder against her skin and he'd tightened his hand on her hip. Olivia wanted to say something, to offer him some comfort, but she knew it was too soon. There was more than that. Men didn't get upset about the rain over just that.

"Only it was crazy. Straight up crazy. They said we had to go by the Astrodome. Said the National Guard was gonna help us. The National Guard. Shit, they wasn't even on the ground. Wasn't no soldiers doing anything. No water, no food, no medical. And my, uh, my daddy—he had a heart attack. If I coulda got him to the hospital, if there'd been someplace to take him, but there wasn't. And the cops wasn't no help. They was running as crazy as everybody else. Shooting at people, trying to keep people away from places. There wasn't no place to take him. Not to get him help."

For several minutes, that was all of the story, but Olivia knew it didn't have a happy ending. His father must have died. If he couldn't get him to the hospital, not even being a paramedic would have helped. Olivia turned her head and kissed his bare arm where it lay tense under her cheek.

"And then there was no way to get back. The levee was busted and the whole place, the whole parish, it was all under water. There wasn't no way I could get back to the house on a jon boat. By the time I managed to get back home, it was two days. Two days I'd been gone and left my mama and my cousin there. I could see right away. The water, it'd fallen some since the levee opened up, but I could see. The house, house I grew up in, it was just one of them shotgun shacks. Nothing but a crawl space in the attic and the water'd come all the way up over the roof."

Despite her best efforts, Olivia's hand trembled where it lay on top of Rindell's. To hide it, she squeezed Rindell's hand. He squeezed back hard enough to pop her knuckles.

"My cousin, he tried, but he couldn't get out. Couldn't get out the attic. And my mama, there wasn't no way."

"I'm so sorry," Olivia said.

There at last was something Olivia was good at. She rolled over to face Rindell and wrapped her arms around him. Nobody wanted to be looked at while they cried, and so the safest place for him to cry was in her shoulder. When the crying had subsided, he smiled at her. Not embarrassed the way Rich got when he cried, but relieved. They lay that way, face to face, but quiet.

Olivia was careful of her silence, to be sure Rindell had as much space to talk as he needed.

"That's enough of that," he said after a few minutes.

"It's okay."

"Nah. Don't do any good to wallow around in it."

Rindell kissed her and rolled onto his back, bringing Olivia on top of him. The bed groaned.

"I'm going to smoosh you," she said with an uneasy giggle.

"Well, get on with smooshing me then."

Pressing on the backs of her thighs to make her straddle him, Rindell coaxed her into rocking back and forth against him. The squeak from the bed springs almost drowned out Olivia's giggles.

Mr. Batson knocked on the kitchen wall and called, "You damn kids need to knock that off. Old man needs his rest."

"Goddamn, old man. Ain't even dark yet."

Mr. Batson grumbled.

Rindell lay underneath her, smiling up at the horrified look on her face. He took her hand away from where she'd clamped it over her mouth and laced his fingers into hers.

"I used to have an extra thumb," Olivia said. It was a lame secret to trade for his tragedy, but it was hers.

"An extra one? For real?"

Olivia turned her left hand to show him the crescent scar where the offending digit had been removed. He drew it closer with a puzzled look as he ran the pad of his thumb over it.

"They had it removed. But when I was a baby, they used to hide it with a mitten, that's why they called me Mitten."

"Aw. That's cute," he said. He brought her hand closer and kissed the scar. Letting go of her hand, he brought his palm to her lower back to coax her back into movement.

"But you know, my mother always lies about it, about why they called me Mitten. She lies about everything. Like her telling you my grandfather was in the Marines. He wasn't. I hate that. I hate all her lies."

Rindell frowned, so that she thought she must have ruined the moment. Leaning over, she kissed him until he stopped frowning and went back to kissing and petting her.

All the same, there was a strange energy about him, the sort of silence she associated with Dan before he stopped calling. Was it that easy to screw things up? To make a man stop wanting her? As she walked home in the light rain, she rubbed the scar where her thumb had been removed. Why would a man want her when there was so clearly something wrong with her?

CHAPTER SEVENTEEN

Jennifer

THE END RESULT of Jennifer's daily interaction with vendors who wanted to make a good impression on TampaFuture, Inc. was that she sometimes forgot why a florist or a caterer might go above and beyond. Not because Jennifer was inherently more special than other people, but because she had something of value to trade: her good opinion and her connections. So she floundered when Olivia didn't jump at the chance to provide her with great service. Or any service.

"I was hoping we could meet at the church to look over the stuff you got from Gayle's boyfriend," Jennifer said.

"I just got home from work," Olivia said flatly. She didn't suggest an alternative.

"I'm sorry, but I was hoping to get it tonight."

"I tried to give it to you at church. Twice."

Caterers and florists never said things like that.

"I'm sorry about that. I really am. It's just that Kevin doesn't want to know I'm still looking into that. I don't want to upset him." Jennifer lowered her voice, as though she were in danger of being overheard, even though she was alone in her car, safe in the shadowed embrace of the parking garage.

After a moment of silence, Olivia said, "Well, you could come here and get it."

It wasn't what Jennifer had hoped for, but she forced herself to smile as she said, "Oh, that would be great. Thank you so much."

Driving up I-275 during rush hour, Jennifer didn't feel particularly grateful until she remembered that Olivia didn't owe her anything. Olivia had already done more to help than Jennifer had a right to expect.

She went into the Holley house, trying to hold that thought, but the Holleys engulfed her.

"Oh, Jennifer! It's so good to see you again! We had such a wonderful time with your parents. Your mother is such a dear. And your father. I'd love to invite them again," Mrs. Holley said, as she hugged Jennifer tightly.

"Yes, please do extend the offer to your folks. We'd love to see them the next time they're in town." Mr. Holley settled for a heavy shoulder-patting. Considering his size, Jennifer was relieved to avoid a hug.

"Dinner will be ready in about half an hour." Mrs. Holley beamed, while her son and daughter hung back in the shadows.

"Oh, no, you don't need to worry about me. Olivia is helping me with a project."

"That sounds exciting! What kind of project?"

Before her mother could horn in any further, Olivia said, "Just a thing. For Mission Week."

Olivia looked uncomfortable. She crossed the living room, cutting Jennifer off from her parents.

"It's up in my room."

Following Olivia up the stairs, Jennifer had warring urges to sympathize and to trump. To say, "You think your mother's bad, look at my mother."

At least Mrs. Holley looked nice. Sure, middle-aged and plump with gray hair, but it was respectably, honestly gray hair. And her clothes were appropriate. A cute pair of red knee-shorts and a gingham blouse. She seemed disappointed as Olivia led Jennifer away, but not batty. Not like Moira.

Upstairs, Olivia retrieved a cardboard box that had originally held fifths of Wild Turkey. Something dark brown had splattered and dried along one end.

"Here it is." Olivia didn't make eye contact as she offered the box to Jennifer.

When Jennifer didn't immediately take the box, Olivia exhaled heavily. A snort more than a sigh.

"I can carry it out to your car for you, if you want." The sharpness in Olivia's voice shamed Jennifer, reminded her of those moments on the phone when she'd been trying to treat Olivia like an employee. She slipped her hands under the box.

"It's not that. I was just wondering if it would be okay if I looked at it here?"

Olivia couldn't hide her confusion and, seeing it, Jennifer closed her eyes for moment, searching for the right thing to say. The thing that would return them to that moment before Jennifer had acted like a spoiled bitch, when Olivia had wanted to help her.

When she opened her eyes again, Olivia was smiling at her. Not soft, but not hard, either.

"The thing is, Kevin is upset with me. He doesn't want me to keep worrying about this. If I take this stuff home with me, he's going to be upset. I promised I would let this go. Could I look at it here, see if there's anything useful in it?"

"Sure. But there's just the dining room table. And that's already set for dinner."

Jennifer had imagined they could dump it out on the bed, but a closer look at the contents of the box made clear that was asking too much. It looked like a box of trash. The quilt on Olivia's bed was some JCPenney floral polyester-looking thing, but it was Olivia's bed. Jennifer wouldn't have wanted that box of crumpled, soiled papers dumped onto her bed.

A growing appreciation for Olivia's discomfort soaked through Jennifer's skin and made her shudder. There Olivia was, living with her parents, possibly not by choice, in a bedroom that was frozen in time. She didn't have NSYNC posters tacked up on the walls, but obviously she hadn't redecorated since she was a teenager. She was essentially living in her high school bedroom.

No wonder she didn't want Jennifer there.

"I'm sorry. I wasn't thinking. I'll think of something else," Jennifer said.

"Dinner's ready, you girls," Mrs. Holley said from the other side of the bedroom door.

"You could stay for dinner and then we could look through it," Olivia said.

"Is that okay?" Jennifer couldn't tell if it was a sincere offer.

"Sure. You can leave that here while we eat."

They went downstairs together, in eerie mimicry of a childhood friendship they had never shared.

Jennifer's job had prepared her for eating with near-strangers who felt it was okay to ask personal questions. So when Mrs. Holley said she wanted to hear "all about" the impending wedding, Jennifer supplied a thousand minute details, even the ones that were just fantasies at that point. Somehow, she sensed that Mrs. Holley wouldn't mind if it wasn't all literal truth.

Mr. Holley's share of the dinner conversation consisted of dire pronouncements about political things Jennifer knew nothing about, but she nodded in politely feigned consternation. Rich interjected random things that only made sense to Mr. Holley. Or if they didn't make sense, they incensed him.

"These damned ACORN people, messing around with voter registration. We need to enact some serious voter fraud laws to keep them from pitching the election to this Obama character," Mr. Holley said, after he'd tried and failed to quiz Jennifer about her political position. She didn't have one.

"No, no," Rich said loudly. He dropped his fork, reached for his water glass, then backtracked to his fork and nearly knocked the glass over, shaking his head the whole time. "Diebold is running a scam. Like in 2000. Easy to do. Easy to do with a machine. Rewrite the code. Easy."

Mr. Holley brought his fist down beside his plate, rattling everything on the table.

"Goddamnit! I'm not listening to that!" he bellowed.

"Oh, honey," Mrs. Holley said, trying to soothe which one, Jennifer wasn't sure.

"Rewrite the code. Say dump these votes, double these votes. Programming...."

"No, not programming! You better eat quick before I send you away from this table with no supper."

"I'm not ten. Can't send me to my room," Rich said.

"By God, you may not be ten, but as long as you live in my house, I'll damn well send you to your room if I like."

Rich stood up, for a moment staring across the room at nothing. Or as though he had forgotten what he intended to say. Then he picked up his plate in a hand that trembled wildly, threatening to send his meatloaf and potatoes au gratin tumbling down his front.

"Sit down," Mr. Holley said.

"Honey, it's okay." Mrs. Holley stood up, too.

"You sit down. Don't be rude to our guest, Rich."

"It's okay," Jennifer said. She felt shaky, too, like a plate held in an unsteady hand. In danger of being broken.

"Sit down!"

"Going to my room," Rich said. He walked away, his plate barely held level.

Mr. Holley hauled himself to his feet, intending to go after his son, but apparently his size was too much for him. After a few seconds, he lowered himself to his seat, wheezing.

"Now you've worked yourself up," Mrs. Holley said.

"I'm fine." His face looked dangerously red. The face of man who would do well to invite a paramedic to every meal.

Jennifer glanced at Olivia, who held a forkful of food over her plate. Her face was nearly as red as her father's.

"Rich gets off track sometimes," Mrs. Holley said. "But he's doing so much better. He's made so much progress already."

Across the table, Olivia lifted the fork to her mouth and ate. Jennifer wished she could leave, but made herself take another bite.

Thankfully, Mr. Holley was a fast eater. In a few minutes, he had cleared his plate and, excusing himself, shifted his bulk to a recliner in the living room. While Jennifer helped Mrs. Holley clear the table, Olivia went to get the box.

For a few moments, they stared at the box in the center of the table. Jennifer longed for Olivia to take charge, but she knew that wasn't fair. Calming her nerves, she tipped the box on its side and sluiced its contents out along the table.

"I'm looking for anything with an address for Renee," Jennifer said.

She didn't mean it to be a plea for help, but she didn't want to be left alone, either. Olivia, who had already taken two steps backward toward the kitchen door, approached the table and picked up the first piece of paper at hand. Torn from a Chinese menu flier, it had a phone number written on the back and a name: Lamar. She set it to the side as possibly important. Jennifer pulled out a receipt for partial payment on an overdue water bill.

An hour later, they had three distinct piles: trash, mementos, and possibly important. The trash pile contained receipts, fliers, gum wrappers, payday loan paperwork, bloated romance novels, and a champagne cork. Among the mementos were a pair of bronzed booties, two yearbooks, Gayle's high school diploma, and several dozen photographs, including a faded picture of Gayle with a slender blond woman who must have been Renee. It explained why Gayle had mistaken Jennifer for Renee. There was a similarity to their eyes and the shapes of their eyebrows.

In the pile of things likely to be important: the Chinese menu, a small spiral notebook with half the pages torn out and the other half scribbled full of dates and state parks, paperwork from Gayle's job, and Shanti's birth certificate. Shanti Williams. Not Shanti Prichard.

Olivia gathered the trash in her perfectly manicured hands and took it into the kitchen to throw away. When she returned, Jennifer blurted out the first thing she could think of: "You have such beautiful hands."

Olivia looked at her hands for a second and then said, "Thanks."

Salvaging the spiral notebook from the other things, Jennifer started copying down all the other information about Shanti and Gayle and Renee. The notebook wasn't anything Jennifer would have picked to carry in her purse, but it was innocuous. She could take it home without arousing Kevin's suspicions. As for the rest of the stuff, she shoved it into the deepest corner of her car trunk. It was unlikely Kevin would ever look there, but better to keep it out of sight.

His suspicions must have been aroused by something else, because when Jennifer got home, he greeted her with a scowl.

"Where have you been? I was getting worried," he said.

"I told you. I had to finish some things at work."

"I didn't think that meant three hours. Did you eat dinner already?"

"Yeah, we ordered in. I told you not to wait on me."

"I know. I know."

Jennifer gave him a kiss, although he didn't invite it. His breath smelled like onions and beer. He'd already eaten, too. And out. They didn't have any onions in the house. So why make a big deal out of how late she was? Steering around him, she went into the bedroom to change out of her work clothes. He followed and stood in the doorway watching her.

"It's just that I'm worried about you," he said.

"Why?" Jennifer tried to toss off a laugh, but it came out as a snort.

"Because I leave for San Francisco next week."

"You what?"

"See? See why I'm worried? Did you forget? NADA is next week in San Francisco. I hate leaving you if … if you're not okay."

"I'm fine." She had completely forgotten about the National Automobile Dealers Association convention. "I'll be fine while you're gone."

"Well, I thought you might miss me."

Kevin gave her the pouty look that was starting to look out of place on him. His hair had started graying at the temples. *Gravitas*, that's what he was getting, and it didn't match the little boy routine. Jennifer saw it all with a cool detachment, just as she saw she was using the wrong tactics, too.

"You know I'll miss you," she said. "How long are you going to be gone?"

Half undressed, she went to him and wrapped her bare arms around his shoulders. Ignoring the onion stink, she went up on her toes for a kiss.

"Just a week. I thought Carrie could look in on you."

"Carrie's not you."

More importantly, Carrie would be in the way. What lay enticingly before Jennifer was a whole week spent alone, doing whatever she wanted. Last year, during NADA, she had spent her evenings moping around and having dinner with Carrie and Nathan, back when they were a couple. This year, she would spend her Kevinless time searching for Gayle Prichard's sister.

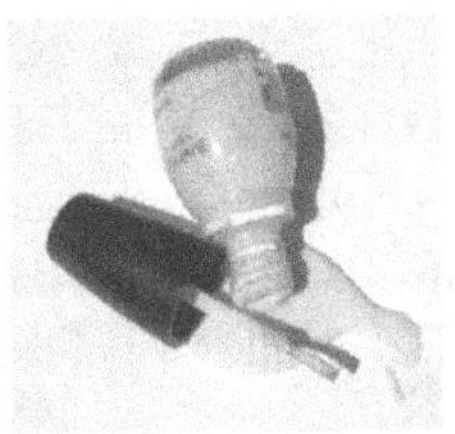

CHAPTER EIGHTEEN

Olivia

THE CHURCH'S YOUTH Director had an aura of cool that Olivia envied. She knew it influenced her, although she wanted to resist it. Marnie had always been one of the cool kids, Christian or otherwise, and when she tossed her hair back and clasped her hands over her modest cleavage and gold cross necklace, Olivia fell for it all over again.

"I have a huge favor to ask you," Marnie said. She didn't say it the way Olivia would have, like a supplicant. She said it with the same inflection she would have used to say, "I have a huge present for you."

"How huge?" Olivia saved and closed the spreadsheet she'd been working on.

"I need another counselor to go on the Double Cross overnight."

It was the sort of opportunity Olivia had once been eager for: participating in the youth ministry, making a difference in the kids' lives, building the future of the church. Once upon a time, she'd been eager to live out all the public relations lingo Marnie used to recruit volunteer chaperones. Then Marnie shut her out, first telling Olivia she was too young to be a counselor and then four years later that she was too old. In short, Marnie didn't want Olivia to be part of "the gang." It felt like high school all over again.

Except now, Marnie needed her.

"I can't. I've got plans with a friend." Olivia reveled in knowing it wasn't an excuse or a lie. She was supposed to see Rindell that night and she'd already promised Jennifer she'd go with her up to Anastasia State Park on Saturday, to help her find that little girl's aunt. Olivia had a full weekend that didn't include work or quilts.

Marnie didn't even blink. "You could always reschedule with your friend. Double Cross only comes once a year and you can't reschedule something special like that."

"I'm sorry. I can't." Olivia didn't care if her bulldog was showing. Marnie's opportunism was so distasteful now that she could see the underbelly of it.

Two hours later, Marnie sent in the big guns. Pastor Lou poked his head into Olivia's cubicle, peering at her over the top of his glasses.

"I hate to put you on the spot, Olivia, but I'd like to ask you to do something for me."

"Double Cross?"

"The difficulty," Pastor Lou said, in the same voice he used to cajole the deacons board, "is that there's no time for us to clear someone through the volunteer protocols. You, however, have already been through it, and you're already on the insurance for the van."

Olivia didn't repeat what she'd said to Marnie, that she already had plans. She didn't mention that she felt pressed into service, taken advantage of, taken for granted.

She said, "Okay, but I have to pack."

"That's no problem," said Pastor Lou. It wasn't for him. "They don't leave until four. You can go home early and get started right now."

Someone had to finish running the Sunday bulletins and someone had to prep the Welcome card folders in the sanctuary since none of the volunteers showed up. When that was done, she sped through traffic to get home, threw some clothes and toiletries into an overnight bag. At 3:15 she was back in traffic, already bumper-to-bumper on a Friday. An hour later, she was behind the wheel of the van, following a convoy of other youth chaperones toward Orlando. Sealed up in the van with nine teenage girls and another chaperone, Olivia realized she hadn't called Rindell or Jennifer.

At the hotel in Orlando, she called them both. She got Rindell's voicemail and left an awkwardly formal message. Jennifer answered on the second ring.

"I'm sorry," Olivia said, after she explained what had happened.

"It's okay," Jennifer said. "I'm being silly. I should be a big girl and go by myself."

Something in Olivia's gut thumped. "No, don't, Jennifer. You're right to want someone to go with you. That's a long way to go by yourself to someplace strange. When I get back on Sunday, I'll go with you then, okay?"

Olivia hung up, not sure what would happen, but fearful that Jennifer would go alone.

By then, the other counselors and youths were trundling their luggage down to their rooms. Olivia followed and discovered the full horror of what she'd been strong-armed into. She would be sharing a room with three teenage girls she barely knew. The adjoining suite held three more girls and another chaperone, Amy, one of the cool kids from the Young Couples Bible Study Group.

"We're in for an adventure," Amy said chummily, touching up her make-up.

"Yeah." Olivia wasn't surprised when they reached the concert venue that she was made to play the adult. While Amy went off to chat with Marnie, Olivia was stuck doling out dinner money, corralling teenagers, and being asked, "Will you keep my lip gloss/cell phone/hairbrush/wallet in your purse?"

The music was nothing like the Christian bands of Olivia's youth, but she preferred the unintelligible lyrics to the MC's strident voice between bands.

"Give it up for Jesus!" he screeched, encouraging the kids to yell as loudly as they could. "You wanna know who the coolest guy in the world is? It's Jesus. He's your best friend, your study partner. He's the man. Who da man?"

The answer came back in chorus: "Jesus is da man!"

It was all more slickly polished than it had been in Olivia's day, and she covered her ears to make it bearable. From somewhere in her purse a cell phone vibrated. As she reached into the bag, searching for a phone that was probably not hers, she glanced up and saw two teenagers pressed together against a wall. They were wrapped around each other, kissing feverishly. The boy was a stranger. Or at least Olivia didn't recognize the back of his floppy blond hair or his sagging jeans, but the girl was one of her own. Erica, in a tiny pink camisole that barely contained her breasts.

"Oh, crap," Olivia said out loud in the din of screaming guitars and teenagers. Her first ever outing as a youth group chaperone and she'd lost a sheep to the wolves.

Her first instinct was to wait for a more experienced counselor to intervene. Her second instinct was to march smartly over to the girl and give her a stern talking to—no, that was more of a fantasy than an instinct. Olivia did in fact take two steps toward the girl, but came up short when the contents of the "stern talking to" failed to materialize.

Her third instinct was to scurry through the crowd and tell Marnie. She found the youth director dancing in the middle of a circle of kids from Church of the Palms. At first Marnie smiled and waved obliviously. Only after Olivia made multiple gestures to her did she approach, frowning.

Leaning close, Olivia shouted into Marnie's ear, "There's a problem."

"What kind of problem?"

"One of the girls is making out with some guy."

Marnie was all responsible adult then. She followed Olivia back through the crowds, and promptly went into action. With a flurry of gestures and words Olivia couldn't hear, Marnie separated Erica from the boy and herded her toward the Church of the Palms crowd. She did it without a single glance at Olivia, leaving her alone on the fringe of the crowd with her vibrating purse.

Back at the hotel, Olivia had plenty of time to repent not following her second instinct/fantasy. Marnie and Amy shut all six girls up in one suite with another chaperone and then they rounded on Olivia.

"How long was it going on before you came to get me?" Marnie said.

"I don't know. I came and got you as soon as I saw it." Olivia was as stupidly surprised at the contempt in the question as she had been in high school, facing down the random viciousness of cheerleaders.

"Why didn't you intervene?"

"I didn't know what to say," Olivia said.

"How about 'stop'?"

"We covered this last week," Amy said. "We talked about abstinence in group last week."

"I'm not a regular counselor. I don't go to group." Olivia hated how plaintive she sounded.

"Well, you can't let them go off by themselves. You have to stay close to them," Amy said.

"I can't believe you didn't reach out to Selena." Marnie shook her head in disappointment.

Selena. Not Erica.

"I don't know her," Olivia said.

"You should have done something." Marnie and Amy shook their heads in unison. That robotic self-satisfaction finally roused Olivia to anger.

"You asked me to do this as a favor!"

Marnie was silent for a moment and then in a low, sneaky voice, she said, "I won't make that mistake again."

She breezed back through the adjoining suite door and, on the other side, she said, "Everybody gather around. We need to talk about something that happened tonight."

Olivia and Amy stood in the doorway, watching as Marnie

wove her web around a teary-eyed Selena. In a few minutes they were all hugging and crying and saying, "We love you, Selena. We want you to love yourself. We want you to respect yourself."

In Olivia's ear, Amy whispered, "Isn't she amazing? She's so good with them. It makes me so happy to think she'll protect them from the mistake I made."

When Olivia glanced at her, Amy looked away, maybe regretting the confession. She separated herself from Olivia and fell into the arms of the crying, praying monster of teenage girls. Olivia stayed where she was, watching the circle she hadn't been invited into and never would be.

Two minutes before lights out, Olivia's purse rang and at long last it was her own phone. She exhaled, put it to her ear and said, "Hello."

"Hey dere, Olivia. Where y'at?" Rindell said.

Olivia was about to say, "Orlando," when she finally realized *where y'at* wasn't a question. It was a greeting.

"Hi. Did you get my message?" Amy was eyeing her and, in a fit of self-consciousness, Olivia went out into the hallway in her nightgown. "I'm sorry I had to cancel."

"That's okay, baby. Things happen."

"How are you?"

"Let's see, you want the whole deal or the highlights? Last night I got four car wrecks, a domestic call with an open head wound, two heart attacks and a tumble down the stairs at an old folks home. Pretty quiet night mostly. Hope tonight's that quiet. How was your day?"

"Long. And awful." Olivia sighed. Her day sounded like a breeze next to car wrecks and domestic violence.

"I'm sorry to hear that."

They went on that way, talking about nothing important until they wound down into silence.

"I missed seeing you today. I was looking forward to it," he said.

"You saw me Wednesday morning." Saying it made her blush.

"That thirty minutes wasn't exactly enough."

She didn't know how to answer and after a moment said, "Would you mind doing me a favor?"

"You bet. You name it."

She explained about Jennifer. She over-explained, aware that he had already done her a favor, that he was mysteriously still interested in her.

"I promised I'd go tomorrow and then I got roped into this. I'm worried she'll go by herself and it's out in the middle of nowhere."

"Sure," he said. "Gimme her phone number. I'll call her, see when she wants to go."

That pleasantly he agreed, but when she gushed, "Thank you so very much," he stopped her.

"O-livia. Baby, I'm happy to do you a favor, but you don't need to thank me. Just so's we're clear, I expect payback for this favor."

It startled her, left her stammering, "Oh, yes. Whatever I can do for you."

"What I'm gonna need you to do is come by me when you get back on Sunday and bring your fine, substantial ass for more than a half-hour quickie."

His voice dropped into a throaty register that made her knees feel squishy, and it took her a moment to process his request. He wasn't just making a sexually suggestive invitation; he was complimenting a part of her anatomy that had always disgusted her.

"We got a deal?" he said.

Dumbly, she nodded and then managed to say, "Okay."

After saying good-bye, she closed the phone and leaned her head against the wall until she had the stupid smile on her face under control. When she reached for the doorknob, it didn't budge. Of course, hotel doors locked automatically and she hadn't bothered to get her room key when she went into the hallway. She knocked lightly on the door, but no one answered.

"Amy?" she called and knocked harder. The sound of muffled giggling answered her.

In her nightgown, she stood in the hallway knocking for a good two minutes until one of the male chaperones came out of his room across the hall to see what the trouble was.

"They locked me out," Olivia said.

He knocked on the door and yelled, "Girls, open the door! I'm not kidding."

A moment later, Amy opened the door, looking red in the face. She said, "I'm sorry. We didn't hear you knocking."

Olivia pushed past her and went to put her phone away. She looked at the bed she would have to share with some strange girl and wanted to cry. Amy stood in the circle of the other girls, looking annoyed.

"We were just having some fun," she said.

"People like you always do think it's fun when you humiliate someone." Olivia had another whole day to spend with these girls and she was done.

Amy looked stung, but she didn't protest or say, "People like me?" She knew what she was, one of the cool kids.

"We're sorry," Amy said, but she was smirking. Two girls giggled.

"Apologies don't count if you're still laughing," Olivia said.

After a moment of uneasy silence, Amy said, "We should pray." They prayed, Amy's voice brittle with insult, Olivia's husky and exhausted.

In the dark, after they were in bed, one of the girls said, "Were you talking to your boyfriend?"

"Yes," Olivia said and regretted it. She couldn't see anything, but she suspected she heard the sound of smirking. She turned on her side to face away from the girl and tried to sleep. Tomorrow was going to be a long day.

CHAPTER NINETEEN

Jennifer

JENNIFER FOCUSED INTENTLY on driving, making minute corrections to the steering wheel.

"Thank you," she said to Rindell for the third or fourth time. They had driven most of the first hour in silence and it was getting to her. They had two more hours of driving to get to Anastasia State Park, then three hours back.

"I appreciate it."

"It's no trouble." He sounded exasperated.

"Thank you." It slipped out unbidden.

"Look, I know you feel like you got lucky. How it coulda been you got run over. I get that. I understand how that feels."

"Do you?" She doubted he did.

"Yeah. When my cousin Rindell died, I felt like I had to make it mean something that he died and I lived. Make it so I deserved to live."

The rawness in his voice startled Jennifer into taking her eyes off the road. He was looking at her with real concern. For an instant they made eye contact, before Jennifer gazed back at the highway.

"I just...." She hesitated, expecting everyone to be as tired of the subject as Kevin was, but Rindell waited for her to speak. "I can't forget how she looked, how she sounded. That's what she was thinking about when she died. If it was that important to her...."

"It had to be important. Yeah, I get you."

They drove in friendly silence after that, until Jennifer said the first thing that popped into her head: "Wait, you have a cousin named Rindell, too?"

"I—yeah. That's weird, right?" When she glanced at him, he was staring out the window.

"A little. Can I ask what happened to your cousin?"

"Nah, let's don't talk about that," he said.

"So how did you meet Olivia?"

He answered her questions, but he didn't offer anything freely. It was like driving alone, except with a stranger in the car, she couldn't sing along with the radio.

Jennifer had no clear expectations of Anastasia State Park, although it sounded elegant enough. She had not envisioned that people *lived* in campgrounds. A small building stood at the park gate, and the ranger on duty gave her a map. He marked an X at Site 48, registered to Renee Williams.

Driving away from the ranger's station, Jennifer marveled at the view out her window. A narrow inlet of water and a narrower strip of sand separated them from the Atlantic, flashing by in the gaps between trees. Rindell perked up, too, looking past her at the stretch of water.

"I never been this far east," he said.

"It's beautiful." Jennifer rolled down her window and the sharp, cool smell of salt brushed away the dense heat they had carried up from Tampa.

"Aw, shit, campground," Rindell said.

"Oh, was that it?"

"There was a sign for it."

Further along to the left, Jennifer swung the car into a parking lot, planning to turn around, but the ocean lay directly before them, past a broad white beach. A convenience store stood at the far end of the parking lot, and Jennifer turned the car toward it.

"Let's get something to drink," she said.

The usual crowd of cranky, sunburned tourists milled around

the shop, finishing out their day at the beach. Mixed in among them were leathery old men and women busy finishing out their lives there. Jennifer excused her way through them, and Rindell followed.

When he reached for his wallet to pay for his own bottle of soda and a bag of chips, she said, "Oh no. I'll get it. I'm the one who dragged you all the way out here."

He shrugged and let her pay. Back outside in the bright light of late afternoon, he raised a hand to shade his eyes as he peered toward the beach.

"Do you want to walk down?" she said.

"Yeah, let's go see what all this fuss 'bout the ocean is." He grinned and took a swig of his Cherry Coke.

Jennifer had thought she was being practical wearing a sturdy denim skirt and tennis shoes, but the wind whipping off the Atlantic onto her legs was cold, and sand drifted into her socks and shoes. Rindell had a similar problem, with his lace-up boots getting mired in the sugary sand.

He soldiered past the dunes to the open beach, where he watched children play while he ate his Doritos. Jennifer sipped her Sprite on a queasy stomach. Soon, they would be at Site 48 and she would have to talk to Gayle's sister about a thing she wished she could forget.

Rindell said something, but it drifted past her on the wind.

"What?"

He turned around, smiling, and said, "I been working too damn much. I need to get out more."

Jennifer returned the smile with the vaguest sense of understanding. She and Kevin sometimes said things like that. *We should go away for the weekend.* In reality, vacation plans almost never panned out, because neither of them could commit to taking time off. They liked working.

"You think Olivia would go camping?" Rindell asked.

"I don't know. I don't know her that well. Just from church."

"She got those fancy nails and soft hands. I don't know if girls with fancy nails go camping." He seemed lost in that thought as he finished his chips.

"Well, maybe if you did all the dirty work. Putting up the tent, building the fire. So she wouldn't mess up her nails," Jennifer suggested.

"Yeah, you right. I could do that. You s'pose we better get on and find this lady?"

"Sure, we better, before it gets dark."

"Yeah, sorry we couldn't leave earlier. It was a long shift last night. Had a hard time getting myself out of bed."

"Oh, it's fine. We have plenty of time," Jennifer said.

They would have found Renee sooner, if Jennifer had let Rindell navigate. Instead she got flustered and lost on the winding roads that led past one campsite after another. Most of them were full for the Labor Day weekend, some housing glossy RV's, while tents and pop-up trailers occupied other spaces. All of the camp sites were overhung by massive trees and hemmed in by palmettos and weedy undergrowth.

Finally, Rindell must have reached his limit, because he said, "Look, see. There's the playground. Only playground on the map."

The children playing on the equipment turned to watch the car roll by.

"Turn up at the next road," Rindell said.

Jennifer obeyed and they started down another curving trail of campsites, until she saw something familiar. In one of the pictures in the box from Gayle's apartment, there had been a snapshot that showed a trailer with a white and red candy-striped awning shading the two Prichard sisters in lawn chairs. The awning must have been new when the photo was taken, but the one Jennifer saw now was faded to pink and tattered along the edges.

"Is that it? Is that 48?" she said.

Before she had completely stopped the car, Rindell opened his door and stepped out. He trotted ahead, looking for the plaque with the site number.

"That's 48, right there," he said.

As dusk fell, the other campsites had come to life. Fires crackled in stone pits while campers chatted and laughed. At Site 48, only the blue glow of television spilled out of the dinged fifth-wheel trailer.

"You want me to go up and knock?" Rindell said.

"Oh, no." Realizing the car was still in gear, she slipped it into park and turned it off, but left the keys dangling in the ignition. "You can just wait. It shouldn't take more than a moment."

The air outside was a steam bath, all the cool ocean breeze blocked by a canopy of live oak that immediately set Jennifer's nose to itching. From the car's trunk she got the cardboard box of photos and mementos. It felt limp with humidity and gave off a stale odor, what she assumed Gayle's apartment had smelled like.

When Jennifer knocked, the whole trailer rattled on its wheels, aluminum clattering against aluminum. Whatever she had expected, it was not the carnival sideshow character who answered the door in a wreath of smoke. The woman's hair was lifeless with three inches of brown roots growing into blond. Her mouth was a narrow frown, framed by a wisp of hair below her chin. Her first chin. The others tumbled below it, one pink roll of fat on top of the next, bridging from a normal human head to a manatee's body. Her upper arms were like hams, her torso mountainous, her legs—Jennifer tried to clamp down on the shock, but she couldn't. What had happened to Gayle's slender blond sister?

"What do you want?" the woman said.

"Are you Renee?"

"What's it to you?"

"My name's Jennifer. I'm a friend of Gayle's." She said it in a rush, afraid she would not be given a second chance to get the relevant details out.

"That supposed to mean something to me?" Renee said.

"I brought this for you." Jennifer hefted the box on her hip. "Some of Gayle's papers. Some pictures. Gayle's boyfriend thought you might want them."

"Why the hell would I want that?"

Jennifer had prepared herself for grief, but not for indifference. Renee didn't know Gayle was dead. Jennifer was bringing the bad news. All of it at once. She said, "Can I come in?"

Renee shrugged. With glacial speed she stepped away from the open door, making the trailer groan. Jennifer followed and, stepping into the trailer, felt the squishiness of the floor underfoot. There were no lights in the trailer beyond what the TV provided. Jennifer squinted and felt along the floor with her foot before transferring her weight.

"Go and get me a cold Coke from the cooler," Renee said. For a moment, Jennifer thought she was speaking to her, and then out of the shadows stepped a young man. He was lean and brown, thirteen or fourteen.

"Hi," Jennifer said.

"Hey. I'm Lamar. You want anything?" he said as he moved past her to the door.

"No, thank you," Jennifer said.

The door slammed behind him and Jennifer took it as her cue.

"Look, I'm not really a friend of Gayle's. I didn't even know her, but I was there when she—passed away. She died. She's dead. And I—I'm sorry."

She had thought there might be some crying, but Renee simply took another step backward and lowered herself to the sofa that took up one wall of the trailer. Like a ship in high winds, the trailer tilted, and Jennifer fought to stay upright.

"She's dead?" Renee's voice was husky.

"I'm sorry, yes. A hit and run, when she was leaving work. It was instantaneous." Now tasked with telling the story, Jennifer saw the attraction of that lie.

Renee was silent, her eyes tracking on the TV to Jennifer's left.

"It's Shanti," Jennifer said. "That's why I'm here, because of Shanti. When Gayle was—the last thing Gayle said was that she wanted you to take care of Shanti. That was her dying wish."

Renee's gaze shifted to Jennifer, and it wasn't a pleasant

experience. The TV turned her eyes an iridescent, insect-like blue. She lifted her lip in a snarl and said, "That ain't going to happen."

"But—I—Gayle wanted…."

"I don't give a fuck what Gayle wanted. I'm sure in your perfect little social worker heart, you can't understand why I'd feel that way."

"I'm not a social worker," Jennifer said.

"Then what the hell are you doing here?"

"I told you. I was there when Gayle died and that was the last thing she said."

"Yeah, she wanted me to forgive her for screwing my husband and getting knocked up. Like I'm supposed to raise the kid that ruined my marriage? Get out. Get the fuck out."

Jennifer left the box on the counter edge beside the TV and inched back across the sagging floor. Coming out of the screen door, she nearly bowled over Lamar, who carried a can of Coke in one hand. He caught Jennifer with the other.

"You okay?" he said.

From the trailer came a shriek and a crash. Lamar jumped up the stairs and opened the door, calling, "Mom?"

Jennifer staggered across the sandy yard in front of the trailer and nearly tripped over the stones around the fire ring. Rindell got out of the car and came toward her.

"Everything awright?" he said.

The trailer door slammed open and Lamar said, "Hey!" He came toward them at a jog, holding up his pants at mid-hip. "She told me to take this out to the trash."

Lamar thrust the cardboard box at them and Rindell took it.

Another scream came from the trailer and then sobbing broke the rhythm of insects in the undergrowth.

"What did you say to her?" Lamar said.

Jennifer wiped her nose on the back of her hand. "I came to tell her that her sister passed away."

"Aunt Gayle's dead?" He teared up and rubbed his eyes fiercely.

"I'm sorry. I came to give her a message from Gayle. She wanted Renee to take care of Shanti, but I don't know where she is."

"My dad's family might know. I haven't talked to them in a while, but I could call." Lamar's face was tense. He was worried about his cousin—no, his sister.

"Maybe you could find out for us? Let us know?" Rindell said.

"Yeah, sure." Lamar shrugged. "Don't take it personal. My mom is still pissed about that whole deal with Aunt Gayle and my dad. Especially after the Jerry Springer thing."

While Jennifer stood by in shock, trying to understand it all, Rindell and Lamar swapped phone numbers. Jennifer was too distracted to mention that she already had Lamar's, scribbled on a Chinese menu in the cardboard box.

After the boy went back into the trailer, Rindell put the box in the car's back seat. When he returned to her side, he said, "I can drive, if you don't feel up to it."

"No, I'll be fine. Give me a minute."

Jennifer thought she would be fine, but failure pressed so hard on her she couldn't breathe. By the time they made it to the main road, dark was falling fast and Jennifer was crying. The crying turned into sobbing, and Jennifer pulled off the road, into the parking lot at the beach. A sign informed her that the beach was closed after dark, but she parked anyway. Inland from the west came the vague glow of St. Augustine, but otherwise it was dark and moonless. A good place to have a meltdown. Rindell was quiet while she cried.

It should have been cathartic, like popping a blister. Jennifer had delivered Gayle's last message to her sister. And failed. The promise wasn't going to be kept.

"Why don't you let me drive?" Rindell clasped her arm in his warm hand, as he reached to unclip her seatbelt.

She made an effort to stop crying and couldn't. When he slipped his arm around her shoulders, it seemed to unleash more tears, and she clutched at him like a life preserver. With her cheek pressed against his, she felt the moment he turned his head, and she turned hers to meet him.

Negotiating the bucket seats and the center console took the most effort. Getting out of her panties was easy. The moment she straddled him wasn't even pleasurable. She was too dry and his zipper scraped against her while a seatbelt buckle dug into her knee. For a brief instant the aloneness abated, before it rebounded more sharply than before. He had kissed her, but after that, he hadn't encouraged her. She had undone his pants, figured out the mechanics of the act. His hands were limp on her hips, not trying to push her away or pull her closer. He probably just needed somewhere to put them.

The worst part, humiliating and sickening at the same time: he wasn't even completely hard.

When she scrambled back into the driver's seat, he opened his door, blinding her with the dome light. In the rearview mirror she saw her ugliness. Her eyes puffy and her hair limp. Rindell was gone for several minutes, and after Jennifer regained her panties and straightened her skirt, she sat dumbly, listening to the door ajar tone.

Headlights washed over the car as someone pulled in behind them. From the open door, she heard Rindell say, "No, sir. We are. We pulled off to swap drivers."

She couldn't hear the other person clearly, but guessed it was a park ranger.

"Yes, sir," Rindell said. "We're getting right back on the road. Going back to Tampa tonight."

With the ranger's lights still on them, Rindell opened the driver's door. Without looking at Jennifer, he said, "I'll drive."

Although they had planned to stop for dinner in Jacksonville, Rindell drove straight through until he stopped for gas in Lake City. He stood with his back to the car while he pumped gas, and all he said to her was what sounded like, "Unidabatroom?"

She stared at him blankly until he said, "The bathroom?" Slowly, like it was a foreign language.

"I'm fine."

After that, they rode the long stretch of I-75 in silence. Staring out at the garish signs advertising adult video stores and real live nude girls, Jennifer must have fallen asleep, because she woke to Rindell saying, "What's the code?"

They were at the security gate for the condo parking garage.

"9674," she said. Kevin's birthday, September 6, 1974. As Rindell parked, Jennifer pulled herself together enough to say, "We don't need to tell Olivia, do we?"

Without a word, he got out of the car and walked toward the entrance where his motorcycle was parked.

Safely inside the condo, Jennifer ran the shower as hot as she could stand it, scrubbing at herself until her skin was raw and the bar of soap was thinner. On her vulva was a zipper abrasion that burned when she soaped it. She stopped the relentless washing when she realized what she was doing—acting like a rape victim. As though something had been done to her, when she was the one who had done something horrible.

She'd never done anything like that. Drunk VIP clients regularly made passes at her and she had never been tempted. So what did Rindell have? Nothing. He was nobody. Not her type at all.

Then she remembered and the remembering sucked all the air out of the room, left her gasping.

During her first year in Tampa, she'd gone to Gasparilla with Carrie. Standing in line to buy a beer, Jennifer met Kevin, who was wearing a UF t-shirt. They started talking to each other like old friends, laughing and teasing each other. Later when they learned they both went to the same church, they'd agreed to pretend that's where they met.

Carrie went home early, but Jennifer stayed to flirt. After she blew out a flip flop, Kevin piggy-backed her home. Standing on the doorstep of her apartment building, they'd kissed and groped each other until they were breathless. Kevin's eyes were bright and urgent when he said, "Can I call you?"

"Yes," she said, a heartbeat away from saying, "No, come in now."

At no point did she think to say, "No, I have a boyfriend."

After that night, she didn't.

Things with Sean had been uncertain anyway since he'd missed graduation, short by six credit hours. It was easy to break up with him, and she never told Kevin the break-up happened after their second date. She'd been practical enough to wait and see if Kevin planned to call her.

Thinking of it, Jennifer felt sick, but she tried to excuse herself by saying, "Well, I was younger then. Besides, I didn't really cheat on Sean. It wasn't like I had sex with Kevin. I didn't even have sex with Rindell. Not really."

She was still telling herself that when the phone rang. She let it go through to voicemail, but Kevin wouldn't give up until he got her. Next he rang her cellphone and then the land line again. She practiced the way to pick up the phone and say, "Hi, honey!"

"Hey, Jenn. What's up?"

"Not much. I just got out of the shower. How are you? How's the conference?"

She kept him going that way, extruding questions and making noises of affirmation or curiosity. Everything was fine. It hadn't gone all the way. It wasn't really cheating.

"Are you okay, baby?" Kevin stopped in mid-sentence to ask and he sounded concerned.

"I'm fine. In fact, I'm great."

"You don't sound it. You sound like you've been crying."

"Oh, it's the pollen count today. I'm super good and I'll tell you why. I took care of the whole thing. I went to see her sister and I told her about what she said."

"How'd it go?"

"It was fine," Jennifer said. "I told the woman's sister and it was fine. And now I've done what I needed to do."

"That's good, Jenn." His voice was warm and friendly. It made her want to cry. Or confess. "I'm happy you got it sorted out. I'm glad you're feeling better."

"Yup and now I'm done. I'm finished with it and everything's fine."

"Good. I've been worried about you."

"Ha!" she said. "You've been mad at me."

"No, I've been worried that you were getting wrapped around the axle about this."

Jennifer laughed forcibly and said, "You have to use a car metaphor for everything, don't you, you nut?"

"Are you sure you're okay?"

"Oh, yeah. I'm just tired. It was a long day."

She made it through the phone call, knowing what it meant. If she didn't tell him now, when would she? And if she wasn't going to tell him, then she needed to find a safe place inside herself to seal it up. That was how people lived with hypocrisy. She would seal it up so thoroughly that when Kevin cheated on her, she would be righteously indignant, untouched by guilt. And she didn't question the likelihood that Kevin would cheat on her. Eventually. It seemed fair. She deserved it.

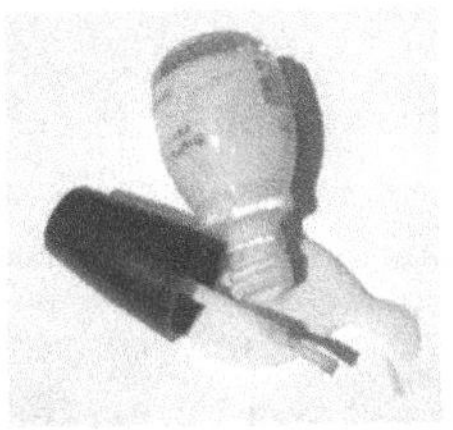

CHAPTER TWENTY

Olivia

OLIVIA TRIED TO leave the church as soon as they unloaded the van, but Pastor Lou said, "Would you please stay? I'd like to talk to you."

While Pastor Lou and Marnie met with Selena's parents, Olivia sat in her cubicle worrying a small hangnail. After half an hour, Selena's scowling parents departed. Selena came after them, head down over a Gameboy.

Pastor Lou beckoned Olivia to his office. Whatever weakness she'd had in the past had been preyed on too much. She felt hard where she'd been porous before. She didn't care what Marnie thought, and seeing Pastor Lou sided up with Marnie, she cared less about what he thought, too. When he started talking about "protecting our children," Olivia tuned him out.

At some point, there was a moment of quiet. A moment for her to speak.

"It doesn't matter. Marnie doesn't want me to volunteer anymore and I don't want to volunteer anymore." From the looks on their faces, Olivia knew they had expected something different. Maybe tears and apologies.

"Well, Olivia, I'm disapp—."

"I want to go home," Olivia said. There was no way she was going to sit there and let Pastor Lou tell her how disappointed he was in her. She got enough of that from her father.

"I wish you'd stay."

"I'm tired. I want to go home." It occurred to Olivia that she didn't need his permission to leave. She stood up, making Pastor Lou frown harder.

"Well, we can talk more when you're feeling better," he said.

"I'd rather not. I'm not going to volunteer again, so it doesn't matter."

"Oh, Olivia," Marnie said.

"That's what you said you wanted, so what do you care?"

Marnie made the sad, pouty face she'd used on Selena and the other teenage girls. It had no effect on Olivia, who crossed the room and opened the door.

As she gathered up her suitcase and purse, Pastor Lou stepped out of his office and closed the door, leaving Marnie inside. He leaned against Olivia's cubicle, blocking her exit.

"Olivia. I don't want you to leave like this."

"Should I come in on Monday?"

"What?"

"Am I fired?" It took everything Olivia had to keep her voice steady.

"No, Olivia, no. As you say, you were just volunteering."

"Then I'm done and I want to go home."

"Okay."

He stepped back, but didn't leave, so that she had to brush past him, mindful of her suitcase. She didn't want to knock it into his bad knee.

"Get some rest, Olivia. I'll see you tomorrow."

At home where she so desperately needed quiet and comfort, her parents were arguing.

"I won't see her left out," Mrs. Holley was saying.

"I'm not suggesting that we 'leave her out.' We need to be sure Rich is taken care of before we worry about anything else," Mr. Holley said.

Olivia set down her suitcase and purse as quietly as she could.

Her parents sat at the dining room table, surrounded by paperwork.

"He'll be taken care of. He's going to get better, so there's no reason we shouldn't divide it three ways."

Their will, that's what they were discussing.

"Damn it. I'm tired of you talking that way. Saying those things. He is not going to get better."

"You don't know! You don't know!" Mrs. Holley wailed.

In the ensuing silence, Olivia almost announced herself, but she had waited too long. Now she was eavesdropping.

"Barb, can we agree to leave Rich the larger share? Say half to Rich? Then split the rest between Olivia and Cynthia? Leave Cynthia the cash and Olivia the house?"

Her father's head came up at that moment, and he saw Olivia in the doorway.

"Olivia! You're home."

"Oh, honey!" Mrs. Holley jumped up from her chair and came to hug Olivia. "Are you hungry? I can heat up the spaghetti we had."

"No, I'm not hungry. I think I'm going to go upstairs and lie down. I'm tired."

"Or I could make you a grilled cheese," Mrs. Holley said.

"No, that's—"

"She said she wasn't hungry," Mr. Holley snapped. "Go up and rest. Your mother and I need to finish talking."

Olivia started up the stairs, but a perverse curiosity held her in its grasp. She paused on the landing, waiting for the conversation to resume.

"I still don't see why we should split it that way," Mrs. Holley said.

"Because Cynthia won't need the house. She has Jeff to take care of her."

"As though Olivia won't find someone to take care of her. She's very serious about that young man."

"I won't have you encouraging her to date that paramedic. You think it didn't get back to me what you told the Dorcas Circle ladies? You've practically got Olivia engaged to him."

Crouched on the stairs, Olivia winced, knowing it was the sort of thing her mother did. For the brief time Dan was in the picture, her mother had painted them as about to get married. No wonder Dan had run away.

"He's a perfectly nice young man. I don't see what you—"

"Good God, Barb. Why would you want to see her marry a black? Do you want colored grandchildren? Is that what you want? To always have people look at you like that?"

"Like what?"

"You see those fat, ugly white girls at the Publix with their food stamps and their pickaninnies. That's what comes of intermarrying with blacks. She'd be better off single."

"You don't have to be that way about it!" Mrs. Holley stood up, her chair scraping on the tile floor. Olivia stood up, too, from where she was squatted on the stairs. Her calves burned.

"Do not have a tantrum. Can you behave like an adult long enough for us to decide on this?"

"I'm not the one being a child."

"What is that supposed to mean?" Mr. Holley said. His voice was hard and threatening. The voice he used when anyone disagreed with him. "I said, what is that supposed to mean?"

"Nothing. I didn't mean anything by it."

"Fine. As I said, I think it's most fair to leave Olivia the house and Cynthia the money. So can we agree?" Mr. Holley harrumphed when her mother didn't answer.

"I just want to be fair to all of them," Mrs. Holley whispered.

"It is fair."

It stuck in Olivia's throat, and after she put her suitcase in her room, she wanted to go down and tell her father she wasn't that ugly. She wasn't so ugly she had to settle for the first guy who would take her. Except maybe it was true. Just because she wanted Rindell didn't mean she'd chosen him out of all her other options. Reaching the bottom of the stairs, she couldn't think of anything to say.

As Olivia opened the front door, her mother called, "Where

are you going, Livvie?"

"I forgot something. At work." Olivia didn't care that it was a lie. She had to get out of there.

Walking down the street, the tears came. They kept coming as she went up the steps to Rindell's trailer. That was how she came to him, sniffling, red-faced, tears dripping down her cheeks.

Whatever she had expected—laughter, confusion, concern—it was not that he would say, "She told you? She asked me not to tell you and she fucking told you?" And then he cried, too. Unshed but hot in his eyes. Angry.

Olivia stared. She had almost forgotten the flood, almost forgotten the complications that existed in Rindell's life. She wanted whatever comfort he might be willing to offer her, but in the small trailer, mud lapped six inches deep around the bottom of the wall, high enough to have invaded the lower cabinets. Rindell held a mop in one hand and rubbed his other palm against his eyes.

Olivia had intended to go straight to him for a hug, but that intention dried up as she looked at his flushed face.

"I suppose she told you it was my fault? Goddamnit! Couldn't even give me a chance to tell you," he said.

Uncomprehending, Olivia imagined there had been some disagreement or some insult. She had asked him for a favor and it had gone badly.

"What happened?"

"What happened is I'm a fuck-up."

Olivia opened her mouth to contradict him, but he shook his head.

"All this time, I thought the world was against me. I thought everything bad that happened was like this unluckiness, like a black cloud hanging over me. Now I know it's me. It's me doing stupid shit. I'm the one who keeps fucking my life up. It's like, Hurricane Katrina was a blessing for me. That's crazy, how messed up that is. All those people dying and suffering and it was a blessing for me. A chance to start over. And I couldn't even manage that, because I'm the one who fucks everything up."

"No, you're not," she said.

"Hear me out, Olivia. I'm a liar and I can't be trusted. My folks didn't die in New Orleans. My mother is long gone and my father's in prison. Yeah, I served in the Marines, but I got a dishonorable discharge for using drugs. My name's not even Rindell. Technically, I ain't even a paramedic."

Olivia responded the same way she would have to a sudden downpour, with a mix of panic and resignation. She edged back toward the door, then stepped forward, trying to undo the retreat.

"I didn't mean to," he said. "I didn't even want to kiss her, let alone anything else. It's bad enough I lied to you about who I am. That I'm not the guy you think I am, but it's like I'm a dog. I got no sense."

"Oh." Olivia was actually flattered. No one had ever bothered to break up with her. The guys she dated just drifted away.

"Goddamn. I am so sorry. You deserve better. I didn't know what to do. It's like she's got this big hole opened up inside her and she needs it filled. I'm so stupid, I did the only thing I know how to do. And I fucked up your friendship. Just don't blame her. She's messed up over what happened. You're like the only person who gives a shit about what happened to her."

Olivia took a deep breath and composed herself. "You mean Jennifer? You and Jennifer. What about Kevin? I thought they were getting married."

"Oh, God. Oh, goddamn. See? It ain't enough for me to fuck up my own life. I gotta go and screw up other folks' lives, too. I thought maybe you'd forgive me if I was honest with you, but then I remembered I pretty much lied to you about everything."

Olivia wanted to say something, but she was struck dumb. It was silly that she'd ever thought he was interested in her. He was much too attractive, and given a choice between her and Jennifer, who would pick Olivia? She thought of it that way, in the third person, setting herself next to Jennifer. Two objects to choose from.

The anger didn't hit until she was at home, when she

remembered what her father had said about ugly white girls marrying black men. She was too ugly even for that. Trudging up the stairs to her bedroom, she didn't know how she had made it home, but hot on the heels of anger came grief.

When Mrs. Holley called upstairs to make another offer of food, Olivia pleaded off with a headache.

"Maybe this diet isn't a good idea, sweetie. You don't seem to be feeling very well these days," Mrs. Holley said.

The diet was a joke anyway, a pathetic joke. In four months Olivia had lost a whopping nine pounds. Even if she lost the weight, she would never look like Jennifer. It was pointless. She sat on the edge of the bed, staring at her reflection in the dresser mirror: bleary-eyed and jowly. A bulldog.

CHAPTER TWENTY-ONE

Jennifer

CONFESSING OVER THE phone was too cold and impersonal, and then, after Jennifer hung up, what would Kevin do? Would he want revenge? There he was in San Francisco, which in her mind was full of well-dressed gay men, but there were surely plenty of available women.

She went to bed on Sunday, not knowing how to tell him, but sure that she should.

On Monday, she saw the real problem with confession. Telling Kevin would require actual words formed into actual sentences that she could speak out loud. She was testing out phrases in her head, when Lucas came in and said, "Do we have the promotional key rings and stuff yet?"

I have something to tell you.

"What key rings?"

I did something terrible—no. I did a bad thing.

"The key rings for the Bay Day promotion," Lucas said.

I love you. I love you so much.

"You did order them, right?" Lucas stood in front of her desk, but Jennifer couldn't bring herself to look up at him.

"Of course, I ordered them," she said.

I'm so ashamed. It just happened. I was upset.

"I was hoping we could take some to the lunch meeting today."

Jennifer could figure out how to say everything right up to the moment she would have to say—*I had sex with this guy. Not really. Just sort of half-hearted.*

Lunch.

"They haven't come in yet. I should call and check up on them. It seems like a long time since I ordered them," Jennifer extemporized.

Trying not to be obvious, she clicked open her calendar. Lunch @ Circles @ noon/Bay Day. In an hour. Below the calendar entry, the to-do list for the lunch meeting scrolled down for a full page. None of it was ready.

"Jennifer?" Lucas was saying. "Everything okay?"

"Yeah. Everything's fine. I'll check with Emily about the collateral."

"Perfect. I figure we'll leave about 11:40. I'll drive."

"Great. Thanks," Jennifer said.

As soon as he was gone, Jennifer went out to the admin's desk. She debated briefly whether she should try a friendly overture. *Hey, did you get a new hair-do*, except that was ridiculous. Emily had perfectly straight brown hair that rose or fell in relationship to her ears depending on seemingly random forces. It might be shorter or longer on any given day, but it was never different.

"Hey, Emily, have you had a chance to print out the sample collateral for the Bay Day event?"

"No." In the middle of typing something, Emily didn't look up.

"Well, we have a lunch meeting about it in half an hour."

"You never sent me the files," Emily said.

"No, I would have sent them to you sometime last week."

"You never sent them."

"I'll resend them, if you can hurry up and make the copies."

"No." Emily looked at Jennifer over the top of her square black librarian glasses.

"Excuse me?" Jennifer wanted to hit a note of indignation, but all that came out was a mousy whisper.

"You know you never sent me the files. Just because you screwed up doesn't mean I'm going to take the blame and bust my ass at the last minute. You know how to use the copier."

Jennifer stood there, waiting for an act of mercy, but it didn't come. Emily went back to typing and the clock kept ticking.

Back at her own desk, Jennifer wasted several minutes staring dumbly at the to-do list. Then she was down to thirty-four minutes to throw together something that looked professional. Her hand shaking on the mouse, she opened the file that claimed to contain official event collateral text. It was empty. She opened an earlier file and began copying and pasting raw chunks of draft text.

With ten minutes to spare, she stood over the copier sweating. When Lucas came to pick Jennifer up, she was stuffing material into folders.

At lunch, she thought she had succeeded, until the rep from Carnelon Construction took his trifold flier out of his promotional packet and squinted at it. He opened it, then turned it over.

"Oh, good grief. I should have known better than to make my copies myself. You got one that's upside down, didn't you? That copier is a bit too smart for me," Jennifer said, trying for adorable incompetence. "Don't worry, that's why the real event collateral is done by professionals."

"Well, let's hope Carnelon is spelled right in the official materials, too," the rep said.

It landed with a thud, like a bowling ball dropped into the middle of the lunch table.

"We may need to reconsider who's doing the proofreading for the materials," Lucas said.

Despite her best efforts to let the threat roll off her, Jennifer felt her face go hot. She had failed completely at what was to have been her triumphant contribution to the meeting. In its current ragged state, the event collateral didn't do justice to the designs and layout for Bay Day. The upside down flier made it hard to appreciate the clever, color-coded flowchart style map.

After the event sponsors had departed, Lucas said, "We need to talk, Jennifer."

"I'm sorry. About the materials. There was a mix-up with the files. It was my mistake, but I didn't realize it until it was too late. I'll have the corrected materials sent by courier over to the sponsors. I know it doesn't make up for it."

"I don't want excuses, Jennifer," Mr. Kraus said.

He was using that trick again where his voice was soft but he wasn't looking at her. Dismissing her even while he spoke to her. He'd probably learned the technique in a management seminar where they made grown men chant self-affirming slogans.

"Do you understand me, Jennifer?"

The sort of seminar where they taught that it was important to keep using someone's name.

She'd done it again. Zoned out.

"Yes, I understand. I'm sorry," she said.

"Did you do what I asked?"

"Wha—ich thing?"

"Did you meet with a counselor?" Mr. Kraus said gruffly.

"Yes. It was very helpful."

"I hope you're still going. I need you to be in top form. This event is important. To all of us. To Tampa's Future."

Jennifer almost laughed out loud. It was too much. He'd actually managed to work the company's name into his lecture.

"I will. I am." She strained to remember what the last thing he'd said was. What was she supposed to be answering?

"Good. I'll see you back at the office."

Mr. Kraus gave her a lukewarm pat on the shoulder, and then Lucas opened the door for him. Together, they stepped through the rectangle of sunshine that cut into the dark safety of the restaurant. Jennifer ducked into the bathroom, where she scrounged through her purse until she found the counselor's card. The one that had *I am not responsible for other people's actions* printed on the back. Because Mr. Kraus had said so, she called and left a message, asking to make another appointment.

She would do whatever Mr. Kraus wanted. She would proof the collateral until it bled. She would call and order the promotional items. She would do some filing. There was plenty of time to make everything right before Bay Day.

After her internal pep talk, she peed, washed her hands, checked her hair, and prepared to brave the rest of the afternoon.

In the parking lot, Jennifer scanned for Lucas' car before she realized she'd been left. Mr. Kraus had assumed she would go with Lucas. Lucas must have assumed she was going back to the office with Mr. Kraus.

"Well, fuck me," Jennifer said out loud.

"Something wrong?" the valet said behind her.

"Can you call me a cab?"

"Sure thing, miss."

She could have called herself, but she liked the separation. She liked how it kept her distant from the act of having been left and needing a ride. When the cab came, she slipped the valet a five, well worth the price of having the cab arrive as if by magic to whisk her back to the office. No one but Lucas knew that Mr. Kraus had reamed her out. She could ascend in the elevator like a princess.

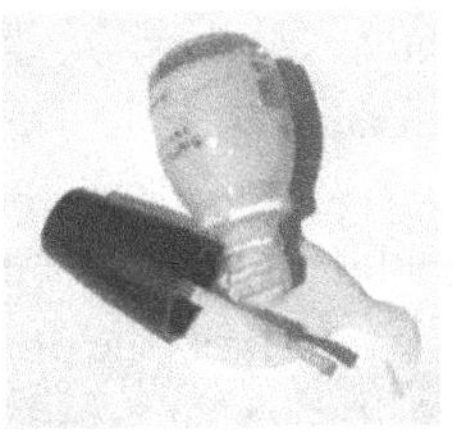

CHAPTER TWENTY-TWO

Olivia

THE WORST OF the grief ran its course the first night. Olivia went into the bathroom to brush her teeth and saw the fashion magazine clipping taped to the mirror. She pulled the picture down and crumpled the glossy paper in her fist. As she pitched it into the trash, she caught the flash of her nails. Pearlescent pink with a double diagonal stripe of mauve across each nail.

Without thinking it through, she pulled out her nail kit. It took a few minutes to cut her nails, almost down to the quick, shorter than she had had them since grade school. It took even less time to clean all the polish off. They weren't ugly that way, just bland. A little yellowed from so many years of polish, although she religiously used a protective undercoat. There was nothing wrong with her nails, but seeing them naked and chopped off, she cried. It was how she felt. Disfigured. Stripped of her dignity.

By Monday morning, she felt better. Impaired, but better. She could breathe, but not as deeply as she used to. On top of her bruised heart, there was the prickling discomfort of having to see Marnie and pretend nothing had happened. When Olivia arrived at her desk, she was sure no one but the pastor and the youth director knew. By noon, she could sense that the rest of the ministry staff had been told. By the end of the day, everyone knew. Olivia considered making a sign to hang outside her cubicle. *Dear Everybody: I screwed up and got banned from being a youth volunteer. Oh and PS: my boyfriend dumped me.*

When Pastor Lou came into her office to discuss a new mailing, she wanted to cry. Between the whole Double Cross nightmare and then everything with Rindell, she felt so drained she couldn't make small talk. At first she longed for Pastor Lou to notice and ask, but if he did, what would she say? Was she in a position to feel betrayed? Had Rindell been her boyfriend? No. He'd never promised any part of himself to her, and if she'd been so delusional as to think he was seriously interested in her, that was her fault. She'd been kidding herself. Men who looked like Rindell didn't fall for women like her.

"Olivia, are you okay?" Pastor Lou said. "You seem like you're in another world."

"I have a lot to think about."

"I don't think you should worry about what happened over the weekend. I'm sorry if you felt pressured to do something you weren't comfortable with."

He said it as though some invisible force had pressured Olivia into going on the youth group trip, as though he'd had nothing to do with it. As irritated as she was with him, she wanted his guidance, because his was the only one she could safely ask for. It wasn't like her mother would have anything helpful to say.

"It's not that," she said.

"Would you like to tell me about it?"

For a moment, Olivia was filled with gratitude. Surrounded by people who needed spiritual guidance, he was willing to listen to her.

"How do you know when you fall in love? How do you know when it's the real thing and not a crush?" It toppled out in one traitorous trip of the tongue.

Pastor Lou smiled a compassionate but tired smile. "You'll know. You will have a light in your soul whenever you're around that person. You'll feel more alive, smarter, more passionate, more godly."

Olivia concentrated, but couldn't imagine the senior pastor's wife producing those feelings in anyone. She was round like an apple, with chopped gray hair. She smelled cabbage-y. In meetings, she dominated and bored people, including her husband. She was profoundly, morbidly, frailly human.

Perhaps sensing her disbelief, Pastor Lou said, "You will know. You'll feel it."

"What if I don't? What if I never have that feeling? Is it wrong to settle?"

"I think it would be wrong to believe that you're settling. Unfair to you and to your husband. There are people who are destined for other lives than marriage. There's nothing wrong with that. Jesus remained unmarried."

Olivia knew Pastor Lou believed gay people were meant for *other lives*. They were supposed to be celibate because gayness was technically a sin, even though he didn't like that word. Did he think she was gay? Without looking at him, she knew he was done. She was on the clock and he needed her to finish the letter. Putting her hands on the keyboard, she glanced down to check her nail polish, but her nails were short and plain. Like her.

She made it through the day wearing her pleasantly neutral mask. The less emotion she revealed, the less she felt. She made it through her lunchtime chat with her mother without letting anything slip. She wasn't ready to face her mother's disappointment or the empty reassurances that she would "find somebody." Her father didn't think she would.

As five o'clock approached, Olivia felt worn around the edges. When her cell phone rang, she looked at it warily. A second phone call from her mother. Did that mean the gossip about Double Cross had percolated down to the parishioners and somebody had told her mother? Olivia let the call ring through to her voicemail. She would be home in half an hour anyway.

Then her desk phone rang and Olivia knew she couldn't dodge her mother. She took a deep breath and picked up the phone.

"Oh, honey, are you still at work?" Mrs. Holley said.

Biting back a smart-assed retort, Olivia said, "Yes, I'm just getting ready to leave."

"Well, you need to pick up Rich on your way home."

"Why? Is there a problem?" The answer to that was invariably yes.

"Rich is being a pill. Davina says he won't get on the bus."

"Well, what makes you think he'll get in the car with me, if he won't get on the bus?"

"Sweetie, will you just go try? You know I can't drive in this rush hour traffic."

That was true. Mrs. Holley had grown up in Tampa, but then the city kept growing without her. Olivia remembered from grade school how the six-block drive to Publix could wreck her mother's nerves for the whole afternoon.

Olivia had been inoculated at a very young age to the steady roar of traffic down narrow streets, and the unforgiving on- and off-ramps of two interstates that converged in the middle of downtown. She grew up immune to the terror that caused her mother's arm to swing out and pin Olivia to the passenger seat at every brake-slamming lurch in traffic. The swerving of elderly drivers who could barely see over the dashboard and the veering of tourists with unfolded maps blocking out half their windshields had no power over her.

The drive between the church and the developmental assistance workshop involved four counterintuitive turns down one-way streets in stop-and-go traffic. When she arrived, Rich stood out front with Davina, the office manager. Olivia rolled down her window and said, "Come on, Rich, let's go home."

"Not riding the bus. Not riding it."

"No, you already missed it. It's long gone," Davina said on the crest of a sigh.

"Come on, get in the car."

"See? Your sister's here to get you. He's been like this all afternoon."

"Don't talk about me like I'm not here." Rich turned away

from Olivia and Davina. He walked back to the workshop's front door and rattled it.

"All locked up, Rich. Time to go home," Davina said.

"I won't ride the short bus!"

The "bus" was in fact an oversized white transport van, complete with a wheelchair lift. For the last five years it had ferried Rich back and forth to work. At least once a year he decided he could drive, but the State of Florida disagreed. He kept trying to get his license back, but he could never pass the tests.

"Look, the bus is gone," Olivia said. "I'll take you home."

He turned back from the shop door and looked at Olivia's Honda.

"I'll drive," he said.

"No, it's my car. I'm driving."

Rich might not accept that his driving days were over, but he was clear on the concept of property and ownership. He got in the car, but refused to put his seatbelt on.

"I won't tell anyone if you don't," Davina said. She wanted to go home, certainly more than Olivia did.

"Deal."

Back in traffic, Rich turned from sullen to talkative.

"I'm not riding the short bus anymore."

"How will you get to work?" Olivia said.

"Not riding the fucking retard short bus. Stupid fucking Brian."

"What did Brian do?" Olivia remembered the name vaguely, and felt guilty for not properly recording his place in Rich's life. How often did she fully listen to what Rich said?

"Retard short bus. Only retards ride the short bus."

"Did he call you a retard?"

"Only retards ride the short bus." Rich stared out the window, while his left hand plucked at his eyebrow.

"And how does Brian get to work?" Olivia said. She doubted that Brian drove to work. All of the people employed at the workshop had serious disabilities.

"A real bus. The city bus. I could come on the real bus."

"Ah."

"I'm not a retard."

"No, you're not," Olivia said. "But you didn't like the city bus. Remember?"

"Nope. I never rode it. Nope."

"You did."

He had. In one of several failed experiments, he got flustered and angry when the bus driver "rushed" him. The driver had a schedule to keep, and when Rich stood on the bus stairs, struggling with his bus pass, the driver yelled at him. Rich yelled back, and the driver booted him off.

"Nope," Rich said again. "Not riding the retard short bus."

"Do you care that much what Brian thinks of you? Is his opinion that important?"

"I'll kill him."

"Don't say that. He's just a jerk. What does it matter what he thinks?"

"I'll smash his stupid head open," Rich muttered and fell silent.

When they got home, Olivia worried that he would repeat the whole tirade for a fresh audience, but he forgot about Brian when Mrs. Holley let him have some chocolate pudding before dinner. Since Rich didn't bring it up, Olivia didn't either. It seemed better, safer, to let the threat go unrepeated.

CHAPTER TWENTY-THREE

Jennifer

AFTER THE HUMILIATING lunch with the Bay Day sponsors, Jennifer threw herself into reparations. She didn't get on top of the planning; she got ahead of the planning. Anything Lucas or Mr. Kraus asked for, she had ready to email. She tried to imagine what they might ask for next, so she could have it at her fingertips. Gasparilla arrest numbers? She had them, in case they wanted to draw similar correlations to security needs. When the promotional items arrived, she hand-delivered them to the sponsors, after checking them to be sure all the names and logos were correct.

She had nightmares about business lunches at exclusive restaurants, where she was dressed in her pajamas or had a folder of old comic books instead of event collateral. Those nightmares pushed aside the ones in which a little girl on a playground sat on a swing alone with no one to push her.

Then there was the wedding.

The invitations were at the printers, and Jennifer's calendar contained three appointments for tastings. A cake maker in Tampa and two caterers. Plus a weekend for dress shopping. There was so much to do she felt panicky.

She talked with the counselor about the pressure, but not about what happened with Rindell. With the wedding only eight months away, it was too late to tell Kevin, so it was better to forget about it.

When the counselor said, "And how are you doing processing Gayle's death?" Jennifer wanted to strangle her. Like she needed to be reminded of that.

Thanks for picking the scab off, she wanted to say.

"I am not responsible for other people's actions," she said brightly.

"Do you feel that's been resolved?"

"Yes."

It had been resolved. Or it had at least been pushed aside until Jennifer left for work one morning and found a slip of paper tucked under her windshield wiper. Her first thought was irritation. Someone had clipped her car and left a bullshit note. She opened the driver's door and tossed her purse in as she reached for the note.

As soon as it was in her hand, she knew it wasn't the sort of note a person leaves when they've hit an unattended car. It was a letter, two distinct paragraphs, with her name at the top. She gave thanks for the fortuitous mathematics of having picked out her work clothes the night before. In two more minutes, Kevin was going to come down in the elevator and leave for work. If she were in the condo getting dressed, he might have seen the note first. Knowing that he was hot on her heels, she didn't even read the note, before jamming it into her purse.

She pulled out of the garage as Kevin exited the elevator. Raising her hand, she blew him a kiss with a jaunty smile she didn't feel.

The note stayed in her purse until after another Strategic Planning meeting, where she scored a small triumph over Emily, the admin assistant. It felt dirty to revel in someone else's failed copy job, but Jennifer was so grateful to be ascendant again, she allowed herself an annoyed sigh when the error came to light. Coming out of the conference room, she shook the offending agenda handout as she approached Emily's desk.

"These need to be redone. You have page seventeen twice and no page eighteen."

Emily took the packet of paper and squinted at the mistake. She sighed.

"Crap. They need them right now?"

Jennifer was about to say something snippy about needing them done right the first time, but Emily stood up and hobbled toward the copy room on one of those surgical boots. Although Emily couldn't see her, Jennifer smiled and said, "Your hair looks cute. Did you get it cut?"

Emily brought a hand up to her hair, as though she needed a reminder.

"Yeah, thanks. I'll bring these in when they're done."

"Thanks."

The world was like a teeter-totter. Every time Jennifer felt like she was rising, she hit a bump and started sinking back down. That was exactly how she felt when she returned to her office after the meeting. Taking out her lip gloss, she dislodged the note.

She had to read it eventually, unless she planned to throw it away without reading it. She unfolded the sheet of white copy paper.

Jennifer,

Sorry to bother you, but I thought you'd want to know that Lamar called me. He said Shanti was with his father's cousin. Her name is Cherice. Not sure if that's spelled right. Her address is 2108 W. Nassau St. here in Tampa. Her number is 813-210-5555.

I'm sorry about the whole deal, but I don't know why you had to tell Olivia. I thought you didn't want me to tell her. It's not like I wanted to keep a secret from her, but it pretty much ruined all that. Anyway, I hope this helps you figure things out.

Rindell

Olivia knew? How? Whatever Rindell thought, Jennifer hadn't said a word. Why would she? In the horror of the moment, she almost ran the note through the shredder, before she remembered to scribble down the name and address of Shanti's father's cousin. Then the mildly incriminating note went through the shredder's blades, turned into slightly less incriminating paper fragments.

She vacillated between anger and gratitude. Like the counselor, Rindell had picked the scab off a half-healed wound. On the other hand, he had solved a mystery for her. Now she knew where Shanti was. Not with Renee like Gayle had wanted, but at least with family. People who loved her and would take care of her. That was what mattered. And honestly, it was better Shanti wasn't with Renee. That wasn't any way to grow up.

Logging into her computer, Jennifer pulled up a map of the address on Nassau street. It was in the 'hood. Or the barrio. She wasn't sure where the lines were drawn in that part of town, but it was a place she wouldn't have normally gone by herself. Except she had burned all the people who might have helped her.

In the magic eight-ball that currently served as Jennifer's moral compass, all signs pointed to her obligation to go see Shanti alone.

As Jennifer turned down the narrow brick street, three kids on bicycles came toward her, riding on the wrong side of the road. The boy in the lead was perhaps twelve, darker than the other two, his hair in cornrows. Behind him came a younger boy and a girl on a pink bike with plastic streamers on the handlebars. For a second, Jennifer's heart skipped. She slowed the car to a crawl as the bicycles approached. She turned to look and the kids did the same, looking in the car window at her curious face.

The younger boy and the girl were as light-skinned as Shanti appeared in pictures, but the girl on the bike was too old. She had to be eight or nine, while Shanti was only five.

Disappointed, Jennifer drove on, scanning the houses until she came to the right number. Like all the others on the block, it was long and skinny, shoe-horned in between its neighbors. It had battered wood siding with the remnants of white paint and a tin roof. A few straggly azaleas grew near the front porch's wrought iron railing.

The front door was open, just a banged up aluminum screen door between Jennifer and the inside of the house. Two children played on the floor of the front room, in front of a blaring TV. The girl looked more Hispanic than black to Jennifer, with her straight brown hair in loose braids. She stared at the TV, sucking on a bottle. The boy had his head shaved and his left arm in a cast. He turned to look at Jennifer when she knocked.

No adult came to answer the door, so Jennifer called, "Hello!" When that produced nothing, she pounded on the edge of the screen door, making it rattle in the frame. From deep in the house, a woman yelled, "Come in!"

Jennifer opened the screen door and stepped inside. The house smelled of smoke and something sweet and greasy, almost like funnel cakes from the fair. The kids looked at her curiously.

"You late, Richard!" the woman yelled down the hallway.

A moment later, she stomped into the front room, straightening a red satin blouse on her narrow hips. Below it she wore tight black capris and strappy black pumps. She was whip-thin, glossy dark brown, with gleaming black hair pulled into a clutch of spiral curls. Her lips, done in a deep red, parted in surprise.

"Who're you?" she said. When she reached the sofa, she muted the TV with a remote and lifted a Gucci purse. She fished out a long, thin cigarette and, as she lit it, Jennifer stared at the purse, disconcerted. Was it real or a knock off? From that distance, she wasn't sure. The Gucci logo looked right.

"My name's Jennifer Palhete. Are you Cherice?"

"Yeah, I'm Cherice. What you want?"

"I'm looking for Shanti. I'm a friend of Gayle Prichard's." Having been told so many times, the lie was almost effortless now. It was almost true.

"Don't be coming around here. I heard about you. Lamar called my mama, said you was snooping around looking for Shanti.

You stirring up trouble. Leo don't need more trouble than he got already." Leo, Shanti's father. Lamar's father.

It rattled Jennifer. Stupid not to realize that the grapevine traveled both directions. When Lamar went looking for information, he was giving it out, too.

"I'm just looking for Shanti. I promised her mother I'd make sure she was okay. I have some pictures and stuff for her. Is she living here?"

"No, she ain't here anymore. And you need to get outta here."

"Well, where is she? I don't know what to do with these pictures and things," Jennifer said.

"Ain't none of your business. And she don't need whatever you got. You need to leave be. Quit snooping around other folks' business."

Cigarette fixed in the corner of her mouth, Cherice stepped around the kids on the floor. Jennifer backed up and fumbled for the screen door latch. The door clattered closed behind her and then the TV volume came back on, the sound of Spongebob Squarepants blotting out anything else.

As Jennifer walked to her car, the three kids on bikes rolled to a stop at the curb.

"You here about Dantez?" the girl asked.

"No. Who's Dantez?" Jennifer said.

"My brother. He broke his arm."

"I'm sorry. I hope he gets better soon. I'm looking for Shanti."

Jennifer took a step closer to the girl and her brother frowned.

"She's not here anymore," the older boy said.

"Do you know where she is?"

The girl shook her head.

"I think her auntie took her," the older boy said.

"Her auntie?" The relief was so sharp, so sudden, it almost hurt. Like the sun breaking through after days of rain. Jennifer reached for her purse, not sure what she intended to do until she had her wallet in her hand. She pulled out a twenty dollar bill and said, “Thanks for your help.”

None of the children moved, but they all looked at the money.

“For you to get a treat or something. A soda or an ice cream. It’s so hot out.”

The screen door opened with a screech and Cherice yelled, “You kids get in here right now!”

The oldest boy and the girl began pushing their bikes up the lawn, but the middle boy dropped his in the gutter and walked up to Jennifer with his hand out. She passed him the bill, pressing it into his rough, sweaty palm.

“Wasn’t her auntie,” he said. “Some social worker took Shanti. ‘Cause of what happen with Dantez.”

That quickly the clouds returned, dark and oppressive. Jennifer staggered back to her car and drove home in a daze.

Kevin was in a foul mood when she arrived.

“Where were you? I thought we were having dinner tonight. I would have stayed at work if I’d known you were going to be late.”

“Work just—there were a bunch of things that kept cropping up.”

The need to lie crushed whatever remained of her happiness. She wanted to tell him about that brief moment of hope and then disappointment, but when he came home from San Francisco, she’d promised him that her priorities would be work and getting married. She couldn’t admit that she was still looking for Shanti.

With nothing to say, she crossed to where Kevin stood sullenly propped against the kitchen island, a half-drunk beer on the counter in front of him.

She slipped off her jacket and let it trail from her fingertips to the floor. When she put her hand on his cheek, he turned to her and kissed her grudgingly. He was so easy, so easily placated, she thought. As she lowered herself to the floor, her knees twinged, the skin tight with fresh scar tissue, a reminder of her promise to Gayle.

Maybe she undid his pants too smoothly. Maybe he saw the calculation in the clever way she reversed the belt through the buckle and popped the button at the same time. Before she unzipped his pants, he pushed her hands away.

"Do you think that solves everything?" he said.

"No, I just wanted to...."

"Are you lying to me? Is that what this is about?"

"I just wanted to apologize for being late. To do something you like," she whispered. She hadn't given up on it, using the husky suggestive voice she'd learned from Tracey.

"Sex doesn't fix everything, Jenn. You can't fuck me into being a doormat."

"There's no need to use that kind of language," she said.

Kevin re-buckled his belt and walked into the living room, where he turned on the TV. When Jennifer followed, he didn't look at her.

"I'm going to the gym," she said.

"Now?"

"You don't want to have sex. You don't want to talk. So yes, now."

"And dinner?"

"I'm not hungry."

She was hungry, and it was a good feeling. A righteous feeling of deprivation. She would lose the pesky fifteen pounds that had been standing between her and perfection since college. She would be her ideal weight for the wedding. That would show—who? Kevin? Moira? Olivia? Carrie?

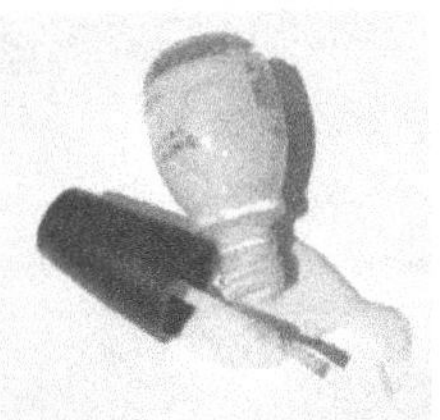

CHAPTER TWENTY-FOUR

Olivia

AFTER THE FIRST week, daily wear dulled the sharpest edges of Olivia's grief. By Sunday, what she thought of as the one week anniversary of her crushing, she discovered she could go for nearly ten minutes at a time without thinking about Rindell. On Monday, she decided to brave her morning walk again. The ambulance was never parked at the river on Mondays or Tuesdays. When Olivia got up on Wednesday, though, she had to admit her cowardice and stay home, or brave that moment when she would see the ambulance.

If Olivia was wounded, she considered make-up a bandage. Dressing up for her walk seemed more ridiculous now that it was over with Rindell than it had been when she was with him, but in the midst of her grief, a spark of pride surfaced. She couldn't stand the thought of him seeing her looking like a slob. Despite that, she almost chickened out a dozen times between the bathroom and the front door.

At the park, she didn't allow her eyes to rove left or right, but the effort was wasted when Rindell stepped out from behind one of the live oaks next to the path. She intended to simply walk past without speaking, until she caught a glimpse of his face. He looked the way she felt: hollow. Pulling the earphones off, she fumbled with her iPod and turned off the music. She tried to look him in the eye, but her gaze caught at his chest where a spray of blood had dried on his shirt and ID badge. She shuddered.

"What am I going to do?" he said.

"I'm not going to tell anyone. I don't even know who I'd tell. Or how. Your secret's safe with me." She assumed it was what he needed to hear.

"But what am I doing? Olivia, what the hell am I doing? What should I do?"

"I don't know." It sounded harsh to her ears. To soften it, or to show some concern, she said, "You have blood on your shirt."

He looked down at himself in surprise. "Goddamn. I didn't notice. Olivia."

"I don't know," she said. Because her wound was bigger than she had realized, she turned and walked back toward home.

"Olivia," he said behind her. Then a little louder: "Olivia, please."

He was there the next morning, leaning against the front of the ambulance. She walked by quickly and he didn't try to stop her. The next morning the ambulance was gone, and the next week she had the park to herself. Every day she turned her music up louder to silence her thoughts. In her mind the splatter of blood on his shirt grew bigger and more gory.

CHAPTER TWENTY-FIVE

Jennifer

JENNIFER FOUND IT easy to avoid Olivia on Sundays. Kevin didn't recognize the ruse behind Jennifer cooking him breakfast three Sundays in a row. It put them heading to the later service with just minutes to spare. Olivia and her family would leave the early service on the church's on the south side, so Jennifer suggested that Kevin park at a nearby restaurant to the north. He seemed happy and unsuspecting.

Three weeks in a row, Jennifer begged off Wednesday night church by working late, and she would have gone on using that excuse indefinitely, but Kevin called her on it.

"Did something happen, Jenn?" He was on the drive home, and she could hear the traffic in the background.

"What do you mean?" She was nearly alone in the office. Even Mr. Kraus and Lucas were gone for the day. She considered faking her end of a conversation, to make her excuse sound more plausible.

"It seems like you never want to go to church on Wednesday night, and you act like you want to get in and out as fast as you can on Sunday."

So much for Kevin's obliviousness.

"Nothing happened. I've just been busy."

"I know you have a lot of work to do, but maybe you could work late tomorrow night and come tonight. I miss us having dinner together on Wednesdays."

She had always liked that Kevin enjoyed sitting around and chatting with people at church. Yes, he was all about the networking, but he would just as happily talk to some random old lady who was never going to buy another car in her life.

"Come with me, Jenn." Kevin was smiling on his end of the call. Wheedling her. She'd played the wrong gambit. She'd been trying to minimize her exposure when she should have been planning a more Machiavellian conversion to another denomination.

"Okay. I'll tell Mr. Kraus I'll stay late tomorrow instead."

"I love you, baby."

"I love you, too," Jennifer said.

She shut down her computer and freshened her make-up, before locking up the office. As she walked across to the parking garage, she wasn't consciously aware of the way she angled the trajectory of her path to avoid the place where Gayle had died.

Wednesday night church was a different animal than Sunday church. Sunday was so ingrained in Jennifer from her childhood that it had lost most of its spiritual element. It was on par with a dozen other weekly tasks. Dishes, laundry, vacuuming, church. Wednesday services meant something more because they required effort. The sacrifice of an evening, a commitment to a Bible study group. The Palhetes had always gone to Sunday services, but they were not involved in their church.

On Sunday, Jennifer could walk into the sanctuary with her head up, brazenly full of sin, or at worst, no more sinful than the average Sunday church goer. Passing through the front doors on a Wednesday night, her conscience prickled with the knowledge of what she'd done. Then prickling awareness turned into a scorching pain. As she and Kevin rounded the corner toward the fellowship hall, they met Olivia leaving the copy room with an armful of mission booklets.

Although she had numbed herself, Jennifer recognized Olivia's wounded state. She succeeded in smiling, but Olivia ducked her head and swerved back toward her office. Jennifer marveled that she would be allowed to pass. She would be permitted to continue next to Kevin as though she had never done anything wrong. Olivia would never say a word.

"I have to talk to Olivia about the wedding." Jennifer almost choked on the nearest lie she could reach. "I'll be there in a minute."

"I'll come with you," Kevin said.

"No, it's girl talk. You go on." Jennifer forced a smile as she stretched up to kiss him.

"Love you," he said.

"Love you."

He paused for a drink at the water fountain, and then he was through the door and into the fellowship hall.

Jennifer's limbs felt detached, her feet nonexistent as she walked the ten feet to Olivia's office. At her desk, Olivia stared at her computer screen, the desktop showing a sand dune. After a moment, she turned and looked near Jennifer.

"Hi. Can I help you with something," Olivia said. It didn't even sound like a question.

"I'm so sorry. I didn't mean to. I didn't. I'm so ashamed."

Whatever remained of Jennifer's infrastructure cracked. Her face felt that way, too, as though some catastrophic fault line had given way to stress. She gasped for air, lost her grip on her purse, and fell into the guest chair. In the dark pit of knowing exactly what she was, Jennifer felt hands on her, soft warm hands on her shoulders and back. The solidity of a human body met her, neck and bosom receiving her head, sturdy torso bracing her.

"I just want to lay down and die. Lie down and die," Jennifer sobbed. "And I'm so stupid I don't know which one."

"It's lie down."

"Lie down and die." It relieved Jennifer to know. "I'm so sorry. I'm so sorry."

Jennifer leaned heavily against Olivia and gave herself up to crying. The comfort that she'd desperately needed, what she'd tried and failed to find with Rindell, what Kevin had absolutely refused her, Olivia gave without being asked. Several minutes passed before Jennifer became aware of people in the hallway, whispering. She hadn't realized the volume of her grief, but Olivia leaned over her, trying to shield her from curious eyes. A moment later, Pastor Lou arrived.

"Jennifer, are you okay?" he said.

She tried to signal him away, but he put a hand on her shoulder, and then Kevin was there, saying, "Baby, what's wrong? What's the matter?"

"Let's give them some space," said the pastor's wife. They converged on her, Pastor Lou, his wife, and Kevin. They pried her out of Olivia's arms, and herded her into Pastor Lou's office. Her cheek felt warm from the pressure of Olivia's shoulder, but someone closed the office door, and Jennifer knew her moment of comfort was over.

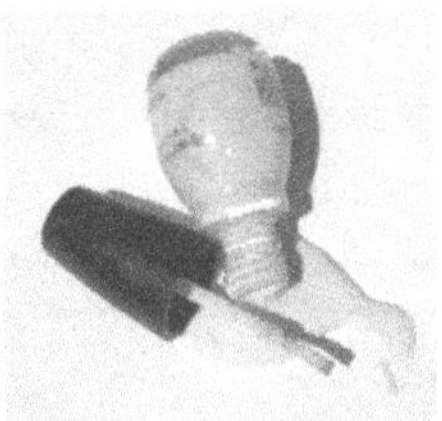

CHAPTER TWENTY-SIX

Olivia

SINCE RICH'S ACCIDENT, it had been Olivia's job to negotiate the outside world for him. By some silent and unanimous agreement that Olivia didn't understand, he became her responsibility. She took him for the original interview with Forward/Ability. She set up his routines. When Tanya returned her engagement ring, Olivia broke the news to him.

With no one else to delegate to, Olivia would have to talk to Brian. After all, she had been taking Rich to work and home since the short bus incident, so who better to talk to Brian? Why would her mother make a special trip to the workshop to talk to one of Rich's coworkers?

The next Monday, after Rich had gone into the workshop, Olivia parked the car and went into the office. Davina was at the front desk and she looked surprised to see Olivia. To see anyone, probably, as she was in the middle of putting on her make-up. She popped up from squinting over a tiny mirror with one eyebrow darkened and the other missing.

"Oh, I'm sorry," Olivia said.

"No, no. You caught me putting my face on." Davina laid down her eyebrow pencil, which Olivia regretted. It was hard to look at her when she was half done. "So, are we ready to put Rich back on the bus? I know it seems easier to keep driving him, because of the whole fuss he made, but it's important for him to have his own routines."

Olivia almost laughed at the misunderstanding. As though she wanted to keep driving Rich back and forth.

"No, you're right. It's better for him to ride the bus. To make his own way. I was wondering if I could talk to Brian."

"Brian?" Davina frowned in puzzlement and, glancing in her compact mirror, seemed to realize how bizarre she looked. She picked up the eyebrow pencil and drew in her other brow.

"That's why Rich doesn't want to ride the bus, because of an argument he had with Brian."

"Oh, they do have their little spats."

"I think it was more than a spat." Olivia bristled to hear the insult against her brother dismissed so out of hand. Was that how she usually treated him, too? As someone who didn't have the wits to have a full-blown argument with someone?

"What exactly did he tell you happened?" Davina said, her mouth contorting as she applied lipstick.

"He said that Brian told him only retards ride the short bus."

"I can't believe Brian would say something like that. He's quite sensitive."

"It's possible Rich misunderstood something Brian said, but if I could talk to him, see if he could help smooth it over?"

"I think that sounds like a good idea," Davina said. "If you want to have a seat down in the lounge, I'll get him."

Olivia waited in the lounge, longing for coffee, but the pot sat on the counter empty and cold. From down the hallway, came a tapping sound that grew closer and more distinct. Then she remembered who Brian was. He hadn't been born blind, because he had been in a life skills retraining program at the same time as Rich. Learning to get by in a world where everyone could look at him, but he couldn't look back.

Thinking of blindness that way made Olivia shiver, and when Brian entered the room, she thought of what incredible bravery it must require to use Tampa's public transportation as a blind person. Olivia had nearly 20/20 vision, but she was too chicken to ride the city buses. Too many routes, too complicated, too unreliable. One of the few times she had ridden it in high school, she'd ended up on the wrong bus and gone nearly ten miles out of her way.

Brian was tanned, with a goatee, and a long blond ponytail restrained in a series of rubber bands. That would be necessary for working around machinery. Other than that, the only thing that stood out about him were his black sunglasses. Not merely big enough to cover up his eyes, but sized to help cover the scar tissue that crept out onto his left temple and his left cheek. Without his eyes to gauge by, she couldn't guess his age. Twenty-five? Thirty? At any rate, close to Rich's age.

Realizing that she was staring at someone who couldn't stare back, she stood up and said, "Hi, Brian. I'm Olivia, Rich's sister."

Brian smiled and held out his hand a good foot too soon, so that Olivia had to take a step forward to shake it. He held her fingers longer than was comfortable, but Olivia didn't think of protesting. How else would a blind man get to know someone?

"You have very soft hands," he said.

"Haha! Well, I'm a secretary. Just typing. No hard work." It flustered Olivia, which was silly. He couldn't see her blushing.

"Davina said you wanted to talk to me."

"About Rich," she said.

"Oh, yeah, I heard there was some sort of problem."

Olivia had stupidly expected an element of apology or at least condolence in her initial encounter with Brian, but he seemed so glib that she wanted to rattle him.

"Rich told me that you said *only retards ride the short bus*. That's why he doesn't want to ride in the workshop van."

"No, I didn't say that to him." Brian laughed and brought a hand up to adjust his glasses.

"Could somebody else have said it? Or maybe he misunderstood something you said?"

"Look—Olivia, right?" Brian gave her a wide smile that paired uneasily with his blank sunglasses. "I know it must be hard, dealing with what's happened to your brother, but the truth is, Rich doesn't have a real good grasp on things. His thinking's off. He—"

"Don't try to tell me about my brother," Olivia snapped. "His thinking isn't so far off that he doesn't know when people are talking down to him."

"You don't work with him every day. I know he used to be some kind of math genius or something, so you're used to thinking of him as smart, but he's not anymore. He gets confused. He makes things up."

"He does get confused, but he doesn't make things up."

"I don't want to upset you," Brian said, still smiling. It dawned on Olivia that he had once been charming. A smooth operator. Now he didn't realize that along with his sight he'd lost whatever had allowed him to charm people.

"I just want you to leave him alone."

"Well, how am I supposed to do that? I have to work with him."

"That's all you have to do. Work. Other than that you don't need to talk to him," she said.

"Oh, I guess you're the boss of me now?"

Brian stood in the doorway, and Olivia considered how to make her exit. She should make nice. Apologize, play the game of *I'm just concerned for my brother*. That would be the easy way to leave, but Rich deserved a better champion. She closed the distance to the door so that she was shoulder to shoulder with Brian.

"I'm telling you to leave him alone. Maybe it's funny to you, somebody like Rich getting knocked down a few rungs. But him being slow, it's not any funnier than you being blind."

"Bitch," Brian said.

"Get out of my way."

"Or what? You gonna knock a blind man down?"

"I might." He must have thought she meant it, because he took a step sideways and let her go.

In the lobby, Davina was back at the desk, this time working on a Sudoku in the newspaper.

"Was Brian able to help you get things squared away?"

"Not really," Olivia said. "I think Rich is ready to try riding the van today, but I want to talk about him moving to a different work station. Something further away from Brian."

"Is there a problem?"

"I don't want Rich getting upset and I think Brian upsets him, whether he means to or not."

"Okaaaay," Davina said. "I can have Mr. Colton give you a call when he comes in. He makes all the work assignments."

"Thank you. That would be great."

Leaving Forward/Ability, already half an hour late for work, Olivia was irritated with herself. And with her family. Mr. Holley would have gotten what he wanted out of Brian. Even Mrs. Holley would have handled it better. She would have been genteel but firm, warm as grits. Olivia had missed that lesson. She was either a doormat or a bulldog. Mrs. Holley was a Southern Belle. Olivia was strictly a Tampanian. What Rich derogatorily referred to as a Tampon Girl. Remembering that made Olivia laugh, but by the time she reached the church, irritation reasserted itself over amusement. If her parents were so good at handling these things, why hadn't they dealt with it?

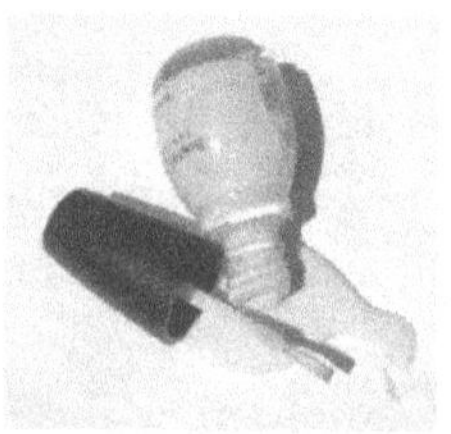

CHAPTER TWENTY-SEVEN

Olivia

IT TOOK THREE more days to convince Rich to go back to riding in the van, and that was what they called it now as a family: the van. Because there were no jokes to be made about "riding the van." Even Mrs. Holley managed to correct herself, although she forgot and called Olivia "Mitten" at least once a day.

Olivia left two more message for Mr. Colton about moving Rich to a different part of the workshop, but he never called her back. With things more or less back to normal, she didn't persist. After all, it had taken nearly two years to train Rich on his current job. It wasn't worth the headache to force him into a new one.

The downside to a return to normal was that Olivia drove home from work alone every day. Without Rich to distract her, she found herself slowing as she passed Mr. Batson's house. Sometimes, she fantasized about stopping to talk to Rindell, but couldn't imagine what they would talk about.

She might have kept driving by and not stopping, except for her mother.

On Sunday, Mrs. Holley was in the education building, where she taught one of the third grade classes. She should have been down in the parking lot already, so Mr. Holley sent his daughter to look for her. They were supposed to go to Sunday dinner with Mr. and Mrs. Irwin.

Mrs. Holley was outside her classroom, talking to Beryl

Magnuson-Croft. Seeing her, Olivia was tempted to return to the parking lot and tell her father she hadn't found her mother. Eventually she would come out, and then Olivia wouldn't have to speak to Beryl. She would have to listen to her father berate her mother in front of the Irwins.

"Mom," she called. "Are you ready?"

"Oh, sweetie. I lost track of the time."

"Well, we're ready to leave. You know how Dad gets."

"Oh goodness, I know. I'm coming."

Mrs. Holley started down the hallway, bringing Beryl in her wake. She said, "So anyway, Cynthia is coming for Christmas and staying through New Year's Eve. So maybe you two can get together."

"I'd like that," Beryl said. "She has my number."

Olivia's older sister wasn't staying that long. She would come in on the twenty-seventh and leave on the thirtieth. Flying down from Atlanta for a lousy three days to see her family. Practically speaking, she and the kids couldn't stay at the Holley house, so they would spend most of those three days at their hotel suite. They would likely come for a brunch and a dinner, and then take the Holleys out for a dinner. The rest of the time would be spent seeing Cynthia's friends or hanging out at the hotel's pool and spa.

Mrs. Holley went on talking about Cynthia, but when she and Beryl got onto the elevator with Olivia, Beryl said, "So, your mom tells me you're dating pretty seriously. Are you thinking of getting married?"

A lifetime of being caught out by her mother's exaggerations and tall tales should have prepared Olivia for that sort of thing, but the question hit her in a place where she was raw.

She forced herself to laugh and say, "I don't know if it's as serious as all that. Mom might be rushing things."

"Oh, well, dating is nice by itself. Married life can wear you down. And then you want to find the right guy,"

Olivia sighed with relief, to be released so painlessly from her mother's lie.

"What boy wouldn't want to marry a girl like Livvie?" Mrs. Holley said.

"Oh, probably nearly all of them," Olivia muttered.

"Pshaw! Don't talk that way."

By then, they were safely to the first floor and Olivia steered her mother away from Beryl, who waved as they went.

During lunch, Olivia remembered that her mother's lie had been launched by Olivia's own dishonesty. She had dragged Rindell into her life, then presented him to her family as a suitor, all based on a reckless lie that she barely remembered.

After the Holleys were home from Sunday lunch, with Rich and his father watching sports, and Mrs. Holley puttering around in the kitchen, Olivia announced that she was taking a walk. A lie of omission. She was taking a walk down to the Eyesore.

Mr. Batson's house was uglier in winter, without its dressing of undergrowth and azalea blooms. Too many naked spots in the foliage revealed the house's peeling paint in an unflattering afternoon light.

Olivia's knock was a nervous stutter and she was about to repeat it when Mr. Batson opened the door.

"Yeah?" he said.

"Is Rindell here?"

"Sure." He shuffled away, leaving her standing in the living room, which she had never seen before. The other times, Rindell had taken her in through the back door. The house was beautiful in its own shabby way, all the original woodwork and brickwork unpainted, the hardwood floors scuffed but handsome. At the kitchen door, the old man turned back and looked at her.

"Olivia, ain't it? You one of the Holley kids?"

"Yes, sir," she said, still a little afraid of him.

"Hadn't seen you in a while. Thought you kids'd busted up."

"Oh, we're just friends."

"When I was a young man, friends didn't make that kinda ruckus on the bed springs."

"I'm sorry." Olivia blushed.

"You come on back," he said.

In the kitchen an old fashioned coffee percolator sat disassembled on the tile countertop. An ancient soot mark traveled up the wall from stove to ceiling.

To her tentative knock on his door, Rindell said, "Yeah, cap."

When she opened the door, he sat up from where he'd been lying on the unmade bed. He wore boxer shorts and a white undershirt stretched tight over his arms. With one hand he held his place in a book.

"Hey there, Olivia," he said in a low voice.

Coming to see him had been an idea, not yet solidified into a plan. Between them lay a topic that didn't seem to admit much small talk. She started with, "What are you reading?"

"Some short stories by this guy."

"Are they any good?"

"Some of them. Olivia, why you coming here?"

"I'll go." The hint was clear enough. She reached for the door knob with her newly manicured hand.

"Wait, wait," he said, but nothing else.

"I haven't seen you in the park for a while and I wondered if you were okay," she said. Those two things were at least solidly truthful. He shifted on the bed, making the springs creak.

"Thanks for even giving a shit about me. I'm okay, but I can't see you."

"I know, I'm sorry. I know it would be too weird with you and Jennifer seeing each other. I just wanted to say—"

He laughed. The back of her neck went hot with shame and anger. She turned the doorknob, but he caught her by the other wrist and held her back.

"That ain't it," he said.

Meaning to get out of his grasp, she turned and found him leaning off the edge of the bed, one bare foot on the floor to balance him.

"What happened with her. That was some stupid damn thing that didn't go all the way, because neither of us wanted it to."

Olivia felt like a moron, staring at him, trying to figure out what he was saying. Was that how Rich felt all the time?

"I don't get it," she confessed.

"The problem is me, what you know about me."

"You're not interested in Jennifer?"

"I don't know her and I don't wanna know her. I hope I don't ever see her again. I don't wanna be reminded of how I messed this up with you. Look, I been putting in applications for some other jobs. One down in Sarasota and a couple in Miami. At least if I was there we wouldn't all the time be in danger of running into each other. I wouldn't be going by your house all the time knowing how bad I messed up."

"I told you, I'm not going to tell anyone. You don't have to move because of me."

He hung his head and let her hand slip out of his.

"I gotta do it for me. Because I can't take seeing you. I saw the look on your face. You know what I done."

"No, I really don't," she said.

"You can't even forgive your mama lying to you. You can't get over what I did. And I can't take seeing you and knowing you know."

"Would you tell me the truth?"

"Why?"

"Because I want to know."

"About Jennifer? I told you—"

"No." Olivia didn't think she could stand to hear anything about that. "About who you are."

"Who I am."

He seemed truly perplexed, his face pinched and miserable. He sank down on the edge of the bed, his face in his hands. After a minute of silence, he dropped his hand to the bed and patted it. She didn't trust herself to sit beside him, but she did it anyway. The way the bed sagged under their combined weight made her heart ache.

"There's this guy. DeVaun James." For another minute, it was all he said, and then he seemed to find the way to start his story.

"So DeVaun, he's a fuckup. But he's lucky, never gets in serious trouble. He's dealing drugs right outta high school, stealing shit, but he always manages to stay clean. He's got this cousin, real straight arrow. The cousin, Rindell, he gets this idea that they oughta join the Marines. See the world, get money for college, all that. Rindell has his shit together. DeVaun, he's just along for the ride, thinking, *I'ma go kill me some sand niggers*. That's how stupid he is at 19. Dumb nigger looking for another nigger to stomp on.

"So, they sign up, the James cousins, and right away, they go to Iraq. Every swingin' dick is going to Iraq when they sign up. Turns out DeVaun is good at one thing. Put a gun in his hand and he don't break a fuckin' sweat. He rides around on a Humvee, running a fifty cal, doesn't blink when the ragheads try to blow him up.

"The cousin, though—Rindell cannot deal with that shit. He can't sleep, can't eat. Jumpin' out of his skin. Turns into a real cheesedick. Useless, scared. Halfway through his second tour he breaks down, won't pick up his gun, won't go on patrol. They ship him home, give him a medical discharge. PTSD, right? DeVaun, though, that dumb bastard, he picks up a goddamn Silver Star for valor in combat. For a while he's in danger of turning into some kinda honest-to-God war hero. Picks up another combat medal and a Purple Heart. Gets a piece of shrapnel in his leg. No big thing, except they dose him with morphine and send him back into Fallujah. Only he gets hooked on the morphine, and when he can't get that, he goes to the next thing. Fucking heroin is rolling across the border from Afghanistan. Cheap, easy to get.

"Next thing you know, Lance Corporal Silver Star gets his ass in a vise over the smack. They hand him a dishonorable discharge. So, there's his life story: the one thing he was good at, he fucked it up, too."

His shoulders slumped, and for a baffled moment, Olivia thought that was it. She had no idea what it all meant. Then he exhaled sharply and glanced up at her.

"So, Katrina was like winning the lotto for DeVaun. I know that sounds fucked up, like I'm a heartless bastard, but the chaos, that's my—that's DeVaun's element. So Katrina come and he spends three days and nights out in a boat with some commando white guys, pulling people out of the water, chopping through roofs to get people out. Saving people, like he's trying to make up for what happened with his auntie and uncle and his cousin.

"He finally crashes, wakes up in a Red Cross shelter, and it's the weirdest thing. Everybody calling him Rindell James, because he's wearing a pair of his cousin's old desert boots with a dog tag in the laces. That's what he pulled on when the water came up.

"It's that easy. Wake up and he's somebody else. He figures he'll buckle down, stay straight, start over clean. Make something outta his cousin dying. And he does. He does."

It sounded like a plea for understanding. Olivia nodded.

"Except inside, he's the same old fuckup, I guess."

"How did you…." Olivia didn't know what to say.

"I kept thinking I'd get caught, but FEMA helped me get a copy of Rindell's birth certificate. Once I had got that, I *was* Rindell. Nobody axed me for more than that. Then I got a driver license and a social security card. This charity down here in Florida helped me move, when I told them I'd been having my EMT certification. Anyways I was close, 'cause I did all the classes with my cousin, but I couldn't pass the drug test. So I knew all the stuff, and these folks said if I relocated to Florida they'd help me get my EMT-4, that's the paramedic certification. And I was clean after Katrina. I been clean for going on three years now.

"I thought the fingerprints might be trouble, except all they do is check for an arrest record in Florida. The way I figured, if anybody got suspicious about the military records, I had an excuse. Me and Rindell, we went into the Corps at the same time. Sat right next to each other when they drew our blood at the physical. Side by side when they took our fingerprints. All I had to say was, 'You screwed up.' Two cousins with the same last name, at the same time, look a lot alike. Perfect excuse. Except I didn't need it."

Rindell sprawled over on his belly, pressing his face into the bedspread. Olivia wasn't sure if he was better or worse for having gotten it off his chest. Muffled in fabric, he said, “You the only person I ever told.”

“Your secret’s safe with me. I won’t tell anyone.”

“Thank you for dat.”

She longed to touch him, but it felt wrong to see him so exposed. He lay face down on the bed, revealing what she had never seen before: a dark purple welt the size of a golf ball on the back of his thigh.

“Take care, okay?” She didn’t think she could live with herself if she injured him. Of course, it had to be illegal; even if his cousin was dead it was identity theft. The lie of it was so enormous that she couldn’t feel angry. He hadn’t told a lie. He’d turned his whole life into a lie.

CHAPTER TWENTY-EIGHT

Jennifer

WHEN JENNIFER WAS small, not yet in kindergarten, she almost drowned. She had been at a hotel alone with her father, which was odd in itself. They weren't on vacation. They'd just driven from Wimauma and checked into a hotel in Tampa. It had been confusing but also magical.

Later, as a teenager, Jennifer figured out how those strange days of hotel swimming pools and restaurant meals fit into her childhood. While she and her father were at the hotel, her mother had been at Tampa General Hospital, watching Jennifer's older sister die of leukemia. At the time, Jennifer knew nothing. Rebecca had always been sick. That was nothing new.

The hotel pool had a lifeguard, and so Jennifer was allowed to swim without her father. Like a big girl she put on her pink one-piece swimsuit with a line of crocheted daisies sewn across the rump, and a single big daisy sewn in the center of the neckline. She'd gotten a towel and gone down to the pool while her father took a nap. Poor Daddy was so tired.

For half an hour, Jennifer played in the shallow end of the pool. She had only passed the beginner swimming class at the Wimauma Municipal Pool that summer, and her father had made her promise not to go in the deep end. After a while, she got bored with paddling around in the shallow end and decided to get out and explore. She found the place where the hotel maids folded all the towels. She found the cigarette vending machine. She also found a glass door covered with steam droplets on the inside.

She was learning to read, but she didn't notice a sign. That was what she remembered later, the hotel manager saying, "The sign says you have to be eighteen to go in the hot tub."

The hot tub was nice at first. Hot and bubbly and quiet. She hopped up and down, bobbing out of the water and then plunging under it. She did it over and over and then suddenly, the firm surface under her left foot gave way, as the plastic grate in the bottom of the whirlpool collapsed. Her foot got trapped in the drain opening and she couldn't pull it out. The water was up past her chin, so that she had to strain to keep her nose above the water and breathe.

She didn't know how long she was trapped like that, but it had seemed like forever. Then came the moment she grew too tired to keep balancing on her one foot, and a man and a woman came in kissing and laughing, and got undressed. The woman had been topless when she found Jennifer and started screaming for help, and the man hopped around on one foot with his penis flopping while he tried to pull his wet swim trunks back on.

While the man went for help, the woman held Jennifer's head up out of the water, and Jennifer remembered the way her breasts floated in the water. Jennifer wondered if she would have been brave enough not to care that people rushed in and saw her topless while they tried to figure out how to get a little girl out of a whirlpool.

Her father slept through the whole thing, only roused by the hotel staff when the fire department came to remove the drain from Jennifer's foot and bandage her up. That kind, bare-breasted stranger, whose name Jennifer never knew, stayed with her the whole time, not caring that every hotel employee and a good number of guests tromped through to gawk at the girl stuck in the hot tub.

In the end, the hot tub had to be emptied with buckets, because Jennifer's foot was caught in the suction of the drain, too swollen to let any water out around it. After they got the water low enough, one of the hotel maintenance men removed the screws that held the drain cover in place. As they tugged on her foot, with the broken grate stuck around it, the last of the water had swirled out, threatening to drag her foot back into the drain.

Jennifer felt like that now, as though a whirlpool of water were swirling around her, dragging her down. And there was no kind stranger to hold onto her and say, "Honey, it's okay. I got you." For a moment, Olivia had, but Jennifer couldn't expect that from her. They had never really been friends and they couldn't be now that Jennifer had betrayed her.

She couldn't expect that from her counselor, who went on saying things like, "Do you feel that this is resolved?" After the third or fourth time, Jennifer realized it was part of a script. She had to *resolve* her patients' problems to meet her goals with the company. That was in Jennifer's annual job evaluation, too. How well she *resolved* problems.

After her breakdown at Wednesday night church, Jennifer lied to Kevin and Pastor Lou about the reason for it: residual shock from the hit and run. She lied to the counselor, too.

"I have a lot of things on my plate right now. At work, and with my personal life. I'm getting married in June."

"Do you find it hard to stay focused on your tasks?" the counselor said.

Those were the magic words, because when Jennifer agreed that she found it hard to focus, the counselor produced a prescription pad. Like a magician pulling a rabbit out of a Danish design desk drawer in a well-appointed corner office on the seventeenth floor. Voilà!

Jennifer went home with a prescription for Xanax, to calm her anxiety about work and marriage, and a prescription for Ritalin, to help her focus.

In addition to her official prescription medication, Jennifer self-medicated. She usually didn't drink around her mother, but after an entire day trying on wedding dresses with Moira, Tracey, and Carrie, she needed a drink or three. Jennifer had balked at the thought of including her mother in the outing, dreading what her suggestions might be. Hideous glow-white fountains of frills or equally awful strapless beige sheaths with enormous bows. To her surprise, Moira declared every dress Jennifer tried on *beautiful*. Her mother also cried half a dozen times, but they were happy tears.

"I want you to be as happy as Daddy and I have been. Getting married to your father was the best thing that ever happened to me. I want you to be that happy. To be married to your best friend," she said in the midst of one of her crying jags.

Jennifer wanted that, too, and she and Kevin were good together. They had the same goals. The same ambitions. The same ideas about what success would be. Unlike her father, Kevin wouldn't let her leave the house looking like a train wreck.

Moira was like a kid included at the adult table, laughing at everything Tracey said. Jennifer wanted it all to be lighthearted and fun, but three drinks in, Carrie scowled and excused herself to take a phone call.

Tracey got silly the way she always did when she drank, but three drinks was early for her to start saying, "You look soooo pretty in your dress." That was another good way to gauge how much Tracey had had to drink—the number of *o*'s on the word *so*.

"And what are you going to wear?" she said to Moira. "It's your special day, too. Your only little girl is getting married. Have you picked out your dress?"

"Oh, whatever Jennifer thinks is best. Whatever she wants me to wear," Moira said. Her smile was so shy it made Jennifer's heart hurt. She was the worst daughter in the world. What did it matter if her mother had hideous taste in clothing? Moira was her mother. Look at how happy she was.

The tightness in Jennifer's chest forced her to stand up and say, "I'm going to step outside and call Kevin."

She didn't really intend to call him. She just wanted a few moments to herself. Out on the patio, Carrie stood at the far end with her phone pressed to her ear. She started when she saw

Jennifer, but smiled and waved, before returning to what looked like an intense conversation.

After a minute of shivering without her jacket, Jennifer decided she might as well call Kevin. It went straight to his voicemail, so he must have been at the gym or something.

"Hey, Kev. I found the dress. Tracey likes it, Carrie likes it, my mother likes it, so I guess it's the one. We're just having dinner and drinks now. I'll probably stay the night out at my folks after I drive my mom back. Love you."

As she turned to go in, Jennifer saw that the food had arrived at their table.

"Carrie, the food's here!" she called across the empty patio.

"Okay." Carrie waved Jennifer off in an annoyed way.

"What did he say?" Moira said, when Jennifer got back to the table.

"Oh, I got his voicemail. I told him we found the dress, though."

"It's soooooo beautiful." Tracey was working on a fresh martini.

"She's going to be a beautiful bride," Moira said.

The two of them nodded sagely at one another while eating from a giant platter of appetizers. They had ordered potato skins, sliders, onion rings, and chicken wings. Jennifer was having a self-righteous grilled chicken Caesar salad with the dressing on the side. Carrie chose some complicated smothered chicken dish, and by the time she came in from the patio, the cheese on top had turned into a nasty congealed crust. She picked at it with a grimace, as though it were the chicken's fault she'd left it to get cold.

"Who was that?" Jennifer said.

"Oh, Nate."

"Are you two getting back together?" By Jennifer's count, Carrie and Nathan had broken up and gotten back together at least six times.

"I don't know. I don't want to talk about it. Where's the waiter?" Carrie said. She actually had the gall to make the waiter take her food back to the kitchen to be reheated. She was silent for the rest of the meal, too, hardly smiling.

Jennifer felt bad for her. Carrie and Nathan had always seemed like a relationship of convenience. Carrie was Jennifer's best friend. Nathan was Kevin's best friend. Beyond that, were they a good match? Carrie must not have thought so, as often as they broke up and got back together. And then, she had never stopped going to the Christian Singles group, even while she dated Nathan. She reasoned that until she got married, she was technically single.

On the drive back to Wimauma, Jennifer told it all to her mother, just for something to talk about.

"She seems unhappy," Moira said.

"Does she?"

"Well, she's not the life of the party, is she?"

"We can't all be like Tracey."

Moira laughed and said, "I'm so happy for you. Soooo happy."

They giggled together and for the first time that Jennifer could recall, she felt like she and her mother had a connection beyond their love for Mr. Palhete.

In her pocket, her phone began to vibrate. Expecting Kevin, she answered without looking at it.

"Hi there!"

"Hey, Miss Palhete? Marco Parmiento here."

"Oh, hello."

Marco Parmiento was a private investigator. She'd found him in the phone book, and in that moment, she felt like an absolute moron for hiring him.

"I got the information that you asked for," he said.

"Oh, that's great." Jennifer was pleased but floored. If she let Moira know what the phone call was about, would it get back to Kevin? Better to play it safe.

"The girl, Shanti, is in foster care. They removed her from her relative's house, like you said. There was some concern that the cousin was overwhelmed with six children in the home. So DCF placed the girl with a family named Vanderbilt. How funny is that?"

Jennifer laughed, although she didn't find it all that funny.

"So the foster mother's name is Amelia Vanderbilt. Her address is—"

"Um, hey, could I have you call me back with this? I don't have anything to write it down with right now."

"Oh, I have a pen," Moira said.

Jennifer ignored her and told Mr. Parmiento, "If you could call me back in a minute and leave the information on my voicemail."

"Sure, I can do that. Your bill's settled. Wasn't too much trouble to get the information."

"Great, thank you so much."

"My pleasure. Take care, doll."

Jennifer frowned quizzically at the endearment, but he had already hung up.

"Who was that?" Moira said.

"Oh, Lucas from work. He was calling me with some information for a project."

"Calling you on a Saturday night? Do they do that a lot? Bother you when you're off work?"

"It's that kind of job," Jennifer said. "It doesn't always fit neatly into nine-to-five."

"I worry about that. I don't like them taking advantage of you."

"It's not taking advantage. They pay me very well." Lying on her thigh, Jennifer's phone began to vibrate again. She glanced at it to be sure it wasn't Kevin. No, Mr. Parmiento calling. She stuffed it back into her pocket.

"Are you going to stay there after the wedding?"

"Why would I quit?"

"Well, you can't work that kind of job once you and Kevin start a family, can you?"

"I don't know." Jennifer and Kevin had talked about that, but only in a hypothetical way. Like a parlor game. When We Start A Family. They'd agreed it would be better for Jennifer to take maternity leave. After that, they would hire a nanny or send the baby to the church's daycare, which was highly recommended.

Jennifer was relieved when she pulled into the driveway at her parents' house. The day was over and, aside from Jennifer's anxieties, it had been a good day. And if no one else knew about her worries, they almost didn't count, did they? As far as Tracey, Carrie, and Moira knew, it had been a perfectly lovely day.

While Jennifer got ready for bed, her father helped her tipsy mother to bed, saying nice but funny things like, "And did you dance on the table after that third martooni, Moira?"

When he returned later, Jennifer was sitting at the kitchen bar, hoping for a bedtime snack. A cup of tea and two fresh-baked oatmeal cookies from his stash of dough in the freezer. He had done that often when she was in high school, waiting up for her when she went to dances or football games. It was always his job to wait up.

While the cookies baked and the tea steeped, he said, "In case she didn't say, your mother is very happy that you invited her today."

"I am, too. It was a good day. We had fun."

He patted her hand and went to peer into the oven. Over his shoulder, he said, "And you found the dress you want?"

"Yes, it's exactly what I wanted. And everyone said it was perfect."

"I'm sure it will be. You'll be lovely." He slid the baking sheet out of the oven and lifted four cookies onto a plate.

They sat at the counter, eating cookies and drinking tea in silence. For the first time in a long time, Jennifer thought of nothing.

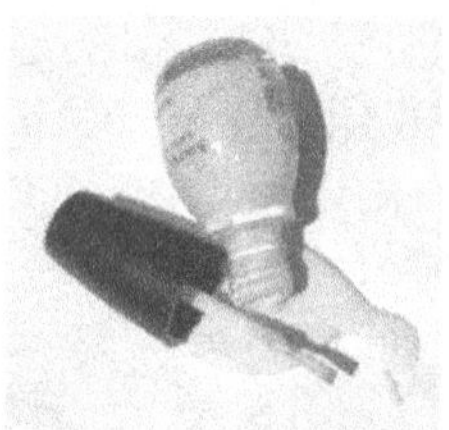

CHAPTER TWENTY-NINE

Olivia

OLIVIA KNEW SHE ought to avoid Rindell. He'd said he couldn't bear to see her, but to Olivia, avoidance was a kind of judgment, and she hated for him to think that she was judging him.

His lie was so monumental that Olivia *needed* to forgive him so that he could go on with his life without feeling guilty. After all, he couldn't undo the lie. The person he'd been before the lie was dead. Literally. Legally.

He didn't spend his breaks at the river park anymore, and Olivia wasn't brave enough to bother him at Mr. Batson's house again, so she went looking for him in other places. Luis' girlfriend lived somewhere east of Nebraska, so Olivia set out on a different route every morning, walking up and down the streets in the neighborhood. On Friday, three days into the project, she found the ambulance parked next to the duck pond south of the grocery store. Rindell's elbow poked out the window, a beacon she focused on as she got closer.

"Good morning," she said as she prepared to walk past as casually as she could.

"Jesus. You spooked me."

She kept walking, trying to keep her hands from shaking.

"Hey, Olivia," he called after her.

She stopped and turned back. His voice was hard to read and the dome light behind him cast his face in shadows. As she approached, he brought his arms to rest on the window ledge. In one hand he held the book he had been reading the last time.

"Are you still reading that?" she said.

"I'm reading it again."

"It must be good."

"I don't know if it is, but it makes me think." He shifted, the door between them like a barrier, but leaning closer to her. She knew she was forcing the conversation, clutching at straws.

"About what?"

"My fucked up life. Here, I'll read you one," he said.

Whatever Olivia had expected of the conversation, it was not that he would open the ambulance door and read her a story, as though he had never said, "I can't stand to see you." He scooted to the edge of the seat and, when she stepped closer, he hunched over the book, so close their heads almost touched.

"The writer is this guy named Lloyd Manley. It's called *Dog's Body*," he said.

> Before the accident, nobody would have described Jarvis as a dog person. After the accident, well, he couldn't help but be one. The four college buddies were out horsing around on motorbikes, a stupid hobby for grown men. Jarvis was always the reckless one, and that day was no different. While the other three were hot-dogging up and down hills, Jarvis decided to go all Evil Knievel. There was a creek that ran through the back of the Mike's property, and Jarvis said, "I bet I can jump it."
>
> "Bet you can't," Smitty said, but it was meant to encourage him. If Jarvis said something was cool, Smitty thought it was cool times two.
>
> "How long would it take for an ambulance to get out here?" Mike said.
>
> "Pussy." Jarvis revved his dirt bike.
>
> Jarvis liked to be in his skin, liked the way his

limbs moved. A lot of people admired that about him. He had his best luck picking up women after they had seen him playing volleyball or riding his dirt bike.

The previous winter's ice storm had brought a guy-wire down across the trail, and spring rain had washed out the trail. Jarvis made the turn with a smooth flexing of his quads, his thighs gripping the gas tank, the bike grips held firmly in his neat brown hands.

At first he thought he'd somehow lost control of the bike, because the earth fell away from him and he no longer felt the handlebars in his hands. The falling went on and then a lurching, tumbling feeling that came to a halt when his helmet cracked against a rock. For an instant, everything went to black and then Jarvis opened his eyes and thought, "I'm dead."

Because he could see himself, lying below the trail, next to the shattered remains of the dirt bike.

There was a pool of blood forming under his body. It was pouring out of his neck, which looked like a nasty joint of meat: gristly white spinal cord and vertebrae where there should have been a head.

"Oh god oh god oh god," Mike said from the hill above, which was convenient. Jarvis couldn't say anything at all, but that was exactly what he'd been thinking.

When Jarvis woke up he assumed it was the afterlife. He hadn't been a likely prospect for Heaven, so Hell, then? The Devil had the same taste in home décor as Mike. Ugly blue carpet and hideous 70s wood paneling.

"Hey," Jarvis said, but his voice sounded odd. A whisper, but coarse.

"Oh wow holy fuck," Smitty said. His face hovered overhead, his eyes wide.

"Is that you, Smitty, or are you the Devil?" Jarvis said.

Smitty laughed, a hysterical series of hiccups, and then began to cry.

The next time Jarvis woke up, it occurred to him to ask the important question: why hadn't they taken him to the hospital?

"Because, dude, because," Smitty said.

"They couldn't have helped you at the hospital," Mike said.

That was probably true. At least, nobody at the hospital would have done what Mike did.

With Jarvis' body broken and trapped down in a crevice by the creek bank, Mike scooped up Jarvis' head, ran it back to the house and did the unthinkable.

He sewed it onto his dog's body.

"I loved Dweezil! I sacrificed him to save your life," Mike said.

"Yeah, don't be an ungrateful douche," Smitty said. "At least you're alive."

That was true. After a fashion. Eventually, with the help of an Elizabethan collar to keep Jarvis from scratching his stitches, the incision healed, and Jarvis was able to get up and move around.

The world from a dog's perspective is odd. Everything is built too tall, above a dog's eye level. Jarvis found himself walking around Mike's house during the day, discovering just how many things he couldn't get to. Countertops. Microwaves on countertops. The freezer where microwave burritos were kept.

Being a dog sucked, always waiting for

someone to feed you or open a door.

There had been a time when Jarvis thought life would be perfect if he didn't have to work. Now that he didn't, he found it wasn't all that great. He couldn't go out and do anything. He spent all day watching TV, and he was reduced to changing the channels with his tongue.

"You couldn't even save me a hand? You didn't think to try that transplant?" Jarvis rounded on Mike after his first full week stuck in the house.

"I didn't think of that," Mike stammered.

"What am I supposed to do? I can't even run a fucking can opener. You didn't think I'd need to wipe my ass?"

The answer was plain on Mike's face. Dweezil hadn't needed hands for that. He simply licked his ass.

Eventually, Mike agreed to install a doggy door, something Dweezil might have enjoyed, if he'd had the verbal skills to lobby for it. The doggy door provided something important to Jarvis: freedom. It was only the freedom to go outside when he wanted, but that mattered. To be able to go out and pee when he needed to instead of waiting for someone to come home. Or worse, being reduced to the disgraceful act of peeing on the kitchen floor. Mike didn't seem to take it amiss when that happened, so maybe Dweezil had done that, too.

Once the flap to the outside was installed, Jarvis quickly located the best place on Mike's property. There was an oak tree on a bluff overlooking the main road to the house, and when the weather was good, Jarvis laid under the tree all afternoon, as though he were a dog.

"Lay," Olivia murmured.

"What?"

"It's lay. Grammatically, it should be *Jarvis lay under the tree.*"

"Really?" Rindell said.

"Yes."

"Well, shit. Printed in a book and it's wrong."

He frowned at the book cover before returning to his place and continuing to read.

> Jarvis might have gone on living like Mike's strange dog, but a girl named Cathy ruined it all. At first it was a bunch of online chatting. Late night messaging sessions that involved Mike hunched over his computer, typing furiously, and occasionally one-handedly. Mike had never had a clear personal boundaries with Dweezil, and that carried over with Jarvis.
>
> The first few times Cathy came over, Mike had been more concerned with the cleanliness of the house than with Jarvis. He'd dismissed the problem of his presence by saying, "Well, jeez, just stay in your room while she's here. That's all I'm asking."
>
> "And what about me? What am I supposed to do in there?"
>
> "I can move that little TV out of the bathroom into there. So you can watch your shows."
>
> In that way, Jarvis was more like an elderly shut-in than a dog. He had a dozen TV shows he watched with an intensity that approached his grandmother's obsession with *Matlock* and *Murder, She Wrote*. That was one benefit of Jarvis' situation: he never had to visit his family.
>
> "Okay, I'll hide out in my room," he told

Mike. "But order me a pizza first and pour some beers in my bowl."

My bowl. That was what Jarvis was reduced to: drinking beer out of a dog bowl. It was that or using a sippy straw.

Six months into Mike's relationship with Cathy, though, it was clear the situation couldn't go on indefinitely.

"She wants to know why she's never met my dog." Mike said. "What am I supposed to tell her?"

"Why does she even know you have a dog?"

"She's seen the bowl and the bed and everything. Every time I tell her you're outside or something." He carried the offending bowl to the kitchen sink and refilled it with water. Jarvis had to give him that: he was a conscientious dog owner. He cared about whether Jarvis had fresh water and a warm bed.

"So what's the problem?" Jarvis said.

"She wants to move in with me."

"No way! She can't move in."

Mike squatted down and leaned back against the kitchen cabinets so he could look Jarvis in the eye. "I want her to move in."

"That won't work."

"I can't keep you a secret forever."

"Then I guess she'll have to meet me."

"Are you crazy?" Mike shouted.

"Well, what's your solution?"

"You'll have to—we'll have to find someplace else for you."

"Find someplace else for me? I'm not a dog, man. You can't just find me a new home, because your new girlfriend is allergic to your fucked up science experiment. What are you going to do, dump me off outside the Humane Society?"

"Well, you can't stay here. Maybe Smitty...."

"Smitty lives in his mother's basement! Do you think she'll be any happier to have me there than Cathy would be?"

"Look, Jarvis, maybe it's just over," Mike said.

"Over?"

"You would have died out there anyway. I mean, you were dead when I—"

"Are you threatening me? What are you going to do? Take me out and put a bullet in my head? Like I'm a dog you don't want?"

"Don't make it sound like that." Mike looked angry. Like Jarvis was being unreasonable. Like this was all Jarvis' fault.

"You did this to me! YOU DID THIS TO ME!"

Mike braced himself to stand up, one hand on the floor, the other reaching up to grasp the counter edge. That was when Jarvis lunged at him.

A dog's teeth, they're dangerous, but the thing most people don't think of is that a dog's claws are nearly as sharp. Dweezil was a boxer-lab mix. He'd been goofy and friendly, but a big dog, nearly 80 pounds.

Jarvis threw himself at Mike, who went down gracelessly and struck his head on the floor. Before he could recover, Jarvis was on him, his claws at Mike's throat, digging with all the fury of a terrier going after a rat in a hole.

The next day Cathy came looking for Mike. She found his body lying on the kitchen floor and made a hysterical phone call to 9-1-1. The police followed the trail of bloody paw prints to the laundry room off the garage. Behind the half-closed

> door they heard heavy panting, almost like sobbing. Rather than go in, they waited for animal control to arrive. The dogcatcher was in for a surprise.

"But that couldn't happen," Olivia said. She didn't want to disturb the magic, or make Rindell think she was belittling the story, but the idea of the Jarvis dog disturbed her. Terrified her. She could see the bloody body, the miserable, weeping Jarvis dog so clearly in her mind, and she needed to banish it into the shadow of fiction.

"The transplant? No way, but that's not what I wanted you to hear. The thing is: Jarvis' friend thinks he's helping, but it blows up in his face. It ruins Mike's life and it ruins Jarvis' life, too."

"But Jarvis' life was ruined anyway."

"No, see, it wasn't. He was gonna die, but fair and square. That's what happened with my auntie and uncle. He wanted to stay with my auntie and we talked him into leaving her and he died anyway, hating himself for leaving her. And she died without him, too. Me and my cuz, we thought we were helping. Sometimes even when you mean to help somebody you betray him."

"I don't understand. I thought you said...." Olivia had not yet figured out where his lies were all lie and where they were part truth.

"When the storm hit Chalmette, we knew we couldn't move my auntie. She was too sick. That part is true. Except it was my auntie and uncle, not my folks. I mean, they was like my folks. They mostly raised me. My cousin and me, we decided since he was an EMT, he'd stay and I'd take my uncle somewhere safe. Find help to get my auntie evacuated. Except my uncle died. And he died with just me there, and he didn't like me all that much. He kinda hated me. Thought I was a douchebag like his brother. My father. But anyways, it was bad enough that they all died, that Rindell died, but the worst thing was my uncle died without my auntie, and she died without him. They shoulda died together, but they died alone, because of what me and Rindell did."

"That's sad," Olivia said, blinking hard to keep tears from

spilling over. When she looked up, Rindell was watching her.

"It woulda been less sad if they died together. When I came back with those rednecks in the boat, I busted through the roof with an axe and there was Rindell. Ain't that fucking crazy? He drowned in the attic. And my auntie—she—she was down in the house. I hope she died before the house flooded, because otherwise, I got to think Rindell had to abandon his own mama to drown, because he couldn't get her up to the attic.

"I shoulda stayed. You know, I shoulda stayed there with my auntie and uncle, and at least they woulda died together, and Rindell woulda lived. That's what happened with Jarvis. Mike shoulda just let him die. There's worse things than dying."

In the choking silence that followed, the edge of the ambulance door blocked the only kind of comfort Olivia knew how to offer. Failing that, she searched for something to say.

"Have you heard about the jobs you applied for?"

"I got an interview in Miami next Tuesday."

"That's a long way to go on your motorcycle. I could drive you," Olivia said.

"Please, Olivia. I can't. I know you mean well. That's how you are. But my stomach is all in knots talking to you. I'd be wrecked by the time we got to Miami."

"You could borrow my car."

"No, really, I can't. Thanks, though. It means something to me that you'd offer. 'Cause I know how you feel about being lied to."

"What else were you going to do? Tell me on the first date? When were you going to tell me?"

"Never. A secret like that, it's too much."

From across the street, Luis stepped out on the front porch of a house and hollered, "Hey, Olivia! You gonna patch up his broken heart? His moping is killing me."

"Not me." Olivia stepped back from the ambulance, blushing furiously.

"Nobody but you," Luis said.

Olivia dared a glance at Rindell out of the corner of her eye.

He looked embarrassed and angry. He said, “Back off, pardner.”

“Take care,” she said.

“You too, Olivia.”

As she walked away, the ambulance started behind her, then rolled up the street past her. Rindell drove, his elbow hanging out the open window. It came to her then: half joke, half pang of conscience.

“I lied, too,” she called.

She thought it was too quiet or too far for him to have heard, but the ambulance’s brake lights flickered. Rindell leaned out the window when it came to a stop.

“What did you say?”

“I said, ‘I lied, too.’”

He smiled and rubbed at his head with his left hand. “I thought you said something else. Take care.”

He waved and drove away, leaving Olivia to wonder what he thought she’d said.

CHAPTER THIRTY

Jennifer

KEVIN WAS JOKING when he suggested hiring a private investigator. That was what you did when you thought your husband was cheating on you, but it turned out to be the best solution. The Department of Children and Families wouldn't tell Jennifer anything, and calling Lamar again would create more bad feelings. Shanti's relatives already thought Jennifer was some ignorant nicey-nice suburbanite. In the end, paying Marco Parmiento two hundred dollars was an absolute bargain. Cheaper than a new purse.

She didn't listen to his voicemail right away, but knowing it existed was a comfort. Mr. Parmiento had found Shanti and that meant she was somewhere safe.

Jennifer saved the message for a moment when she could have some real privacy: in the parking garage at work on Monday.

Camouflaging what it was, she added the foster family's address to her dayplanner. It wasn't like Kevin flipped through her planner looking for suspicious entries, but she'd taken the same precaution with Mr. Parmiento's number, too.

One act of spy craft led to another. Knowing where Shanti was made Jennifer feel better, but it wasn't enough. It felt *unresolved*. Jennifer told herself she was resolving the issue when she drove by the Vanderbilts' house. If she saw that Shanti lived in a decent home, her obligation to Gayle would have been met, as best she was able.

Driving by the house the first time and looking at the lights in the windows wasn't enough, though. Jennifer needed to see Shanti.

The next day, she left work on time and was rewarded. On the front lawn, where the night before there had only been a wrecking yard of toys, five children played. Jennifer scanned them as she drove by, splitting her attention between traffic and the kids.

Two boys and three girls, all in hoodies against the evening chill.

Feeling like a stalker, Jennifer circled back, this time more slowly. One of the girls was white with blond hair peeking out around the edges of her hood. The other two girls were brown, but in the growing dark, Jennifer couldn't see their faces.

One of the girls kicked a red rubber ball toward the boys, and the car behind Jennifer honked at her. The kids' heads swiveled toward the sound, and for an instant, Jennifer had a clear view of the girl with the kickball. Shanti. She was there. She was okay.

As quickly as they had been distracted, the kids went back to their game.

Jennifer took one more loop around the block, in time to see the foster mother call the kids inside. Shanti was the last one up the steps, the kickball tucked under one arm.

Driving on to the gym, Jennifer felt relieved. More than relieved. Elated. Transcendent. She did an hour on the elliptical and didn't even feel it.

At home, she was so cheerful that Kevin gave her a funny look and said, "What's got you so keyed up."

"Life!" Jennifer said. "Glorious life!"

"Dingbat."

He didn't protest any of the by-products of her newfound happiness, and after they had sex, she booted him out of the bed, and stripped off the sheets. Sometimes she thought her happiness could be gauged in clean sheets. In the nadir of her worst weeks lay a crumpled bed with sour smelling sheets and yellowing pillowcases. At the height of her joy, crisp clean linens and a freshly fluffed duvet dressed the bed. She went to bed in clean pajamas that night, and slept dreamlessly.

Now that she had seen Shanti, Jennifer decided to deliver the box of photos and mementos from Gayle's apartment. If she could meet Shanti, let her know she was the last thing her mother was thinking of, that would be nice. If that wasn't possible, Jennifer would drop off the box with Shanti's foster mother, and consider her task completed.

She went back the next evening. The kids horsed around in the front yard, the only place for them to play. The house backed up to a drainage ditch along Hillsborough, and a garage/workshop filled the back yard. That night was warmer and the kids wore school uniforms: khakis and navy blue polo shirts. The blond girl looked like the oldest of the five, maybe as old as twelve. The two Latino boys were clearly brothers, possibly twins, and the other little girl looked like she might be their sister. She and Shanti were about the same age.

Jennifer's phone rang. Kevin. She ignored it. She'd told him she was going to the gym after work, so he couldn't be expecting her to answer. He probably just wanted to let her know he was working late. It was a good time of year for evening sales, with people planning to buy their spouses a new car for Christmas.

Circling the block again, she scouted for a place where she could park and watch the kids. The joy of seeing Shanti was addictive and she wanted more of it.

At the gym, warming up on the elliptical, Jennifer listened to Kevin's voicemail. He sounded distracted. "Jenn, hey. I'm gonna work late. I'll catch you at home." That was it. She dialed his number, but it went straight to voicemail. He must have been with customers.

Laying her phone aside, she flipped open a new issue of *Bride* magazine and increased the speed on the elliptical. At the rate she was going, skipping dinner and getting in a workout every day, those extra fifteen pounds were going to melt away. She would look like a princess for the wedding.

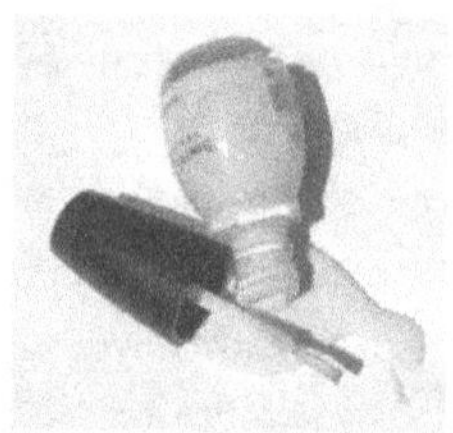

CHAPTER THIRTY-ONE

Olivia

THE WEEK BEFORE Olivia's older sister visited was spent in industrious preparation. "Sprucing things up," Mrs. Holley called it. They even cleaned house on Christmas Eve. Olivia was used to working on Christmas Day, regardless. Before she was a church employee, she had volunteered to help organize the poinsettia tributes, but now she had to proofread and print the service bulletins, three altogether for three services, each with a different pastor and a different choir.

After she finished at church, Olivia went home and detailed her father's car. He had once done it himself, making the car showroom clean before he picked up Cynthia from the airport. His size had finally made it impossible for him to do the detailing. Now he struggled to get in and out of the car. Olivia had suggested several times that Rich could do the car, but her father negated the idea with a gruff, "I don't want it messed up." Without even a please, Olivia inherited the task of preparing Cynthia's chariot.

After the car was clean, Olivia helped her mother shampoo the living room carpet. Then they decorated a mountain of cookies and packaged them into tins for neighbors and friends.

The holiday had lost most of its magic since Olivia was a child, but one thing remained special: the Christmas Eve candlelight service. After the chores were done, and everyone else went to bed, Olivia showered, did her hair, and dressed in a plain ivory blouse and a dark green skirt. Then she sat down at her vanity and repaired her nails, ragged and dirty from detailing her father's car. For Christmas, it was tempting to go with red or green, something flashy, but she chose a simple ivory with a hint of glitter in it. Her manicure kit held the perfect accessory: a sheet of silver snowflake decals. She applied one to each nail, and sealed them with a coating of clear enamel.

A little after eleven, she left the house, balancing eight tins of cookies in her arms. The night was cool, but Olivia abandoned her sweater in the car as she walked up the front steps of Mr. Batson's. As late as it was, she'd planned to simply leave the tin of cookies on the porch, but the TV was on in the front room, and the chandelier lit up the dining room windows.

She tapped lightly enough that it could be ignored, but almost before she'd lowered her hand, Mr. Batson opened the door, wearing a violent scowl that made her take a step back. When he saw who it was, he smiled. She couldn't remember ever seeing him smile. Mostly, she remembered him shouting at her the one time she accidentally rode her bike off the sidewalk and onto his lawn.

"Miss Olivia Holley!" he said, as though she were someone worth announcing.

He swung the door open wider, and she saw that she'd been wrong in assuming Rindell would be at work. He was very much at home, sitting at the dining room table, a book spread open in front of him. His uniform shirt was draped over the back of his chair, but he wore his uniform pants and an undershirt.

Jerking her gaze away from him, Olivia said, "Hi, Mr. Batson."

"Come on in, missy."

"Oh, no. I'm on my way to services. I just wanted to bring these cookies. My mother and I made them today."

"Well, that is real sweet." He reached out and took the tin, polite enough not to mention that the Holleys had never given him holiday cookies before. "You sure you don't want to come in?"

"No, thank you. I need to get going. Merry Christmas!"

"Merry Christmas to you, too," Mr. Batson said.

As Olivia went down the stairs, she heard the door close. She was already in her car, reaching for the seatbelt, when the front door opened again, the light cutting across the porch and through the windshield.

Rindell came down the steps in two jumps and was at Olivia's window before she could get the key in the ignition. It left an awkward gap as he waited for her to start the car and roll down the window.

"Hey, where you going so late?" he said.

"To church. For the candlelight service."

"That is a whole lot of churching." He laughed.

"I won't go tomorrow. Tonight is my favorite service all year."

"Yeah? What makes it so special?"

Olivia hesitated.

"It's a simple service. No sermon, just music. All the traditional songs. They light the sanctuary with candles. It's the same every year, and it has been ever since I was little. So it's like—it's like a time machine."

She dared to glance at him. He had come out in his undershirt and he was shivering.

"It sounds good," he said.

"Do you … want to go?"

"I gotta go to work. I'm on duty in like half an hour. So you just come to bring the old man some cookies?"

"I bet he'd share them with you," Olivia said.

"I bet he won't. Old man a sugar junkie. I bet he's in there now eating them up."

"Do you want some cookies?" It would mean stiffing one of the ministry staff, for whom the other tins of cookies were intended, but Olivia didn't think Marnie would care whether she got cookies from Mrs. Holley.

Rindell grinned at her. "Now are these homemade cookies?"

"Yes, made with my own two hands." Olivia lifted her hands off the steering wheel to display them. The snowflakes on her nails caught and reflected the lights from the dash. Embarrassed by her vanity, she let them drop to her lap.

"You got a lot of different talents, don't you?" Rindell said.

He was flirting with her. What did that mean? To avoid thinking about it, she reached for the top tin, which held the cookies that had turned out best. Pastor Lou would have to settle for the second prettiest cookies. When she passed the tin to Rindell, she did it one-handed to be sure his hands wouldn't touch hers. She didn't want to look like she was inviting more flirtation.

Rindell pried the lid off the tin and inhaled.

"Damn, O-livia. That's butter I smell."

"Absolutely. Because it's not really Christmas unless you gain ten pounds."

He laughed again, smiling at her.

"I better go. I don't want to be late for the service," she said.

"Yeah, you right. You better get on. Thanks for the cookies."

"You're welcome. Merry Christmas."

"You too."

As she backed out of the drive, he stood there, holding his cookies, watching her drive away.

Finding the church offices empty, she went around leaving tins of cookies on desks. In Marnie's office, she could see the cookies wouldn't be missed. Plates of holiday treats lay in drifts on the youth director's desk.

Olivia took her time delivering the cookies, because no matter what she had said to Rindell, she wanted to be late to the service. If she arrived too soon, she would have to make small talk. She might get corralled into sitting with other people. Christmas made people want to reach out.

The sanctuary was nearly full, but hushed. The candlelight glinted off the night-dark stained glass windows, casting jewel-toned winks of light. Pine wreaths hung at the end of each pew, filling the room with a sharp woodsy smell. Like holding a church service in the forest. On every available surface, poinsettias crowded next to each other.

All Olivia wanted was a quiet place to sit. Dismissing the pews out of hand, she tiptoed to the side of the sanctuary, where four carpeted steps led up to the sound booth. Seated on the second step with her feet tucked up out of the aisle, she was nearly invisible.

She had told Rindell the midnight service was a time machine, but if he'd asked what time it returned her to, she wouldn't have had an answer. She remembered no specific Christmas of particular magic or splendor. It was more that the candlelight service returned her to a mindset she had lost along the way. Sitting in that narrow stairwell, her hands clasped together over her knees, she was a little girl who did not yet have worries. Not yet fat enough to attract the attention of bullies. Not yet aware that her mother was a liar and her father a bigot. Not yet heartbroken over her brother's destruction or her sister's defection.

The candlelight service lasted only forty-five minutes, but they were minutes in which Olivia was still a child whose biggest problem was that she'd once had an extra thumb.

CHAPTER THIRTY-TWO

Jennifer

FOR SEVERAL YEARS, Jennifer had made a point of buying her mother the latest fashion accessory, but that Christmas, she didn't waste money on designer handbags or sunglasses. Instead, she bought her mother a box of her favorite chocolates and a thirty-dollar shopping tote embroidered with ladybugs. Her mother raved about it, as she never had over any of the high dollar gifts.

Part of the decision was a matter of economy. The money she might have spent on her mother, Jennifer spent on Shanti. She started simple and practical: a new hoody, bright red with fleece and embroidery around the pockets, hood and cuffs. Then she added a youth soccer ball with David Beckham's signature, plus a DVD of *Bend it Like Beckham* and a Mia Hamm jersey. To finish, Jennifer bought a photo album at the craft store and put all the loose photos from Gayle's box in it. Jennifer packed everything up, including Shanti's bronzed baby booties, and included a note to the foster mother.

Dear Mrs. Vanderbilt:

I was a friend of Shanti's mother, Gayle. I wanted to send Shanti some Christmas gifts, and I'm including a small album of family photos and a few mementos. They are things her mother would have wanted her to have. Shanti was very much on her mind at the end, and I hope you'll let her know that her mother loved her very much.

I'm also including a gift card that I hope you'll use to purchase presents for the other children in your care.

Merry Christmas and Happy New Year!

Jennifer

She ended up with two identical version of the note. One signed simply "Jennifer", the other with her full name and her phone number. In the parking lot of the post office, four days before Christmas, she chose anonymity, and sent the note with only her first name.

Because of the hectic schedule of flying to visit Kevin's family, it was after New Year's before Jennifer saw Shanti again. The public schools were on break, so the kids played out in the Vanderbilts' yard. It was a small house to have five kids underfoot.

Shanti wore her new hoody, and tried to get the boys to play soccer with her. She wasn't a natural athlete but she was passionate. When she ran to the ball she often overshot it, and when she kicked it hard, it was as likely to veer off course as it was to go to her intended target. Jennifer held her breath each time the ball rolled toward the road and Shanti chased after it.

Although the muffler shop was open, Jennifer sat in her parked car for half an hour, watching. Shanti had lost her mother, but it hadn't cast a dark shadow over her. She smiled often and quickly, laughing as she ran around the yard with the other kids. Jennifer drove away feeling like one of Santa's helpers. She might not have done exactly what she'd promised Gayle, but she was helping to make Shanti's life good.

After the New Year, Jennifer cut her visits to Shanti back to once a week, occasionally timing her lunch hour to the recess period at the nearby elementary school. Shanti was easy to pick out with her bright red hoody, running or jumping rope or working a swing along with a row of other girls.

The weekly glimpse was enough, and Jennifer planned to use Shanti's upcoming birthday to contact the foster mother again. It seemed like something Jennifer could do: Christmas and birthday gifts, a note to let Shanti know someone from her mother's life was thinking of her. Shanti wouldn't need to know that Jennifer had been part of Gayle's life after the fact. Sitting in her car, sipping coffee, Jennifer imagined herself as a doting aunt, since Shanti's real aunt wasn't interested.

Jennifer invented elaborate fantasies about how it all might play out. She needed that fantasy because reality had developed a nagging habit of disappointing her.

The wedding dress that everyone agreed was perfect lost its luster. Whenever she glimpsed the fitting picture Tracey had snapped on her phone, it looked childish. Like a dress-up costume for a little girl playing at being a bride. Was that how they all saw her? Everywhere she went, she saw pictures of wedding dresses that looked sleek and sophisticated. Elegant. She should have picked something like that instead of a ridiculous, princess dress.

She took on more of the wedding planning as Kevin lost interest in the details. The catering briefly held his attention, but as soon as they moved from food to flowers, his eyes glazed over. The same for the thousand other things that went into making a wedding happen. Like hotel arrangements for his family, which he seemed to think would magically appear for the ceremony and then *poof!* disappear when it was over. As though they wouldn't have to be fed, accommodated, and entertained.

"Well, what about our honeymoon?" she said. He could delegate all the small things to her, but surely he had an opinion about that. He was watching basketball on TV, and didn't bother to look away from the screen to answer.

"I dunno. I figured we'd do a weekend at Don CeSar."

Jennifer tried to see it as a romantic suggestion. After all, he had proposed to her on a weekend getaway to the Don CeSar Resort in St. Petersburg. It was a great place for a proposal, but for a honeymoon, it lacked something.

"A weekend in St. Pete for our honeymoon?" Jennifer said. He wasn't being romantic; he was being lazy. That was what a weekend at Don CeSar lacked: sincerity.

"Well, where do you want to go?"

"Someplace special. The Caribbean. Turks and Caicos."

"Jenn, baby, for real? We couldn't do that in a long weekend."

"Of course not. We'd need a week at least."

"I can't take a week off work." Kevin looked away from the game and frowned in annoyance.

"Somehow, I imagine Mr. Grange will let you take time off for your honeymoon." She hopped off the kitchen stool and stomped over to the fridge.

"He'll let me take the time off, but I can't be gone that long. I'll lose commissions."

"Probably so."

Jennifer opened the fridge and peered in. Three bottles of beer. Leftover spaghetti sauce that made the whole space stink of garlic. Yogurt. Salad ingredients. No junk food. There was never junk food when she needed it.

Kevin came up behind her, slipping his arm around her waist as he reached into the fridge for another beer. His head bobbed toward her, and she pulled back, too late realizing he'd meant to kiss her. With a shrug, he carried the beer bottle to the counter and opened the drawer to get out the bottle opener.

"I just think our honeymoon should be something special," she said.

"Baby, so do I, but I can't take a week off to go sit on the beach while Galliday racks up a shit-ton of sales that ought to be mine. Because seriously, that guy is a douche. I don't want to lose my spot on the roster to him."

"You're not going to lose your spot on the sales roster in a week."

"You'd be surprised how fast it can happen," Kevin said.

"So, that's it. A weekend at Don CeSar?"

"Jeez, don't make it sound like I suggested a weekend at Motel Six."

Jennifer slammed the fridge door closed and walked back to the bar, where she had spread out a dozen different brochures for the Caribbean. She wanted to take them and throw them in the trash under Kevin's nose, but didn't want to be accused of being childish or passive-aggressive. She put the brochures back in the folder.

"Don't pout. Come on. We'll do a real honeymoon some other time," Kevin said.

"What other time? When won't you be worried about losing your spot on the sales roster?"

"Look, we're gonna be married for the rest of our lives. There'll be time to take a trip like that. Okay?"

"Yeah, it's okay. I think it's totally romantic that you want to sell cars instead of go on a honeymoon with me," Jennifer said.

"You're not going to let it go, are you?" He said it like she'd been nagging him for weeks. After a few moments of silence, he wandered back to the couch and the basketball game.

Jennifer climbed up on the bar stool and went back to arranging guests at tables for the reception. Making diagrams and buying favors was simpler. Like planning an event for someone else. Sure, the commemorative tchotchkes would be engraved with Jennifer and Kevin, but they could have been any Jennifer and Kevin.

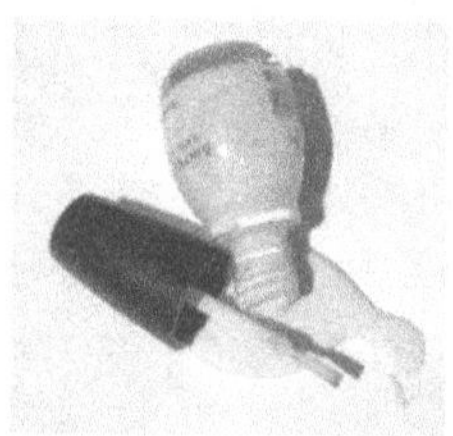

CHAPTER THIRTY-THREE

Olivia

MRS. HOLLEY SPENT Christmas Day fretting over the grandkids' presents. What she wanted to do was admire them again, but once they were wrapped, the only excuse to do that was to fret over the wrapping job. One by one, she set about re-wrapping them. As much as Mr. Holley's Official Cynthia Christmas Ritual focused on his car, Mrs. Holley's focused on the wrapping of packages.

For Rich there were new sneakers and a new computer game, puzzles appropriate for ages 9-12. From the sounds of frustration coming from his room by dinner time, Olivia worried that she'd over-gauged his abilities.

Rich insisted on opening his presents on Christmas morning, but Mr. and Mrs. Holley declined to open their presents, preferring to save them for what they referred to as "the family Christmas," a thing which required Cynthia's presence.

Olivia played along, primarily because she knew what her carefully wrapped packages contained: some nail polish, a scarf, and a new travel coffee mug. Rich had given her his gift back at Thanksgiving. Eight perfectly matched, sanded, and stained wood blocks that he attached to her vanity's legs to raise it three inches. He had devised the idea himself, seeing her paint her fingernails with her knees wedged against the front of the vanity.

"Needs to be taller, so your knees fit," he'd said. And that was what he did. He might be stumped by computer puzzles designed for ages 9-12, but he was an engineer at heart.

The day after Christmas, the Holleys were reduced to thumb-twiddling, four wise men awaiting an immaculate birth. When Olivia woke on the twenty-seventh, her parents were bustling around downstairs. Her father dressed the way he did for important work meetings. Good suit, crisp shirt, tie with a diamond tie tack, a silk hanky in his suit pocket.

"Good morning, Olivia!" he boomed.

While she ate her yogurt, he chatted excitedly, killing time before his trip to the airport.

After he picked up Cynthia and the kids, he would bring the kids back to the house to spend the afternoon with Grandma. Then he would take Cynthia to lunch at The Columbia. It was her favorite place to eat in Tampa, and tradition for him to take her there alone.

By the time Cynthia and Mr. Holley came home from lunch, Mrs. Holley had a roaring headache, and responsibility for the kids had devolved to Olivia. Seth was ten, Jacob seven, and Lilly five. Nice kids, although she didn't see them often enough to feel confident that they would obey her. The boys were being rowdy, so she convinced Rich to take his nephews upstairs to play computer games. Lilly followed them, and that seemed to solve the problem. For nearly half an hour, the house was quiet enough for the older Holleys to slip into their usual after lunch doze.

A thud and a wail from upstairs brought everyone out of their stupor, but Cynthia bolted up the stairs first. Maternal instinct.

Overhead, Olivia heard her sister say, "What happened? What did you boys do?"

When Olivia and her mother reached the landing, Cynthia held Seth's face in her hands, peering at him closely. Jacob and Lilly bunched up next to her, so that Rich stood alone in the doorway of his room.

"Is everything okay?" Mrs. Holley said.

"Rich punched Seth," Cynthia said.

"What?"

For a moment, Olivia worried that in Southern Belle fashion her mother was about to get the vapors.

"I am not a retard!" Rich said.

"Did you say that, Seth?" Olivia got a glare from Cynthia for asking the question.

Seth was too busy blubbering to answer, and by then, Mr. Holley had begun his arduous journey up the stairs. For some awful reason that dated back to their childhoods, they all stood in wretched silence, waiting on his arrival.

"Richard, you better get in your room!" Mr. Holley bellowed, when he heard what had happened.

"You can't make me."

"Rich, honey, please, go in your room," Mrs. Holley said.

"I am not a retard!"

"Well, you're acting like one!" Cynthia shouted.

Seeing the bug-eyed look on Lilly's face, Olivia said, "Why don't I take the kids downstairs and put some ice on Seth's eye?"

Lilly came to her like she was leaping over an abyss to safety.

In the kitchen, Olivia made an icepack for Seth. He wasn't badly hurt, but he was going to have a black eye. Something he'd be proud of once the initial shock wore off.

After that was taken care of, Olivia set out a plate of Christmas cookies. The boys went for the cookies with both hands, but Lilly carefully selected a single cookie and began to nibble on it.

"Seth, tell me the truth. Did you call Uncle Rich a retard?" Olivia said.

"No."

"Liar," Jacob whispered.

"He did," Lilly said, still working on the top edge of her cookie.

"Do you know that's not nice? Not ever. It's not ever nice to say that to someone. It's especially not nice to say that to Uncle Rich."

"But he's so dumb! He can't do anything!" Seth said.

"You know a bad thing happened to him. You know that, right?"

"A motorcycle wreck," Jacob said.

"That's right. He had a motorcycle accident and it hurt his brain. So he can't do the things he used to do. That's why it's not nice to say mean things to him. It makes him remember that he used to be smarter. It makes him feel bad."

Seth's defiance leaked out as Olivia talked and the ice pack drooped into his lap. After a moment his shoulders heaved and Olivia knew he was crying. She scooted her chair closer and slipped her arm around him.

"Is he going to get smarter again?" Seth said.

For an instant, Mrs. Holley's lie hung in Olivia's mind. *He's getting better*, she always said.

"No, he isn't. So you have to act grown up and be nice to him. Even when you get frustrated. Can you do that?"

Seth nodded and across the table, Jacob nodded, too, like his little mirror. Lilly sat with her hands flat on the table in front of her, not a crumb in sight.

"Do you want another cookie, Lilly?"

After a moment's hesitation, Lilly said, "Mommy says I'm only 'lowed one cookie a day. So I won't get fat."

Like you. That was what her niece was too polite to say. *Mommy says I'm only allowed one cookie a day, so I won't get fat like you*.

"Well, fat isn't the worst thing you could be in life, but if you only want one cookie, there's no reason to eat a second one."

Lilly looked longingly at the plate of cookies.

"But if you wanted a second one, you could have it. I don't have any rules like Mommy."

Lilly's hand darted out and lifted another green tree from the plate. Olivia took one, too, and while the boys devoured what was left, she and her niece nibbled their second cookies like mice.

Upstairs the argument was going strong, and as Olivia approached, she heard Cynthia say, "—can't allow the kids to be around him if he acts like that."

"I don't think one incident represents the whole situation," Mr. Holley said.

Rich must have been in his room with Mrs. Holley, because only Cynthia and their father stood at the top of the stairs.

"How's Seth?" Cynthia said when she saw Olivia.

"He's fine. He admitted that he called Rich a retard."

"I don't care what he called him. Rich punched him. He's going to have a black eye."

"It's no worse than what Seth and Jacob do to each other," Olivia said.

"Except that Rich is a grown man! He could have seriously hurt Seth."

"Cynthia, he has impulse control issues."

"Then he can't be left unsupervised with the kids. If he can't act like an adult, he can't be treated like an adult."

Maybe she was right, and they had been trying too hard to let Rich keep his position as a grown up in the family. Olivia was about to concede that until Cynthia said, "Daddy, I think you need to start considering other solutions for his long term care."

"Don't think I haven't," Mr. Holley said.

Olivia's jaw dropped, and for a moment she was at a loss for words. When she could speak, she said, "What does that mean?"

"I don't want to hash all this out right now," her father said.

"I just want to know what you mean by you've thought about it? About putting Rich in a home?"

"He can't stay here indefinitely. There's going to come a day when he'll need to be in a facility where he can be taken care of."

"Well, then what was the point of...." Olivia had been about to say, *What was the point of me staying at home to help with him if you're going to put him in an institution?* Except, she hadn't made any sacrifice to stay at home, so what did it matter?

Mr. Holley started down the stairs, clinging to the railing, and Olivia let him go. If he didn't want to hash things out, they wouldn't get hashed out.

Although Seth and Rich were eager to forgive and forget, the incident cast a cloud over the rest of their visit. On the day they had planned to go to Busch Gardens, Cynthia called from her hotel and said she didn't want Rich to come. So instead of the whole family going, Cynthia took the kids, and Rich stayed home playing his computer games, while Olivia helped her mother cut out another quilt. The day after that, Cynthia and the kids flew home to Atlanta.

On New Year's Eve, Olivia moped around the house, first trying to work up her nerve to walk down to Mr. Batson's house, then talking herself out of it. What good did it do to let Rindell flirt with her, knowing nothing would come of it? He could flirt all he wanted, but in the end, he didn't want her. He wanted to leave.

At midnight, with everyone else in the house asleep, Olivia lay in bed reading one of her mother's cast off mystery novels. She didn't fall asleep until almost three o'clock, and at the time she normally would have gotten up to walk, she heard a sound that made her heart leap: an ambulance siren. It roared by, directly outside her window. Rindell and Luis must have gotten a call on their break.

She thought of what Rindell had said, about how chaos was his element, and she smiled to think of him driving into the dark morning to rescue someone.

CHAPTER THIRTY-FOUR

Jennifer

EVENTUALLY BAY DAY loomed on the horizon, blotting out everything else in Jennifer's life. Her days became a death march of event planning. She got up earlier and went to bed later, and her day planner seemed to gain every pound she lost, until it grew to the size of a newborn baby. It was as heavy to lug around and, without the benefit of a baby stroller or one of those Scandinavian snuggli things, the weight strained at her arms and shoulders until the muscles in her neck grew as taut as guy-wires, threatening to snap.

The dayplanner required as much attention as a baby, too. Every day, Jennifer removed old pages and inserted fresh ones, rewriting her to-do lists and her calendar dozens of times each week. It seemed like every hour, Lucas gave her something to keep track of, and he called her so often, she developed Phantom Phone Syndrome. Even when her phone wasn't ringing or vibrating, she imagined it was. After wrestling it out of her pocket or off her nightstand, she would look at it dumbly for a minute before realizing no one had called.

January and February melted away, and then the beast named Bay Day swallowed March whole. One day, Jennifer was thinking about gifts for Shanti's sixth birthday, and the next day, or so it seemed, she had already missed the date. An opportunity to make contact lost, and Jennifer was too overwhelmed to do more than regret it. A belated card with some cash would have been better than nothing, but as Jennifer thought that, she was three weeks late for the birthday.

The last time she thought about Shanti's birthday was the day the rental service called to tell her she had asked for the impossible.

"The math doesn't add up," said Tim, the sales rep in charge of the Bay Day account.

"Okay, what's wrong?" Jennifer hoped it was something simple, as she pulled out the folder of property rental plans and event service layout.

"The whole food pavilion."

"The whole thing? You're kidding me."

"Look, you're showing fifty six-foot rectangles and forty circles. But there's not enough room."

"No, it works," Jennifer said.

"It doesn't."

Tim had started the conversation sounding friendly. Now he sounded exasperated. Jennifer felt for him. She truly did. Staring at the layout Lucas had drawn, she could see that all the tables fit inside the horseshoe shape of the food vendor stalls. She started counting tables, lost track, and started again, hardly aware that she was counting under her breath.

"I'm not saying the tables don't fit in your drawing," Tim interrupted. "I'm saying your drawing is wrong."

"But I…."

"Your scale is wrong."

Jennifer and Lucas had worked together on the layout, but his drawing had ultimately been forwarded to the rental company. The scale was wrong.

As Jennifer scrambled to reconfigure the food pavilion, the intercom notice on her phone beeped. Mr. Kraus. She picked it up, but before she could offer a greeting, Lucas snapped, "Get down here now!"

The two men were leaning over Mr. Kraus' desk, and when Jennifer walked in, they turned to her. No, they turned *on* her.

Lucas was pale, but Mr. Kraus looked florid under his golf course tan.

"Laying at the confluence of the Hillsborough River and Tampa Bay?" Mr. Kraus said.

"What?" Jennifer had never thought it was good text. It tried too hard to sound sophisticated. Who used words like *confluence*? She was pretty sure it didn't mean what Lucas thought it meant.

"Laying? Laying?" Mr. Kraus roared. He rattled a copy of the event brochure at her. "We're not fucking the Hillsborough River!"

Jennifer stepped forward and took the brochure Mr. Kraus thrust at her. The offending word was circled in his signature blue fountain pen ink, which had smudged on the glossy paper. Jennifer had seen the brochure text a million times by that point, but with a slowly dawning disbelief, she identified the mistake. *Lying*. It should have been "lying at the confluence."

How many people had looked at the collateral materials? A dozen? Two dozen? And yet the error landed squarely on her shoulders. Or rolled over her like a bus, one that Lucas readily threw her under.

"Jennifer, I cannot believe you missed something that big. I know I corrected that on an earlier proof." Lucas shook his head in a show of disappointment.

Jennifer longed to denounce him, to retrieve the file of proofs that she kept from every stage. On none of the proofs had he or anyone else corrected that error. Instead of wasting time defending herself, she said the thing that Lucas himself had taught her to say: "It's not too late to fix it."

"The hell it's not," Mr. Kraus said. "We have a dozen boxes of that brochure piled up in the conference room."

"And there's still time to have it reprinted."

"Oh, I see, so I'm supposed to drop another ten thousand to correct your mistake?"

"No, it's my mistake. I'll pay for it," Jennifer said.

Lucas scowled. He hadn't been prepared for her to step up to the plate. She was beginning to see that Lucas only shone when things went right. When they went wrong, he rarely solved problems, just pointed them out.

"Don't waste my time with bullshit. Just fucking fix it." Mr. Kraus turned back to his desk, dismissing her.

Jennifer would pay for the corrected brochures, if only to show Lucas up. Paying for the botched brochures would mean changes for the short term. No more extravagances. A lot of economization.

Jennifer had gone to the mat for a Caribbean honeymoon, but it wasn't too late to get the honeymoon money back. They'd lose the deposit, but that would save almost five thousand. The other five thousand could be made up with Jennifer's bonus money and some credit card debt. Kevin would be furious, but he would understand why it had to be done. He knew about making good on professional obligations.

In the conference room, Jennifer snatched up a bundle of brochures and peeled one off. She went through it word by word, reading it aloud, to be sure that was absolutely the only error in it. What she found was that two of the staging areas had been mislabeled. Stage 4 should have been Stage 7 and vice versa. That was Lucas' mistake, too. He had insisted on doing all the planning for the bands. When she was sure everything was correct, she took out her phone and called the printer.

Jennifer didn't leave work until after seven, and by then she needed something to cheer her up. She drove to the Vanderbilts' house without thinking. For a blissful fifteen minutes, she watched Shanti kick her soccer ball against the side of the house, dashing back and forth to get it when it rebounded. She kept up a steady pace, never losing the ball, until the front door slammed open.

A woman stepped out on the porch. The foster mother, Amelia Vanderbilt. Standing under the porch light, she looked about fifty with longish gray hair in a braid. She wore a pair of sloppy sweatpants and a pocket t-shirt. She wasn't wearing a bra or shoes. She yelled at Shanti. About the ball being kicked against the house? Shanti captured the ball under one foot and stood with her hands on her hips. Defiant.

Abruptly the woman reached over the railing and grabbed Shanti's arm. With a jerk, she brought her up the porch steps. The soccer ball rolled free and came to rest beside the minivan's tires. The foster mother shoved Shanti through the front door, swatting her backside as she did.

The front door slammed and the porch light went off. Jennifer realized she had been holding her breath. Today, of all days, she needed to see Shanti happy and playing, not alone and then punished.

In search of relief from the day's stress, Jennifer drove on to the gym. She ran on a treadmill until she thought she might fall over. Afterward, in the locker room, trying to untie her gym shoes, her hands trembled. Then she remembered. The brochure problem had blown up before lunch. She'd never eaten lunch, and she'd been too rushed to have anything but coffee for breakfast. No wonder she felt weak.

She'd been skipping more meals. Eating required five minutes to sit and put food in her mouth. A luxury these days. The self-righteous voice in her head encouraged her to skip dinner again, but the internal voice tasked with absorbing the body blow of Mr. Kraus' anger and Lucas' betrayal was stronger.

In the anonymity of her car, she went through a drive-thru and devoured a bacon cheeseburger and fries, washed down with an enormous Coke. Not diet.

At the condo, she detoured to the parking garage trash to dispose of the sickening, shameful evidence, but she could smell it on her hands: grease and lies.

All she wanted was to take a shower and go to bed, but Kevin was waiting for her when she walked through the door. He had taken off his tie, but he still wore his work shirt and pants. His laptop sat open on the coffee table.

"Where have you been?" he said.

"At work. I told you. God, Kevin, Bay Day is in less than a month. You can't imagine what today was like. Just, please, be nice to me for once."

"Am I so awful you have to tell me to be nice to you?"

She sighed. "I didn't say you were awful. I have had the crappiest day you can imagine, and I can't—I can't do this."

"What is *this*?" He held out his hands like he was showing off a fish he'd caught.

Jennifer started peeling out of her clothes. She was sticky with sweat from the gym and the stink of the burger on her hands was suddenly nauseating.

"This, where the first thing you say to me is *Where have you been?* You know where I've been."

"At work, right? That's your story? That's where you've been for the last two hours?"

"And then the gym."

"Yeah," he said slowly. "The gym, right after you spent half an hour parked at a muffler shop over on east Hillsborough."

Jennifer turned to him with her mouth hanging open.

"Did you follow me?" she said.

"No, I just used your GPS."

"My GPS? What does that mean?"

"I used your GPS system to track where you went." Kevin's gaze shifted to the laptop.

Jennifer approached and stared down at the screen. It showed a little blue triangle on a map of Davis Islands. She squinted harder and realized she was seeing her car parked downstairs.

"You used my stupid car computer thing to spy on me?" Jennifer hadn't wanted GPS installed in her car, but he'd said it would make her safer. From what?

"Do you have any idea how crazy you've been acting lately?" he said.

"Yes! Of course, I do! My job is driving me around the bend and I'm trying to plan a wedding! And—and Gayle Prichard is still dead and—and—and you're spying on me!" Jennifer knew she was screaming and she didn't care. "Is that why you installed it? So you could watch me? So you could keep track of me?"

"Jenn, don't. Don't."

"Don't what?" she shrieked.

"Don't be upset."

"Why would you do that?"

"I thought you were cheating on me!"

Jennifer ran for the bathroom, her face slick with sweat and her mouth gushing saliva. She nearly tripped over the threshold and slammed her hip against the door frame. She reached the toilet in time to vomit the burger and fries all over the closed lid.

"Jenn, I'm sorry," Kevin whispered behind her. "I'm sorry. I don't mean it the way it sounds. I was just worried and I thought…."

"You thought I was cheating on you!" The horror of it was the same, whether she was innocent or guilty, and she wasn't sure which she was.

"You've been lying to me. About where you're going. About the thing with Gayle Prichard. About what you're up to."

"Not about that!"

"I'm sorry." He cried. Actual tears.

Jennifer had never seen him cry before. It seemed like she should cry, too, but she was too numb. Not knowing what else to do, she began to wipe uselessly at the vomit with a wad of toilet paper.

After a few minutes of silence, Kevin got a roll of paper towels and some kitchen cleaner. Under normal circumstances she never would have let him clean up her vomit, but she watched him mop up the mess.

All the energy she had left was spent on a shower and brushing her teeth. Once they were in bed, Kevin said, "I'm sorry, Jenn. I didn't know what to do."

"It's okay." It wasn't, but she thought it was the fastest way to make him leave her alone. When he put his arm around her, she didn't object.

"But what are you doing? Why are you going over to that muffler shop every day?"

"It's not every day," she said.

"But a lot of days."

"How often do you watch me?" Had he tracked her GPS on the day she drove to Anastasia State Park?

"No, baby. I just—I didn't know what to do. I didn't know where you were going. So what's at the muffler shop?" He wasn't going to let it go.

"Nothing. It's just a place to park."

"Why?"

"So I can watch her, Gayle Prichard's little girl." Jennifer sighed, relieved to have it said, but she felt his consternation in the way his arm muscles tightened.

"I thought you were over all that business."

"I am *over all that business*. I just like to see her. To see that she's happy and safe."

"So that's what you've been doing, all these times I couldn't get ahold of you or you said you were working late? You're driving halfway across town to spy on this little girl? Do you know how crazy that is?"

"Fuck you," Jennifer said. She didn't want to placate him anymore. "You spied on me because you thought I was having an affair. So fuck you."

"Fuck me? Nice. Nice."

Jennifer rolled over, pushing his arm away. He let her go.

"Oh, and you'll be glad to know, we don't have to go on a honeymoon, because I fucked up at work and we're going to need the money to pay for my fuckup. So, that should make you happy."

"Jenn, don't be that way," Kevin said.

"I am that way. I just am."

It felt like a profound truth, but a frightening one. She was the way she was, and if Kevin was going to marry her, he needed to accept that.

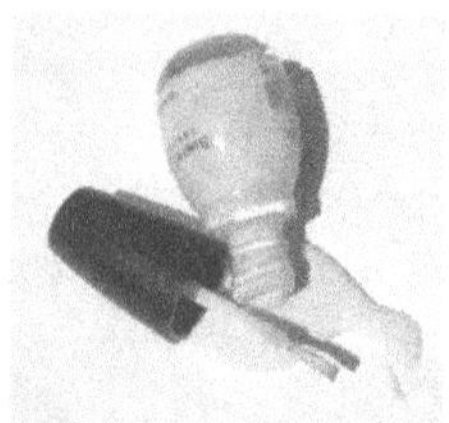

CHAPTER THIRTY-FIVE

Olivia

OLIVIA EXPECTED THE phone call to be her mother's usual mid-day call: ten minutes of chatter about what she'd seen out the front window, what was on TV, and what she thought she might cook for dinner.

Except the call was half an hour early and for the first two minutes, Olivia couldn't understand anything her mother said.

"—and I can't get Daddy on the phone." That part Olivia understood.

"It's okay, Mom. I'll come home and you can tell me what happened."

"It's Rich again," her mother sobbed.

"I'm coming home. Just wait."

Olivia hung up, but she didn't go home immediately. First, she pressed her hands together hard to stop them from shaking. Then she called the Forward/Ability office and when Davina answered, she said, "This is Olivia Holley, Rich's sister...."

"I'll put you through to Mr. Colton."

Click.

Olivia listened to a moment of dead air, then thirty seconds of crackly Vivaldi, before Mr. Colton came on the line and said, "Miss Holley? Have you spoken to your mother?"

"I did, but she's very upset. She couldn't tell me what happened. Has Rich had an accident?"

It was all Olivia could think of: the room full of power tools, where Rich used a big saw to cut bookcase shelves.

"Not an accident so much," Mr. Colton said. His voice sounded raw, almost like he had a cold, or had been crying. "He's been in a fight with one of the other guys."

"Brian?"

"Has he mentioned Brian to you?"

"Just that they work together," Olivia said. Just that Rich had said he was going to kill him. The lie of omission came effortlessly, even though Olivia's throat felt dry. "Is he—is Rich in jail?"

"He's at the hospital, Miss Holley. At TGH."

"Is he okay?"

"I don't know."

She went to the hospital first, imagining it would calm her mother, if Olivia could say, "I saw him and he was fine."

Except that he wasn't. In a horrible echo of his motorcycle accident, he lay in a hospital bed with his head swathed in bloody bandages. Unlike that earlier hospital stay, a pair of handcuffs held Rich's left hand to the bed railing. Taking his free hand in hers, she squeezed his fingers. They were swollen from IV fluids and he didn't squeeze back.

"Rich, it's me, Olivia. Can you hear me?

"He's heavily sedated," the nurse said. "He was combative when he came in."

"How is he?"

"He looks worse than he is, but he's pretty banged up. I'll get the doctor to come talk to you in a couple minutes."

The nurse was turning to go, when Olivia said, "What about the person who came in with him? Brian?"

"He's in ICU."

Afer waiting half an hour for the doctor, Olivia decided to go home. If Rich wasn't in any danger, she could wait to talk to the doctor. Pulling out of the parking lot, Olivia tried her father's phone again, but got no answer. As soon as she disconnected, her phone rang. It was her father, sounding angry and out of breath.

"Your mother expected you home half an hour ago," he said.

"I went by the hospital first, to check on Rich."

"You need to come home and take your mother to see him. I have to go meet with Dale Edgerton."

Dale was a family friend, but he was a lawyer, too. If Rich had put someone into ICU, he would need a lawyer.

"I'll be home in fifteen minutes," Olivia said.

At home, Mr. Holley was already gone, and Mrs. Holley was crying. Her lunch sat on the table: a sandwich and a cup of cold coffee with a scummy layer of milk on top. Olivia felt too shocked to cry, but she stood with her arms around her mother, her face buried in Mrs. Holley's unwashed neck.

"Do you want me to take you to the hospital now?"

"I'm sure I look like a mess," Mrs. Holley said.

"I don't think that matters."

At any rate, she couldn't wear her pajamas to the hospital, so Olivia encouraged her to shower and do her hair. The longer it took them to get there, the better. Mrs. Holley would worry less if she didn't see him in the ER with bloody bandages on his head.

"Have you called Cynthia yet?" Olivia said.

"No, I didn't want to worry her."

Once again, Cynthia got a pass, but today wasn't the day to complain about that. Instead, Olivia helped her mother get ready and drove her to the hospital.

They spent the afternoon and the evening there, with Rich sedated and handcuffed to the bed. The doctor came to talk to them. Another head injury. Swelling, risk of further brain damage, another shunt.

Olivia was eager to escape. The smell of disinfectant and the muffled squeaking of shoes and beeping of machines made her feel suffocated. Leaving Mrs. Holley with Rich, Olivia ventured out to find dinner for her mother. Then she went back to the church to finish the materials for a missioning conference scheduled for the morning. Over a hundred people were expected, most of them from outside the church.

Once upon a time, when Olivia started at Church of the Palms, there had been two other administrative staff. Lisa, who had been part time, wasn't replaced after she quit. Kyle had been promoted to a ministry staff position, and they hadn't hired a replacement for him, either. In a pinch, Bernadette could have made copies and put together the materials, but not without Olivia to supervise. It was easier to do the work herself.

Relieved to find no one else at the church, Olivia unlocked the door, turned off the alarm, and went into her cubicle. What needed to be a hundred color-coded folders of training materials was still a disordered pile of papers to be collated.

She worked until her phone rang. Mrs. Holley, asking for a few things from home. Olivia locked up and went by the house to pick up a pillow, a sweater, her mother's medicine, and a crossword puzzle book. It felt like a reversal of roles, from when her mother had packed her book bag for school.

When she returned to the hospital, it was after midnight, and Mrs. Holley was watching TV, absently patting Rich's hand where it lay on top of the blankets.

"I went for a walk to stretch my legs and I saw your beau," Mrs. Holley said.

"Who?"

"That young man you're seeing. Rindell?"

"We're not dating anymore." Of all the cruel, random things in the universe.

"You're not? Well, that's awkward. I invited him to dinner. At least you could have told me you weren't seeing him anymore," Mrs. Holley said, as though she alone suffered from the embarrassment of it.

"What did he say? Is he coming to dinner?"

"Well, I assume so. I invited him."

Olivia stepped into the hallway and walked down to the bank of windows that looked over Davis Islands. There she had enough signal to call Rindell. She knew she should have deleted his phone number, but there it was. She didn't think of the time until he answered with a sharp, “Yeah?”

“I’m sorry. I’m sorry. I forgot you’d be at work.”

“Olivia?”

“I’m sorry I bothered you,” she mumbled, facing down the prospect of having to find the nerve to call him again.

“It’s okay. I can talk for a minute.”

“Oh, okay.”

“So you didn’t tell your mama?” he said.

“No.”

“She asked me to dinner.”

“I know. I’m sorry. I should have told her. It’s okay. I told her you weren’t coming.”

“Oh, okay,” Rindell said.

Olivia hesitated, unsure of what he meant by that. “Were you going to come?”

“No. No. I just didn’t—it’s okay.”

“Right. Again, sorry to be a bother.”

“What was your mama doing down at TGH this time of night?”

“Something happened with my brother. An accident.” Olivia wondered why he asked, when she was sure she’d already run out the clock on her allotted minute.

“I’m sorry to hear that.”

“It’s—I’m sure it’ll be okay. Thank you.”

Olivia was trying to decide how to end the call when he said, “Well, you take care, Olivia. Thanks for those cookies. They were real good.”

Before she could answer, he disconnected.

At home, Mr. Holley’s booming snore greeted her at the top of the stairs. However he had managed to get to sleep, Olivia hoped she would, too. She set her alarm for five o’clock, planning to go into the church and finish up the mission packets before anyone else came to work.

When she got there at six o’clock, Pastor Lou’s car was in the front lot, along with a car from the security company. The senior pastor and a security guard stood in the lobby, puzzling over the alarm panel.

"Is there a problem?" she said.

"It looks like the alarm wasn't active when you came in, sir, and so when you punched in the code, it armed instead of disarming," the security guard said.

"I did it. I must have forgotten to arm it when I left," Olivia said.

"Oh, Olivia, I wondered. I thought we'd had a break in," said Pastor Lou.

"I left the lights on. So it wouldn't be dark when I came back. And then I was too tired, so I tried to sleep. I didn't think about the alarm."

With the mystery solved, Pastor Lou walked the security guard out to his car. When he came back, he poked his head into Olivia's cubicle.

"How's your brother? I heard he had an accident at work."

"Yes. I don't know. Mom's at the hospital with him."

"You should go, be with your family. You don't need to be here."

"I do. This is the stuff for the missioning conference."

"Oh, oh," he said. "Well, can't someone else do it for you?"

"No, not really."

Olivia finished the packets with half an hour to spare. She walked them over to the fellowship hall, where steam from fresh-brewed coffee filled the air. After unloading the stacks of folders on the nearest table, she went to the urns and siphoned off a Styrofoam cup of coffee.

By the time she finished setting out the files, the first of the conference participants started arriving. They wandered around the fellowship hall, choosing places, and then descended on the table of pastries. Olivia slipped away, thinking of Pastor Lou's suggestion that she should go home.

It wasn't to be, though. As soon as she made it back to the main office, Luanne the accountant said, "Oh, Olivia, can you go do tickets for the conference? Mrs. Bondurant was supposed to, but she hasn't come yet. We've already got people arriving and nobody to take money for registration or lunch tickets."

It wasn't a question. Luanne had the cash drawer in her hand. As Olivia accepted the dented, beige steel box, it dawned on her that only she saw herself as a bulldog. Everyone else viewed her as a pack mule.

CHAPTER THIRTY-SIX

Jennifer

BAY DAY UNFURLED upon downtown Tampa like the grasping tentacles of a Leviathan. Orange and white police barricades threaded through the streets, delineating boundaries, while banners and flags rippled over white tents. At six o'clock in the morning, Jennifer had already been awake for two hours. She rolled through the dark streets in a golf cart, checking the list on her clipboard against what remained of her brain. At seven, a light mist fell, justifying the extra expense of awnings for the welcome booths. When the staffers arrived, corrected brochures lay in orderly mounds on the table, as neat and dry as the Great Pyramids. At seven-thirty, Lucas arrived, and Jennifer read in his face a concern that reflected her own. Did the citizens of Tampa want a civilized outdoor festival squeezed in between the raucous debaucheries of Gasparilla in January and Guavaween in October?

By noon, they had their answer. The welcome booths had clocked nearly two hundred thousand entrants and the headlining acts had yet to take the stage. All those empty store fronts spruced up and occupied for the month looked like hot properties, and the foot traffic was heavy.

Jennifer had been in touch with Lucas all morning, but then Mr. Kraus texted her to tell her to meet him at the VIP balcony. All she could think was that something else had gone wrong and Lucas was dumping it on her again.

When Jennifer passed through security, she knew she'd done good work. She had come up with the idea of the VIP *balcony*. Instead of an indoor VIP lounge, she'd given the important people a gorgeous suite on the third floor with a view of the main stage, where the crowd was densest. The suite's interior was as sumptuous as any VIP lounge she'd ever seen, thick carpets on bamboo floors, glittering crystal, wood paneling softened by heady-smelling gardenia bushes in terra cotta pots. The deep leather loungers and chairs were nearly empty as people gathered on the balcony, peering down at the crowds and the stage, about to come to life with one of the headline acts.

As Jennifer approached the balcony, a man in khakis, polo shirt, and deck shoes turned toward her and cried, "Jennifer!"

Mr. Kraus, incognito as he hobnobbed with investors, a hundred-dollar cigar clenched in his perfectly veneered teeth. To Jennifer's eyes, he looked naked without his suit.

"Here's the lovely lady who helped plan today's festivities," he said to the man beside him. Jennifer recognized him from television, but she blanked on his name. He was dressed in ridiculously bright colors and his toupee was so over the top that it redefined the word *bigwig*.

"Well, I thought you were exaggerating when you said she was cute as a button, but now that I've seen her I'll have to reconsider all the other things I thought you were exaggerating about." Mr. Bigwig pumped Jennifer's hand, pressing the flesh a little too familiarly. She could see that if she wasn't careful, he would be hitting on her after another cognac, and his glass was dangerously close to empty already.

"Have you seen the numbers from the welcome booths?" she said.

"I have," Mr. Kraus said.

Someone from the balcony called, "You know, all we're missing is beads. I'm pretty sure if we had beads to give out, we could see some skin."

So much for a civilized outdoor festival. Jennifer identified the would-be Mardi Gras pirate as Mr. Carnelon of Carnelon Construction. Spelled correctly on all the event collateral, thank you very much.

Bigwig guffawed loudly and Mr. Kraus joined in for a few seconds before saying, "Excuse me for a minute."

He caught Jennifer by the elbow and drew her back into the lounge. She was suddenly aware of being lightheaded. Too much heat and not enough water. Not enough food, either. There had been a bagel at some point, but she'd only managed a few bites.

"Is there a problem?" she said.

"Far from it. Aside from the fact that our male-to-female ratio is a bit skewed, and for which I take full responsibility, I think things are going perfectly." He patted her on the shoulder and then fished in the cargo pocket of his khaki shorts. "And none of this nonsense about you paying for those brochures. This is something to say thank you."

Jennifer's instinct was to smile and effuse mindlessly. *Oh thank you so much!* Then she registered what he was handing her: an envelope from the travel agency he and his wife used for their vacations.

"I want you to have a nice long honeymoon, so you'll come back refreshed and ready to tackle the promo events for The Lofts."

The Lofts. A project that had been under discussion for as long as Jennifer had worked at TFI.

"They're going ahead?" she said.

"Back on schedule." Mr. Kraus tilted his head toward Mr. Bigwig. "I know Lucas has you running down a list as long as your arm, but just one more thing: do you have a few single girlfriends you could invite down?"

After a moment's hesitation, he laughed and she joined him.

"I'll get right on that."

As she turned to go, he tapped her arm with a cigar. "Give that to your young man."

"Thanks."

She trotted back down the spiral staircase to security, the cigar and envelope clutched in her hand. Caught up in the excitement of the moment, she called Kevin, but got his voicemail.

"Hey, you! Looks like we're having a honeymoon after all. Mr. Kraus just gave me...." She opened the envelope and scanned the pages inside. "A ten-day trip to Martinique. Holy shit. All inclusive. The flight, the hotel, everything. Anyway, things are crazy, but if you come down, we could get some dinner together. Call me. Love you."

She was nearly back to the command post, when Mr. Kraus' joke sank in. Was he joking? Or had he asked her to find some women to populate the VIP room? Too many powerful men had left their significant others at home to come out for what at least Mr. Carnelon seemed to think was going to be a wild party.

Puzzling it over, Jennifer called Tracey. She had gotten no further than the words "VIP" and Mr. Bigwig's name, when Tracey squealed.

"Oh my God, yes! I can be ready in like half an hour."

"Take a cab. There is no parking down here. If you can scare up a couple more friends, TFI will cover the cost."

Tracey kept her word. In less than forty-five minutes, she arrived at the VIP lounge with her cleavage artfully displayed, and her handmaidens in tow. Jennifer didn't know the other two women, but they were not all that different from the ones Tracey brought to Nathan's parties. The women Nathan called Brides of Dracula. Somehow ancient and ageless, but perfectly preserved. Divorcées with expensive clothes and no visible means of support. Ten more years and another divorce, and Tracey might be a full member of the club. Maybe she would find Ex-Husband Number Three in the VIP lounge.

"Agnes and Marisol," Tracey said, as she glided past Jennifer on her way toward Mr. Bigwig.

"Oh, going straight for the gold?" Agnes or Marisol said.

"Go big or go home," Tracey whispered.

When she reached the balcony, she inserted herself into the *tête à tête* between Mr. Bigwig and Mr. Kraus. Within two minutes, she had them both leaning in toward her. A waiter cruised by to prime her martini hand. Agnes/Marisol followed suit. One skimmed Mr. Carnelon, and the other snagged a paunchy lawyer wearing a Cartier watch with his weekend casual clothes.

Watching the three women ooze effortlessly into the gaps of the party, Jennifer wasn't sure how to feel about her role in their presence. Did this make her a pimp? Was she okay with that? Did she have the energy to care? No.

Belatedly, Jennifer thought of Carrie. She wasn't Dracula's Bride material, but if she wasn't back with Nathan, maybe she would like to come to the party, too. On her way to the command post, Jennifer dialed Carrie's number, but got her voicemail. She left a message, and then Lucas called with her next mission. A pallet of propane tanks delivered to the wrong place and needed at the food pavilion.

The whole day melted away like that. An endless circuit from the welcome booths, to the command post, past the stages, to the VIP lounge, back to the command post, with regular interruptions for emergencies and check-ins via walkie-talkie with the security head, who was making a similar but less glamorous circuit.

At one point, Jennifer snagged a handful of hors d'oeuvres from the VIP lounge and choked them down with the dregs of a bottle of tonic water. She was past the point of trying to impress anyone. With giant sweat rings under her arms, what did it matter if she got caught guzzling out of a two-liter?

After the last act left the main stage, the party in the streets grew more chaotic, as drunks looked for their cars or a last-minute hookup. Like the awnings for the welcome booths, the extra money spent on security was worth it. Relying on the police exclusively would mean all the misbehavior made it into the newspaper, and in its inaugural year, Bay Day didn't need bad publicity.

Sometime after three o'clock, Jennifer coasted home in a daze of elation and low blood sugar. Whatever problems had preceded it, Bay Day was a success. She had her tired feet and a Caribbean honeymoon as proof.

Finding the apartment empty, she was surprised and then concerned. Where was Kevin? She tried his phone again, but he didn't answer. She had intended to take a shower and go straight to bed, but not knowing where he was, she paced, trying to decide what to do. She dialed Nathan's number but it went straight to his voicemail. Just as she was starting to get frantic, the front door opened and Kevin walked in.

"Well, crap," he said. "I missed you at every turn."

"I was starting to worry." Jennifer went to hug him but got a side hug, where he squeezed her with one arm while he did something else with the other. In this case, he was looking at his phone.

"I went down to see if I could meet up with you. Took me forever to find parking, and then my phone battery crapped out."

"You should have come up to the VIP lounge, I would have found you there."

"I know, I know! But...." He tapped his phone against his forehead. "Like an idiot, I forgot where you told me it was going to be. So I basically wasted the whole night wandering around looking for you."

"Silly, you should have come home and charged your phone. And why'd you drive into that mess?"

"I wasn't thinking." He tucked his phone into his pocket and gave her a full hug. He rocked her back and forth the way he did when he was in a good mood, and kissed her on top of her head.

If she hadn't been so tired, she might have led him on to something more, but instead she fished the travel agency envelope out of her pocket. As he looked over the details, Kevin gave a long, low whistle of admiration.

"This is going to be so awesome," he said. "I can't wait."

After all his efforts to talk her out of a long honeymoon, now he was excited about it. Part of her felt cranky about his sudden reversal, but she was mostly relieved. They had made it out the other side. Bay Day was over and she could finally focus on the wedding. They were going to be so happy together.

CHAPTER THIRTY-SEVEN

Olivia

AT TUESDAY STAFF meetings, Pastor Lou started offering prayers for Rich, even before Olivia could ask. She could tell how quickly gossip worked its way through the church from the way sympathy took on the taint of horror. People who had been unstintingly concerned for Rich and the Holley family on the first day grew more circumspect once they knew Rich had put someone else in the hospital, too. The condolences shifted from *I'm so sorry* to *It's so horrible*.

Olivia didn't blame them. She was horrified, too.

Mr. Holley spoke to the police and to Mr. Colton at the workshop, but they had more questions than answers. What had started the fight? Who had done what to whom? Nobody seemed to know. Mr. Colton had been in the office when it happened, and of the three other employees who witnessed the fight, two were blind and the other was non-verbal.

Only Brian and Rich knew what had happened, so it was a matter of waiting for one or both of them to recover enough to talk to the police. The whole first week, Rich was unconscious, and the doctor couldn't say what level of damage he had sustained. By the second week, he was sometimes conscious, but not lucid.

After his motorcycle accident, he had been unable to communicate, so they'd had no way of knowing if he understood what happened. This time, he didn't seem to have lost all his words, but it was clear he didn't understand what was happening. The police removed the handcuffs, but when he regained consciousness, the nurses put restraints on him to keep him from getting out of bed or hitting people.

When he muttered, "Prison," Mrs. Holley interpreted that as a fear of going to prison, but Olivia wondered if Rich believed he was already in prison. Maybe that was why he kept yelling at the nurses.

At least Rich regained consciousness, even if what he said made no sense. He told the police a bear attacked him. Then later, that an asteroid hit his head.

Brian remained unconscious. And alone. Olivia sometimes walked by ICU in the evening, peering down the dim corridor. The only time she saw someone outside Brian's room, it was Davina and Mr. Colton from Forward/Ability. Olivia approached to ask, "Is he okay? Is he getting any better?"

"Not that the doctors can tell," Mr. Colton said.

"They're not sure he'll wake up at all." Davina turned away and started toward the elevators, before Olivia could respond.

"It's a terrible situation." Mr. Colton squeezed Olivia's shoulder. For a moment, he looked after Davina's retreating back, then said, "I hope Rich is doing okay."

"He's awake, but he's not making much sense. What exactly happened?" Olivia hoped it sounded neutral rather than desperate.

"I don't think—I think it's better if we don't talk about it. Our attorney doesn't want us to discuss it, because of the legal issues."

"Oh, okay. I'm sorry."

Olivia never saw anyone else visit Brian. Not that she was there every moment of the day, but it seemed unlikely that people would visit during the day but not in the evenings.

At the next staff meeting, where Olivia once would have hunkered down in her pew, half-praying, half-drowsing, she cleared her throat and said, "Please pray for Brian, my brother's coworker."

Pastor Lou added Brian to the flow of his prayer, and Olivia focused all of her energy into that prayer. *Please let Brian be okay.*

Please let Brian be okay. She wanted Rich to be okay, too, but it seemed more pressing for Brian to get better, because if Brian didn't get better, what would happen to Rich? Whatever happened, it would be Olivia's fault for not doing more to prevent their fight.

The prayer for Brian became a mantra, as persistent as the need to check her fingernails for chipped polish. She focused on her prayer so intently that when her office phone rang, she slammed the file drawer closed and snapped off her thumbnail. As she stared in disbelief at the sheared off nail, the phone rang again. Stuffing her throbbing thumb into her mouth, she picked up the phone and mumbled, "This is Olivia."

"Olivia, there's a police officer here to see you," Bernadette said.

A police officer. Olivia shivered under her sweater.

"I'll be there in a second."

She put the phone down, but didn't go out to the lobby immediately. First she took out her clippers and trimmed off her ragged thumbnail. It looked blunt and offensive, like an outward manifestation of her guilt.

In the lobby, the policeman wasn't in uniform. He wore a suit and handed her a business card as he introduced himself. Detective Vance.

"Is there somewhere we can go to talk, Miss Holley?"

"Um, I think the conference room is open."

It was empty and dark, but rather than turn on the overheads, Olivia pulled up the blinds. She didn't want to be alone in the room with the detective, and the open blinds let the outside in.

"Miss Holley, I wanted to ask you a few questions about your brother."

"Okay."

The questions started out as she expected. How had Rich seemed lately? Had there been changes in his behavior? Did he get along with his co-workers? Any problems at home?

It distressed Olivia that her first instinct was to lie.

"Back before Christmas, he went through this period of not

wanting to ride the van to work. Forward/Ability has a van, and they pick Rich up, but for a while he wouldn't ride in it."

"Do you know why?" Detective Vance said.

"He got in an argument with somebody at work."

"Do you know who that might have been?"

"I don't know the people he works with very well," Olivia said. Technically, that was true, but it avoided the real meat of the question. A natural liar, like her mother.

"But you were the one driving him to work when he refused to take the van?"

"Yes."

"And Rich didn't tell you about the argument?"

"He said that someone was being a jerk."

For several minutes, the detective looked down at his notes, glancing back through the pages that preceded his conversation with Olivia.

"Did he ever mention Brian Kelly to you?"

Her stomach lurched up to her throat. Under the table, her forefinger tested out the rough edge of her shorn off thumbnail, like the unpleasant sensation would help her.

"I'm sure he did, but I don't remem—"

"Davina Rogers said that you came into the office at some point and spoke to Brian Kelly," the detective said, relieving Olivia of the temptation to lie. "So you've met Brian Kelly?"

"Yes."

"And what did you talk about?" When Olivia didn't answer, the detective tapped his ballpoint against the paper, as though the ink had stopped flowing. He glanced up at her and said, "Did you and Brian talk about Rich?"

"Yes. He'd hurt Rich's feelings and I asked him to be nicer. That was all."

"Did you ask Bill Colton about having Rich or Brian reassigned to a different place in the workshop?"

"Yes. He said it wasn't necessary. He never called me back," Olivia said, hearing the defensiveness in her voice.

"Miss Holley, I'd like to show you something to see if you recognize it."

Detective Vance shifted the notepad to reveal a file underneath. After Olivia nodded her agreement, he opened the folder and took out a photograph.

Framed by a ruled square on a white backdrop, the object in the photo appeared to be a broken table leg and a length of chain. Honestly puzzled by it, Olivia turned it upside down. Yes, a table leg, but not broken. Cut in two. The chain was attached with what looked like eyebolts, one screwed into each section of table leg, with the chain strung between.

"Is this a...."

"It's pretty much what it looks like. A homemade pair of nunchucks."

"*Nunchakus*," Olivia corrected. Rich had owned some when they were kids. He'd been quite proficient with them until he got in trouble for using them on the crepe myrtles in the back yard.

"You do recognize them, then?"

"No. I know what they are, but I've never seen these before."

"You've never seen them in Rich's possession?" the detective said. "In his room maybe?"

"No."

"You're sure? Absolutely sure?"

"I'm sure. Were these what—I mean, is this what was used? In the fight?"

"Yes."

The table legs were stained a dark oak, but there were a few darker stains on the wood as well. Blood? Olivia felt light-headed at the prospect. The detective withdrew another photo from his file and laid it on top of the other.

On the right side of the second photo were yellow and white stripes painted on concrete next to a pair of green metal feet. The safety zone around one of the pieces of woodworking equipment at Forward/Ability. A glistening red-black puddle of blood took up the center of the photo. Soaking in the middle were the table-leg *nunchakus*. Bits of skin and long blond hair clung to one end.

The next photo was so grotesque, Olivia knew she would be able to recall it for the rest of her life. A lumpy jack-o-lantern of a head, with slits for eyes and swollen, black cheeks. The skull was covered in pulpy divots that left bald spots in freshly shorn hair. It didn't even look human. Brian.

Before her brain could check her response, Olivia stood up from the conference table, knocking her chair to the floor. She backed away and found herself against the door. Desperate, she fumbled at the handle.

With the air going thin around her, she yanked the door open hard enough to stub it against her own toe. She plunged into the hallway and ran into someone. Without stopping to see who it was, she kept walking.

She didn't know where she was going, but sunlight and escape beckoned from the lobby doors down the hallway. Behind her, the detective was calling, "Miss Holley! Miss Holley! I didn't mean to upset you. Calm down!"

Then someone else said, "Olivia? What's the matter? What happened?"

A hand grabbed her arm and she fought back, slapping her open palm uselessly at empty air. An alarm sounded and two hands grasped her shoulders and pulled her around. She staggered backward and her head knocked against something hard. The alarm kept ringing.

"Miss Holley! It's okay. You're okay."

The detective pushed her toward one of the lobby chairs.

"Sit down, Miss Holley. Sit down."

Olivia sat down hard, and slowly the outside world began to seep back in around the edges of her panic. What she had thought was an alarm was the telephone ringing, unanswered while Bernadette stood behind the front desk with her mouth hanging open.

"Is she okay? What happened?" That was Pastor Zach, the new associate minister. He held a hand over his nose and when he took it away, there was blood on his upper lip.

"I'm afraid I gave her a shock," the detective said.

"Who are you?" Pastor Zach said.

They swapped introductions and Bernadette brought a handful of tissues for Pastor Zach to wipe his nose. His first week at the church and this was his welcome?

"I'm so sorry," she whispered. "I'm sorry, Pastor Zach. Did I hit you?"

"Just with your head. It's okay. I stuck my nose in where it didn't belong. Are you alright?"

Olivia nodded, although her miscellaneous injuries were beginning to announce themselves. Smashed thumb, stubbed toe, and the back of her skull where it had made contact with Pastor Zach's head.

"Miss Holley, could we finish...." the detective said.

"No. I don't want to talk to you anymore. I wish you'd go." She felt woozy, but strangely calm.

"I understand. I'm sorry about what happened."

He went back to the conference room to get his notepad and his folder of pictures. When he returned to the lobby, he stood in front of Olivia.

"I'll leave you my card, in case you think of anything else you want to tell me."

He held the card out, and when she didn't take it, he laid it on the arm of the chair. After he left, she threw the detective's card into the trash.

CHAPTER THIRTY-EIGHT

Jennifer

JENNIFER WOKE UP untethered on the Monday after Bay Day. She had a never-decreasing list of promotional events to be prepped—home tours, open houses, meetings about The Lofts—but the great monolith of Bay Day no longer provided sustaining pressure. Like a deep sea creature brought to the surface, Jennifer felt quivery with the sudden space for expansion.

The wedding approached, only six weeks away. In the madness of Bay Day, Jennifer had made wedding decisions with a precision and efficiency that she could no longer muster. Faced with a mound of RSVPs, she shuffled them like playing cards, struggling to tally up the final numbers for the caterer.

For the first time since Kevin learned about her secret, she drove to the muffler shop, in time to see the minivan roll into the driveway. The foster mother got out first in her usual sweat pants. The blond girl hopped out of the front passenger's seat, her head down over a handheld game. Then the back door rolled open and the two brothers and their sister jumped out. Jennifer waited for Shanti to come out next, but the younger brother heaved the door closed and dashed up to the front door. No Shanti. Was she home sick?

On Tuesday, Jennifer tried again, with the same result: no sign of Shanti coming home from school. Trying a different tack, she went early on Wednesday morning, and saw the progression from the house. First, the foster father driving away in his truck. Then the foster mother and the four kids loading into the minivan. Were they leaving Shanti home alone? Jennifer thought back to her own childhood, but couldn't remember being left home sick by herself before middle school. One of her parents had always stayed home with her.

Knowing that Kevin would label her behavior "crazy," Jennifer pulled out of the muffler shop and turned into the foster family's driveway. Going up the sidewalk to the house, she tried out different phrases in her head. *I was a friend of your mother's. I knew your mother.* She regretted not having anything to excuse her presence, like a late birthday card. Not completely sure what she would say, Jennifer knocked.

After waiting a few minutes, she knocked again, but no one came to the door. Maybe Shanti wasn't supposed to answer the door when she was home alone. She might be inside, listening to Jennifer knock. Walking down the length of the porch, Jennifer came to the end of the big front window and found a few of the blind segments turned backwards. She glanced around, and then put her hand up to the glass to peer in.

She had a view of the edge of a recliner and an entertainment center. The television was dark, which seemed odd. All Jennifer had done when she stayed home from school sick was watch TV. Shanti must not be there.

Returning to the car, Jennifer backed around the side of the house and turned around. As she pulled into the street, she saw something unsettling lying in the ditch next to the storm drain across the street. Pulling back into traffic, she returned to the muffler shop.

She crossed the parking lot to the edge of the ditch, where a muddy drop-off drained rainwater away from the trailer park to the east of the muffler shop. The flash of white that had caught her eye from across the street was round, cantaloupe-sized.

As she worked her way down the incline into the ditch, spring mud squelched onto her toes through the cutwork of her Jimmy Choos. She should have backtracked and tried to salvage the shoes, but she knew what was in the ditch. The soccer ball she'd sent to Shanti for Christmas. Before it had come to rest in a ditch full of mud, Shanti had valued it enough to write her name on it in magic marker. The letters were childishly irregular but large. A stamp of ownership. The ball's whole bottom half was muddy, but Jennifer picked it up and carried it back to her car.

She was leaning into the trunk, in search of something to clean the ball with when she heard someone approach.

"You got a problem, lady?"

The man was a muffler shop employee according to his maroon t-shirt, which had *Manny's Mufflers* emblazoned in white script. He was forty-ish with tattoos on his brown arms, and one on his neck. Maybe he was Manny.

"I—no, I'm fine. I saw this in the ditch and thought I better rescue it," Jennifer said, carelessly bumping the muddy ball against her skirt.

"Uh, okay. You come around here a lot. Just looking for soccer balls?"

"No, no." She'd been stupid to think the people at the muffler shop wouldn't notice her. Possibly even the foster family had noticed. Manny was waiting for her to explain herself. "Do you know the people who live across the street there?"

"What's it to you? You ain't a cop. You a private eye or something?" Manny said.

"No. I'm Jennifer. One of the kids who lives over there, they're her foster family. I knew her mother, who got killed last year. Sometimes I come by, so I can make sure Shanti's okay. That's the girl. I like to check on her."

"You park here to look at her?"

"I know that seems weird."

"Yeah, you was a man, coming around watching a little girl, I'd kick your ass."

"I'm not a weirdo. Just a friend. But I don't know the foster family," Jennifer said. "Do you see them? The kids playing over in the yard?"

"Sure, they out there all the time. Foster kids, huh? I wondered how come they had the white girl and the black girl and the three little beaners." He grinned.

"The little black girl. That's Shanti."

"Oh, yeah? I seen her, out there playing." His gaze dropped to the muddy soccer ball. "That hers? Think I seen them kicking it around."

"I gave it to her for Christmas. That's why I wanted to get it out of the ditch."

"Oh, okay. Well, you know, seeing you park here, I just wondered what was up."

Manny took a step back, about to return to the shop. Before he could get too far away, Jennifer said, "Have you seen her lately?"

He shrugged.

"I came on Monday and Tuesday, and I didn't see her. Or this morning."

"I don't pay so much attention." He frowned for a moment, gazing at the soccer ball in contemplation. "The two boys mostly is all I seen."

"What about the week before? I didn't come then," she said.

"I know. You been gone a while. Was surprised to see you back again today. But I don't know if I seen her then. Like I said, I don't pay so much attention. Just see 'em out the front window sometimes."

"Thank you," Jennifer said. "I'm sorry about being a bother, parking here and stuff."

"No, it's cool." He shot her a quick grin before turning and walking to the shop door. When he got there, he called to her: "You know, she might've went to a new foster home. That shit happens." It sounded like the voice of experience.

"Thank you!" The idea had crossed Jennifer's mind, and it was the reason she'd gone into the ditch to retrieve the ball. If Shanti had to leave suddenly, maybe she hadn't been able to get the ball before she left. Jennifer found a plastic shopping bag in the trunk and slid the muddy ball into it.

As she drove back to the condo to change clothes, she scrolled through her phone contacts with her muddy hand. She was glad she hadn't deleted Marco Parmiento's phone number yet. When she told him what she wanted, he said, "I won't charge you for this one, doll. It'll just take a quick phone call to my guy at DCF. Probably have it back to you by tomorrow."

At home, before she changed clothes, she popped the soccer ball into the tub and scrubbed the mud off. When she finished, it was ready to give back to Shanti.

CHAPTER THIRTY-NINE

Jennifer

AS PROMISED, MR. Parmiento called on Thursday, while Jennifer was walking clients around a property. They were opening an art gallery. She excused herself out of the booming confines of a loft with thirty foot ceilings. The only place to go was the loft's elevator, where Jennifer got the phone to her ear on the last ring.

"Hey, doll," Marco said, making her wonder how they'd gotten on such familiar terms. She imagined him as one of the Mario Brothers. A paunchy little Italian man with a mustache.

"Hi. Did you find out anything?"

"Nothing new. My guy at DCF says she's with the same foster family. Amelia and Dan Vanderbilt."

"But I haven't seen her there."

"You been going by, huh?"

"I didn't for a while. Things have been crazy the last few months. But I went by on Monday, and she wasn't at the house. Are you sure they haven't moved her to a new foster family?" Jennifer said.

"Guy faxed me a copy of her file. Social worker visits her every month. Looks like he signed off on a visit on Tuesday."

"So, this week?"

"This Tuesday. Reports Shanti's fine. You sure she wasn't there?"

"I don't know." Shanti could have been home in bed. That

wasn't great, but probably it wasn't illegal to leave her home alone.

"You want me to go around and ask? I can go buzz their doorbell, if you want."

"No. I don't know. I'll see if she's there next week."

"Okay, doll. You play it how you want. Just let me know if you want me to go by. And you know, if you decide you want a job. I can always use somebody who likes sitting around in cars watching people."

He said it as a joke, but it made Jennifer blush.

When she stepped back into the loft, she found the clients whispering to each other in the kitchen. She hoped that meant they were close to a decision, but they were looking over a print out of a different property. Another phone call, another drive, another property. In all, she showed them three more places before they were done for the day.

After she dropped them back at their own car, Jennifer debated her next step. If she drove over to East Tampa now, she wouldn't get there until after six. The dinner hour. The Vanderbilts might be eating, but they would be at home. Without another thought, she pulled out of the parking garage and headed north.

It wasn't until she saw the minivan parked in the Vanderbilt's driveway that she knew she was brave enough to do what she needed to do.

Jennifer expected the foster mother, Amelia, but the Latina girl answered the door. It seemed like good luck. Kids were usually more open.

"Hi. My name's Jennifer. Is Shanti here?"

"Not here," the girl said.

"Where is she?"

"Gone."

"Is your mother here?" When the girl didn't answer, Jennifer amended it to, "Your foster mother?"

The girl nodded and walked away from the door. She left it standing open, so Jennifer stepped into the front room. The house was clean but shabby. The plaid couch sagged in the middle, and the coffee table was splintered on one end, like it had been chewed by a dog.

Down the hallway, the girl shouted, "Amelia?"

The foster mother appeared in the passage to the living room and said, "What can I do for you?"

"Hi. My name is Jennifer Palhete. I'm a friend of Shanti's mother. I just wanted to stop by and see her."

Amelia frowned and flicked her braid back over her shoulder.

"She's not here anymore. Some DCF caseworker took her."

"When did they take her?" Jennifer felt so deflated she couldn't control her reaction. Her face sagged and her shoulders drooped.

Amelia rolled her eyes, annoyed.

"I dunno. Two months ago."

"Two months? That can't be right," Jennifer said.

"What's going on?" Mr. Vanderbilt—Jennifer didn't remember his first name—asked from the kitchen doorway. He was balding with a dense salt and pepper beard that framed his scowl.

"She's here looking for Shanti," his wife said.

"You with DCF?"

"No, I'm a friend of her mother's," Jennifer said.

"I was just *telling* her that DCF came and took Shanti a while back," Amelia said.

Mr. Vanderbilt grunted.

"You don't know for sure when DCF took her away?"

"Why don't you ask them?" he said.

"I did. They told me she was here." Now Jennifer was annoyed.

"That's bullshit. They came and took her. It was back in March," said Amelia.

"That can't be right," Jennifer said.

Mr. Vanderbilt stepped out of the kitchen and crossed to stand beside his wife.

"You need to leave now. You don't have any business here."

Jennifer turned, about to go, when she saw the coat hooks mounted behind the front door. They were crowded full of sweaters and windbreakers, including a bright red hoody with fleece trim. Shifting the coats beside it, she pulled the jacket out.

"You let her go without her coat?" It was a ridiculous accusation in May in Florida, except that in March, when they claimed she had left, there would have been mornings when Shanti needed a sweater.

"I told you to get out," Mr. Vanderbilt said.

"I'm going."

As Jennifer walked back to her car, she felt the Vanderbilts watching her. Getting into the car, she tossed the hoody onto the passenger seat, and the sight of the hoody and the soccer ball together was too much. She took out her phone and called Marco Parmiento. He answered without preliminaries: "So, you decide you want me to go around to check on the little girl?"

"Not quite, Mr. Parmiento."

"Call me Marco, doll."

Mr. Vanderbilt stood inside his front door, glaring out at Jennifer.

"I went myself. To the foster family. And she's not there. They said DCF came and took her away in March."

Marco made a low humming noise and then grunted. "Hang on, lemme look."

He came back a minute later, clearing his throat.

"Yeah, like I told you, this caseworker for DCF, his report shows him visiting Shanti at the Vanderbilts' house every month, going all the way back to—December. Visits in January, February, March, April, and this Tuesday."

"Well, if he says he saw her on Tuesday, he's lying. I was here on Tuesday and she wasn't. She's not here now. Can that happen?"

"I imagine caseworkers lie sometimes," Marco said.

"But could she be moved to a new foster family, and have it not be in her file?"

"That seems unlikely. If DCF moved her, that'd be in the file."

"The coat I sent her for Christmas, it was still in their house. And the soccer ball I gave her."

"What are you thinking?"

"I think something happened to her. I think she's supposed to be here and she's not. Or she's there and they won't let me see her for some reason. Like, I don't know, maybe they hurt her. I think they're lying. Or the DCF caseworker is lying. Or maybe both." As Jennifer said it, she looked up and saw Mr. Vanderbilt open the front door and step onto the porch.

Marco let out a long sigh.

"What should I do? How do I find out where she is?" Jennifer said.

"I hate to say this, but if you think something hinky is going on...." He faded off and Jennifer heard him breathing at the other end of the line. Hesitating.

"What?"

"How sure are you? I don't mean what you *think*. I mean in your *gut*, how sure are you that something's wrong there?"

Aware of Mr. Vanderbilt watching her and Marco waiting for her to answer, Jennifer's throat closed up. Before she could stop them, a handful of tears escaped, and her nose began to run.

"In my gut?" The tears came faster as it sank in. Suppressing a sniffle, she said, "I'm sure."

"Okay, doll. You got a pen? Paper?"

"Yes." She expected him to give her someone to call at DCF, but what he gave her was a case number.

"That's Shanti's file with DCF. Call the police and tell them you want to report a missing child. They won't want to hear it, and they won't want to follow up with DCF after hours, but if you dig in, they'll do it. You may not get any answers today, but it'll start the ball rolling."

"Okay." She took a deep breath, trying to prepare herself. "Who do I call at the police? What number?"

"Doll, just dial 9-1-1. That's what I mean about being sure. If you're sure something's wrong, this is worth calling 9-1-1 for."

He was right. If something had happened to Shanti, it was an emergency. After Jennifer hung up with Marco, she dug in her purse for a tissue to wipe her eyes and blow her nose. She was about to dial 9-1-1, when Mr. Vanderbilt came down the steps and approached her car.

"You better get the hell out of here," he snarled.

"Where's Shanti?" Jennifer said.

"If you don't get off my property, I'm gonna call the cops."

"Go ahead. I wish you would. Go call the police and tell them I'm trespassing."

The last of her doubt dissipated at his reaction. He still looked angry, but the aggressive set to his mouth went away. He wasn't going to call the police.

"You better get off my property," he said, but he was already retreating to the porch. Once there, he shot another glare at Jennifer before going inside and slamming the door.

She pushed the Call button on her phone and a moment later was talking to an emergency operator.

The police responded more quickly than Jennifer expected. Thanks to the magic words "missing child," she supposed. In less than ten minutes, two uniformed officers pulled up in a patrol car. Officer Denker was younger than Jennifer and he wore his head shaved and his uniform too tight. Thiessen was older and quieter. He hung back, letting the younger man ask the questions.

Denker must have expected a worried mother, and he wasn't thrilled to find a private citizen reporting a missing foster child. He wrote down the details, but when he finished, he snapped his notepad closed and said, "We'll have someone from DCF come check it out."

Thiessen shook his head. He still held the photo Jennifer had handed him when they arrived. She had kept the picture of Shanti on the playground, because she didn't want to give it to her with her mother's blood smeared on it.

While Denker turned, about to go back to the patrol car,

Thiessen walked toward the Vanderbilts' front door.

From where she waited next to her car, Jennifer couldn't hear the exchange, but she saw the warring emotions on Mr. Vanderbilt's face. Anger and fear. He kept shaking his head, and when his voice rose, it was to say, "Get a warrant then."

On his way down the drive, Thiessen bypassed Jennifer and walked to his patrol car, where he had a conversation that ended with Denker getting on the radio and Thiessen coming back to Jennifer.

"Miss, I'm going to need you to leave. Mr. Vanderbilt says you're trespassing. You just need—"

"That's it? This little girl is missing and all you care about is me being parked in his shitty driveway?"

The way Thiessen winced, Jennifer knew she was being loud. *Hysterical*, that was the word Kevin used when he wanted her to shut up, but Thiessen didn't say it.

"Miss Palhete, I understand you're upset. And I'm worried, too. If what you're saying is true, there's something wrong here. I don't want things to get confused. Legally speaking. I want us to be able to focus on this girl, not whether you're trespassing."

"I can't go home until I know something."

"You don't need to go home, just off the Vanderbilts' property. Maybe you could go across the street there?"

Jennifer turned to look, as though she weren't already intimately acquainted with the muffler shop.

"We've got a call into DCF," Thiessen said. "We're going to get this sorted out. We need to get the girl's info into the system, so we can start looking for her. If you'll go over there and wait, I'll let you know what's going on, okay?"

"Okay. Thank you."

Thiessen opened her car door and guided her into the driver's seat. Jennifer had a moment of fear as Denker backed the police car into the street to let Jennifer out of the drive. What would she do if the cops simply drove away? Thiessen, however, remained where he was, waiting for Denker to pull the patrol car back into the Vanderbilts' driveway.

From her vantage point at the muffler shop, she watched Thiessen pace back and forth, occasionally talking into the radio on his shoulder.

It seemed like an eternity, but after an hour a plain beige sedan pulled in behind the patrol car. Thiessen approached and introduced himself to the woman who stepped out. She was dressed in what Jennifer thought of as sloppy business casual: rumpled skirt, baggy cardigan, and flats. The woman slung a big purse over her shoulder and then hauled a briefcase out of the back seat. She followed Thiessen to the Vanderbilts' front door, where she was allowed in. The police officer remained outside.

In the next hour, two more cars arrived and two more people went into the Vanderbilt home. Then another patrol car came. Seeing all the activity and not knowing what was going on made Jennifer so agitated that she got out of the car and unconsciously began to mirror Thiessen's pacing. While she was out walking, a blue and white Mustang pulled into the muffler shop lot. The man who got out walked straight to her and held out his hand.

"Jennifer, right?"

"Yes, and you are…"

"Marco Parmiento. Nice to meet you, doll." He squeezed her hand warmly between both of his. He was Italian, but not short or pudgy. He was tall and wiry, with a neat black mustache and an oily black ponytail touched with gray at the temples.

Marco jerked his thumb over his shoulder toward the Vanderbilt house.

"You see this shit? You just pulled off something even the governor hasn't been able to do—you lit a fire under DCF. My buddy over there says the phones are ringing off the hook. Pulling files. Looking at visit logs."

"What about Shanti? Where is she?" Jennifer said. For all the activity, all the fuss, there should be some news already.

"Nobody seems to know. DCF says she's here. Foster family says DCF took her away. You were right to call the police, because that little girl is really and truly missing."

"How could she just disappear?"

Marco looked at Jennifer for a long moment. In a soft voice, he said, "I don't imagine she *disappeared*."

Jennifer knew he meant to break the news in the nicest way possible, but it felt like a punch in the stomach. She walked slowly backward until she bumped against the side of her car, something solid to lean against.

"What are the police doing?" she said.

"Well, so far, a whole lotta nothing. The Vanderbilts won't let the cops in the house, so they're waiting on a search warrant. How many civilians have you seen go in?"

"Three people with brief cases. From DCF maybe? A woman, about forty, an older man, and a younger man."

"They all still in there?"

"Just the woman."

Marco's smile showed gold in his teeth. "You got a good eye for this kinda work."

"I just want to know what's happening."

"I feel for you. Now, I gotta go, but I'll check back with you if I hear anything, okay? I'd tell you to go home, but I been married enough times, I know not to tell a woman what to do."

After Marco left, there was a lull in the action. No one came or went, no matter how hard Jennifer tried to will something to happen.

As darkness fell, the street lamp next to the muffler shop flickered on, jarring her out of her reverie. She slid into the driver's seat and checked the time on her phone. Almost eight-thirty, and her phone cheerfully informed her that she had two missed calls, both from Kevin, but no voicemail.

Then she remembered that it was Wednesday. He must have called to ask about church, and she hadn't answered. He'd probably gone by himself.

She started the car and pulled into traffic before she called Kevin back. It would help to sell the lie, whatever lie she came up with. She didn't even consider the truth, because she didn't want to disturb the fragile peace they'd made around the topic of Shanti. Jennifer hoped she would get his voicemail, but when he answered, she gave him comforting lies. Lucas, demanding; clients, crazy; traffic, snarled; phone battery, dead, charging while she drove.

"It's okay," he said. "Why don't I pick up some Thai and meet you at home?"

"Are you at church?" She'd been prepared for his anger, so she hardly knew how to answer his calm.

"No, I didn't go. I had a long day, too. What do you want? Some coconut chicken soup?"

"Please. And some *yum woon sen*."

"Which is that?" he mumbled. He wasn't listening, distracted by something else.

"It's the noodle salad. I better drive. I'll see you in a bit."

"Okay, yeah. Bye."

As she drove, Jennifer kept seeing Mr. Vanderbilt's face, snarling at her.

Angry. But afraid.

Afraid of what?

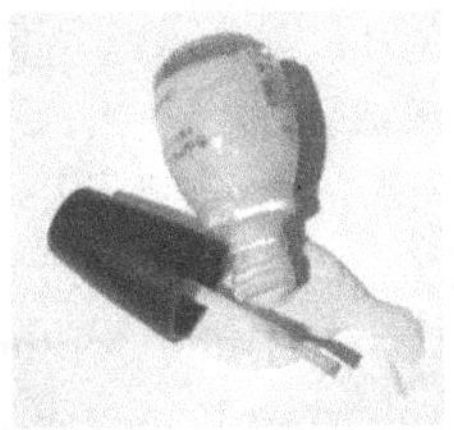

CHAPTER FORTY

Olivia

THE NEW COPIER repairman arrived toting his toolbox and complaining about the heat.

"What heat?" Olivia said as she led him to the copy room.

"Oh, not you, too," he groaned. "Everybody keeps telling me it's going to get worse."

"It's only May. It's going to get a lot worse."

"This isn't what I was promised."

"What exactly were you promised?" Normally, Olivia would have been on her way already, but the repairman winked at her as he squatted in front of the open copier. As flirtations went, it was small, but Olivia congratulated herself on making an effort.

"I'm pretty sure my contract promised white sandy beaches and girls in bikinis."

"That's the Miami office. This is Tampa," Olivia said.

"Man, that's a cruel trick. I traded in my moose for this."

Clueless but amused, Olivia giggled. "Your moose? Where are you from?"

"Alaska. Hi, I'm David."

"Olivia. Sorry Florida isn't working out how you planned." She intended to leave him to his work then, but as he ducked his head to consider the copier's innards, he said something that skewered her to the spot.

"On the upside, apparently Tampa's got curvy secretaries with serious hair." It hung in the air for a few seconds, and then he bobbed his head back up and smiled.

Olivia blushed and stammered, "I'll let you get to work."

"I'll see you when I'm done. Where's your office?"

"Just, um, down this hall and to the left." Olivia scurried away, before she could embarrass herself any further.

An hour later, he came past her cubicle and said, "It was the imaging drum. All fixed up now."

"Great, thank you so much."

When he handed her the clipboard to approve the repairs, she pulled a pen out of her hairdo and signed.

"So, do you keep other things in there or just pens?" David said.

"Pencils, too. And a pad of post-it notes."

For half a second, he frowned quizzically, reminding Olivia why she so rarely made jokes. People couldn't tell if they were jokes. Then David laughed and pulled a business card from his shirt pocket.

"Here. You're part of my route now, so you can call me instead of dispatch."

"Thanks. And try to stay cool."

After he was gone, Olivia stared at the business card. Call him, instead of dispatch? Was that typical? No. Olivia could not remember any copier repairman ever saying that. So, if that wasn't what he meant, what did he mean? Did he want Olivia to call him?

She was trying to decide what to make of the flirtation, as she rode up in the elevator at Tampa General Hospital to meet her parents. She had expected to arrive early, because Mr. Holley would have to leave work and swing by the house to pick up Mrs. Holley, whereas Olivia was only a few blocks away. When the elevator doors opened, though, her parents were sitting in the lobby chairs in front of the nurse's station. Her mother was crying, her eyes red as she crumpled up one wet tissue after another. Mr. Holley looked grim, his lips pinched together. His hands rested on his knees as his enormous belly spilled down between his spread legs. Olivia walked faster, her heels clicking against the waxed linoleum.

"Did something happen?" she said.

"He died." Mr. Holley barked it out.

Olivia ran the twenty feet from the nurse's station to Rich's room. He looked awful, his face bloated and covered in fading bruises, but he was alive.

"Olivia!" In answer to her father's call, she went back down the hallway to her parents. She had run to check on Rich, but returning, she walked slowly, heavy with dread.

"Brian?" she said.

"Yes. He died about four hours ago. Dale says there's a good chance they'll charge Rich with murder. At the very least manslaughter. We're waiting for the sheriff to send someone down. And Dale's on his way."

"He didn't murder him!" Mrs. Holley said. "It was a misunderstanding."

As Olivia tried to push away her memory of what Rich had done to Brian, the image of the homemade *nunchakus* came to her in a flash of recognition. They were so familiar, it felt like she could reach out and take them in her hand.

"I want you to drive your mother home. I'll stay here and wait for Dale," Mr. Holley said.

Her mother protested, or that was what it sounded like to Olivia. It was hard to make out words in the sniffling, whimpering noises, but when she put her arm around her mother's shoulders, Mrs. Holley let herself be led away.

At home, Mrs. Holley wandered around the living room, picking things up and putting them down. Then she went into the kitchen and looked at laundry hampers. She must have abandoned laundry day in midstream to go to the hospital. Olivia opened the washing machine and started putting clothes in.

"You don't need to do that, Livvie."

"It's okay, Mom. I'll just start a load."

With her mother hovering at her elbow, Olivia went through the clothes mechanically, checking pockets for change and candy wrappers. Out of one of her own skirt pockets came a neat white rectangle of paper. For a confusing moment, Olivia thought it was the copier repairman's card. Except that it couldn't be. She had left that card at work, and besides, she'd worn this skirt more than a week ago. Turning it over, she had an even more unnerving thought. The police detective's card was haunting her. She had thrown it away and there it was again.

The irrational thought gave way to memory. Detective Vance had given her two business cards. One when he introduced himself, and a second when he left. She had thrown away the second one, but she'd put the first one in her pocket. Stuffing the card into the pocket of the skirt she wore, she started the washing machine.

"I'm going out to the garage for a minute."

"I'll come with you," Mrs. Holley said.

That was the last thing Olivia needed and she reached for the nearest distraction: the phone. She hit speed dial number one and handed the phone to her mother.

"Here, Mom. You need to talk to Cynthia."

"Oh, I don't want to trouble her. She's so busy."

"You're not troubling her. She needs to know what's going on." Olivia didn't honestly care whether Cynthia knew what was going on, but she got what she needed—space—as soon as Cynthia picked up.

"Oh, honey, it's Mom." Mrs. Holley's face relaxed at the sound of Cynthia's voice. She didn't even look up when Olivia went out the back door.

In the garage, Olivia dragged the ladder over to the storage loft. The ladder swayed under her as she went up, teetering in her high heels on the narrow rungs. The air in the loft was stifling and dusty. Boxes of Christmas decorations sat at the front, the most recently used items. Behind them were boxes of toys and tax records. A mousy stink rolled out of the boxes as Olivia tried to shift them, but then she saw the route someone else had used:

footprints going over the top. Hiking her skirt the way she did to ride on Rindell's motorcycle, Olivia mounted the pile and, on the other side, found what had made those *nunchakus* so familiar.

Standing upright, the table would have reached mid-thigh on Olivia. A table for children. Its top surface, which lay visible to the side, had crayon marks and scratches from the years it served as the Holley kids' project table. It lay on its side, however, because one of its legs had been removed. Olivia ran her hand over one of the remaining legs. Solid oak with simple curves lathed into it. Saw one in half and you would have two ready-made handles for a pair of nunchucks.

She crawled back over the boxes to the ladder. On the ground, panting, she didn't know where to go, but once she left the garage, she kept walking.

An hour later, she had completed a lap of the river park and circled back almost to Mr. Batson's house. For once when she knocked on the door, Rindell answered. His smile faltered when he saw her.

"Olivia, what's wrong?"

"I don't...."

"Come here. Come in here."

The same way she had steered her mother around, Rindell walked Olivia through the living room, and into the kitchen, where Mr. Batson sat at the table. They were in the middle of preparing dinner. There was a pot on the stove and a mixing bowl on the counter.

"I'm sorry. I didn't mean to interrupt."

"You not interrupting. You okay?"

Olivia shook her head. She was not okay.

"You want some dinner? We just about to eat," Mr. Batson said.

"I made some gumbo and we got corn bread coming outta the oven here in a minute." Rindell's hand was steady on her lower back, no longer steering but providing support.

"I don't think I could eat."

"Why don't you lay down for a bit? See if that don't clear your head."

In response to pressure from his hand, Olivia moved toward Rindell's bedroom. He closed the door behind them and guided her to the bed. She sat down, aware of him watching her, but couldn't meet his eyes. Behind them in the kitchen, a timer chimed.

"Can you get that cornbread out?" he called.

"Will do," Mr. Batson said. His chair scraped against the floor and the oven door creaked as he opened it.

Rindell squatted down in front of Olivia and lowered his voice to a whisper.

"Look at you, got your legs all scratched up." His hands were gentle, running down her calves, checking her for injury. That was his job. Then he eased her shoes off and said, "Why don't you lay down? I'll go have my dinner and you rest for a while."

"I'm all dusty. Your sheets."

"They'll wash. Don't you fret about that. Lay down."

She did. Rindell pulled the sheet over her bare legs and went out to eat his dinner. For the first few minutes, Olivia lay there thinking she should go, but weariness crept in, muscle by muscle. She sighed and nestled her head into Rindell's pillow, which smelled of his aftershave, something woodsy. Turning on her side, she let herself go further. After she finished crying, she sank into sleep.

When she woke, it was dark outside. The wedge of light that came in from the kitchen when Rindell opened the door woke her. He closed it immediately and the room was dark again. The bed dipped under his weight when he sat down, and the shift in the mattress left Olivia's belly pressed against his lower back. He probably wanted her to go. To delay that she laid her hand on his thigh, nearly to the crotch of his jeans. She was trying to work up her nerve to move it further when he said, "Olivia, I don't know what to do for you. Can you tell me what's wrong?"

"Will you lie down with me for a while? Then I'll go."

She tensed herself, ready for him to push her hand away, but he did what she asked. He stretched out beside her and drew her into the curve of his armpit before pressing a kiss to her cheek.

"You had you one of them days, huh?" he said.

"My brother."

He kissed her jaw and pulled her closer.

"He doing okay?"

"The guy he beat up—did I tell you?"

"You said he had some kinda accident," Rindell said.

"It wasn't an accident. He got in a fight, and he beat up this guy at work. A blind guy. Rich killed him. My brother beat him up and killed him."

Rindell let out a long breath and squeezed Olivia tightly.

"Goddamn, that ain't good. I'm sorry. If I can do anything for you, you say so, okay?"

"Can we pretend none of the stuff that happened happened? All the stuff with Jennifer and the other things? Can we pretend it never happened?" She had wished it so many times it was embarrassing, but in the dark, she was more afraid of going home than she was of confessing it.

"But it did," he whispered against her neck. It seemed to Olivia that he was trying to say yes and no at the same time.

"But can we pretend it didn't? Just for tonight?"

He kissed her, and after a few minutes of that, he lifted her left knee over his hip. Pushing up her skirt, his hand skimmed up her leg to her panties. For a while, he stroked her through the cotton, and then he pushed it aside and slid his fingers into her. She lay panting against his mouth while he worked his fingers in and out of her. It was two minutes of forgetting, but after she came, she felt disappointed. That was it?

He sat up and turned on the lamp on his nightstand. She closed her eyes against the light, but he was silent until she opened her eyes and looked at him.

"You still wanna pretend?" he said.

"Yes."

Leaving the lamp on, he started kissing her again. His hand found the top button on her blouse and undid it, then the next. Once they were naked, grinding against each other, with the sheets thrown off, it was easy to forget. Olivia erased months of confusion and misery, clinging to him, clutching at his lower back, her legs squeezing the hard muscles of his thighs. Braced above her on one hand, he slipped his other hand to the back of her neck and into her hair, pulling it loose, using it to tilt her face to his. He kissed her deeply and then pressed his face into her neck. They were slippery with sweat together and there was a world of forgetting in the way he said her name. She opened her mouth to answer him, but hesitated. Rindell or DeVaun? In the end, she said neither.

Afterward, an unpleasant memory tried sneak in, but Mr. Batson cleared his throat reproachfully from the kitchen. Rindell laughed against her skin, where his head rested on her breast. Memory receded into the darkness.

At eleven, Rindell got up and showered, then dressed in his uniform.

"I should go," Olivia said, although she had the sheets drawn up to her chin.

Shaking his head, Rindell leaned down to kiss her. His hand slipped under the sheet, stroking her legs, her belly, then her breasts. Drawing his hand back out of the covers, he said, "You oughta get some sleep."

He kissed her forehead, pressing his lips there for a good twenty seconds.

"Okay," she said.

"You forgot a while, didn't you? But not all of it. You can't forget I ain't Rindell."

"I don't know. I'm sorry. I didn't mean…."

"Ain't your fault," he said, but it felt that way. It felt like he had put something very fragile—the truth was that fragile—in her hands and she had dropped it and broken it.

CHAPTER FORTY-ONE

Jennifer

IN A PREVIEW of what it would be like maneuvering her wedding dress down the aisle at Church of the Palms, Jennifer walked from the dressing room to the fitting area, where she climbed the two steps to the dais without being able to see her feet.

"You can't lose any more weight before the ceremony," the dress fitter said around a mouthful of pins, as he marked final adjustments on the gown.

"I won't," Jennifer said, but she felt a thrill at his disapproval. As of that morning, she was two pounds below what she had always considered her *ideal weight*.

"Don't make it too tight. We're going to stuff ourselves with sushi after this," Tracey said.

When Jennifer's phone rang, Tracey squinted at the screen, and said: "Marco Polo?"

"Haha. Parmiento."

Normally, it would have been Carrie who retrieved the phone, but she was too busy tapping out a text message on her own phone, frowning while she did it. Tracey held the phone out, but Jennifer shook her head. She needed to focus on the wedding and not get sidetracked by Marco.

"So who's Marco Polo?" Tracey said.

"Potential buyer for a downtown property. That's why he gets to call me on Saturday." Jennifer had the lie ready in case Kevin ever asked, but she hated to leave it hanging in the air, so she looked for the nearest distraction. "The real question is: who has Carrie been texting all day?"

"Yeah, Carrie. Do you have a new boyfriend or something? Because I know you're not spending all that time texting Nathan," Tracey said, but Carrie wasn't paying attention to them.

"Earth to Carrie, come in Carrie," Jennifer said.

"What?" Carrie's head jerked up.

"Who are you texting?"

"Just a friend."

"And will this friend be your plus-one at my wedding reception?"

Carrie gave Jennifer a brittle smile and stuffed her phone into her purse.

After the dress was pinned to the fitter's satisfaction, Jennifer wished the day was over, but they'd made plans for a girls night. Sushi and drinks at Jacksons. They got a table on the patio, where a breeze came in off the bay. Yachts and sailboats bobbed against the backdrop of the setting sun, like a tourist postcard. On the south end of the patio, twenty or so small tables stood empty with number placards on them. When the waitress came to bring their drinks and get their sushi order, Tracey said, "Are they speed dating tonight?"

"Yeah, but you have to register beforehand. They fill up fast!" the waitress said.

"Oh, I was just wondering. We came here once, didn't we, Carrie?"

Carrie was texting again, and Jennifer had the overwhelming urge to take the phone and throw it over the railing into the water. Kevin was like that, at times so absorbed in his phone that he couldn't make polite conversation.

Tracey lifted her martini glass and said, "To losing weight and looking fabulous in your wedding dress!"

"I'll drink to that." Jennifer raised her glass and they clinked them together without Carrie. On a whim, Jennifer leaned over and put her arm around Tracey, who responded with an enthusiastic hug. Whatever doubts she had had about making Tracey part of the wedding party faded away. She'd already done more than Carrie, the maid of honor.

Of the two, only Tracey seemed interested in the wedding or in anything else. To fill the silence of Carrie's empty presence, Jennifer grilled Tracey about Mr. Bigwig, even though the details made her cringe a little. There had been a *hookup* and promises of a trip to the Hamptons for Memorial Day.

"But don't worry. No matter what he offers to seduce me away, I will be back in time for the wedding."

"You're a doll," Jennifer said, borrowing Marco's word. She had always thought of it as an unpleasant diminution, but applying it to Tracey, it felt warm, affectionate.

Just as the sushi arrived, Carrie got a text that made her exhale loudly in agitation.

"I'm going to the little girls room." She got up from the table and walked away, her phone clutched in one hand.

"What is going on with her?" Jennifer said, as soon as Carrie was out of earshot. She had tried asking Carrie and been ignored.

Tracey picked up a chunk of lobster roll with the chopsticks clutched uneasily in her cigarette hand. Frowning in concentration, she conveyed it to her mouth, which seemed too small but then opened wide, like a snake unhinging its jaw, to admit the sushi.

"I don't think we should talk about it right now," she said, after she swallowed the mouthful.

"Is it Nate? Or some new guy?"

"Seriously, not while she's here."

"But she's not here."

"She's coming back." Tracey pointed with stage drama toward Carrie's purse.

In Carrie's absence, Jennifer and Tracey worked on the sushi. If everything tasted that amazing, Jennifer wouldn't be losing weight.

A few minutes later, Carrie came back. Without a word, she

plopped her purse up on the table, and started to dig through it for her car keys.

"I have to go."

"Why?" Jennifer said. Tracey gave her a meaningful look out of the corner of her eye.

"Something came up with work."

"On Saturday?"

"I don't want to talk about it. Some idiot I have to go rescue."

Jennifer opened her mouth to ask another question and Tracey kicked her under the table.

"I'm sorry, Jenn," Carrie said. She slung her purse over her shoulder and leaned down to give Jennifer a quick hug. "You look gorgeous in your dress. I'll talk to you later."

"Okay, what's up?" Jennifer said, as soon as Carrie had crossed the dimly lit dining room behind them.

Tracey put a finger up to her lips, her shiny red nail polish filling in the gap where sushi had worn away her lipstick. She scurried away on her Prada-clad feet. The sight made Jennifer giggle. What was tiny alcoholic Barbie doing?

Tracey followed Carrie's course through the main dining room, before returning. She looked worried as she sat down and pulled out her cigarette case.

"What's going on?" Jennifer said.

"I wanted to be sure she was really gone."

"Is she?"

Tracey nodded as she lit up and inhaled. She didn't speak until her cigarette was half gone.

"Okay, look, I don't know exactly what's going on, but there's something I need to show you. And I don't know if you should see it here or someplace more private."

"You can show it to me here."

"Yeah, but I don't want you to freak out."

"Why would I freak out?" Jennifer said.

"I know you and Carrie have been friends a long time. I don't want you to hate me after you see this. I'm not some kind of bitch. I didn't go looking for this." Tracey stubbed out her cigarette and brought her hand up to pinch at the bridge of her nose. To Jennifer's astonishment, a tear slipped out of Tracey's eye. She wiped it away immediately, and it left no trace in her make-up.

"I won't hate you. Just show it to me," Jennifer said.

Behind them, a bell rang to start the speed dating and Tracey jumped in her seat. She pulled her phone out of her purse.

"I got this new phone with the camera, see?" She laid it on the table next to Jennifer's sushi plate. "When this happened, I didn't know what to do, so I took a picture."

"Show me."

Tracey nodded and tapped at a few buttons on her phone with one fingernail. Jennifer leaned closer to look. The photo was of another cell phone's screen. The lighting on the patio was too dim, so Jennifer shifted her chair and raised the phone to catch the last of the sunset. The picture showed four entries of a text exchange. With a little more squinting, Jennifer could make out the words.

> *ME: Can you come tonight?*
> *KD: Yeah J is at her event shell be there alnight*
> *ME: I want you. Do you want me?*
> *KD: Cant stop thinking bout u b there in half hour*

Jennifer shook her head, trying to shake off the booze.

"Whose phone is this in the picture?" she said.

"Carrie's." Tracey lit another cigarette. "And you know who KD is."

"I do?"

"KD? Kevin Dean?"

"You can't know that," Jennifer said.

"See? I was worried you'd be mad. Nobody likes the girl who gives you bad news." Tracey tapped her cigarette nervously against the ashtray.

"KD could be anybody."

"KD with a girl whose name starts with *J*? who's going to be at her *event* all night? And the date on the texts was Bay Day, okay?"

"Well, how did you see these texts?" Jennifer's head hurt, on the fast track to a hangover.

"Carrie called me and wanted to go out a couple nights after Bay Day. She was upset about something. Kept looking at her phone. Like she wasn't texting with somebody, she was just looking at a text she already had. Then she got upset and tossed it in her purse. She went out to the restroom, and when the hostess seated some people at the table next to ours, Carrie's purse got knocked off her chair, and her phone fell out. I didn't look at it on purpose! I just—I picked up the phone and the screen came on and I saw the texts. Those were the last texts. That's why she was upset, because those were the last texts from him. So I took the picture. I didn't know what to do, but then today, I think she was texting him."

Tracey puffed hard on her cigarette while Jennifer stared at the texts, trying to decide whether she believed KD was her Kevin. Yes, he used the abbreviation *u* for *you*, but a lot of people did that. The way the texts ran together without punctuation made her mouth go dry. Kevin did that. It drove her crazy. One sentence tumbling into another, leaving her to sort the syntax.

"Do you think that's where she went? To meet him?" Jennifer said. The sushi had turned toxic in her stomach.

Tracey nodded, but looked away, watching the commotion of a table change at the speed dating event. She was crying again. Wiping at her cheeks, she said, "I'm sorry."

"It's not your fault."

"I'm sorry. My second husband cheated on me, so I know what it's like, finding out something like that. It sucks."

"How are we doing here?" the waitress said.

"You want another drink?" said Tracey.

"Just the check," Jennifer said.

"Another Cosmo for me." Tracey lit her next cigarette off the one she'd just finished. "I'll drink it fast."

The waitress brought the check and Tracey's drink at the same time. Jennifer held up a credit card for her to take.

"Oh, wait, wait." Tracey reached for her wallet.

"No, it's on me. It's my wedding dress fitting," Jennifer said.

Saying the words *my wedding* broke the clog in the back of her throat. As the waitress took the bill away, Jennifer started to cry. To her relief, Tracey did what she'd promised. She plucked the lemon rind curl off the rim of her glass, and drained the drink in two gulps. When the waitress came back, Jennifer didn't even try to do math. She scrawled a forty dollar tip and her signature.

"What do you want to do?" Tracey said.

"I want to go see him." Jennifer had expected she might have to justify herself, but the little blonde nodded and waved the waitress back to the table.

"Will you have the valet call us a cab?"

CHAPTER FORTY-TWO

Jennifer

JENNIFER AND TRACEY huddled together in the back of the taxi, their arms locked together.

"So you girls out partying tonight?" the cab driver said.

"Not anymore." The chill in Tracey's voice shut the driver up for the rest of the trip.

"There's her car," she said, as the cab pulled into the apartment complex.

Sure enough, Carrie's car was parked front and center of the building. So much for a work emergency taking her away from dinner.

"This it?" the taxi driver said.

"I don't see his car," Jennifer said. "Will you pull around to the back?"

"Sure thing."

On the backside of Carrie's building, Jennifer saw the thing that destroyed any deniability: Kevin's Lexus.

"Stop here," she said. As soon as the cab came to rest, she opened the door and Tracey scrambled after her.

"Ladies!" the cab driver shouted. "I got fares to make."

Tracey opened her purse and pulled out what looked to Jennifer like a hundred dollar bill. She shoved it at the cab driver and said, "Just wait, okay? You'll get that plus your fare."

"Whatever you say," he said.

Leaving the cab door open behind them, Jennifer and Tracey walked over to the Lexus.

"You're sure it's his car?"

Jennifer looked through the windshield at what hung from the rearview mirror. It had come on a necklace Jennifer got at Gasparilla, but the tribe of brown plastic monkeys on a string of banana-shaped beads had been reduced to a single sun-faded monkey. The last souvenir of their meeting that Kevin couldn't bear to part with. When he got the new Lexus last year, he made the Transferring of the Gasparilla Monkey into a kind of ritual.

"Yes, it's his car," Jennifer said. "Wait here. I'm going up."

Leaving Tracey with the cab, Jennifer walked up the back stairwell of the apartment building, wishing she hadn't had so much to drink. With one hand on the wall and the other on the railing, she stumbled up the cheap, stained carpeting on the stairs. Carrie's apartment was on the third floor, almost to the end of hallway, close to the trash chute.

Light came out from under Carrie's apartment door and touched the toes of Jennifer's shoes. She stared at the peephole, wondering what she would look like to whoever came to the door. Carrie or Kevin? Her first knock was half-hearted, like she didn't want anyone to hear. She knocked again, three times, loud enough that it couldn't be ignored.

When there was no response, she knocked again. It might take a while to get out of bed and come to the door, after all. Eventually, a shadow broke the light coming out from under the door, then retreated. She had been seen.

She was about to knock again, when she remembered something. Reaching into her purse, she pulled out her house keys. At one point Carrie and Jennifer had traded keys, in case one of them ever got locked out. Eliminating all the keys for work, the condo, and her parents' house left Jennifer with Carrie's key. It slipped into the lock easily, but as she turned it, someone inside grabbed the doorknob and twisted.

"Hey, what's up?" Carrie said. She opened the door far enough to peek out. Her hair was tousled and she wore a bathrobe.

"I thought you had a work emergency," Jennifer said.

"Yeah, I—I just don't feel very good. That's why I left. I'm sorry."

"I want to see Kevin." Jennifer laid her hand on the door and pushed until she felt Carrie pushing back.

"What are you talking about?"

"I'm not stupid, Carrie. His car is parked in back."

"I don't know anything about that."

"Stop lying to me!" Jennifer pushed harder on the door. Hard enough that Carrie fell back a step. Her robe slid open to reveal bare skin. As she tried to fix the gaping robe, Jennifer pushed her way into the apartment.

"Why would Kevin be here?" Carrie hugged her robe tightly to herself.

"I just want to see him."

Jennifer swept her gaze over the apartment, looking for any sign of Kevin—his car keys or wallet—but she saw nothing.

The apartment was neat but cluttered. Stacks of books and magazines covered the coffee table, with a few angel figurines crowded in. The window sills were the same, full of ordered ranks of plants, angels, and sun-catchers. Half a dozen tote bags were scattered around, full of Bible Study materials and knitting projects, if Jennifer had to guess.

"Is it okay if I sit down?"

"I'd rather you didn't," Carrie said.

Jennifer ignored that and wobbled her way over to the couch. She shifted a tote bag full of pink and blue yarn, and sat down where it had been.

"Baby afghan?" she asked.

"Yeah, for Nina Domanski's baby."

Jennifer nodded and took out her phone.

Will the cab wait? she texted to Tracey.

The response came back a moment later: *Yes. Everything ok hon?*

Jennifer didn't answer.

"What do you want?" Carrie stood in the kitchen doorway, her arms crossed over her chest. Her eyes jumped back and forth between Jennifer and the closed bedroom door.

"I'm not going until I see Kevin." Jennifer wished she felt as sure as that. She knew her voice was shaking, as much as the rest of her. It was the reason she'd had to sit down. She couldn't keep standing up, feeling as shaky as she did.

"Well, you're going to be waiting here a long time."

Carrie sounded so confident that for an instant, Jennifer almost faltered. Maybe the texts were to a different KD. Maybe someone else with a 2007 Lexus ES 350 in Moon Shell Mica with a plastic monkey hanging from the rearview mirror just happened to know someone who lived at these apartments.

"I'll wait."

Carrie paced between the kitchen and the front door, her bare feet scuffing over the carpet.

"We were friends, weren't we?" Jennifer said. "I mean, I thought we were. Maybe you never really liked me, though."

"Of course, we're friends! I don't know where you got this crazy idea, but it's not true."

"So you're saying if I sit here all night, Kevin is never going to walk out of the bedroom?"

"No, he's not!" Carrie pressed her palms to her forehead, a gesture Jennifer recognized. Carrie had always done that when she was preparing for final exams in college. When she was stressed.

At the five minute mark, Carrie said, "This is crazy, Jenn!"

At the ten minute mark, Jennifer's phone trilled inside her purse. An incoming text message. She debated telling Tracey to go on without her. She could always call for a cab later. As she was about to unzip her purse, the bedroom door opened.

Kevin stepped out, fully dressed, as though that was any counter argument to the fact that he'd been in Carrie's bedroom.

"Jenn, this isn't what it looks like," he said.

"What do you think it looks like?"

Whatever he'd expected her to say, it wasn't that, because his mouth hung open uncertainly.

"We were just talking," he said.

"Ten minutes and that's the best you could come up with?"

"Please, Jenn, don't be mad."

"I'm not mad." She was ashamed, not angry. Kevin would have known what to do if she were yelling and crying.

"Just let me explain," he said, like she'd been trying to stop him.

"Okay, explain." Jennifer folded her hands in her lap and looked up at him expectantly.

"I mean, let me take you home, so I can explain."

"Oh, I think you should explain here. I imagine Carrie wants an explanation, too. Am I right, Carrie? Don't you want to hear Kevin's explanation?"

Carrie stood in the kitchen doorway, looking like she might cry, so that Jennifer felt bad for being so flippant. Except it was funny. Pathetically funny. Carrie was the only one who seemed to be hurting, because she was the only real person involved. Jennifer felt like a cardboard cutout, while Carrie looked absolutely lifelike, clutching at her cheap bath robe, as the first few tears rolled down her cheeks. Poor Carrie. She'd had an affair with the cardboard girl's cardboard fiancé and now the cardboard couple was having a pretend fight in her apartment.

It was so heartbreaking and uncomfortable, Jennifer couldn't stand to witness any more of it. She stood up, still a little shaky, and walked past Carrie to the front door.

"Jenn!" Kevin called after her.

Slamming the door, Jennifer walked as quickly as she could toward the stairwell. As she started down, she heard the door open and Carrie saying, "Wait, Kevin!"

In the parking lot, Tracey leaned against the cab's bumper, smoking. She dropped her cigarette and said, "What happened?"

"Let's go," Jennifer said.

Tracey took the hint; she didn't ask any more questions on the drive back to Davis Islands. Only after the taxi had been paid and they were standing in the parking garage under Jacksons did she say, "What can I do for you, sweetie? Do you need a place to stay tonight?"

"Are you sober enough to drive?"

"I am now."

"Would you drive me out to Wimauma?"

"Where?" Tracey said.

"To my parents' house."

"Oh, absolutely."

Tracey's car smelled of cigarettes and a heavy vanilla air freshener. That was the flimsy reason Jennifer had never been better friends with her. She didn't like the smoking and its olfactory aftermath. Tonight it hardly mattered. She sank down in the seat and rested her head on the door.

The darkness and the steady hum of tires on the road brought back a memory of the trip to Anastasia State Park to see Gayle's sister.

"I totally deserve this," she said.

"That is bullshit! What? Because you've been busy? Well, fuck that. So you've been busy with work." Tracey took a deep breath, about to rail indignantly against Kevin.

"No. I cheated on him."

For a few minutes, Tracey was silent. Then she said, "Oh. Well, did you sleep with Nathan?"

"No!"

"Because that's what Kevin did. He slept with your best friend."

"I don't think she is," Jennifer said.

Tracey pushed in the lighter in the dash, and when it popped back out, Jennifer rolled down her window. For the length of Tracey's cigarette break, they didn't speak. The thick swampy air was cut with a tinge of wood smoke. A wildfire somewhere to the north. The blast of air made Jennifer's eyes water and she let them.

"So, who did you sleep with?" Tracey said.

"A guy. I don't even know his last name."

"Just the one time?"

"Yeah. It didn't even go all the way."

Jennifer felt like a weasel for trying to downplay it, so she told Tracey the whole mortifying story of betraying Kevin and molesting Olivia's boyfriend.

"Wow. You church girls," Tracey said. "Anyway, it's not the same as what he's done. Or what Carrie's done."

"How do you figure?"

"Because it's been going on for weeks. Months. Your thing was one stupid night when you were upset. And it wasn't like you even got off."

They reached the Palhetes' house after ten. Her parents seemed drowsy and confused at finding their daughter on the front step unannounced. Already in their pajamas, they ushered Jennifer and Tracey into the kitchen, where Mr. Palhete began to bake cookies.

Too late, Jennifer realized she wasn't in high school anymore. They were wondering why she was there. When cookies and tea had been shared all around, her father said, "Is everything okay, Jennifer?"

Tracey came to the rescue: "She had a fight with Kevin."

"Oh, honey." Moira reached across the kitchen table like she might touch Jennifer's arm, but then withdrew.

The question hung in the air, unasked: *a fight about what?* In the end, the Palhetes didn't ask. Jennifer put it down to Tracey's presence. Although the tea cup and oatmeal cookies didn't seem to fit exactly into her hands, she took to them readily. With Jennifer silent, trying not to cry, Tracey ate cookies and kept up a stream of pleasant, empty chatter. When Moira said, "There are two beds in Jennifer's room, if you girls want to spend the night," Tracey didn't demure, the way Jennifer expected her to.

"That would be nice. It's a long drive to Tampa. I can stay and take Jenn back in the morning, so you don't have to." Her hand, warm from the tea mug, came to rest on Jennifer's back and patted out a little circle.

It had been a long time since Jennifer had a sleep over, but once they were dressed in some of Moira's animal print satin pajamas and tucked into the twin beds, she was glad for Tracey. Jennifer had silenced her phone on the drive to Wimauma, but in the quiet of her childhood bedroom, it buzzed in her purse repeatedly. Tracey got up in the dark to turn the phone off.

A wall of worries rose up before Jennifer—Kevin, Shanti, a wedding to plan or cancel—but she silenced them like Tracey had silenced the phone. Tomorrow would be soon enough to worry about Kevin. Tomorrow would be soon enough to worry about Shanti.

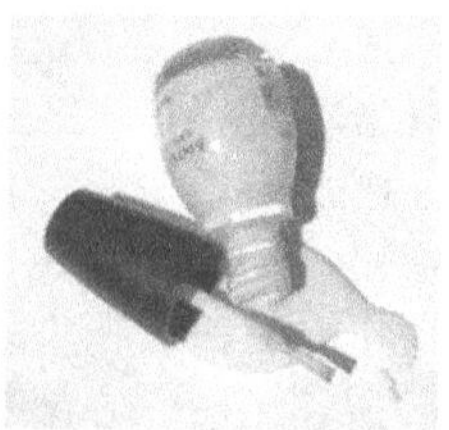

CHAPTER FORTY-THREE

Olivia

OLIVIA ROLLED OVER, looking for her alarm clock, but the movement brought a crisp cotton sheet sliding across her bare breasts. The sensation was as effective as a dousing with cold water. She never slept naked. She sat up, wide awake. Glancing around the room, she found Rindell's alarm clock, showing it was after six. On the bureau, her clothes had been folded up in a neat pile.

Acutely uneasy at her nakedness, she got dressed. In the pocket of her skirt, the detective's card crinkled. Hoping to use the bathroom without waking Mr. Batson, she picked up her shoes and stepped out of the room, but she needn't have worried about making noise. Mr. Batson was at the kitchen table, reading the morning paper.

"Good morning, Miss Holley." Although she couldn't see him behind the paper, he had a smile in his voice.

"Good morning, sir."

"You want some coffee? A couple eggs?"

Olivia hesitated, thinking of possible outcomes for her morning. She would have to go home and face her parents. Then she would have to go to work. None of it was conducive to coffee or breakfast.

"If it's not any trouble," she said.

"No trouble at all."

"Is it okay if I use the bathroom?"

"Help yourself." He folded the paper and nodded his head toward the hallway behind him.

She wanted a shower, but made do with washing her face and straightening her hair. When she returned to the kitchen, Mr. Batson was at the stove. A second cup of coffee stood on the table across from his place. Olivia took a grateful sip and waited for her eggs.

While they ate, she snuck furtive looks at Mr. Batson. He glared at the newspaper through a pair of bifocals.

"Had a rough night of it?" he said around a mouthful of eggs and toast.

She nodded. What kind of night had it been for Rich. Had he been arrested?

"Mr. Holley come around here looking for you."

"He did?" She choked out the words on the end of a swallow of coffee. "What happ—what did he say?"

"Just wanted to know if you was here. I told him you was sleeping. I imagine you'll hear all about it when you go home."

"I'm sorry for being a bother," she said.

"His huffing and puffing don't bother this little pig." She stifled a giggle, but when she looked up, he was smiling. "Yep, that boy of yours is an odd one."

Her mind on her brother, Olivia blanked before she realized Mr. Batson meant Rindell.

"Restless. All the time talking like he going to leave, get a job somewhere else, but then he stays. I suppose that's down to you."

"I doubt it," she said.

He shrugged and began to mop the egg yolk off his plate with a piece of toast.

"War done a number on him. Wish he was back out in the trailer sometimes, way he comes awake in the middle of the day, hollering and the like. The war getting its teeth into him while he's asleep. I suppose that's why he likes to work nights."

"Were you in the war—a war?"

"Yes, I was."

Olivia waited for him to say more, but after a few minutes of silence, she realized that was all he had to say. It made her think of the way Rindell had described his experiences. *This guy Rindell. This guy DeVaun.* Like something that had happened to someone else.

"Thank you for breakfast, Mr. Batson."

"You are surely welcome."

"I better get home and get ready for work."

"You take care, Miss Holley."

She put her shoes on and stood up. After a moment's hesitation, she dared to do what her child self would have cowered from. As she stepped past him on her way out the kitchen, she patted his shoulder.

Olivia braced for her father to shout the house down. He was capable of it. As much as she wanted to go upstairs and get ready for work, she walked directly to the dining room, where Mr. Holley was finishing his breakfast. He didn't even raise his voice to say, "You ever pull a stunt like that again and you won't be welcome in this house."

When she didn't answer, he added, "If you want to humiliate yourself chasing after that black boy, that's your business, but don't you humiliate this family in front of our friends and neighbors."

Olivia had expected to be raked over the coals. *You worried your mother. Your family needed you. Didn't you even think about your brother?* Any of those things she would have apologized for; she had run out in a time of crisis. All her father cared about was the neighbors thinking she'd spent the night with Rindell.

She refused to apologize for sleeping in his bed while he was at work. She had completed her first walk of shame and was unashamed.

With "I'm sorry" off the table, Olivia went up to her room without answering her father. All the bedroom doors were closed. She could think of half a dozen occasions when her mother had stayed in bed that late, only when she was sick. Careful not to make too much noise, Olivia went into the bathroom and started getting ready for work.

Half an hour later, dressed and her hair done, she knocked on Rich's door.

"Wha?" was the answer.

When she opened the door, he sat up in bed and rubbed at his face.

"Time for work?" he said.

"For me. You go back to sleep."

"Good." He flopped back on the bed dramatically.

Olivia crossed the room to stand next to his bed, and he looked up at her with a puzzled expression.

"What happened yesterday?" she said.

"Came home from the hospital. We had pizza. You missed pizza, even though it wasn't pizza night."

"Too bad for me."

"And Pastor Lou. And Dale."

"What about the police? Did the police come here?"

"Nah, at the hospital," he said.

"What happened?"

"We had pizza, even though it wasn't pizza night. Dad was mad at you for running off."

Olivia leaned over and kissed his forehead, making him grimace.

"Richie, you know I love you," she said.

"Yeah."

"Do you know what you did to Brian?"

"It was a misunderstanding. That's what Mom said."

She should have expected it. After all those weeks Mrs. Holley had spent alone next to Rich's hospital bed, of course he would parrot back what she kept saying. A misunderstanding.

"Did you…." Olivia hated to ask. "Rich, did you make those *nunchakus*? The ones the police have."

"I had some when I was a kid. Remember? Remember how I worked that tree over and Dad was pissed?"

"Yeah, and you were like George Washington. *I cannot tell a lie.*"

He giggled and she joined him, forcing herself to laugh.

"Did you make them out of our old table? The one up in the garage?"

"I dunno," he mumbled. "Go away. Lemme sleep."

Olivia didn't know what she'd expected. That he would deny it or that he would admit it. She should have known that he had inherited the lying and avoiding gene from their mother, too.

CHAPTER FORTY-FOUR

Jennifer

JENNIFER SPENT THE drive back to Tampa hoping Kevin would be gone when she reached the condo. She didn't care where he went: Carrie's, church, work. She just didn't want to see him. There was his car, though, parked next to her own. Everything had changed and he was still parking in his usual spot.

"I'm serious. You can stay with me," Tracey said.

"No, it's okay. I have to see him eventually. Thanks for everything."

"You're welcome. Call me, okay? Let me know how things are."

Jennifer leaned over the center console to hug Tracey, before getting out of the car. Riding up in the elevator, she tried to imagine what Kevin would say. Everything seemed to hinge on what he said.

He was asleep and didn't hear her come in. She hadn't realized she wanted an advantage, but seeing it, she took it. Picking out fresh clothes, she went into the bathroom and locked the door. Although she heard Kevin try the knob while she was in the shower, she didn't unlock the door until she had showered, styled her hair, done her make-up, and re-dressed. She was ready for church, unless Kevin called her bluff.

When she came out of the bathroom, he was sitting on the edge of the bed. Her side of the bed. He looked terrible.

"Jenn," he said plaintively.

"Good morning, Kevin."

Jennifer hadn't found her anger, but she found something else when she went to her closet to swap out her pumps for sandals. On the closet floor lay Shanti's soccer ball, like an accusation.

"I'm so sorry, Jenn." He said it from right behind her, so close that she jumped.

For a moment she thought the time had come to say, "It's okay, Kevin. I cheated on you, too."

But if she said that, why would she be saying it? To make him feel better? Or to make him feel worse? She breathed in and out, counting her heartbeat up to one hundred. Telling him now wouldn't be a confession. It would be revenge. An elaborate time-travelling revenge. That wasn't what she wanted.

"I'm sorry," he said again. "I know how bad I screwed up. Things got so complicated I didn't know what to do. I went there last night to break it off."

"To break what off?" Jennifer wasn't looking for a detailed confession, but she found his word choice fascinating. Did one break off a fling? Or did an affair require the violence of *breaking off*?

"What happened … with Carrie."

"So if you went there to *break it off*, why was Carrie naked under her bathrobe?" Jennifer knew she would regret asking. Like opening a container of ancient leftovers in the fridge, there wouldn't be anything pleasant in there. Better to throw it out without looking.

"It just—it got complicated."

"Never mind. I don't want to know. Is it over with her?"

"Yes. Yes! It's over," he said.

He was so close behind her, Jennifer could hear him snuffling, about to cry. She closed the closet door and turned to walk out of the bedroom.

"Please, please don't leave me. Please," he said. "Can we try to—to fix this?"

"I'm not leaving." Until she said it, Jennifer wasn't sure, but now that he had suggested the possibility of her leaving, she knew she couldn't. This was her life. The condo. Kevin. The wedding.

There she found a twinge of anger. As stupid and selfish as she was, at least she hadn't been that stupid and selfish. Rindell was nobody to Kevin. Carrie was her best friend. Sort of.

"Oh my God, Kevin. Carrie is supposed to be my maid of honor. My maid of honor! What am I supposed to do?"

"What about Tracey?" Kevin said.

To hide her reaction, Jennifer walked into the living room, but Kevin came after her, still snuffling. Tears would make sense to him, but her urge to laugh, he wouldn't understand that. Tracey would be perfect as the maid of honor. It was the pragmatic answer Jennifer would have found eventually, the answer that had nothing to do with the real issue. That was why she and Kevin were together. They had the same perspective on the world.

"We'll go to counseling," he said.

"No."

"No?"

"I don't want to go to counseling. If I wanted anyone to know, I'd go on one of those stupid TV shows." Under the tears and the nervous giggle that she choked down, Jennifer found another vein of anger. "I can't believe you turned our life into a Jerry Springer episode!"

"I'm sorry."

"My maid of honor. How would you feel if I slept with your best man? It's so unbelievably tacky. And cheap. And—and—and tacky."

More than anything, in that moment, Jennifer wished for a better vocabulary. There had to be a dozen other words to describe the situation, and she was stuck on *cheap* and *tacky*.

"Jenny, I'm sorry. I'm so sorry."

"Tawdry," she added. "And what do we do now? Change churches to avoid her?"

"She won't come anymore."

"Did you ask her that? Was that how you broke it off? *Oh, and by the way, could you change churches?*"

"We talked about it. It's okay. She isn't—she doesn't—She's embarrassed, too."

The accordion file of planning materials for the wedding lay on the coffee table in front of her. When the folder was new, Jennifer had drawn hearts on it. Now the folder was scuffed all around the corners and bulging with the detritus of wedding planning. It was too late to go back. The wedding would go on with a new maid of honor.

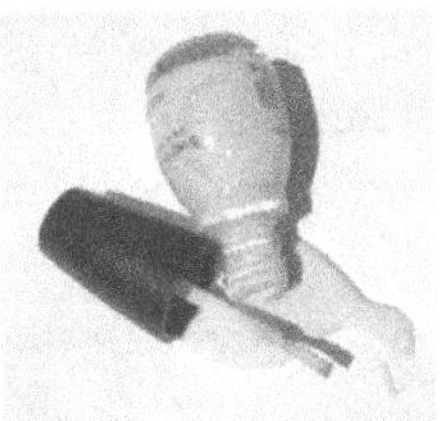

CHAPTER FORTY-FIVE

Olivia

OLIVIA TOOK THE pan of muffins out of the oven and tipped them into a basket, while her mother scrambled the eggs. It worried Olivia that Mrs. Holley wanted to make a *special breakfast* this morning, like Rich's arraignment was a special occasion. Dale Edgerton said that attending Rich's court appearance as a family would look better to the judge. Olivia wasn't convinced, considering how her parents looked these days. Mrs. Holley quivery and anxious, and Mr. Holley scowling and more bloated than ever.

When her father came to the dining room table, he looked ill rather than angry. As Olivia put a plate of bacon on the table, Mr. Holley put a hand up to his mouth to cover a belch.

"Are you okay?" she said.

"Just some indigestion. Think my dinner didn't agree with me last night."

"Do you want some Tums?"

"Yes, if you'd go up and get me a couple?"

"Tell Rich breakfast is ready while you're up there," Mrs. Holley called from the kitchen.

Olivia dutifully went upstairs, got the bottle of antacids from the bathroom cabinet, and then knocked on Rich's door.

"Come down and eat!"

"Yeah, okay," came the mumbled answer. Since his arrest, he spent most days alone in his room playing video games. He had nothing else to do. Olivia had called Mr. Colton to ask where to send flowers for Brian's funeral service and, although she didn't ask, Mr. Colton made it clear Rich couldn't come back to Forward/Ability.

"It would be too troubling for the other folks," he said.

Olivia couldn't argue with that. As she started down the stairs, Rich's door opened and he followed her to the dining room.

The TV was on in the living room, turned to the morning news. Mr. Holley glared down the length of the table toward something about a planning commission report. Having the TV on while they ate irritated Olivia, but she ignored it, hoping for a calm breakfast. Instead she got a frown from her father, who had eaten half a cinnamon apple muffin. The other half lay on his plate, unbuttered. It wasn't like him.

"You can't wear that to court," he said.

Olivia looked first at Rich, who wore a suit and tie, but then realized her father was talking to her.

"Why not?" Olivia knew she'd made the wrong response, leading with weakness instead of confidence. She'd bought the outfit expressly for this court appearance. Courtesy of all the stress about Rich, she had gone down two dress sizes. She'd never expected to get back into a size eighteen, but all her other clothes looked like bags on her.

As for the outfit itself, it was nicer than anything she'd owned before. A black pencil skirt with fine gray stripes, a silk blouse with a watermark-like cherry blossom pattern, and a perfectly cut gray jacket with princess seams and a peplum.

"It's too tight," Mr. Holley said. He put his hand to his mouth and burped again. "You look like a slut."

"I do not."

"Wear something different."

Olivia sat down, as her mother came in with the coffee pot. Mrs. Holley was in her housecoat, although her make-up and hair were done. Had she heard what Mr. Holley said? If so, she didn't mention it, just poured everyone more coffee and sat down. As

Olivia expected, the special breakfast was wasted effort. None of them were hungry, and she could hardly get anything but her coffee down. She'd been worried about the hearing, but now the word *slut* burned in the back of her brain.

Rich fumbled under the table, the tell-tale motions of his Gameboy at play.

"I told you to leave that in your room," Mr. Holley grumbled.

"You can't take that to court," said Mrs. Holley.

Rich made some unintelligible response.

Her father picked up the other half of his muffin and stuffed it into his mouth. An instant later, he spit it back out.

"Is something wrong with the muffins?" Mrs. Holley said.

"No, just my damn stomach." He wiped his mouth fastidiously and then covered the muffin's corpse with his napkin.

"I better get dressed," Mrs. Holley said. "Olivia, will you clear the table?"

"No, she needs to go upstairs and get changed."

"I thought she looked—"

"And I don't want you going into court with those sleazy nigger nails."

"Daddy! I can't believe you said that." Beyond the initial shock, like a slap to the face, Olivia wasn't honestly surprised. By the word, but not by the sentiment behind it.

"I think her nails look pretty," Mrs. Holley whispered.

Mr. Holley belched again, this time not even bothering to cover his mouth. He pushed his tie aside to press on his belly.

With *sleazy nigger nails* still hanging in the air, he said, "Where's the antacids? My stomach is rotten."

"They're in the kitchen," Olivia said. Let him get them himself.

"Well, bring them in here, and then go take that crap off your fingers."

Mrs. Holley got up from the table, like she was relieved to go. She brought back the bottle of antacid tablets.

"You don't like my clothes. You don't like my fingernails.

Would you rather I didn't go?" Olivia said.

"What I want—" Another burp interrupted him. "—is for us to go to court and look like a decent, white family."

"If Olivia doesn't go, I'm not going," Rich said. He stood up and carried his plate into the kitchen.

"Goddamnit. Richard, it's your hearing." Mr. Holley was pressing on his stomach again.

"No way. I'm not going if Olivia doesn't go."

Rich came back through the dining room, Gameboy in hand, headed toward the stairs.

"I'm going, Rich. Daddy's just fussing. I'm going," Olivia said. She wished she weren't, but she wanted to make peace, even if that meant taking off her nail polish and wearing a sloppy outfit two sizes too big.

From upstairs came the sound of Rich's video game console, the game with the bouncing balls and squares that made boinging noises.

Mr. Holley coughed and said, "We need to leave soon."

"I'll go get dressed," Mrs. Holley said.

Ignoring her father's orders, Olivia started to clear the table.

She assumed that by the time she finished with the dishes, her mother would have dressed and wrangled Rich downstairs, but when she came back to the dining room, the TV was still on and the sound of Rich's game was coming down the stairs. Mr. Holley sat at the head of table, looking sweaty and gray.

"Jim!" Olivia's mother called.

Coughing, Mr. Holley pushed back from the table and started toward the stairs at a laborious pace. Then her mother shrieked and a door slammed. Olivia would have rushed upstairs, but her father blocked the way, huffing and panting.

"I wasn't making a joke," he muttered under his breath. "Clean that crap off your nails."

That crap was a reverse French manicure with tiny flower decals. No rhinestones or bright colors, but it wasn't this particular manicure he was upset about. He was thinking of the times she'd done her nails for dates with Rindell.

"And change into a skirt that doesn't show off how fat your ass is," he added.

Olivia choked back the first retort she thought of: *I would, if your fat ass weren't in my way.*

Then Mr. Holley reached the top stair, and began shouting, "You damn well will go! Now put your jacket and tie back on! Right now!"

Rich's answer was full-throated: "Leave me alone! I'm not going! You can't make me!"

Mrs. Holley's part of the fight was drowned out entirely.

Not knowing what else to do, Olivia got a sealed acetone wipe from her purse. She stripped her nails, clearing away the decals in tiny shreds, and then the layers of polish, until her nails were bare. Her broken nail had mostly grown back.

She folded her thumb up next to her fingers to hide the scar from her long lost thumb. Taking out her cell phone, she checked the time. They needed to go. They had to find parking at the courthouse. She picked up the remote control and muted the television.

"Why do you have to be so hard on him?" Mrs. Holley was asking upstairs, her voice raw from crying.

"Hard on him? This is your fault. Always babying him. Always letting him get away with his attitude."

"My fault?"

"Now put your tie back on. Right now!" There was a scuffling sound and Mr. Holley shouted, "You son of a bitch, you'll do what I say! I can still whip you!"

"You can't! I'll whip you! I'll whip you!" Rich's voice cracked with emotion.

There was a thud and a crunch, and her mother screamed, "No, Jim! Don't! Don't!"

Olivia stood up, hoping it wasn't too late to intervene.

"You don't think there are consequences for this? You're only here because I put up bail. You can go sit and stew in a jail cell."

"Oh, Jim, no!"

Olivia started up the stairs, but at the landing, she met her father, his face purple with rage. Above him, Rich stood on the top step, holding a big black box in his hands. He threw it at Mr. Holley's retreating back, and as it bounced off, Olivia recognized it. Rich's TV game console with the wires torn lose.

When the console struck his back, Mr. Holley staggered and roared like a bear. He spun around, and started back up the stairs.

"How dare you? I will kill you, you son of bitch. I will—goddamn. Oh goddamn."

With a groan, he went down on one knee. He reached for the banister to support himself, and half-turned in the narrow stairwell. Olivia hurried up the steps, just as he lost his grip and fell toward her. She put her hands out to try to catch him, but the impact slammed her into the wall. Her right foot slid off a step and her ankle twisted under her, sending a hot bolt of pain up her leg. She landed on her backside and slid down three more steps, with Mr. Holley half on top of her.

For a few moments, Olivia lay stunned, before she took stock of herself. Nothing broken. She sat up, straining to keep Mr. Holley from continuing his descent down the stairs.

"Mom?" Olivia called, but there was no answer. Her foot was trapped under her own weight, and with her father's upper torso in her lap, she couldn't get it free.

Mr. Holley groaned and brought his hand up to his chest. This time, Olivia saw that he hadn't been rubbing his stomach. He was rubbing at his heart.

"Hurts," he said.

"Your chest? Your chest hurts?"

"Like it's on fire. Oh God." His breath was short and ragged.

"Mom? Mom?" Olivia yelled.

There was no answer but Mrs. Holley whimpering. A moment later, she appeared at the top of the stairs and looked down at her husband. She started crying harder.

"Richie, what did you do?" Her voice was tiny and scared.

"I think he's having a heart attack," Olivia said. "He has nitroglycerin, right? Somewhere? That little metal tube of pills. Where are they?"

"I don't know."

"Daddy, where's your nitroglycerin?"

"Don't know. Nightstand. Or the car."

Mr. Holley coughed and shuddered, making his shoulder press harder into Olivia's thigh. Her ankle twinged sharply enough to bring tears to her eyes.

With most of her father's admitted four-hundred—and truthfully more—pounds sliding down the stairs with nothing to stop it but Olivia's body for a chock, she couldn't think of any way to go look for the pills.

Trying to shift her weight off her aching ankle, she dislodged Mr. Holley, and they both slid another agonizing step down, twisting his body more tightly into the stairwell. The antennae of her cell phone gouged at her thigh. She worked it out into her hand, like squeezing frosting out of a tube. Maybe her skirt was too tight.

Clutching the phone for an instant, she dialed the first number that came to mind. Not 9-1-1, but Rindell. He answered after two rings.

"Are you—are you home?" she said, trying to keep her voice steady.

"Olivia? Where y'at?"

"I'm—are you at home?"

"Yeah," he said.

"My father, I think he's had a heart attack."

"You call 9-1-1?"

"No, I didn't know if—"

"Call 9-1-1. Right now, Olivia. Hang up and call 9-1-1. I'm coming."

She obeyed, and was grateful the emergency operator was able to coax the address and important details out of her frantic brain. The operator said, "Stay on the line, ma'am. We're sending help."

The front door slammed open and Rindell skidded around the

corner. He was panting, but then he must have run all the way from his house to hers. Even though he wore shorts with no shirt, and tennis shoes with no socks, she could see how he must look at work: calm, ready to take action. In his left hand he clutched a stethoscope. He dashed up the stairs and knelt down to check her father over. Grabbing Mr. Holley's tie, he loosened it and pulled it free. He pressed the stethoscope to several places on Mr. Holley's chest and then pulled the ear pieces down to talk.

"Sir, you with us? You hear me?"

"I can't … get up," Mr. Holley said.

"You got pain or pressure in your chest? Your arm?"

Mr. Holley nodded to both.

"How you been feeling this morning?"

When her father didn't answer, Olivia said, "He had indigestion. He couldn't eat his breakfast."

Taking the phone from Olivia's hand, Rindell spoke to the dispatcher: "This is Rindell James, I'm a paramedic. Live down the street from the Holleys. Yep. Caucasian male, early sixties, morbidly obese. Myocardial infarction. You need to dispatch a bus with a hydraulic lift." Rindell gave Olivia a reassuring smile as he listened to the operator.

"Probably five hundred pounds, maybe more. Yeah, five hundred. I'm gonna administer some aspirin, try to get him comfortable. Get back with you if things change."

He tossed the phone onto the stairs and said, "Olivia, can you get the aspirin?"

"I can't get up."

Rindell looked at the precariousness of her balance on the stair, her arm straining up to hold onto the banister. "Okay. Where the aspirin?"

"Upstairs. In the bathroom medicine cabinet. The left side."

He looked up the stairs to where Mrs. Holley was crumpled, sobbing.

"Mom! Mom! Get the aspirin," Olivia shouted, but her mother didn't answer.

He glanced around, calculating, and Olivia followed his gaze as he took in the massive obstacle of her father. Like a manatee in a laundry chute. There was no route up that didn't involve stepping on Mr. Holley.

"Mom! Now! Get the aspirin now."

Mrs. Holley raised her head and looked down at Olivia with bleary confused eyes.

"Fuck it," Rindell muttered under his breath. He grasped the banister and pulled himself up, bracing his opposite foot and hand on the wall. Olivia heard the crunch of plaster as his foot pushed against the wall. He slipped half an inch, then got his right foot up to the banister, too. Olivia marveled, like watching Spider-man, as Rindell scaled the staircase over her father.

He ran up the rest of the stairs and Olivia heard him say, "Hey, man. Hey. Remember me?"

"You're Olivia's boyfriend."

"Yeah, you right. I'm Rindell, remember? What you doing, man?"

With a lurch, Olivia realized Rindell spoke so cautiously, because he was worried about what Rich would do.

"I gotta go in the bathroom, okay?"

"I don't wanna go to court," Rich said.

"No, that's cool. You don't have to." Rindell was right. They wouldn't be going to court.

"I don't?"

"No, why don't you go on in your room there, while I take care of this?"

"Can I play my Gameboy?"

"Sure, sure you can, pardner." Rindell called down the stairs: "Olivia, how are things down there?"

"Daddy? How are you?" she said.

"Hurts." Mr. Holley's face was slick with sweat and his lips looked blue.

A moment later, Rindell appeared on the stairs above and rattled a pill bottle in his hand.

"I'm gonna throw these down. Take two and put them in his mouth. He needs to dry swallow or chew them up. Get them working in his system."

"Alright."

"You doing okay?"

"I'm okay."

Leaning forward, Olivia managed to let go of the banister railing without slipping. She held her hands up and Rindell pitched the bottle into them. She pried the cap off the bottle and tilted it over her palm. Half a dozen aspirin scattered loose on the stairs, but she managed to get two pills into her father's mouth, shuddering at how cold his tongue felt against her fingers. He moaned, his eyes rolling toward her.

"Chew those up, Daddy. There's no water."

Mr. Holley made a gurgling choking noise, and his eyes fluttered closed.

"Damn. Damn," Rindell said. He reversed his Spider-man ascent, one of his shoes skidding along the baseboard before he managed to catch himself with the banister. He repeated the processing of checking Mr. Holley with the stethoscope.

"What is it? Is he...."

"He's in arrest."

"Oh my God." Olivia knew her hands were shaking and she couldn't stop them. Rindell's hand by contrast was firm as he squeezed hers.

"Don't panic on me," he said.

"What's happening?" Mrs. Holley lifted her head from her lap, and Olivia was worried by the look on her mother's face: terror and hysteria.

"Olivia!" Rindell said sharply. "Can you help me roll him over to his back?"

"Yes." Olivia shifted to get a better angle, but as soon as her knee lost contact with her father's back, he slid further down the stairs, sending her tumbling to the landing.

"You okay?"

"Yes, yes." As quick as she could get up on her knees, she scrambled back to her father.

"Push there. Harder."

The two of them together were able to shift Mr. Holley from his side to his back, but his legs lay above him, tangled together.

"You gonna breathe for him, okay? You had CPR, right? For your church volunteer thing, right?" Rindell guided her hands in place and then clambered over her father, straddling his chest.

Olivia had the vaguest memory of taking CPR classes to qualify as a volunteer for the youth ministry. Watching Rindell's twined hands plunge against her father's chest, the compressions seemed to be in fast forward.

When he said, "Breathe," she did what she was told. Some memory came back, and she remembered why she was supposed to keep her father's head tilted back, to be sure the air went to his lungs. She focused on breathing, and tried not think of the coldness of his mouth under hers.

Suddenly there was a rubber glove clad hand on her shoulder and a man in a crisp uniform shirt said, "I'll take over here."

"He's in full arrest. No pulse. Been doing compressions for a little more than three minutes," Rindell said.

Olivia gave way to the paramedic, who used a plastic bag device to squeeze air into Mr. Holley's lungs.

"Damn, he's big," the man said. "We need to get him out of here."

"Need to get him stabilized first," said another paramedic on the landing.

"We need the paddles and we gotta get him off these here stairs," Rindell snapped, panting between compressions.

After that it was all a rush, the three men talking in short hand, and one of the paramedics muttering into his walkie-talkie.

"Four of us. Five of us," Rindell said. "We can move him down to the living room."

"Us three and the girl? Who else?" the paramedic said.

"Rich! Rich! Hey, man!" Rindell shouted up the stairs.

"What?" To Olivia's surprise, her brother poked his head around the corner.

"Get down here, man, and give us a hand."

"Olivia's boyfriend," Rich said.

"Yeah, you right. Same as I was before."

"Dad doesn't like you."

"I don't reckon he does. Now get down here and help us move your daddy."

The five of them dragged Mr. Holley down the steps and into the living room, with Olivia hobbling on her aching ankle. As soon as they had him flat on the floor, they continued CPR while one paramedic prepped the paddles. When they were ready, Rindell dismounted and one of the paramedics cut open Mr. Holley's shirt.

When the paramedic muttered, "Clear," Olivia closed her eyes and heard her mother give a stifled scream.

They shocked Mr. Holley again, while Olivia and Rich sat on the couch, holding hands like children. The muted TV flickered with the local news, showing an image that was familiar to Olivia. Down the dark, quiet tunnel of her shock, she stared at the TV. In the photo, a little girl stood on a playground, her hands on her hips, looking defiant.

"Damn it," Rindell said. "Hit him again."

CHAPTER FORTY-SIX

Jennifer

WHEN JENNIFER'S PHONE vibrated on the conference table a second time, Mr. Kraus frowned. Without looking at the screen, she tucked the phone back into her briefcase. Kevin called her all the time now. During his lunch hour, while he was driving home from work, between customers. Like he needed to prove at every moment that he wasn't with Carrie.

As for Lucas, he acted like Jennifer had decided to get married and go on a honeymoon just to inconvenience him. He piled work on her at every opportunity. By the time she left the meeting, she'd agreed to three seventy-hour workweeks in a row.

On the way back to her office, Jennifer checked her phone and found the usual call from Kevin. "Just checking in." The other call wasn't from him.

"Hey, doll. Marco here," the second voicemail said. "You been around to the Vanderbilts today? Something going on, but I can't get over there...."

In mid-stride, Jennifer came to a stop. Without waiting to hear if there was more to the message, she called Marco's number, but it went to his voicemail. Lucas approached her in the hallway, carrying a cardboard box. He held it out to her.

"Fliers for Del Ray," he said.

"Del Ray?"

"The open house this afternoon."

"Right." Jennifer took the box under her arm, juggling it with her briefcase into the door of her office. With her other hand, she punched back to her voicemail and listened to Marco's whole message. Something going on and he'd call her later.

She played the message a third time, listening intently to the tone of his voice. Was it high? Good news? Low? It seemed low.

If she skipped lunch, she had time to drive by the Vanderbilts' house. Stuffing her purse and phone into her briefcase, she picked up the box of fliers, and headed for the parking garage. On the drive over, she tried Marco again, but he didn't answer.

Long before she got through traffic to the muffler shop, Jennifer understood what Marco meant by "something." Police cars and panel vans clogged the Vanderbilts' driveway and overflowed onto the front lawn. The muffler shop parking lot was crowded, too, and not with customers. Two news vans parked front and center, almost blocking the drive. The news crews watched Jennifer pull in and park, before deciding she was nobody.

Although half a dozen uniformed officers milled around outside the Vanderbilts' house, nothing seemed to be happening. Jennifer stayed in her car, running the air conditioner and watching in the rear view mirror, while she bounced her cell phone against her leg. After half an hour, she needed to go. The open house started at one, and if she left now, she would be on time.

Ten minutes later, another white panel van arrived. It was marked with a logo for the Department of Children and Families.

Jennifer was going to miss the open house.

Half an hour later, the Vanderbilts' front door opened and a woman came out, leading four children behind her: the blond girl and the Latino siblings. They carried no luggage, and it saddened Jennifer to see that none of them looked particularly upset. As Manny the muffler guy said, "That shit happens." The driver got out and opened the side door on the passenger van. One by one the brothers and sister got in, followed by the blond girl, playing her video game. The woman got into the passenger seat, and a moment later, the van drove away.

Jennifer got out of the car and walked toward the street, intending to talk to the police, but before she made it to the curb, both news crews were in her face.

"Are you involved in the investigation into this missing child?" one of them asked her. He was sweating under a heavy layer of make-up.

"No. I don't know anything," Jennifer said. "I'm waiting for someone."

She retreated to the car, but she was tired of watching in her mirror. Once the reporters lost interest in her, she sat up on the car trunk and waited. For a long time, nothing happened, unless she counted the game of musical cars. Patrol cars left and were replaced by others. Panel vans came and went, carrying people in jumpsuits with plastic tackle boxes. Men in suits rode away in Suburbans and other men in suits came in unmarked sedans.

Jennifer felt the way she had when Kevin took her to a Devil Rays game. She didn't know anything about baseball, and she got a sunburn. The same elements held sway here. She didn't know what was going on, and she was getting sunburned. The sun reached its zenith and blared down on Jennifer until she soaked her blouse with sweat.

"I wondered if you'd show up," a man said behind her. Manny the muffler guy, with a hand up to shield his eyes from the sun. As he approached her, he held out a can of soda. When she took it, he said, "Jupiña."

Jennifer didn't know what it was, but she was thirsty, so she opened it and drank. In the first sip, the sweetness overpowered everything else, but in the second swallow, the pineapple taste hit sharply, making her pucker her lips.

"So, what's happening?" Manny said.

"I don't know. How long have they been here?"

"Cops showed up around ten this morning. The news people showed up before noon. They don't know nothing, except they said there was a foster kid missing. The little girl you was looking for?"

"Shanti," Jennifer said.

"Yeah. Well, let me know what you find out."

"Thanks for the soda."

He nodded, already heading back into the muffler shop.

The pineapple soda left Jennifer's mouth feeling coated in sugar. Her head throbbed from the heat and she hadn't had any lunch.

At five o'clock, the news crews did a broadcast and departed, leaving a lone man with a hand held video camera. Giving up on watching discreetly from a distance, Jennifer walked to the curb and stared across the street. A few people in the trailer park were doing the same. As suddenly as the van had come and taken the children away, there was a commotion at the front door, and a phalanx of uniformed police officers walked the Vanderbilts out of the house. Amelia's face looked more pinched than usual. Mr. Vanderbilt's scowl had been replaced by a stunned look.

They were handcuffed. Just like in the movies, a cop rested his hand on Amelia's head as she ducked into a patrol car. Mr. Vanderbilt got into another cop car.

Beside Jennifer, the guy with the video camera was trying to film and dial his cell phone at the same time. "You gotta get back here," he panted into the phone. "The cops just cuffed them. No, I got it. I got footage."

The Vanderbilts were still waiting in separate police cars an hour later, when Marco Parmiento drove up. He parked at the front of the lot, where the news vans had been, and waved for Jennifer to get in. After so many hours standing in the heat, she was relieved to sink into the air conditioning. The car was clean but lived in, with two drive-thru soda cups in the center console. Instead of the radio, Marco had a police scanner on low in the background.

"Here. Bet you didn't have lunch." He reached into the back seat for a fast food bag.

"I'm okay."

"No, you look like a stiff breeze could knock you over. I got you chicken. You look like a girl who eats chicken." Taking out a sandwich, he unwrapped it for her. He tapped the soda cup next to her. "That's a diet Coke for you."

The sandwich was a fried chicken patty on an enormous puffy bun, with a fat dollop of mayo. It was hot and Jennifer ate it quickly. Marco ate his own dinner, a double decker bacon cheeseburger, with the practiced air of someone who often ate in his car.

When they finished eating, Jennifer reported everything she'd seen, like they were on a stakeout together. He nodded while she spoke, but didn't ask any questions. Maybe he already knew it all.

"You don't need to be here. I appreciate all your help, but I'm sure you have more important things to do," she said.

"Don't worry, doll. I'm not charging you for this. You uncovered a thing like this, I wanna stick it out, see what happens. Seems like the least I can do for that little girl."

After a few minutes, he plugged a headset into the police scanner and popped one of the earbuds in. While he listened to the police scanner, Jennifer stewed inside her own thoughts. Marco's words gnawed at her. *The least I can do.* That was what Jennifer had done. The very bare minimum. The inside of her head felt like a mouth full of sore and loose teeth. No matter where her thoughts wandered, they landed on something painful.

Marco sat up straight in his seat and pressed the ear bud more firmly into place.

Jennifer watched his face, but couldn't read him. She said, "Is there something…."

"Hang on." Removing the ear bud, he opened the Mustang's door and stepped out. He turned his back and took out his cell phone.

Jennifer needed to pee. The physical sensation of pressure on her bladder brought her attention back to her own life. She hadn't showed up for the Del Ray open house; Lucas would be furious. Kevin would have called her by now, probably several times, but she'd left her phone in her car. And she needed to pee.

As she got out of the car, intending to ask Manny if she could use his bathroom, two men in blue windbreakers came around the side of the Vanderbilts' house. They walked down the driveway from the garage, one of them leading a yellow Labrador retriever in a harness. Jennifer slammed the car door and walked around to where Marco hunched over his phone.

"Is that a dog?" she said. It was a stupid question, so she tried, "What's the dog for?"

Marco didn't answer, and he took half a dozen steps away from her, like he needed more privacy. With her heart thudding uneasily against her full stomach, Jennifer followed.

"It's for a friend. You know I won't drop anything to the media," he said into the phone. "True. Well, thanks, Joe. I appreciate it."

When he turned to her, his face was set in a frown.

"Did you find out something?" Jennifer said.

The man leading the dog had reached one of the police panel vans. He opened the back door and the dog jumped inside. Marco watched the dog, too, and when his gaze returned to Jennifer, he smiled. A fake smile.

"Why don't you go home for the night, doll? They're not gonna know anything tonight," he said. "Tell you what, I'll call you if I—"

"Just tell me."

Marco shrugged, nodded, and tucked his phone away.

"It's not much, but the cadaver dog got a hit in the garage."

"That's a cadaver dog? Does that mean—is there a body in the garage?"

"It means there was at some point. Not now. The dog hit on a cabinet in the garage, plus a hit in the house and in Vanderbilt's truck, too. Like a body got moved. The thing is...."

Marco kept talking, but Jennifer couldn't listen anymore. She had promised to take care of Shanti. Across the street, the panel van with the dog pulled away, and then the patrol car carrying Amelia Vanderbilt began backing across the front lawn toward the driveway.

Jennifer stepped off the curb into the street. In answer to blaring car horns, she held out her hand and kept walking. She was nearly to the patrol car when the first cop reached her, shouting, "I told you people to stay off the property. No fucking reporters!"

She didn't bother to correct him, but sidestepped and kept walking. Using her open palm, she slapped the rear passenger window of the patrol car. Amelia Vanderbilt jerked her head up in surprise and met Jennifer's gaze. Her eyes were wide and bloodshot.

Jennifer hit the window again, this time with her closed fist.

"What did you do to her? You were supposed to be taking care of her! What did you do to her?" she screamed. When Amelia looked away, Jennifer pounded on the window.

She would have hit the window until it or her hand broke, but a police officer grabbed her by the arm and yanked her backwards hard enough to knock her off her feet. Her palms hitting the hot asphalt was sickeningly familiar. This time no unseen hand flicked a switch to tell her what was the right thing to do. Jennifer scrambled to stand up and pushed the cop away from her.

"Lady!" he shouted. "Who the hell is this? What's she doing?"

Before Jennifer could reach the car again, more hands grabbed her and pulled her away. She fought back, but someone lifted her off her feet and carried her backwards, away from the car. It pulled out into traffic, with Amelia slumped in the back seat. Then the patrol car with Mr. Vanderbilt, his bearded face a blur. Seeing the cars go, Jennifer stopped fighting. Too late.

"You know her, Parmiento?" someone said.

"Yeah, I got her. I got her."

"Get her outta here before I have to arrest her."

"Aw hell," Marco said. Or Jennifer assumed it was Marco talking in her ear. Holding her up when all she wanted was to lie down and die. She was crying too hard to be sure whose arms were around her or who was stroking her hair.

Like Gayle Prichard once had to do, Jennifer gave herself up to the kindness of a stranger. Jennifer had been too much of a coward to tell Gayle the truth, to say, "You're dying and I'm not your sister."

Marco had no such qualms. Blocking traffic, with Jennifer's head tucked into the crook of his shoulder, he whispered, "I know. Life is a goddamn bitch at every turn. Everything goes to hell and people die who don't deserve it. I know, doll. It's all a goddamn pile of shit."

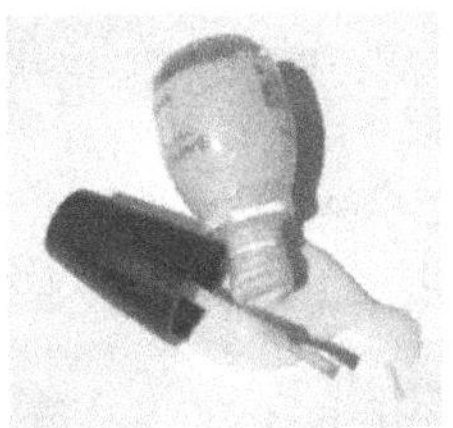

CHAPTER FORTY-SEVEN

Olivia

OLIVIA STARED AT the little girl's picture on the television, until she figured out why it was familiar. The girl on the news was Shanti, the girl Jennifer had been looking for. At the bottom of the image, blue letters scrolled past: *DCF Investigates Missing Girl Amid Claims of Fraud by Foster Care Case Workers.*

"Got him," Rindell said.

Olivia pulled her gaze away from the TV and back to her father.

"Got a beat?" said the paramedic with the electrical paddles.

"Yep, let's go."

By then a second ambulance and two more paramedics had arrived. The five men loaded her father onto an oversized gurney. Mrs. Holley stood at the foot of the stairs, her face slack and smudged with tears. When the paramedics rolled her husband out the front door, she said, "I want to go with him."

"There's room for you to ride with us, ma'am."

Olivia let go of Rich's hand and followed her mother to the front porch. After her father was loaded into the ambulance, the paramedics helped Mrs. Holley in. She was still in her housecoat.

"I'll follow in the car. I'll bring your purse and some clothes," Olivia said.

It was a relief to watch the ambulance pull out of the driveway, to have the immediate burden of her father's life out of her hands. She sat down on the top step and started to remove her shoes.

"You do that falling down the stairs?" Rindell knelt in front of her and gave a low whistle. "You twisted that good. Gonna swell up like grapefruit."

Once her shoe was off, he took her foot in his hand.

"Yep. Didn't break it, but you sprained it real good. Need to get some ice on it." He held her foot a moment too long, saying, "You and your itty bitty feet."

"Is he going to be okay?" Olivia said.

"We got him restarted pretty quick. Wish it'd happened earlier. Me and Luis woulda been right to hand."

"Thank you for coming, though. I realize it's not your responsibility."

"I was glad to help," he said. "You need me to do anything else?"

"No. I just need to catch my breath."

Sitting down on the step beside her, Rindell laid his hand on her arm. She let it rest there, a calming presence.

"How important do you think the truth is?" she said. It was the question she couldn't stop asking herself.

"I don't know if I'm the best person to answer that."

"Maybe you are more than most people."

"Why? Because I told such a whopper?" Rindell asked.

"Because, I don't know. Because you had to decide. About something important."

Rindell nodded. "There was that point, where I either had to tell the truth and go down one road, or I could let the lie ride and go down another."

"Did you make the right decision?"

"I think so. For me. Going the other way, I wasn't gonna end up nowhere good. That don't mean it's always the case. Most times telling the truth is prolly better."

"I know," Olivia whispered.

"There something particular you trying to decide about?"

It had been on her tongue for weeks, waiting to be said.

"I think my brother killed him. The man he worked with. I think he killed him on purpose. I think he planned to do it."

"And you don't know whether you ought to tell the cops that."

"I'm sorry. It's not your problem," she said. He squeezed her arm gently.

"It's okay. You know I can keep a secret."

She smiled at him and then remembered the thing that had been pushed aside by her father's heart attack.

"What time is it?" she said.

He pulled his cell phone out of his pocket. "Quarter of ten now. I know how it seem like time—"

"Oh my God."

"What?"

"We were supposed to be at the courthouse by now. Rich's arraignment is at ten."

Olivia stood up, letting Rindell's hand slip off her arm. He stood up, too, a step down from her.

"You need anything?" he offered again.

"No, you've already done so much. I don't want to trouble you."

"I took a job in Miami."

For a moment, Olivia squinted at him, not understanding. There were too many other things going on for her to process it.

"I'm supposed to start next Monday. I was gonna tell you, only it was never a good time. And this ain't either," he said.

"Oh. Oh."

"It's okay, Olivia. You got a whole lot to worry about. You take care, okay?"

"You, too."

As he walked down the drive, she limped inside, carrying her shoes, and retrieved her cell phone from the stairs. Thumbing through her contacts list, she found Dale Edgerton's number. She hesitated before pushing the call button and walked back into the living room. Shanti's photo flashed on the television screen.

Rich hunkered over his Gameboy, pushing buttons furiously.

"What happened?" Olivia said, but he didn't look up. "Rich?"

"Ambulance came."

"No, upstairs, what happened? Why'd you throw your game at Daddy?"

"Stupid jerk," he muttered. "He broke it. He told me to stop acting like a retard. Then he smacked me, so I smacked him back harder. He broke my Nintendo. So I threw it at him. He shouldn't have done that."

When they were kids, her father's idea of *smacking* had been a quick slap on a leg or a shoulder. Petty, annoying, but not painful.

"How did you hit him?" she said.

"Whack!" Rich raised his arm and lowered it in a karate chop. "Showed him he couldn't whip me."

"You shouldn't have hit him."

"Asshole retard. He's the retard. I didn't mean to hit Mom, though."

"You hit Mom?"

"On accident. Not on purpose. I don't have to go to court, do I? It's boring." Rich looked up from his Gameboy and gave her a plaintive frown.

"I don't know yet. You stay here. I'm going upstairs for a little bit."

He grunted in acknowledgement.

Upstairs, Olivia surveyed the aftermath of the fight in Rich's room. The entertainment center with the TV off-center and loose wires dangling where the game console had been ripped out.

In her bedroom, she closed the door and sat down at the vanity. Her ankle emitted a dull throbbing pain, but she ignored it. When she thumbed her phone back to life, Dale Edgerton's number was there, waiting to be dialed. He was expecting them at the courthouse. Soon, he'd start calling, wondering where they were.

Olivia opened her vanity drawer and took out a business card. With one bare fingernail, she pecked in Detective Vance's phone number and, after a deep breath, hit the call button. While she waited for him to answer, she picked out the two bottles of polish for her reverse French manicure. In the time it took her to put two coats of polish on her nails, she told Detective Vance everything: how Rich had threatened to kill Brian, how he'd made the set of nunchucks, how he'd thrown his game console at Mr. Holley. When she finished, the house phone was ringing.

"I need to go, Detective."

"Is everything okay there, Miss Holley?" the detective said. He breathed heavily into the phone.

"I think my brother's lawyer is calling to find out why we're not in court yet."

"I can be at your house in fifteen minutes. Do you need me to send uniforms there?"

"What?"

"What I mean is, is your brother calm right now? Are you safe?"

"He's fine. He's playing video games. It's better if you come alone. I'll tell his lawyer to come, too."

"That's a good idea. And Miss Holley? Thank you for telling me the truth."

"It isn't."

"What?" The detective's voice rose in alarm.

"It's true. What I told you is all true, but that doesn't make it The Truth. I don't know what The Truth is. Okay?"

"Okay, Miss Holley. I'll be there in fifteen minutes."

After she hung up, she looked down at her nails. They were all wrong. She cleaned them off and then she called Dale Edgerton. While she explained to him why they weren't coming to the courthouse, she pulled bottle after bottle of polish out of her drawer, and set them on the vanity. The glass bottles clinked together musically, a sound that had always cheered Olivia up. Now it teased her as she tried to decide on a color. What was the color of betrayal? What color was The Truth? After all the bottles were lined up before her, she could see that whatever the color was, she didn't own a bottle of it.

CHAPTER FORTY-EIGHT

Jennifer

IF JENNIFER HAD had fallen apart in February, she could have been alone in her parents' house. Her mother would have gotten up in the dark to go drive a school bus, and her father would have gone to teach. Because everything happened after the end of the school year, Jennifer hid out in her childhood bedroom, while her parents tried to get on with their summer vacation.

In the first week after the Vanderbilts' arrest, the television was guaranteed to flash Shanti's picture every hour on the hour with the latest updates. Interviews with former foster kids who made thinly veiled accusations against the Vanderbilts. Neighbors, co-workers, distant relatives, everyone was eager to be on TV. The news crews were like mice. They could squeeze in anywhere to do an interview, including the visitation room at the Georgia penitentiary where Shanti's father served time on a larceny charge. He was a handsome man, with wide, deep-set brown eyes. Jennifer knelt in front of the television in rapt attention, waiting to hear what he would say.

"Murmbathumlawhermanun Shanti." That was it. Mumble mumble mumble Shanti. He talked like he had a mouth full of cotton. How had he managed to seduce both of the Prichard sisters?

Then came the interview that ended Jennifer's ability to watch the news: Renee Prichard Williams, with her seven chins and her beady eyes, railing against the Department of Children and

Families, and threatening to sue the State of Florida. The TV survived its encounter with the remote control, but the remote disgorged its batteries and a handful of plastic and wires. It never worked right again.

After that, Jennifer stuck to home decor shows and shopping channels. Cardboard people against pretty backdrops. They played all night long, which was perfect, because Jennifer worked the night shift of depression. It was safer to sleep through the morning and into the afternoon. When she was awake during the day, she could hear her father talking on the phone.

Just as he had managed her childhood dance classes and social activities, now he managed the disintegration of her life. At first, it was the daily calls to Lucas, to explain that Jennifer was still *under the weather*.

That was the nice thing about being an adult. When her father came in to check every morning, Jennifer didn't have to provide proof that she was too sick to go to work. She could stay home in bed without puking or have her temperature taken, and Mr. Palhete would deliver the news to Lucas.

One morning, after she'd delivered her verdict, Mr. Palhete carried the phone into her room and said, "You need to talk to him."

Jennifer shook her head, but her father laid the phone down on the pillow beside her. When she didn't pick it up, he did. But instead of leaving, he brought the phone back to his mouth and said, "Here she is, Mr. Cavuto."

He held out the phone and Jennifer took it, ashamed of herself.

"Jennifer, we're worried about you," Lucas said.

"I know."

"We need you. You're an important part of this team. We're all concerned about what's been going on with you."

"Thank you." Those canned phrases were all Jennifer had.

"But we need you to be on the team. We need you here today. There's a big planning meeting for The Lofts launch and we need you here for it. The meeting's at two, but I want you to come earlier so we can go over some things. Okay?" Lucas said.

Jennifer checked her little collection of words. If she said, "Okay," she would have to get out of bed, take a shower, get dressed, and go to Tampa. Mr. Palhete would drive her if she asked. He and Moira would call it a *fun day trip*.

Closing her eyes, Jennifer went over the steps in her mind. She could see herself getting up, doing her hair, going into the condo, picking out work clothes. She could see all of that, but couldn't see herself walking down the sidewalk past the Bank of America building. When she tried to picture herself crossing the street to TFI, a river of blood flowed across her path.

"Jennifer, do you understand? We need you here today," Lucas said.

"I can't."

"That is not an acceptable answer. If you have a medical condition, you need to provide documentation. We have been more than understanding, but this is the limit. You need to come to work and do your job or we'll begin proceedings to terminate you."

"You don't need to. I quit."

She got the gasp of disbelief in stereo, from Lucas and Mr. Palhete.

"You're officially resigning from your position?" Lucas said.

"Yes."

Mr. Palhete sank down on the edge of the bed with a sigh. Jennifer kept her eyes closed to avoid seeing his sad, disappointed look. When she held the phone out, he took it from her.

"This is her father," he said to Lucas. Then after listening for a while: "I understand. Yes. Good-bye."

"Have they found her body yet? You'd tell me, wouldn't you, if they'd found her body?" Jennifer said.

"Yes, of course I would."

"Because they probably won't. Those people probably buried her somewhere. Or they threw her in the Everglades. Or maybe the bay. They killed her and they dumped her somewhere and the cops will never find her. And you know, maybe it was an accident. One of those stupid things. Maybe she hit her head and they panicked."

"Jenny, please, don't," Mr. Palhete said, but she couldn't stop herself. Courtesy of cop shows on TV, she had played a thousand scenarios in her head. Ones where the Vanderbilts were abusers and pedophiles and monsters and murderers. Ones where the Vanderbilts were careless and scared. Jennifer had imagined Shanti dead a hundred different ways, disposed of in as many more, but dead was dead. It almost didn't matter how.

Some days, her father tried to comfort her, but that day, he simply left. He didn't come back until he brought the phone for Kevin's daily call.

"I'll try to come this weekend, but you know I'm busy at work," he said.

"I know."

"Even in good traffic, it's a two-hour round trip out to Wimauma."

"I know," Jennifer said.

Kevin must have finally noticed that he was defending himself against an accusation she'd never made, because he fell silent before asking, "When are you coming home?"

"Never."

He laughed.

"I'm not coming back."

"Don't say that. I'll come see you this weekend, okay?"

"Don't," Jennifer said. "I don't want to see you."

"But we need to talk about the wedding."

"There's not going to be a wedding. We're not getting married."

She hung up without waiting to hear what he would say. When the phone rang, she pulled the back off and unplugged the battery. Now that she had quit her job, it was easy to leave him. Kevin, the wedding, her job. Take one leg off a three-legged stool and it falls over.

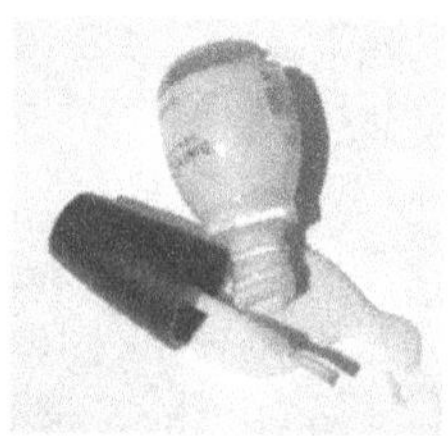

CHAPTER FORTY-NINE

Olivia

OLIVIA CHOSE HER church outfit with an eye to appeasing her father. A khaki skirt two sizes too big that fell to mid-calf. A pink linen blouse, also two sizes too big, buttoned all the way up, and then for an extra measure of safety, covered with a sweater vest. Her nails she did in a soft pink with no embellishments. Let him find fault if he could.

They had not actually spoken to each other since he came home from the hospital. Talking had fallen out of favor altogether at the Holley house since Mr. Holley's heart attack and Rich's second arrest. Olivia stopped having her meals at home. She stocked the refrigerator at work with yogurt, and got her coffee from Palm Avenue Sandwich or the Fourth of July Café. Lunch was a microwave meal at work, dinner a Publix salad or sushi, eaten in her car in the grocery store parking lot.

After two weeks of that, Olivia knew she would have to make an effort to return what was left of the family to normalcy. Wearing her careful church clothes, she went downstairs to cook Sunday breakfast. Although she had always waited for her mother's guidance, she knew the steps. Eggs were a given. She picked ham over bacon, and waffles over pancakes.

At the hospital, a dietician had lectured them about Mr. Holley's eating habits, but when the time came to buy groceries, he insisted on his favorite foods. Olivia listened to her mother's tremulous attempts to follow the dietician's guidelines, but didn't interfere.

When the ham was hot and three waffles had come off the iron the right shade of brown, she put the eggs in the pan, and went into the living room.

"Breakfast is ready!" she yelled. She knew her parents could hear her, but no one answered.

It made Olivia think of the ridiculous Rapture movie she'd seen as a child, where people woke up to find that their families had been *taken up* while they'd been *left behind*. She remembered a scene in which a bouffant-haired housewife was raptured while using her mixer. Her sinner husband came into the kitchen and found the mixer running unattended. At age ten, Olivia had found the movie terrifying. The thought of being left alone fueled her nightmares for months. Now she thought it would hardly cause a bump in her life.

Going back to the kitchen, she finished scrambling the eggs and turned off all the burners. She allotted herself small servings of ham and eggs, and retrieved one of the waffles from the oven where she'd kept them hot. She doctored it with butter and syrup, and sat down at her usual place. She was half-finished with her breakfast when Mr. Holley lumbered into the dining room. He lifted his nose like a dog and sniffed.

"There are more waffles in the oven." They were the first words she had volunteered in days. Her father answered with a grunt on the way into the kitchen.

"Is Mom getting ready?"

"Not going," Mr. Holley said, as though complete sentences were more than Olivia deserved.

Leaving her half-eaten breakfast at the table, she went looking for her mother. She found Mrs. Holley in the Florida room, still in her housedress, re-reading a coverless mystery novel. Olivia tried to remember if she'd seen her mother get dressed and leave the house any day that week. She'd been so focused on avoiding her father's glowering anger that she hadn't noticed.

The room was sunny and cheerful, but her mother's mouth

was set in a glum frown. Olivia sat on the rattan sofa across from her mother, who didn't look up from her book.

"I made breakfast. You still have time to get ready for church."

"I'm not going," Mrs. Holley said.

Pastor Lou had come a few times and prayed with them, but they hadn't been to church as a family since Mr. Holley's heart attack. There had been too many other things to worry about.

"Don't you need to meet with the Dorcas Circle ladies?" Olivia said.

"They'll be okay without me."

"That's not true, Mom. You do twice as much as anyone else does. They'll miss you."

"I don't care." Mrs. Holley groaned and tossed her book onto the side table. "All the things I told them and now they'll know it's not true."

"What's not true?" With her mother, it was likely anything and everything. What didn't her mother lie about?

"All of it. All the times I told them Rich was getting better and now they'll know he's in jail! All the times I told them you were going to get married and you never are!" It came out on a wail, like an accusation. Mrs. Holley kept her head turned away, looking out the window at the vacant bird feeder.

"Why would you tell them that?" Olivia said.

"Because I thought if I wanted it enough, it would happen. Now they'll know everything. And they'll know Cynthia's getting a divorce."

"Wait! What?" Olivia leaned across and grabbed at her mother's knee, trying to make eye contact. "Cynthia and Jeff are getting divorced?"

"Oh, she told your father all about it. It's just awful! And everyone at church will know now. They'll know everything."

Surprise made Olivia laugh. Hadn't that been her whole reason for asking Rindell out? To avoid the shame of being discovered in a lie? She empathized with her mother in the same instant she was exasperated by their shared stupidity. Feeling bad for laughing, she patted her mother's leg. Mrs. Holley still wouldn't look at her.

"Oh, Mom, they already know anyway. Not about Cynthia yet, but it doesn't matter. I mean, Pearl Bennett, her daughter got divorced. And good grief, Mom, Marsha Delancey just got a divorce. Weren't you her maid of honor like thirty years ago?"

"But not my family! Not my children! And now Rich in jail! And Cynthia! And then you're going to be an old maid. I made it seem like you all were doing so well and now they'll know. I can't face them." Mrs. Holley sobbed and buried her face in her hands. Olivia gave her mother one last pat and got up to leave.

Mr. Holley had started on a second waffle in the dining room. When Olivia asked him about church, he mumbled, "Someone has to stay home with your mother."

"Okay, well, this old maid is going to church." She didn't wait for his answer before gathering up her purse and keys.

At Church of the Palms, she'd intended to go straight to the sanctuary and sit in back. She wasn't embarrassed to be seen. After all, she had to be seen there every other day of the week, so she didn't have the luxury of hiding out from her family's shame. She just didn't feel like fielding questions. No sooner had she walked through the front office than Pastor Zach said, "I'm so glad to see you, Olivia. Would you mind handing out bulletins? We're short on greeters this morning."

Olivia went to it grudgingly. Standing outside the main door of the sanctuary, she first tried to hand out the bulletins with a silent smile. After half a dozen people had stopped to offer their concern and condolences about Rich or Mr. Holley, Olivia realized she needed a different approach. To the next person who came through the door, she said, "Good morning, Mrs. Gamble. How are you?"

Then no matter what Mrs. Gamble said, as soon as the door opened, Olivia greeted the next person. People couldn't dawdle and condole her, if she greeted the people behind them.

The first few were easy, early arrivers she had known for years.

Then she began to challenge herself to see how many names she could get right. How many people did she know? As the crowds got heavier, she had to think fast to get her greetings out.

Across the foyer, the other two greeters watched her with puzzled smiles. Mr. and Mrs. Lambert had been volunteering as greeters for as long as Olivia could remember. Considering she'd been baptized at Church of the Palms twenty-seven years before, that was a long time.

"Good morning, Mrs. Lambert! Good morning, Mr. Lambert!" Olivia said during a lull.

After she greeted the last of the stragglers, Olivia followed them into the sanctuary, where the organ began the opening hymn. As always, the sanctuary was beautiful. Wooden beams cut the high white ceiling, and sunlight, filtered through stained glass, winked off the brass appointments on the altar. As Pastor Lou welcomed the congregation, Pastor Zach stood on the sidelines, looking nervous. Today, he would deliver the sermon at his new church.

Opening the bulletin she had printed on Friday jogged Olivia's memory. When she should have had her head down in prayer, she was subduing a giggle. Pastor Zach's first sermon to the congregation of Church of the Palms was "When the Truth Is Hard." Where had Pastor Zach been when she needed him?

The prayer ended and the congregation rose to sing the next hymn. Olivia stood, too, but she didn't reach for a hymnal. Looking around, she marveled at how many people in the room she knew. There was Beryl Magnusson-Croft and her husband. They must have come in from the side chapel. Olivia scanned the crowd for Jennifer Palhete, but didn't see her.

As she calculated all the people she knew and how long she had known them, Olivia realized that she had done what her mother cautioned her against when she went to a classmate's tenth birthday party. She had stayed at the party too long. She knew all these people and yet she knew none of them well. They didn't know her either, except for whatever truths they managed to glean from her mother's lies.

The hymn finished with a grand crescendo from the pipe organ. As the rest of the congregation resettled in the pews, Olivia laid her bulletin on the seat and walked out.

Driving north on Florida Avenue, Olivia passed the Palm Avenue Baptist Church, where parishioners streamed down the high brick-red steps on their way to their cars. Further on stood the bland façade of an evangelical church whose name she didn't know. Then came the store front church, Solid Rock of Jesus, with its barred windows and yellowing blinds. Across the street from it was a church Olivia had admired since she was a child. It was a tiny block chapel, painted white now, with moss growing in the cracks. When she was little, its arched window galleries had held stained glass, but twenty years of vandalism had led to them being boarded up. As 10:30 approached, people crossed the fenced parking lot toward the building. Without thinking it through, Olivia signaled and pulled in.

Just like at Church of the Palms, greeters stood inside the front door: two Latino men dressed in dark suits. In the narrow chapel, the temperature was already soaring, and ladies fanned themselves vigorously. One of the greeters offered Olivia a program sheet.

"*Buenos dias!*" he said. "*Ha estado aquí antes?*"

Olivia froze for a moment, staring down at the order of services for Iglesia de Dios Refugio.

"*No, es mi—hoy es mi primero tiempo,*" she said, unsteady but gaining confidence. She knew *tiempo* was the wrong word for *time*, but the greeter responded with a broad smile and a handshake.

"*Bueno! Bienvenida, mi hermana en Cristo.*"

"*Gracias.*"

Olivia found a place on the narrow unpadded pews and, like the ladies around her, used the order of service to fan herself. As the greeter walked to the front of the church and transformed into the minister, she remembered the right word. *Vez*, which was feminine. Drowned out by the opening hymn, she whispered it to herself: *Hoy es mi primera vez*. Today is my first time.

The exciting buzz of that moment carried her home, singing *¿Nos Veremos Junto al Rio?* under her breath, even though she was missing about every third word.

"Where have you been?" Mr. Holley said as soon as she stepped through the front door.

"At church."

"You should have been home by now. Your mother needs you. I'm tired of you acting like you don't have any obligations to this family."

"When have I acted like that? I wanted us to go to church together. I made breakfast, so we could—"

"Oh, you made one lousy breakfast and you think you're somebody special?" Mr. Holley snarled.

Halfway to the stairs, Olivia turned to face him, a hot flush running up her neck and into her cheeks.

"Is that what you think I've contributed to this family? One breakfast?"

"You could cook a thousand breakfasts and it won't make up for what you did," he said.

Her father's face looked as red as Olivia's felt. Remembering the day of his heart attack, she was about to apologize, to calm him down. Then she decided he probably wasn't going to have another heart attack. He was just going to go on saying hateful things as long as she was willing to put up with it.

"What I did?" she said.

"It's your fault your mother is upset. You destroyed this family. You did this."

"Somebody had to do it."

"Cynthia never—"

"Oh, bullshit! Cynthia moved to Atlanta to get away from us."

"Cynthia is coming home," Mr. Holley bleated like an injured sheep. Olivia laughed.

"Well, then I guess Cynthia can take care of things around here."

"Oh, you think you can go on living here and doing nothing?"

"No," Olivia said as she went up the stairs. "I don't think that at all."

In her room, she grabbed the coverlet on her bed and savagely ripped it off. The sheets and pillows followed. Once they were on the floor, she trampled them. Then she flung open her closet door and started yanking her fat clothes off their hangers. The boxy beige skirts and baggy blouses. The Mom jeans with stretch waistbands. The shapeless sundresses with matching sweaters to hide her fat arms.

When her temper tantrum petered out, the only things left in her closet were the half dozen new outfits she'd bought in the last month. From the closet shelf, she took down her suitcase and matching overnight bag. It surprised her how quickly she could pack her life and how little space it took up. She dismissed the handful of boxes marked Grade School, Junior High, and Plant High. Nothing worth keeping there. She used her nightgowns to wrap a couple of breakable trinkets. Lastly, she packed her bank records and her nail polish.

Slinging the overnight bag over her shoulder, she picked up her manicure box in one hand and her suitcase in the other. She had imagined simply walking out the front door, but Mr. Holley was in the living room when she went past.

"Where do you think you're going?" he said.

"I'm leaving. I'll be back later this week to clear out my room. You'll need it for Cynthia and the kids."

"Oh, you're running away? Don't be such a child."

Olivia stopped at the coat rack long enough to get her purse and her car keys.

"You'll be back," he said.

"Yeah, to clean out my room."

Olivia struggled to keep her voice steady. She wasn't going to give her father the satisfaction of seeing her cry.

She loaded her bags in the car and backed out of the drive, knowing her father was watching from the dining room. Since she'd left home with no plan, she went to the one place she thought she might be welcomed without an explanation.

"Miss Holley," Mr. Batson said when he answered the door. His threadbare undershirt seemed somewhat cleaner than usual.

"Hi, Mr. Batson. Would you be willing to rent me your spare bedroom for a while? I'll pay whatever Rindell was paying."

"Sure, sure. Say two hundred a month?"

"That seems fair."

"When was you thinking of moving in?"

Olivia blushed. "Would now be okay?"

"Right this minute then?" He laughed.

"Right this minute, if that's okay."

"Come on in, and I'll see about some clean sheets for that bed."

Mr. Batson swung the door open, welcoming her in.

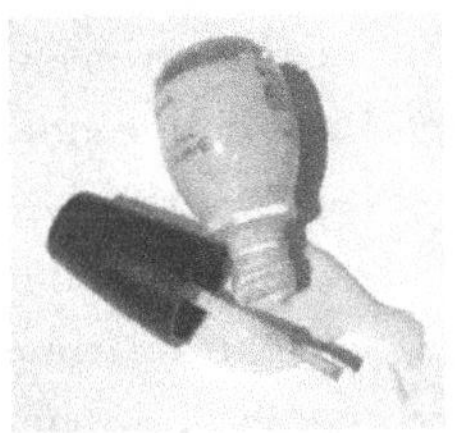

CHAPTER FIFTY

Olivia

THE INTERVIEW WENT better than Olivia had imagined possible. In some small corner of her mind, she'd been prepared for the interviewer to ask why she was wearing such slutty clothes. After all, she wore the same outfit she'd once planned to wear to Rich's arraignment. She hadn't toned down her nails either, using a sparkling plum as the backdrop to her lavender flower decals. Here and there, she'd used pink rhinestones to highlight the flowers. Where her toenails peeped out of her nude slingback pumps, they were painted to match.

Almost the first question the interviewer asked was about why she wanted to change jobs. Olivia weathered the question with something like the truth. She was stagnating in her current job. Dry mouthed and queasy, she answered a question about her strengths and weaknesses, and then reached up to tuck a stray wisp of hair behind her ear.

The interviewer, Helena, who was a stout Latina in a bright red suit, made a little gasping sound.

"I love your nails!" she said. "Where do you get them done?"

"I actually do them myself."

"Really?" Helena reached across the table and, in a moment of recklessness, Olivia offered her left hand. The scar was irrelevant to Helena, who clasped Olivia's fingers and admired her nails up close.

"They look amazing. You have great hands."

After that, the conversation went off in a dozen different directions. When the next interview candidate arrived, Helena and Olivia were still talking. As she walked Olivia to the lobby, Helena said, "I'm pretty sure I'll be talking to you later this week, chica."

Outside the office, in the glaring sunlight of a Miami afternoon, Olivia released the nervous laughter she'd been holding in. She felt so elated, she wished she could go to her next interview immediately, but it wasn't until the next day. While she had daylight, she practiced the drive from her hotel to her other interviews.

After it got dark, she ate a Cuban sandwich from a shop in the strip mall down the street from her hotel. She tried to take a nap, but all she could manage was a few hours of lying quietly in her darkened room. By ten o'clock she was already fretting about her clothes. The same old debate about one button or two buttons undone? Prim or slutty? If what she had seen so far was any indication, nobody in Miami would blink at her version of slutty.

On the drive to the hospital, she worried about everything. What she looked like, that she hadn't called ahead, that it was midnight in a strange town. Walking across the parking lot to the ambulance bays, she worried most about what Rindell would say.

"Olivia? O-livia?" The way he said it, astounded but pleased, made her blush.

He had been in mid-conversation with another paramedic, who also turned to look at her.

"Hi," she said.

After a second, he turned back to the other paramedic and said, "Hey, Josh, I gotta go. Ya'll drive safe tonight. Full moon and all."

They performed a mysterious handshake maneuver, and then Rindell's attention focused entirely on her. He ran his hand over his forehead into his hair and took a step toward her.

"What you doing here?" he said.

"I came for a job interview."

"In Miami?"

She nodded.

"How'd you know where I was?"

"Luis told me," she said.

"Do you wanna go somewheres and talk?"

"That's the reason I'm here. Here." She pointed to the ground to tether herself at that spot. "Do you want to get some dinner? Or would it be breakfast for you?"

"Yeah, we could go by Little Havana. Place down there stays open this late. Not too late for you, is it?"

"No, my next interview isn't until ten tomorrow."

At his suggestion, Olivia drove them both to the restaurant, leaving his motorcycle at the hospital. When they were on the road, he tilted the two nearest vents on himself and sighed.

"That's good. Get me some air conditioning." He started to settle back in the seat with his hands behind his head, and then sat up and said, "Oh, damn. Why didn't you tell me I stink like an old bum?"

"You're fine."

"You made of stern stuff, Olivia Mae Holley. This stink could knock a buzzard off a shit wagon."

Once, she would have chattered to fill the silence, but his admonition all those months ago had stuck with her. She didn't have to always talk. In fact, it was easier to focus on the driving and let him talk.

At the restaurant, with their meals ordered, they ran aground on silence. He had either talked himself out on the drive, or he was waiting to see what she would say.

"Anyway, I came for a couple of job interviews," she offered.

"How's that gonna work? You gonna move outta ya mama's house?"

"I already did. I couldn't live there anymore." She hoped he would speak again, but he took a deep drink of his beer and waited for her to continue. "My brother, Rich, he's probably going to prison. They revoked his bail."

"What did you tell the police?" Rindell said.

It was on the tip of Olivia's tongue to say, "The truth," but then she remembered how *true* was different from *truth*.

"I told them that he planned it. He told me he was going to kill Brian. He said it just like that. 'I'll kill him.' I didn't believe him. I thought he was just saying that, the way people do. My father always says that."

The waiter interrupted, setting down an elaborately dressed hot dog for Rindell and a plate of Niçoise salad for Olivia. Rindell raised his empty beer bottle and nodded for another.

They busied themselves with their food, Rindell eating and Olivia moving things around in her salad. At the table beside them, three drunk women rounded on a fourth for being *so stupid*. From what Olivia could gather there was a man who liked her, but the stupid girl kept sending the wrong signals. Olivia sympathized.

"So you come down here to get away?" Rindell said.

"Yes. Today's interview was with a children's non-profit organization. Tomorrow is with a mega church, which I don't want, but I'd take. I like the children's charity. They liked my fingernails."

He laughed and reached across the table, his first attempt at physical contact. Again, she offered her left hand and he took it in his condensation-damp palm, making a show of looking at her fingernails.

"That's classy. I like that. But you always look classy," he said. "Don't know why you'd wanna be seen out with a slob like me, wearing his sweaty uniform."

"Have you heard about Jennifer?" Olivia said.

Abruptly he let go of her hand. She was an idiot to bring it up that way. Mentioning Jennifer made him defensive. He ducked his head and took a large bite of his dinner.

"I mean, have you heard on the news, about what happened to that little girl? Shanti Williams?"

His head bobbed up and he gave her a curious look. He finished chewing and wiped his mouth, before he spoke.

"Yeah, I heard that. How she just gone? Cops think she's dead, but they can't find the body."

"That's the little girl. When you and Jennifer went to visit the dead woman's sister? The woman who got run over? Shanti is her daughter."

"Damn. That was her? That's—that's hard. I gone out on a domestic last week. Guy stabbed his wife. She lived, but they were a couple of meth-heads. Kids got picked up by DCF. I couldn't help thinking about how scary that was. Woulda been me if it wasn't for my auntie and uncle. Like those kids might get a good foster family, but then what if...."

At the table behind them, laughter rose and drowned out what he was saying. For a few minutes, he focused on his food and Olivia tried to do the same.

"What did you mean?" he said. "That day when you said, 'I lied, too.' What did you lie about?"

The question caught her unprepared. She had nearly forgotten telling him that.

"When I asked you out that first time, I only did it because I'd lied. I told somebody that I was dating you," she said.

"Me? Why'd you tell somebody that?"

"Not you exactly. I hadn't been on a date in a long time, and I didn't want to admit it. So I said I was dating a paramedic. Because I saw you every day. Then I felt stupid for lying. So I asked you out, to make it so it wasn't a lie."

"Damn." Rindell's beer bottle met the table with an alarming clunk. Any harder and it might have broken.

"What?"

"That's hard core. You asked me out so it wouldn't be a lie?" he said, sounding winded.

"I know. It's pathetic. I just wanted you to know. It's not like I tell the truth all the time."

"Just when it counts, right? You tell the truth when it matters."

It sounded so harsh that she couldn't answer, and they didn't speak again until the waiter brought the check. Before Olivia could even offer, Rindell handed cash back to the waiter. Then he stood up and said, "Well, if you'd give me a ride to my place, I'd appreciate it."

"You don't need to get your bike?"

"Drank too much beer. I'll take the bus to work tomorrow and get it then."

He didn't speak except to tell her where to turn, and then to say, "Yeah, gone from living in a trailer to a tent. Weather's good and it gives me a chance to figure out what I wanna do."

The campground was right there in the middle of Miami, at the edge of the zoo, according to the signs. At two in the morning, a single street light held back the night where they turned into the drive. Rindell's camping spot was all darkness under a canopy of trees. It spoke to Olivia of fairy tales. Hansel and Gretel lost in the woods. Little Red Riding Hood fleeing the Big Bad Wolf. She was about to mention it when he opened the door and stepped out. He slammed the door behind him.

"Okay, good night," she called out her open window. What else was there to say?

In the dark, she couldn't see him, and his voice was nearly lost as she pulled away.

"That day, when you told me you lied," he said. "It's stupid, but I thought you said, 'I love you.'"

She reached the campground's exit before it sank in. He had thought she loved him, and it hadn't seemed ridiculous to him. When she circled back to his campsite, a camp lantern glowed on the picnic table next to his tent. He came out of his tent in shorts and flip-flops, carrying a plastic bucket.

"I always wanted to go camping when I was little," she said.

"I didn't figure you for a camping girl."

"I've never been. I just like the idea of it. Sleeping out at night, campfires, sleeping bags."

"Mosquitos. Walking down the road for a shower." He set his plastic bucket on the table and took a few steps toward her car.

"Um, maybe not that so much."

"O-livia. Why *are* you here?"

The way he said it, he didn't sound angry or annoyed. It was a question that needed an answer. It was an invitation, too. Olivia got out of the car and approached the picnic table.

"I don't want to be there anymore. At home or at the church. Or in Tampa. I don't want to see those people anymore."

"Those people?" he said. "Like your mama?"

"Or my father. My parents are never going to forgive me for telling the police about Rich. Maybe I don't deserve forgiveness."

"Hush with that kinda talk." Rindell reached out, effortless as always, and drew her close to him. A comforting hug she was prepared for, but she gasped in surprise when he kissed her. After all the talking and the uneasy silences, was it that simple? He braced her with one hand along her jaw, while his other hand slid down to her hip. Inhaling, she got a head full of the sharp tang of a day's sweat in the Miami summer. She closed the gap between them with one step and kissed him harder. When his erection pressed against her belly, she brushed her hand down his side and used her thumbnail to trace the boundary of his waist band.

As she was thinking of doing more than that, he broke off the kiss, but didn't let her go.

"I can't do this," he whispered into her ear.

Her heart dropped into a hollow place. She stumbled backward, breaking his hold on her.

"I'll go. I'm sorry I bothered you."

"If alls you want is another night of pretend, I can't do that."

"I'm not here to pretend," she said.

"Whatever kinda guy you deserve, I ain't him. I lied about everything to you."

"But you were right."

"I'm one big ole walking lie. You don't even say my name because it's a lie."

"Rindell. Rindell. Rindell. Listen to me."

He squatted in front of her, his head sunk between his shoulders, both hands clasped to the top of his head. The lantern on the table cast a glow on his bare back, as slick with sweat as she felt. To be closer to him, Olivia sat down on the picnic table bench, her knees a few inches from his jutting elbows.

"I'm listening," he said.

"Maybe you don't agree. I know my father doesn't, but I know I did the right thing, to tell the truth about Rich. If I hadn't told the truth, he might have hurt someone else."

"True. True dat."

"Shh. Listen," she scolded.

"Yes, Miss Olivia."

"I was right. But you were right, too. If you were still DeVaun, would you be here?"

"No way. No how. I'd be in New Orleans, fucking up my life. Or maybe I'd be dead. Or in prison like my daddy."

"Then you were right to lie, because if you'd gone on being DeVaun, you wouldn't be doing anybody any good. Not you, not all the people whose lives—"

"But if I died and Rindell lived, he'd be doing good."

"No," she said.

"Yeah, he would."

"No, because your cousin is dead. Your lie didn't kill him. If you were still DeVaun, Rindell would still be dead, but because of you, Rindell is still doing good. Your lie made something good happen."

Olivia laid her hand on the back of his neck. He arched against her palm like a cat, but when he spoke, his voice was tight from fighting tears.

"But what if you can't forgive me? It ain't a one-time lie. I'm telling that lie every day!"

"I don't have to forgive you. All I have to do is accept it," she said. "I'm glad you lied. Otherwise you wouldn't be here. I never would have met you."

He slid one of his hands to the back of his neck, not to push her hand away, but to hold onto it. After a moment, he raised his head and pressed a kiss into her palm. His cheek was damp with tears but when he looked up at her, he was smiling.

"You still here trying to make your lie true?" he said.

"I already made my lie true. I'm here because I miss you, Rindell."

CHAPTER FIFTY-ONE

Jennifer

"WAKE UP, HONEY. You need to shower."

"No." Jennifer rolled away from her father's hand and tried to burrow more deeply into her bed.

"Jenny, I'm serious now. Get up and take a shower."

She knew she would have to obey, because he used his stern teacher's voice. When she sat up on the edge of her bed, he said, "Good!" like Jennifer was a baby, just learning to sit up by herself.

In the shower, she swabbed at herself with a soapy bath pouf and made a half-hearted attempt to wash her hair. Enough to keep the stink off, but not enough to get truly clean. Her legs and armpits had gone Neanderthal and she didn't care.

As she stood under the water, blanking on what she was supposed to do next, someone knocked on the bathroom door. Her father called, "Jenny?"

"I'm sorry, do you need in?"

"No, no. You've just been in there for a while."

She twisted the shower handles, ending up with a scalding and then a dousing with cold water before she managed to turn it off.

Jennifer stepped out of the shower and looked around at the familiar bathroom with its tiny white tiles, like so many Chiclets. Not for the first time, she wondered what Moira had done that night when Jennifer was in second grade. When Mr. Palhete was pounding on the door and calling for her, what had Moira been doing? Had she taken pills? Or slit her wrists? Thinking of it gave Jennifer a sick feeling, like the ghost of Moira-that-was still occupied the space. A lost mother, like Shanti's. Not dead, but a ghost all the same.

Was Jennifer turning into a ghost, too? Was that why her father smiled so anxiously, as she stepped out of the bathroom wrapped in a towel?

"I'm sorry I took so long," she said.

"It's fine, honey. I was just starting to think you'd gone down the drain."

She managed a wan smile at the joke as she shuffled down the hallway to her bedroom. Sitting on the edge of her bed, she stared helplessly at the mound of clothes that occupied the other twin bed.

Her furniture and other things were wedged into the Palhetes' garage, but her father had brought all the boxes marked CLOTHES to her bedroom. Jennifer had haphazardly opened boxes until she found her underwear and some pajamas. They were all she needed.

"Oh, good for you! All showered and ready to get dressed." Moira came into the room without knocking. She never could hit the right note. Either too familiar or too distant. The same way her clothes never hit the right note. She wore a zebra print blouse with lace insets and a pair of hot pink spandex exercise pants. Her hair was a deep auburn that glowed purple when the sun hit it. She carried a basket under her arm which she set at Jennifer's feet.

"Fresh from the laundry for you!"

"Thanks, Mom."

"Come on, get dressed. We got company coming."

"I don't want to see anybody." Jennifer recoiled. Who had her parents invited?

"Weeeellll," Moira said. "They're already on their way, so I guess you could stay in your room. But you need to get dressed."

Unable to offer a counter argument, Jennifer took off her towel and let Moira dress her. Whatever Moira took out of the hamper, Jennifer put on. A pair of pink satin Valentine's panties and some khaki capris that were too big.

"And I got this on sale for you." Moira lifted up a t-shirt for Jennifer's approval. It was bright teal with sequined sea turtles. In her old life, Jennifer never would have worn it, but she obediently pulled it on, frowning down at the turtles swimming across her chest.

Moira must have seen the puzzled look on Jennifer's face, because she hurried to say, "I thought you'd like it, you know, because you love sea turtles. You got the license plate and everything."

Jennifer did have a Save the Sea Turtles license plate on her car, but she'd never considered that it signaled a love of sea turtles. She did like them.

"Thanks, Mom."

"All decent in there?" Mr. Palhete called as he rapped on the bedroom door frame.

"Hey, Daddy." Every time Jennifer looked at him, she wanted to apologize.

"Your first guest has arrived," he said and made a little flourish with one hand.

"Hi hi!" Tracey came into the room with all the exuberance of a stripper leaping out of a bachelor party cake. When Jennifer stood up, Tracey enveloped her in a smoky, perfumed hug. "I'm so glad to see you."

"Me too," Jennifer whispered, and it was true. She clung to Tracey for a moment, feeling like someone who'd been adrift on a lifeboat and had just been rescued.

The doorbell sounded.

"Why don't you girls go out to the sunroom and I'll get that," Mr. Palhete said.

Jennifer followed her mother and Tracey down the hallway, feeling shaky. Had her parents invited Carrie? Prepared for the worst, Jennifer was relieved to see her father in the foyer with anyone who wasn't Carrie. Even if it was Olivia Holley.

"Oh, you don't need to carry that," Olivia said as Mr. Palhete took a plastic cosmetics case from her. In those seconds when Olivia was distracted, Jennifer marveled at her transformation. She'd put blond highlights in her hair and piled it up in lacquered curls, leaving her dangly peacock feather earrings unobstructed. Her turquoise dress was a clingy jersey knit wrap that Jennifer never would have dared to wear. It revealed every curve and bulge.

Shame flushed Jennifer's face, so sharp she thought she might cry. She was about to retreat to her bedroom when Olivia smiled.

"Hi, Jennifer."

Moira crossed the living room to hug Olivia, and in the midst of introducing Tracey to Olivia, Jennifer let go of the lump of embarrassment in her throat. Olivia had come, because she was truly transformed. Not just her hair, but all of her.

They were arranging themselves in the sunroom, when Mr. Palhete brought out a tray with glasses of iced tea. With him came someone Jennifer had hoped never to see again.

"Hey, doll, it's good to see you," Marco said. He came toward her, planning to shake her hand or hug her, but she shrank back into the porch glider defensively.

For the first week after it all happened, she had waited for him to call and tell her it was all a mix-up. The cadaver dog made a mistake. A DCF worker took Shanti and she was okay. The call never came. Jennifer knew Marco didn't deserve it, but she still blamed him. If Olivia was a painful reminder of mistakes she'd made, Marco Parmiento made her stare down the worst failure of her life.

For a moment Jennifer wished she had the strength to fake a hug and a happy greeting. It would have been better than the pained look Marco exchanged with her father.

"Alright, Marco and I are off to the ballgame. We'll leave you ladies to your beautifying. Not that any of you need beautifying," Mr. Palhete said. He leaned down and kissed Moira, who giggled.

"Oh, you charmer. Have fun!" she said.

Jennifer clenched the arm of the glider, listening for the sound of the front door. Once the men were gone, she turned on her mother.

"What is he doing here? Is he going to the game with Daddy?"

"Oh, he and your dad hit it off. And then he's been a huge help. I don't know what we would have done without Marco."

"What do you mean? What would you need his help for?" Jennifer knew it sounded hysterical, but she had an awful feeling that all around her, people were keeping secrets. Or it was the realization that while she lay in bed crying, the world kept going.

"Who did you think helped pack up all your things and move?" Moira said.

"Mr. Parmiento helped Daddy move me?"

"You know I can't lift anything heavy since I hurt my shoulder. Your daddy says Marco's a modern Philip Marlowe."

"Well, I think you should have told me. That he was—that you.... Has he—is he...."

Jennifer didn't even know what she was accusing her parents of, but Moira looked sympathetic to Jennifer's anger and confusion. In the silence that followed the outburst, Olivia started opening the latches on her cosmetic case and setting out bottles of nail polish.

"Oooh! Can you show me how to do decals like yours?" Tracey said.

While Tracey and Olivia sorted through nail supplies, Jennifer drank her iced tea like it was liquor. Her stomach gurgled, as though it had finally decided to complain about her recent eating habits. The other three women exchanged furtive glances that Jennifer understood. Whatever she did, they were going to pretend it was okay. Even if she sat there brooding in silence for the half hour it took Olivia to do Tracey's nails.

Then came the moment Olivia turned to Jennifer.

"You like a French manicure, right?"

"You don't need to do my nails," Jennifer said.

"Oh, that's what I came for. A girls day, your mom said."

"I'm doing makeovers," Tracey said. "As soon as my nails are dry."

"You don't need to." Jennifer tucked her hands into her lap. They were a ragged mess.

"It's okay. Truly, it is," Olivia said.

Jennifer understood the code, what Olivia wouldn't say in front of Tracey and Moira. She had forgiven Jennifer, but Jennifer couldn't stand the thought of her doing her nails. It was too intimate. Too nice. Jennifer didn't deserve that.

"What about you, Mrs. Palhete?" Olivia said.

"Oh, yes! But call me Moira."

She looked through Olivia's nail polish, but decided they were all too quiet. She went into the house and returned with a brand new bottle of polish in a throbbing purple color. Olivia didn't bat an eye at it, just set to work on Moira's nails.

Jennifer slumped on the porch glider, pushing off restlessly to keep it moving. She closed her eyes and tuned out the other women's chatter. Everyone made noises of awe when Tracey dropped Mr. Bigwig's name, and Moira re-told an old story about the Palhetes' first anniversary. The hotel had caught fire and they'd spent the night in a park. It all faded to a soft buzz until Olivia said, "And Rindell is working third shift now, so we manage to overlap for part of every day."

"As long as you overlap in bed, that sounds like a dream," Moira said.

Olivia and Tracey laughed.

Jennifer sat up and opened her eyes. Tracey was standing over Olivia, fussing with something. Plucking her eyebrows?

"Are you girls hungry? I have some mini egg rolls. And these puff pastry things with spinach artichoke dip." Moira lowered her voice like she was sharing a dirty secret. "And I got some of that frozen margarita mix that comes in bags."

"Oooh, margaritas," Tracey said. "I'll help you."

Tracey padded after Moira, wads of tissue separating her freshly painted toes. She walked so awkwardly that Jennifer wondered if she ever wore shoes without heels. Left behind, Tracey's black Hermès Crocodile Birkin looked immaculate, like it had just been taken from a display case. Removed for her pedicure, her eight-inch platform stilettos stood in front of her chair, as though a poised but invisible Tracey occupied them.

Jennifer must have stared at them too long, because Olivia said, "I don't think Tracey would agree to be raptured without her shoes."

Startled out of her reverie, Jennifer gave a bleat of laughter. Olivia blushed.

"I think I'll go help them." Jennifer didn't want to be rude, but she was uneasy at being left alone with Olivia. What were they supposed to talk about? As she got to the sunroom doorway, Olivia reached out to stop her. Her hand hung in the air, threatening to make contact with Jennifer's arm.

"Wait. Can I ask you something?"

Jennifer assumed it would be a single question and nodded, but Olivia patted the chair Tracey had occupied to have her nails painted.

Once Jennifer was seated, Olivia put several bottles of polish out on the side table.

"You don't need to do my nails."

"I want to. Besides, I need to ask you for a favor. What color?"

"A favor?" Jennifer reached out blindly and picked up a bottle of polish. Her hand was shaking, and it didn't stop until Olivia took hold of her fingers to begin filing her nails.

"My boss and I have been talking a lot about Shanti. I mean, I know everyone is following it on the news but my boss wants—"

"Pastor Lou?" Jennifer said.

"What? Oh, no. I'm sorry. I'm telling this in the wrong order. I took a job in Miami. With Child Advocacy of Florida. I do newsletters, mailings, things like that. And my boss, Helena, she's the director. She's been invited to the Governor's Task Force on Child Welfare. Do you know about it?"

"No."

Olivia finished filing and uncapped a bottle of undercoat.

"They're having a hearing in Tallahassee. Helena wants CAF to testify at the hearing, to shape policy. You know, to improve the way DCF tracks and supervises the children in their care."

"Oh, that's good," Jennifer said dully.

"We want you to testify at the task force hearing," Olivia said.

"So how do you like Miami? You and Rindell are living there together?" Between reopening the wound of Rindell or Shanti, that seemed like the lesser of two horrors. Olivia frowned over Jennifer's nails, either in concentration or puzzlement.

"It's different from Tampa, but I like it. And my Spanish is getting a workout. "

"I didn't know you spoke Spanish."

"It was my minor in college, but it's pretty rusty."

"And Rindell's still working as a paramedic?" Jennifer said.

"Yeah. We just rented an apartment by the beach."

"Is it noisy? I mean, with people partying on the beach and stuff." Jennifer thought she sounded almost normal if she stuck to saying vapid things.

"Well, we haven't moved in yet, but the apartment's on the fourth floor, so maybe it won't be too bad. But you can see the ocean from our balcony."

"That's nice. So how's your family?" Jennifer said, desperate for harmless conversation while her nails dried.

"They're okay, considering. My sister's back home and my brother is in jail." Olivia blew lightly on Jennifer's nails, a thing no nail technician in a salon had ever done. It made goosebumps stand up on her arms and brought back the hot flush of guilt. Why did Olivia have to be so kind?

"Oh, that's ni—" Jennifer caught herself on the verge of telling Olivia that it was nice her brother was in jail. "That's not good."

"I think his lawyer is working on a plea deal, but no one tells me anything anymore. Since I left home, they're not talking to me."

"I'm sorry." Two inadequate words to cover such a broad topic, but Jennifer couldn't think of anything else to say. She expected Olivia to smooth it over, but she was silent as she painted Jennifer's nails. "So, what was it really like working at the church?"

"Some good. Some bad," Olivia said. "I didn't mean to booby trap you, coming here."

"What?" Jennifer looked down at her hands, and realized she'd picked Moira's bottle of polish. The obnoxious purple.

"But your mother asked me to come, and I wasn't sure if you'd ever return my phone calls."

"I don't—I haven't looked at my phone in a while," Jennifer said.

"So, I'm sorry, if it seems like I'm pressuring you, but I've been learning a lot about lobbying at my job. Helena, my boss, she says that in hearings like this, narrative can make a big difference in how people understand things. Senators don't pay as much attention to statistics and data. They like stories, and Shanti's story is important."

"Who wants a drinky?" Tracey sang as she carried in a pair of margarita glasses.

Jennifer used the distraction to stand up and move away from Olivia. She felt boxed in and the chemical smell of nail polish made it hard to breath.

"Oh, everything's taken care of, sweetie. Sit down and have a drink," Tracey said.

"I'm just going to the bathroom."

"Your nails are wet," Olivia called after her.

It didn't matter that her nails were wet, because Jennifer wasn't going to the bathroom. She didn't want to be alone with the ghost of Moira-that-was, and it was the only bathroom in the house. If she went there, she might be interrupted. Instead she went to her bedroom. Heedless of her freshly painted nails, she moved her desk chair in front of the door. The chair back wasn't high enough to latch under the door knob, but it would at least alert her if anyone opened the door.

Sealed up alone, she found she'd brought the claustrophobia with her. That suffocating feeling was part of her. Lying down on the bed, she laid her hands on her belly and tried to force herself to breathe deeply.

Jennifer woke up to the thunk of the door hitting the chair. Usually, Moira would have retreated after finding the chair in place, but she pushed the door open, sending the chair toppling onto the rug.

"Are you okay, honey?"

"I'm fine, Mom. I just needed some space."

"Olivia was telling us about the governor's hearing thing. I really think that would be—"

"I don't want to talk about it! Why did you invite them here?" Jennifer snapped.

Moira sat on the edge of the bed and reached out to pat Jennifer's shoulder. The gesture was familiar for its uncertainty, as though Moira expected her affections to be rebuffed.

"Because I don't want you to make the mistake I did."

"What mistake?" Jennifer said.

"How I went away after Rebecca died, I gave up on everything. I abandoned you."

"You didn't abandon me." Jennifer rolled over, wanting to dislodge Moira's hand from her shoulder, but it stayed.

"I did! When your sister died, I abandoned you. I curled up inside myself and stopped caring about anything else. The next thing I knew, you'd already learned to read and to ride a bike. I missed out on those things, and it was my fault. I don't want you to do that, to give up on your life."

"I'm not," Jennifer said. Moira had begun crying.

"I just want you to try. To get out and see people. Look for a new job. Have a life."

"I will."

"Promise me." Moira sniffled. When Jennifer didn't answer, Moira wailed, "Please, honey. Don't do what I did. Promise you'll try. I know you don't owe me anything, but will you promise me that?"

"I promise," Jennifer said. The words terrified her, reminded her of the promise she'd made to Gayle Prichard.

"Hey, Palhetes. Everything alright?" Tracey said. She stood in the doorway, frowning.

"I'm being an idiot like always." Moira stood up and wiped her eyes with her shirt, smearing make-up on it.

"Oh, Mrs. P., it's okay." Without her enormous shoes, Tracey had to reach up like a child to hug Moira. It looked so effortless that Jennifer felt ashamed and confused. Why hadn't she hugged her mother?

From the hallway came Olivia's soft voice: "I'm sorry. I don't want to disturb you. I just wanted to say good-bye."

"Oh, you're leaving already?" Moira said.

"I need to get on the road. I don't want to drive through the Everglades in the dark."

It jarred Jennifer, the reminder that Olivia wasn't making the trip back to Tampa. She had driven all the way from Miami to talk to Jennifer.

"Wait. I have something for you." After weeks of physical and mental inactivity, Jennifer had to concentrate to make sense. "What size bed do you have?"

Olivia tilted her head in confusion.

"Is it a queen size? Or what?"

"I—we don't have one yet. We have to buy one."

"Oh, good."

Now everyone gave Jennifer a funny look. She thought it would be easier to find the box than to explain, but the boxes were piled four deep behind the other bed. Most of them were marked CLOTHES, although a handful were marked BEDROOM. With her nails already smudged, Jennifer tore tape off BEDROOM boxes and dug through them, feeling more ridiculous by the minute.

Still in its Nordstrom bag, the bedding set had been packed so tightly that the air was squeezed out. It began to poof up as soon as Jennifer opened the box. She tried to drag the box free from behind the bed, but as she tugged on it, the side ripped open and out spilled half a dozen pairs of shoes and a soccer ball. The ball skidded off the pile of clothes and bounced against the nightstand.

Jennifer stared at it in horror. She had felt the same way when her purse popped open at her first high school dance and spilled her spare maxi pad on the gym floor. A secret she didn't want anyone else to see. As Olivia bent over and picked up the soccer ball, Jennifer dumped the contents of the Nordstrom bag onto the bed.

"It's new. I bought it...." For after the wedding, that was what she'd bought it for. "But then I never used it. So it's brand new. It's a duvet, and sheets, in queen size, and pillow shams, and a dust ruffle maybe, and...."

Jennifer fell silent as the items spilled out on the bed, because the bedding was as pretty as she remembered. Silver-gray silk, shot through with navy and burgundy slubs and abstract floral embroidery.

"And since you're getting a new place, I thought you could use it," she said. Too late she remembered how she had refused Olivia's offer to do her nails. How she'd said, "You don't need to." What if Olivia said, "Oh, no, I couldn't"?

To her relief, Olivia laid down the soccer ball and picked up a sealed package of pillow cases. With a gracious smile, she said, "Thank you. I don't have anything for the new place yet. They're so pretty."

"You're welcome." Jennifer reached for the soccer ball, hoping to tuck it out of sight, but Olivia followed the movement. Her hand fell back on the ball, before Jennifer could reach it. Her nails glittered incongruously against the dirty white leather.

From the living room came the sound of male voices. Marco and Mr. Palhete. A reprieve.

"Oh, Daddy's home," Moira said. She scurried out of the room to greet them.

Pretending nonchalance, Jennifer began to put the bedding into the shopping bag. Olivia turned the soccer ball over in her hands. Jennifer held her breath, pushing down to force air out of the duvet.

"This was hers?" Olivia said.

When Jennifer looked up from making herself busy, Olivia was tracing her fingernail over Shanti's name.

"I gave it to her for Christmas."

"I know you don't want to talk at the hearing. I understand that. If you wanted to talk, you would have already been on TV a hundred times. Your mother told me all the true crime TV shows called to try to set up interviews. So I know you don't want to talk about it."

"I can't."

Olivia might as well have suggested Jennifer run a three-minute mile. It was a physical impossibility.

"I'm the one who turned my brother in. I turned him into the police," Olivia said. "If his lawyer doesn't make a deal with the prosecutor, I'll have to testify against him at the trial."

"I'm sorry. That's got to be hard."

"I'm not any braver than you. Don't think that. But the hardest things are what you do for other people. Like forgiving Rindell for what happened, that was easy. Do you know why?"

Jennifer shook her head. She'd always known that Olivia was a better person. A better Christian. No amount of church or praying was going to make her as good as Olivia.

"Because it was for me. Forgiving him was for me. So I could be with him. It was selfish. Telling the police about my brother, that was for my brother and for the man he killed. And for my parents, too. It was hard. It would have been so much easier to keep my mouth shut. So I know I'm telling you to do a hard thing, but you need to talk to the governor's task force."

Although she hadn't asked a question, Olivia turned the ball over in her hands, like she was waiting for an answer.

"When's the hearing? When would she have to go?" Tracey said.

"The first hearing is Tuesday, August 4th. And we would pay for transportation and a hotel up in Tallahassee."

Tracey took out her phone and opened the calendar. Jennifer bristled at them making plans around her, but as she reached for the phone to make Tracey stop, she saw the bright blue square that indicated the day. June 13. In another life, today would have been her wedding day.

"What's the point of going to this hearing? Shanti's dead. I could have saved her, but I didn't. It won't do any good now," Jennifer said. Saying it out loud felt like crawling back into the safety of a cave.

Olivia kept her eyes down, squeezing the ball between her palms. "You're right. She probably is dead. On the news they keep talking about how a murder trial works when there's no body. I don't know if you could have saved her. If you could and you didn't, I'm sorry. Even if you couldn't have saved her, but you thought you could, I'm sorry."

"Yeah, you're sorry. I'm sorry. We're all so sorry," Jennifer sneered. Standing up, she reached for the soccer ball. She couldn't stand to watch Olivia touch it anymore. She thought she would simply grab it and take it away, but Olivia held tight.

"Whatever you wish you'd done for Shanti, this is the only thing you can do for her now."

"I can't," Jennifer said.

"Who else is going to do it? I've seen her aunt on the news. Renee. The one who didn't want her. Do you think the governor's task force will listen to her when all she's interested in is getting money from her lawsuit?"

"Leave me alone!"

When Olivia let go of the soccer ball, it rebounded against Jennifer's solar plexus, hard enough that she sat back on the bed beside Tracey. Jennifer rolled the ball in her lap until Shanti's name was framed between her hands. The obnoxious purple polish glinted on her nails. It was not the nail polish of someone who wanted to lie down and die.

"What would I tell the task force?" Jennifer said.

"Everything you know about Shanti's story. All of it."

"So from the beginning?" From the moment she watched Gayle Prichard die.

Jennifer tried to wrap her brain around the idea of leaving the house, traveling to Tallahassee, and getting up in front of strangers to tell the whole story. When that was too much to think about, she bit off the smallest piece of the process and chewed it.

"What would I wear?"

"Anything you want," Olivia said.

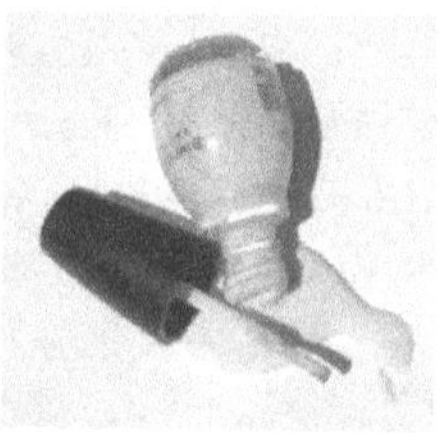

CHAPTER FIFTY-TWO

Olivia

"I LIKE THIS kind of camping best," Olivia said. She was rewarded by Rindell's sleepy chuckle. She felt a little guilty, because he needed to sleep before he went to work, but she wanted another moment of pleasure lying awake next to him. He slid his hand down her side, then back up it, before bringing it to rest on her breast again.

"You don't miss the tent?" he mumbled against her shoulder.

They had managed almost two months living out of the tent and Olivia's car while they hunted for an apartment. Putting down Rindell's Miami post office box address on the first day at her new job, Olivia had explained about the situation. The moving. The tent. She hoped it didn't look like homelessness, but she prepared for her new boss to make a disapproving face. Instead, Helena had said, "Oh my God, Olivia! You packed up and moved here to be with him? That's so romantic!" Later, Olivia overheard her telling the story to someone else. *Adventurous* was the word she used. Olivia was officially *adventurous*.

Four stories up, with the balcony doors open to the night air, Olivia felt adventurous, but she didn't miss the tent. Once she was sure Rindell was asleep, she got up and put her nightgown back on. Then she smoothed the twelve-hundred thread count top sheet over him.

Jennifer's fancy sheets had already served a dual purpose.

They'd been used to officially christen the new mattress and they were the only sign of civilization in the current chaos. The apartment looked like an IKEA warehouse, piled with boxes, shopping bags, and unassembled furniture. For their first night, Olivia made up the mattress on the floor, because the bed frame was in a box.

Closing the bedroom door, she padded out to the kitchen to start washing new dishes. If she worked for the two hours until Rindell's alarm went off, she could make him some breakfast before he went to work.

She had always imagined shopping for cereal bowls and hand towels with her mother, but she found her new co-workers eager to wander through department stores, helping her pick out all the things she needed. Quiet, boring Olivia had never made friends. Adventurous Olivia already had several.

Once she had the drainer full of freshly washed plates and bowls, she clipped the tags from a pile of new towels and started a load of laundry. Then she cut shelf liner for the kitchen cabinets and unboxed the parts of a table to fit in the dollhouse-sized dining nook. That had been the tradeoff for a bay view balcony. By the time the alarm went off at ten-thirty, the table was mostly assembled. Seeing it on its top with three legs attached gave Olivia a chill. She reached for the fourth leg and hurriedly used Rindell's socket set to wrench it into place.

He must have hit the snooze, because as she was setting the table up on its legs, the alarm sounded again. When she went into the bedroom, he was awake, sprawled on his back in the middle of the bed. It was going to work out, them sleeping in different shifts. They would each get the bed to themselves with time in between together.

"Rindell, do you want some breakfast?" she said.

"That'd be nice. Just give me ten more minutes."

"Okay." She turned, intending to leave him to sleep, but he caught her by the ankle and held her back.

"No, I meant give me ten more minutes. Come back to bed."

She slipped under the sheet, surprised by the contrast between his sleep-warm skin and hers, cooled from ceiling fans and the ocean breeze coming in through open balcony doors. He rolled onto his side and curled against her.

"I like laying here with you," he said.

"I like lying here with you, too."

"That's not right, huh? It's not laying?"

"No," she said, embarrassed.

"I can always count on you to know which is which, but that's weird. *Lying*. I don't like how lie has the two meanings. I don't want to lie here with you. Been enough lying already. Why does it mean two different things?"

"I don't know."

"If it's okay, I'm just gonna keep saying *lay*. I like laying here with you," he said.

"I like laying here with you, too."

ACKNOWLEDGEMENTS

I would like to express my gratitude to the people who saw this book in various states of undress: Norma Johnson, Clovia Shaw, George Berger, Lisa Brackmann, and Madison Jones.

To the secretaries who will always type 85 wpm in my heart: June Greenwood, Emily, Sherry, Brianne, Cara, Cynthia, Jennifer, Rhonda, Rae Ann, Dora, Eileen, Missy, Lori, Lydia, and Cindy.

To the people who propped me up or inspired me in myriad ways: Liberty Greenwood, Erica Greenwood, Deirdre Alexander, Robert Ozier, Emily Nelson, and all of my Vox Peeps.

To the people behind the scenes in making this book a reality: Ken Coffman, Stacey Benson, Chris Benson, Guy Corp, and all the rest of the Stairway Press crew.

To Jimmy Fashner, whose photograph graces the cover.

To my fellow writers, be they Purgatorians, Lurkers, Pitizens, or CDSers.

DISCUSSION GUIDE

1. What would you have done, if you had witnessed Gayle's death? Would you be willing to make the same promise to a dying person? If so, how far would you go to keep that promise?

2. Both Olivia and Jennifer treat themselves to luxuries. Olivia's are small: painting and decorating her own nails. Jennifer's luxuries are expensive and name brand: Coach handbags and Louboutin shoes. Which of them enjoys her luxuries more? Why? What does this disparity say about them?

3. During Olivia's ill-fated trip as a church youth group volunteer, she uncovers another counselor's secret—that she didn't wait until marriage to have sex. Neither did Olivia. How does this element of "do as I say, not as I do" play into Olivia's own attitudes about sex? How does she feel about losing her virginity? About her sexual activity with Rindell? Is it at odds with her religious upbringing? Or is it in keeping with her need to go along and please people?

4. Lies are a major plot element and means of characterization in Lie Lay Lain. Which lies are the most damaging? Which lies do you find most offensive or shocking? Toward the end of the book, Olivia asks Rindell, "How important is the truth?" In the novel, what are the consequences of telling the truth? Is there such a thing as *The Truth*? Within the story, who is the most truthful character? How do you measure it?

5. Olivia frequently seems passive or even cowed, but faced with her brother's terrible crime, she displays great strength. Has

this strength been in her all along? Where else do we see it? Or is this strength a new growth? Stemming from what? Conversely, Jennifer comes across as "in control," with an orderly life. What compels her to try to control so many things? Is this a strength or a cover for weakness?

6. The narrative suggests that if Jennifer had been walking more slowly, she might have been the one struck and killed as she crossed the street. How might the lives of the other characters have developed, if she and not Gayle had died? What if Jennifer had left work a few minutes earlier and never witnessed Gayle's death?

7. We're familiar with the idea of cliques and mean girls in the public school system. How did you react to the discovery that the "cool kids" continue to dominate Olivia's adult working life and even her spiritual life at church?

8. Olivia feels suffocated by her parents, while Jennifer feels disconnected from hers. As much as she loves her father, after all, he remains *Mr. Palhete* in her narrative. How have they developed these patterns, and how do parental relationships shape the way Jennifer and Olivia respond to other people?

9. Rindell has served his country, survived a horrific natural disaster, and is serving his community as a paramedic. Does his sacrifice or his suffering ultimately earn him the right to use the events of Hurricane Katrina to erase his past life? Is his past truly erased? Will it ever be?

10. How is Olivia changed by learning that Rindell is not who he claims to be? How does it affect her perception of her own identity?

11. Returning from their trip to the state park, what prevents Rindell from rebuffing Jennifer's sexual advances? Surprise? Old habits? Low self-esteem? Is it likely that he'll continue this pattern of behavior, or have things changed for him by the end? Why or why not?

12. How do Olivia's issues of self-esteem and body-image affect her feelings for Rindell and her perception of his feelings for her? How does his self-doubt affect his perceptions of their relationship? In the end, how has Olivia's sense of self-worth changed? What about Rindell?

13. There are multiple instances of infidelity in the story. What would have happened if Olivia had never learned about Rindell's infidelity? If Jennifer had remained ignorant of Kevin and Carrie's affair? If Kevin *had* learned of Jennifer's misdeed?

14. What changes for Jennifer, after she is certain that Shanti is dead? Why does she give up on everything? How is she likely to emerge from this experience? Stronger and more independent? Or do we see the beginnings of a long-term cycle of depression and co-dependency? What do you think she will do after Olivia's visit?

15. The Greater Tampa Bay Area has a population of over four million people. How does living in such a large metropolitan population center enable Rindell's reinvention as his cousin? For Olivia, however, Tampa is her hometown, where she is surrounded by people and landmarks from her childhood. How does that affect her ability to grow or change? What does the move to Miami offer her?

16. Tampa continues to pass through cycles of urban growth, decay, and gentrification, creating tensions between the rich and the poor. Where do we see those tensions played out in the novel? How are the cycles of growth and decay reflected in the trajectories of the characters?

17. Beyond socio-economic issues, what racial tensions are evident in the novel? How do the characters perceive and interact with characters of other races? How do those perceptions and interactions change?

18. Although *Lie Lay Lain* is a work of fiction, the book is dedicated to the memory of Rilya Wilson, who went missing out of foster care in Florida at the age of four, and is presumed dead. Her 18th birthday would have been September 29, 2014. Hers is sadly not the only recent case of children being mistreated by those entrusted with their care. How do you feel about the current conditions for children in foster care in America?

ABOUT THE AUTHOR

After a seven-year stint in Tampa, Bryn Greenwood now lives in Kansas with a pair of rescued boxers and two condescending hairless cats. She is married to a never-ending home remodeling project. *Lie Lay Lain* is her second novel. Visit her at www.bryngreenwood.com.

CPSIA information can be obtained
at www.ICGtesting.com
Printed in the USA
BVHW071658280220
573632BV00004BA/498